gondolin press

Elisabetta Sala

THE EXECUTION

OF JUSTICE

A NOVEL

gondolin press

THE EXECUTION OF JUSTICE – *Elisabetta Sala*

Original title: *L'esecuzione della giustizia* (2017)
First published in Italian by D'Ettoris editori (CR)

Translated from the original by Mary Anne Robertson

© **gondolin press**

1915 Aster Rd.
60178 Sycamore IL

www.gondolinpress.com
info@gondolinpress.com

2022 © Gondolin Institute LLC

ISBN 978-1-945658-30-3 *(soft cover)*

First U.S. edition: December 2022

To Peter Milward, S.J. (1925-2017)
To my father (1941-2015)

PART I

City of London, 30 January 1606

Day had not yet come. Along the narrow winding streets, the uneven profiles of the buildings, all pressed against one another, were slowly emerging from the night – dark timber against light walls, slated or thatched sloping roofs. Every minute made things more visible: the colourful sign of a shop or an alehouse, a window, a dormer. Here and there, rickety stairs, tiny balconies, low, irregular wooden porches. Despite the early hour, and the biting cold, and the icy drizzle, the route to St Paul's Cathedral was crammed with excited, noisy people thronging together.

Jack suddenly found himself with his nose buried in a faded red kerchief covering the head of a fat woman commoner, trapped between her huge behind and the legs of an aged craftsman wearing a rough, foul-smelling shirt. He did not like being so close to all those unwashed human bodies. Wincing, he struggled to catch a breath of fresh air. He moved again. Slowly at first, then wriggling like a little eel, ducking and re-emerging, he made his way forward, until he came to a position of absolute privilege: just behind the sharp halberd of a soldier, who blocked the way but not the view.

Adam, his old servant, had managed to elbow his way up almost right next to him. He was trying his best to follow Lady Mary's order to watch over the boy, although he wasn't half as nimble as him. Milady herself was somewhere in that crowd with her younger children. She was poorly dressed, so as not to stick out, and also certainly trying to get as close as possible to the spot where the horses were due to arrive.

Jack shivered. He felt the chill seeping through his skin into his bones. He wrapped himself up more tightly in the black cloak Adam had lent him and stretched his numbed fingers, reddened with the cold: he blew on them, his breath rising like smoke towards the greyish sky. He strained to see. Time went by, but the light of day above that thick, cloudy shroud still struggled weakly to dispel the darkness of those murky alleys.

Suddenly, the crowd grew even more restless and started to push forward while the dull hum of voices mounted in waves, turning into one loud clamour. An unexpected jostle threw Jack against the soldier's shoulder, whose elbow, in response, went sharp into his chest. Jack gasped for air. Well done, boy, he thought. Now there were at least two men in front of him: a young one nibbling at an apple with his few rotten teeth, and a middle-aged fellow wearing a cobbler's leather apron. He craned his neck over to the left, freeing his eyes from a wisp of brown hair soaked with rain, until at last he saw the first horse's head.

A bay horse; as it got closer, Jack could see its neck moving up and down, its muzzle lowered, vexed by the drizzle. It was now so close that, despite the noise, Jack could clearly hear its stamping hoofs on the muddy street and even smell the warm reek of its sweat. He then pushed his way beyond the two commoners, who did not take much notice of him, and brought his eyes to a sort of chink in the crowd which he deemed perfect. He soon realised that his eyes were dangerously close to the soldier's halberd, barely an inch from its shining sharp blade. He stood still, hoping that the soldier would not shift around, and waited the few seconds that remained.

The horse passed, led by another soldier. It was dragging a sort of stretcher, actually a hurdle of rushes, on which a man lay outstretched, his hands crossed on his breast. This was not the one he was waiting for. A young red-haired woman hurriedly placed a little leather purse into the halberdier's hand, who pretended not to see; she threw herself on top of the man, clinging to him and crying. He did not cry; instead, he murmured something about a certain sum he had hidden in a certain place for her and the children. The woman kissed him and vanished back into the crowd.

"God bless thee, Martha!" the prisoner cried after her.

The second horse came: this time it was him. A longish beard and a swollen face made him almost unrecognisable; yet his clothes were fine and new, though soaked and muddy. From his horrid stretcher, the man spotted Jack in the crowd and smiled. This was all Jack had hoped for. A smile, a final farewell.

All of a sudden, a two-year-old boy slipped between the soldier's legs shouting enthusiastically: "Tata! Tata!" Jack recognised Robin, his brother, from the blond curls sticking out below his cap; he crouched down, leaned over and grabbed the little boy by the wrist. Then he lifted him and passed him back into the crowd where Lady Mary emerged for just a second, gathering the child into her arms and crying out to her husband to be brave and pray.

As soon as the horse had passed, Jack called out to Adam to follow him, then started pushing his way back into the human wall, which was eagerly awaiting more horses. Again, he lost sight of his mother and the children. He would find them later: now he had to hurry. He cut through a maze of lanes and headed for the cathedral yard, actually a great square, where the gloomy procession was headed.

There, between the spotted trunks of two massive plane-trees standing like two great stone towers, an imposing scaffold had been set up, surrounded by more soldiers. All around, though the rain was now falling even harder, the crowd was even thicker than down the street. Jack knocked on a very narrow door looking onto the square, three blows in quick sequence followed by two. The door was opened at once, but only by a few inches, by a freckled-faced, bright-eyed, ruffled-haired blond boy more or less his age, who bolted it as soon as he and Adam had slipped in.

"Thanks," said Jack succinctly, putting a golden angel into the lad's hand. What a stroke of luck, in his misfortune, meeting this boy by chance a few days before, while wandering miserably in the City streets. The boy silently led them up a steep and dark little staircase to a chilly little room with a sloping ceiling, where the space was occupied almost entirely by a huge bed in which a human form was just barely visible in the dim light of that dark dawn. The small window beyond the bed offered a good view of the spot upon which everyone's eyes were fixed. The three of them stood motionless at the window and looked out, impervious to the sudden gusts of wind and spurts of rain. Only now did Jack notice that beside the scaffold a small stand, not unlike a stage, had been erected: that was certainly for court dignitaries, judges, aristocrats and all those who, thanks to what was to take place, would be sleeping more soundly and peacefully in their beds from now on. Many people even said that the King in person wished to take part in the show. But then he would be disguised, of course, for His Majesty was – officially – not vengeful by nature and would not stoop to being personally involved in the annihilation of his foes.

And so it was: slowly, one by one, and according to the right of precedence and Palace etiquette, all the seats on the stand were occupied by great noblemen and country gentlemen, courtiers and lawyers, municipal authorities and guild representatives. Among the higher ranks Jack could make out a boy like him, the most richly clad he had ever seen, wrapped up in a snow-white cloak all lined with fur. Although it was not the royal ermine, Jack recognised Prince Harry, the monarchy's rising star, the king-to-be. He too had miraculously been spared death. His pale handsome face was expressionless, stonelike, as if he did not belong to this world. And maybe he didn't.

Until just recently, this boy had been Jack's hero: that is, the time he still thought heroes existed. Handsome and of noble heart, the young prince had rallied a group of passionate young men around him, rather along the lines of the Knights of the Round Table. Jack had only met him once, a couple of years earlier, when his father had taken him on a hunting party in which the King himself had been present. Even if he had only been a child, the prince possessed a splendid falcon and at one point Jack, his heart trembling, had exchanged looks and shared a knowing smile with him. Sir Everard had not excluded the prospect that his son could aspire to the position of Gentleman of the Prince's Chamber, if the boys were given the opportunity of spending more time together. Which would mean, in the not too distant future, being one of the new King's most intimate friends.

"Thou lackst nothing, son, to get there," he had told him. "Beauty, class, education, riding and sport skills, honesty and, I would say, charm." The prince, he had added, would surely need such trustworthy people around him.

Jack knew there *was* one thing he lacked: the Oath to the Supremacy. But that was only a detail, a formality, for, in those early days, the King had appeared tolerant of everyone. Now, instead, after all this, there would be no respite. That dream had slipped away and the young Sun of Britain, sitting on that platform not thirty yards away from the window, was now farther away from him than ever.

Dawn had given way to a dreary, grey, dull day; after the downpour, the rain had finally stopped. No horse, no wretched consignment had yet come, but the spectators – like one multicoloured monster – had already started screaming insults at the condemned men. Some had even climbed onto the damp, slippery roofs.

"Traitors! Demons! Murderers! Death to you! Death!" Some had brought drums and beat on them adding force to every new abuse. But, from the little window above, Jack, Adam and the blond boy could see a few others uncover their heads and cross themselves silently. Behind them, the person who was in bed had timidly approached the window.

The first prisoner was untied from his bonds and hoisted onto the scaffold, where the executioner and his apprentices, along with a cleric in his surplice, were waiting for him. Jack recognised his father, and his heart began to pound. His legs were trembling. He forgot what he had been supposed to do as his thoughts were sort of erased at that moment: he was all eyes, all ears and nothing else. Sir Everard was as white as a ghost and his eyes were heavy, but he tried to be as gallant and good-natured as he had always been. With a kind gesture he refused the cleric's assistance and, as was the custom, asked for permission to speak to the crowd; which, as was the custom, was granted to him.

A deadly silence fell: the entire *piazza* was holding its breath. Everybody knew that this speech could decide his lot: that his total and unconditional repentance might even obtain for him His Majesty's pardon at the very last moment, even with a noose round his neck. Or, maybe, it would transform his execution into a quick beheading, which was no small thing. But his refusal of the cleric's prayers did not leave room for much hope; besides, his crime was too heinous. Jack tried therefore to smother that thin thread of hope still lingering deep down in his heart.

"I have come hither this morning to die," His voice sounded loud and clear, though slightly trembling, "Because I well know that I have broken the law. Although..." The crowd broke into a cheer "... Although my conscience has nothing to reproach me for." Everybody started yelling. He waited for the clamour to subside. "I therefore ask forgiveness..." He raised his voice. "I therefore *beg* God's forgiveness, and my King's, and the entire kingdom's. And I also beg you all to forgive me." Loud cheer: the crowd liked this. "But I also beg mercy for my family: they have done nothing wrong, nor did they know anything." Yells. "My death speech ends here. But I wish to say one last thing. Please, remember one thing." People hushed one another, but many were still murmuring. "I want to say, and I swear this upon my soul, which shortly will be before my Maker..." He paused, waiting for complete silence. He breathed deeply to give more strength to his voice, then spoke out clearly: "... That *no one else*... No one on earth is involved in the matter. That neither John Gerard nor Henry Garnet nor any other Jesuit has had any part in all this, and that none of them knew anything about it." The crowd was confused and started chattering loudly, exchanging opinions; because everybody knew that the superior of the English Jesuits, Henry Garnet, had already been arrested and was now on his way from Worcestershire to London.

Old Adam covered his face with his hands: "This seals his fate. No more quick beheading, now... And they won't even let him hang till he dies! Let's go, Master John, let's get away from here!"

"No," Jack said firmly. "I want to stay. He would want me to stay. When it's done, I want to tell everything about this to those who ask me. See? He is dying a brave man's death. Help me, I beg thee." Adam just placed a hand on his shoulder. The blond boy was silent: wide-eyed, he bit his lip and didn't miss a single word.

The prisoner gently refused again the spiritual assistance he was offered and started instead to pray, probably in Latin, moving his lips slightly. Lastly, he said farewell to his peers, his former friends, who were now looking at him from their seats on the stand. He addressed them as their rank required, from the higher to the lower, as if he were departing for a pleasant excursion. Some of those courtiers uncovered their heads and betrayed their uneasiness: Sir Everard had truly been one of them in pleasant times of recreation and amusement, now gone forever.

The hangman did not kneel, as was the custom, to ask for his pardon before dispatching him: too grievous was his crime. He just had him mount a stool and put his head into a noose. The prisoner made the sign of the cross for the last time. Then, amid yells of excitement, the real show began. They kicked the stool away and Sir Everard began to swing. But he was not left swinging for long before the rope was cut. The hanging was part of the procedure, even for a few seconds, for thus had died Judas, the prince of traitors. Only those who were particularly cherished by His Majesty or the very high-born were allowed to hang until death. On the other hand, the hangman might do a clumsy job, hanging his man too violently and killing him instantly. But for this occasion, someone had been chosen who really knew what he was about and was certainly expecting rich compensation for a clean job well done. So, Jack saw that his father was still perfectly conscious when he was quickly stripped, stretched, and tied to a sort of table next to the gallows, then slowly and with precision castrated, drawn open, his entrails taken out, one by one, and thrown into a boiling cauldron. Jack' eyes were glued to that glutting orgy of blood.

A big final clump, or lump of something, slowly rolled onto the straw below leaving a last red streak on the black wood. Then that hulk of a hangman in his gory apron, masked face covered in spurts of blood and arms dripping to the elbows, raised Sir Everard's still beating heart up in the air and shouted triumphantly: "Behold the heart of a traitor!"

"God bless the King!," the mob answered in one voice. They were mad, drunk with blood. When his axe had chopped off the head, the hangman raised that as well and shouted another ritual phrase: "Behold the head of a traitor!"

"Traitor! Traitor!"

Then, helped by his apprentices, he went on to cut to pieces what was left of the body, whose quarters were to be exposed over several of the city gates. The head was blanched in the cauldron where the entrails were still boiling, then it was dressed up to be impaled on London Bridge, Traitor's Gate, together with all the others. Jack rolled his eyes over that bubbling broth of triumphant people below; his gaze lingered on one old woman who was crying, beads running through her fingers. His thought then darted to his mother and the children, in the hope that they had stayed back, that they had not managed to get close enough to see the horror, that the throng had somehow shielded them.

His eyes skimmed the crowd again: it looked like a vast coloured sea, waves surging, and he felt as he had that time when his father had taken him out on a boat in a rough sea. Like then, he now saw everything moving round him, and felt sickness mounting from his throat. He leant out of that small window and puked on the crowd; then he sagged back into Adam's arms.

He did not see, therefore, the executioner meticulously fold his father's fine muddied clothes and put them into a satchel to take them home. He did not see the perfunctory cleaning job, with brooms and straw, which got the scaffold ready for the second of the four executions.

On that dreary late January morning, John Kenelm Digby became a man. He learnt to reflect before airing his opinion. He learnt to consider who he was talking to and, if necessary, hold his tongue. He learnt to pretend he was strong, to choke back tears for the sake of his loved ones. He wanted to learn to be really strong. As strong as his mother, who had cried her eyes out in secret but in front of them had not shed one tear.

To him, that day marked the beginning of a new age, as if the sun of his childhood had been obscured by an eternal thick cloud: it became a watershed dividing history into before and after. It was the end of a golden age, of the Edenic innocence in which only now did he realise he had always lived. It marked a new Fall for mankind, as if the simple, peaceful world that had been there only three months before had sunk down into a sort of foul, primordial Chaos in which what had always been good, true and beautiful had turned uncertain, dark, foul. The world had lost its crystal-like transparency of yore, in which everything was as it had appeared. Good had been defiled by a mire of filth and what had emerged from it was Evil – pure, groundless, despairing evil which lies at the bottom of every man. And who had unleashed this horror? Who had opened the gates to Evil, who had lifted the dam so that Evil had flooded life, invading the innocent places of the past and bringing about only sorrow, desolation, confusion? The very father he loved so much and almost worshipped. Surely, the Fall from Heaven could not have been more excruciating.

In those first weeks, however, he happened to forget. Early morning slumbers led him to believe that it had all been but a bad dream. He longed to wake up once again in his four-poster feather-bed, up there at Gayhurst, between lavender-smelling sheets, sunlight filtering through the heavy embroidered curtains, birds singing in the park oaks, his siblings laughing and playing with servants in the garden downstairs, and Adam asking him where he would like to break his fast and whether he wanted his pony saddled. His only disturbing thought, back then, had been how to revise his Latin or Italian lesson better.

On waking up, he wished all that horror had been nothing but a terrifying nightmare. But not so: even before he opened his eyes, the hard pallet on which he lay and the chill running down his spine told him that it was all true and that the golden world of his childhood was gone forever.

Above all, he missed his father. Just recently, Sir Everard had begun to take him along with him more and more often, teaching him to be a man. He missed the young cheerful, smiling gentleman and courtier who had never hurt a fly! His father was no more; what was left of him had been scattered to the four winds and could not even be buried. The man who had always been his model, his mirror, had dared do something not worthy of the most devilish mind of the worst murderer in the world. This was why he had been taken from him forever. And Jack's eyes filled with tears even before he opened them. A fiendish treason, conceived in the entrails of the earth, had deprived him of past and future in one stroke.

On other nights, instead, his survival instinct prevailed. He dreamed he was running in blind terror through never-ending, winding tunnels and dungeons, chased by black-hooded men who, once they got him, threw him into a prison full of filthy water and rats. He could hear his mother screaming and his siblings crying while he was being led to the same bloody scaffold to be quartered alive. And, as he struggled to escape, he woke up with a start, panting, gasping.

Lady Mary and the children had fallen too far behind and had not been able to see the execution, but they had heard Sir Everard's last words. Immediately after that, she had taken them to pray in the first church she found.

"I know it's been horrendous, Jack, but I hoped for thee to see it," she told him as soon as they could embrace again. "Now what's important for thee is to remember; so that, when I too am dead and gone, thou canst tell thy siblings, and then thy children and thy children's children. No one must ever forget."

Though her voice was trembling, Lady Mary did not cry: not even this time. His father used to tell him, in case he died before Mother, to console and support her; but at the moment he was the one being consoled and supported. It was Jack, not Mother, who could not stop crying.

"What shall we do now, Mother? Will they arrest us?"

"Again? I don't know. We must be ready: anything may happen. But I believe that, were this what they wanted, they wouldn't have released me. If we can, we'll go back to Gayhurst and just wait. One can never tell. If they do arrest us, however, just think of thy father and bear what thou hast to."

Why did he have to? But Jack did not ask. He just knew that life would no longer be the same for any of them.

"I will, Mother."

While devotedly kissing her hand, he noticed that all her beautiful rings had gone too.

They remained in London for several more days, for Lady Mary had many things to see to, now they had fallen into poverty. She would have liked, at least, to get Gayhurst back, as she had told him. True, traitors' property was forfeit to the Crown; but Gayhurst Manor had been her own dowry. If they begged the right people, they might manage to have it restored to them.

"Mother," Jack told her one day, "I am not sure, after all, that I want to go back to Gayhurst: that would remind me even more cruelly about the happy days. And then they've looted it, haven't they?"

"They have, son. Its bare walls would be all that is left to us, and I don't know how much of the land or the park. Not a piece of furniture, not any tapestry or panelling. But 'tis our home, as well as my family's seat, and your father would want us to make it alive again. And anyhow, where else could we go? No one will host us, now that we are attainted and our name means disgrace. I don't want to rely on friends to support us: as you know, almost all of them are as poor as we are, now. But if Gayhurst is given back to us, we shall withdraw there and, little by little, we'll be forgotten and left alone. Then we'll have to think about a decent future for each of you; but one thing at a time. However it goes, you all must be strong, now that your father's gone, and be worthy of him.''

And his mother, still so young and fair, had gazed into the distance, as if exploring new horizons, and had smiled bitterly, slightly narrowing her large, velvet-like brown eyes. What she was actually doing in those days was trying to gain audience with some powerful man so that the King would have mercy on her and not take away her children.

"Worthy of him," she had said: what could that mean? How could Jack wish to be worthy of his father, one of the worst criminals in history? His heart told him that this could not be true; his mind, instead, had shown him that it was. Loving a traitor meant sharing his guilt, didn't it? If it did, should he then hate his father's memory, he who had given him life and everything he had? Did loving the King mean hating Sir Everard? And was it true that, as was being proclaimed from all the pulpits of the kingdom, all the souls of the conspirators were now burning on one stake in deepest Hell, to be torn apart by unimaginable torments for all eternity? Jack didn't dare ask his mother anything about all this and just nodded. His mind could not explain it, but this was what his heart most longed for: yes, he wanted to be worthy of him.

As even their London home had been seized by the authorities, they had found cheap lodgings at the *Mermaid,* the inn and alehouse where Sir Everard used to meet his degenerate friends and accomplices. Bill Thomson, the owner, knew them well and wouldn't cheat them, as innkeepers often did with naive and helpless travellers. Thomson had nothing to fear from the law now, and took them in willingly, for he had already been questioned by the Privy Council and had told them everything he knew: not much, in truth, but fortunately they had believed him and let him go.

One evening, while they were having a quick supper at a table in the far corner, high-pitched little Meg suddenly gave voice to what they were all thinking:

"Was my father a traitor, Mother?"

Lady Mary was silent, looked down and then said: "Ay, that he was."

Meg opened her big black eyes wide. "And are traitors bad?"

"Not always, dear," her mother had lowered her voice, "And not all of them are like that."

The little girl had raised hers, instead: "Was my father a *good* traitor, then?"

"I can't explain this to thee now, Meg; but I will, when thou growest older."

"As old as Jack?"

"Even a little older. Now you all eat."

A few seconds later, as she was nibbling unenthusiastically at a piece of hardened cheese, Meg went on: "But if Father was good, who are the baddies? Those who killed him?"

"Eat your supper, Meg."

While the little girl was prattling, Jack noticed a well-dressed stranger sitting all alone, in half-shadow, at a table not too far away. He had paper, ink and pen and was writing. Of course, he had heard the conversation: he had just looked at them. His mother too had noticed him, but both had seen him too late. Was he an informer? A secret agent? Jack panicked but then started to repeat to himself till he was deeply convinced that they had actually said nothing wrong, absolutely nothing. As long as he had written the very words they had spoken and not something he had made up... In those dangerous times, even the smallest transgression would be enough to bring you before the King's Privy Council and then straight into the Tower. But what would they do? Arrest Meg who was only seven, and a girl too? Girls don't really know what they are talking about.

Their fears were alleviated in the following days, when they were not summoned to explain the conversation at the inn. So much the better: maybe Jack and his mother had mistaken for an informer someone who was only an innocuous customer, or even a poet following his muse, and he might not even have heard them. Or else, the man might well be an informer, but he had not deemed their words worthy of note. Or else again, but Jack did not dare put this thought into words even to himself, those words of Meg's had just been recorded and filed by the government for future reference, if necessary, later on.

That night, in the rather squalid, big cheerless room they all shared, Jack waited for his siblings to fall asleep and then went back to the matter with Lady Mary, who was lying with the two girls, Meg and

Muriel, in the bed next to his. "Mother, my father did not truly tell you anything about his plans?"

His mother's voice was a barely distinguishable whisper in the darkness of the room. "He chose to keep me out of it, Jack. So that, when they questioned me, I didn't have to lie: in truth, I knew nothing at all about the whole matter. I believe, and I told them so, that thy father had only entered the plot in very recent times, and even he may not have known everything about it. And, of course, when they allowed me to visit him in the Tower it was better not to speak a word about it. That is exactly why they gave me permission to meet him: so that they could listen and learn something more. But we did not even mention the subject. By then, of course, it had no more importance: nothing in the world could save him."

"But who contrived this powder treason?"

"Two men who were killed during capture and could reveal nothing: Robert Catesby and Thomas Percy, gentlemen, friends of thy father's and of all the others. Catesby was actually his dearest friend; 'tis him who got us to rent Coughton Court from the Throckmortons, where we were staying when the whole thing was discovered. Percy I did not know personally, but he belonged to His Majesty's Gentlemen Pensioners, a kind of bodyguard, as thou knowst, just like thy father."

"And what about Guy Fawkes?"

"I didn't know him either. He was staying here in London, on Percy's orders, when they found him, ready to light his slow match. He can have been an artificer... I believe no one on earth has ever been so grievously tortured. Thou didst not see his execution – it took place on the following day, next to that House of Parliament that he would have blown up. Poor thing, he could not even mount the scaffold. Luckily, he didn't survive the hanging and his sufferings ended there. Thy father instead... Thou'st seen."

"I have, and I will remember it forever. But not everybody in the crowd had it against him, even if all the others were shouting like mad. Mother, don't we have anything at all to cling to defend Father's name and ours?"

"Nothing, Jack, apart from his being a man of honour: I don't doubt this in the least. This is why all that follows is not so important: even in death, I keep on trusting him. Although I do not know why he did it. That is: of course it was because of the penal laws, but I still can't believe he came to that. But in the end, if we consider things well, they did not hurt anyone but themselves…"

("… And us", Jack thought, but said nothing).

"As for our good name… there's nothing more to defend, Jack, let's realise that. But we must tell the children again and again never to speak a word about the whole matter: 'tis too dangerous."

Lady Mary closed her eyes. Her family was destroyed, together with her life, like a precious, antique vase flung violently to the ground. All she could do was pick up the pieces and try to keep them together as best as she could. Without stooping too low, though. Therefore, she added:

"These are cruel times, Jack, and I am sorry that thou and thy siblings must grow up thus, like reeds shaken with the wind. These are times when the oaks protecting the earth, and hosting the birds of the air, and sheltering the lowly shrubs and bushes, are ruthlessly chopped down at the roots. Only those survive who bend like willow boughs; those who follow the wind like blades of grass."

"Therefore, what must we do, Mother?"

"'Tis difficult, son." Lady Mary paused as if looking for words. She herself felt like a vine which, deprived of the great tree to which it clung, was now forced to grow all her grapes on the ground, a prey to the boar and the wild beasts of the forest. "We mustn't bend too low and, above all, we must preserve our inner purity. Not defile ourselves… Let's just give them what they want, but not our souls. When it comes to this, though, even just staying alive may be quite a complicated duty."

Jack was puzzled: he heard Lady Mary trying to smile. "I am not sure thou canst understand this, son: thou wilt, when thou growest older. Thou seest, we are surely not as stout and strong as the oak is, but not as important either: perhaps in a short time no one will notice us any longer. There: we should be like the little daisies of the fields, neglected by the great and the powerful, which know how to bend but then stand up at once and always bloom, even after they are trodden down."

Jack gazed in the dark, beyond the small window, at the starry night. Life appeared to him as a long struggle between bravery and fear, light and darkness, order and chaos. And no one could tell which would win.

That afternoon, as soon as it stopped snowing, Jack asked old Adam to walk with him to the house of the boy who had helped them on that fateful day. He wanted to thank him and maybe give him some more money for the trouble he had taken: he was ashamed of fainting like a milksop without saying a proper goodbye.

They knocked on the narrow, battered door. The boy opened cautiously and started slightly; then he stood aside respectfully and led them to the small room up the creaking stairs. He was alone: his widowed mother was out delivering the sewing and embroidery work which was their bread and butter. Jack noticed that the room was really poor, besides being very cold: the walls and ceiling were made of simple wood beams and the only pieces of furniture were the big straw-mattressed bed and a trunk, on which the boy now laid the tallow candle he was holding. That feeble, guttering flame threw its light on several frameless prints, some of which rather old and faded, hanging on simple nails hammered into the wood; they mainly showed flowery patterns or mythological characters. On a nail above the bed hung an old little wooden rosary, as you could still often see in poor homes. On the trunk, next to the candle, Jack spotted a booklet, brand new but with no cover, lying open, face down, as if to mark a page. Jack was surprised to find someone who could read in such poverty.

"I've come to thank thee for everything, and for helping me when I... uh... passed out. Unfortunately, I haven't got another coin on me like the one I gave thee then: all I've got today is just a few groats."

"It don't matter, y' Lordship: let's say everything was included in the price!" The blond ruffle-haired boy, his quick dark-blue eyes overlooking a sea of freckles, smiled at him.

Jack smiled back. "What's thy name?"

"Timothy Rice, Milord. Just Tim to friends."

"I'm John Kenelm Digby," he said, reaching out his hand.

"I know." The lad took Jack's hand into his and smiled more shyly.

"Just call me Jack. Art thou not afraid of reprisals for letting me in?"

"Nope. The Gov'ment has no time for us! What will you do now?"

"Maybe we can go back to Buckinghamshire, and then we'll see. What about thee? Hast got a job?"

"Me ma' would like to send me to a printer as a 'prentice, one of me da's friends that is, to learn the trade." He then added, as if to excuse himself: "You know, when me da' was 'live we wasn't this poor." He was silent, as if not sure whether or not to go on, and finally spoke up: "But I don't want to be a printer: I want to tread the stage!"

Jack frowned: "What meanst thou? Dost like a player's life?"

And then it was a stream of words: "I love it! But me ma' says 'tis not a safe job, with the puritans and town authorities all against it, and the plague making them close down every other day, and then the players have to tour the country. She also says all players are knaves and rascals, but, I say, this is just what all those preachers've nailed into her head, but she don't trust'em anyway. And then, besides being a far more beautiful job, it fills you with money in no time, 'specially if you manage to get into a good company. Meanwhile, what I do is go to the Globe every day, down in Southwark, and look after gentlemen's horses, so, while I bring something home, I also try to make mysel' known to the players. You know, I'm memorising some soliloquies, my fav'rite ones, so that if they happen to call me, I know how to recite aught for them. I'll have to specialise in female parts, 'course. But there are some male parts I love, that is those declaimed by the heroes, even if I could never dream of getting one right now!"

"But that would be a tough life, and a very uncertain one: thou knowst they get thrown out of town every time that a plague is heard of. And in recent times, the way the wind is blowing, every now and then they are sent away from villages too, because they don't want anything to do with tumblers and braggarts. Last year it went just like this in Milton Keynes, near my family home: they had to load their carts again and go. The puritans don't like to have a good time and a good laugh, thou knowst, neither in town nor in the country."

"Some players, though, *have* got rich: far richer than any printer in the world. I want to be a wonderful actor, like Ned Alleyn, like Dick Burbage."

"Then, declaim something to me now," Jack suggested with curiosity, "And I'll tell thee if thou'rt good."

Tim's eyes went brighter. "D' you really mean this? Have you ever been to a theatre?"

"Not popular ones; but now and then, when my father was a man of honour, companies used to come to our manor and play for us and all our friends." He sighed. "When we had a lot of friends and a lot of money, I mean."

"One of the finest plays I know is very old, I've never seen it performed. The playwright himself was quite old when they stabbed him to death, 'cause he was an adventurer. 'Tis about a scholar who turns into a necromancer and sells his soul to the devil."

Jack's face darkened. "Like my father and his friends? I tell thee 'tis a lie!" Actually, he was far from certain about this.

"No, Master Jack, I swear I did not mean this at all. 'Tis just the play! Now I'll declaim it for you. You see, he's sold his soul to Lucifer so he could have four and twenty years of absolute power and forbidden knowledge. And now he must die and go to Hell and doesn't want to, can't believe it, still wants to control Nature like the wizard he'd been, maybe he even wants to deceive the devil himself, like in the tale of the cunning little tailor, to out-devil the devil! But he fails, and fiends come to take him away. Hellmouth opens on stage, I believe, and eats him up. Listen to this, then, Milord." Tim's face was all lit up, his quick blue eyes bright with excitement.

"Canst call me Jack, I say. Go!"

"Gentles all, take your seats!" Jack and Adam sat on the bed. And the young lower-class lad who had first looked so shy and self-effacing became even more lively, as if he had turned into someone else, and started to recite a perfect soliloquy in iambic pentameters, stressing the right syllables, pausing when he had to, now lingering, now running, and all this in an accent worthy of Oxford and Cambridge.

> *Ah, Faustus!*
> *Now hast thou but one bare hour to live*
> *And the thou must be damned perpetually.*
> *Stand still you ever moving spheres of Heaven*
> *That time may cease, and midnight never come.*
> *Fair nature's eye, rise, rise again, and make*
> *Perpetual day. Or let this hour be but*
> *A year, a month, a week, a natural day,*

That Faustus may repent and save his soul!

Now he lowered his voice, now he raised it, now he stopped short, sighed, sobbed. In the final part, Tim had entered the role so deeply that one felt as if this boy's eternal salvation or damnation were really at stake. After the final scream, when the wretch was being carried away by a crew of devils, the lad had tears in his eyes. But, as soon as he had done playing, he came out of his character and bowed to them. "What d'you think?"

"Thou'rt a genius!" said Jack enthusiastically, his own tragedy almost forgotten for a minute. Even old Adam seemed amused. "Shouldst declaim thy lines to thyself, while tending the horses, and hope for some of the players to hear and hire thee. And should they ask thee to let them hear something, this is the thing! Even if, 'tis true, in the end thou'lt have to learn women's parts."

Tim smiled. "Thank you for the encouragement, Master John."

"Who taught thee to read?"

"I taught mesel', Sir. Actually, I am not as good at writing, but that's 'cause I've never tried hard enough."

Though Jack was not particularly well dressed, Tim was aware of the class difference between them, and not only because the young lord spoke differently and with a different intonation, far more similar to the one they used on stage. He even moved differently. And then, he had white soft hands like a girl's, not rough and hardened ones like his. He glanced quickly at his own nails, all broken and dirty, and tucked his hands under his waistcoat.

Just then, they heard steps up the creaking stairs: it was Tim's mother coming back with a basketful of new work. "Still talkin' to thysel', Tim? Light a bit o' fire, me lad, 'cause now 'tis real cold," she said as she came closer. She was still young but wasted by fatigue and worry. Her eyes widened in shock to find the young lord and his servant. She laid the basket down, curtseyed and tried to tidy up her hair. Once she had got over her surprise she grinned, her face all creasing with wrinkles; Jack noticed a missing upper tooth. "I apologise, Your Lo'ships, but I thought my son was talkin' to himsel' as usual."

"That's because he must rehearse his parts," Jack, amused, explained to her. "Did you know, Dame Rice, that your son is really very good?"

"Really? At times he looks a bit dotty to me." She tapped her temple and shook her head. "And you, young Lord, what do you say? Shall I let 'im try and go wi' th' players, if they call him?"

"Your son has good talent: if I were you, I would."

"We'll see, we'll see…" The woman was clearly pleased by the young gentleman's approval.

When Jack and Adam said farewell, Tim went down with them to bolt the door and whispered to him: "Thanks for supporting me!"

Jack was happy to breathe some fresh air, after the stifling atmosphere of the little room. He was even happier that the blond boy had not asked him one question about his father, nor about his family. And also because neither Tim nor his mother seemed to despise him and not even to be afraid or embarrassed in his company, considering that he was the son of one of the worst criminals of the moment. One that, together with other gentlemen, had planned to blow up the whole House of Lords, down in Westminster, during the opening ceremony of Parliament.

Many old friends who, like them, were suffering under the laws had been so scandalised that they wanted to have nothing more to do with them. Many others had been entangled into it unwittingly and then fined, imprisoned or worse, only because they knew them and shared their faith. The persecution would be relentless, now; and this was all Guy Fawkes' fault; and Catesby's, Percy's and all those desperate men's fault, of whom Sir Everard was one.

Feeling at least as little as his sister Meg, Jack then addressed his old servant as they walked: "Adam, was my father a wicked man?"

"He wasn't, Master John, bless my soul! Rather the opposite: he was good and generous to everybody, including us servants. You may not have noticed how, while he was on the scaffold, some of his friends sitting on the stand cried silently for him."

"How could he do this, then?"

"I don't know, Master John: we're all confused… Maybe 'tis Catesby and his cronies as convinced him it was the only thing to be done to stop the persecution." Adam stopped walking, leant towards him and lowered his voice: "Because now they say the King had vowed no tolerance, but I know this to be a lie! Before he came to the throne he'd promised it sure as death! But I'd better not speak about such things 'cause 'tis not my place." He sighed. "Think not about all this, Master John," he then said as he laid, as always, one hand on his shoulder. Jack went on, though: "But why on earth kill so many innocent people, if they were only against the king?"

Adam was silent and just shook his head despondently.

Jack's thoughts lingered on the plot: on the group of men ready for anything, on the secret oath, the magnificent swords forged for that occasion, the mysterious tunnel, the barrels of gunpowder slowly and patiently hoarded. As for Guy Fawkes, he was said to have been a mercenary abroad, to have the body of a hero, and to be full of war scars, all of them on his breast, not one on his back. But then he had committed this cowardly deed, plotting to destroy the innocent and guilty together: why? And why, oh, why had Sir Everard let himself get involved? All that was left of him, now, ran in Jack's veins, and in the veins of his little brothers and sisters: was it a good man's blood, or else the blood of a ruthless murderer? As for himself, who was his father's heir, what would become of his life? Where exactly were Good, Beauty and Truth? Did they still exist? Was it still possible to build anything over the ruins of that bloody explosion which had never taken place?

As he was listening to his own steps on the frozen snow, dirty with the tread of a thousand feet, Jack's thoughts went back to the lost world of his childhood, in which good and evil always fought on opposite sides, and all the good ones were also beautiful, and all the bad ones were but monsters to be overthrown, and combats took place in the open field, and dragons were killed by pure-hearted heroes, until Evil was destroyed forever, and all lived happily ever after. Now, instead, good and evil seemed to mesh in a kind of grey-zone which was real life, where a tyrant could reign undisturbed and a good man suddenly be transformed into the worst of bloodthirsty traitors. Jack was not sure he wanted to be part of that world.

At that very moment, the only concrete reality was Adam's hand on his shoulder; but he would have longed for his father's hand to guide him, instead, and give him a clear, convincing explanation. He bent down and picked up a handful of virgin snow from the side of the street: this white had been his life until that accursed fifth of November. It could never be like this again. The only thing he shared with this snow, now, was the coldness inside him.

Lady Mary Digby dressed with greater care, this morning, than she had done for a long time: she matched an amaranth silk dress (she had no black ones left) with a black fur-fissured waistcoat, large and stately sleeves and a ruff that was almost new. She covered it all up, though, with a very commonplace long brown cloak and instead of a plumed hat she just lowered the wide cloak hood over her raven-black hair, which she had fixed up in a high bun with a sprig of rosemary; the hood hid her face almost completely. Then she borrowed an old basket from the alehouse pantry, so that she looked like a common housewife running her errands, and she walked out together with faithful old Ellen, Adam's wife. She didn't want anybody to notice her on the way to that decisive appointment: she didn't want any curious eyes upon her, nor hear any wiseacre remarks.

It had been snowing all night and all sounds were hushed, all filth covered by a thick blanket of white. Nobody could see the dirt, but it was there, of course. She stood aside to give way to a cartful of peat which made almost no noise and left long furrows in the pressed snow. She tightened the worn-out cloak round herself and looked up, among the houses, to the first wisps of black smoke against the white sky. Two large ravens winged over her head crowing dismally. Perhaps they were coming from London Bridge, or from another of the town gates: perhaps they had flown past what was left of him... Perhaps they had even eaten some of his flesh. She looked down again on the snow, now soft and fresh, in which her feet sank up to the ankles, and tried not to think: she just kept right on walking through the narrow lanes of that freezing morning.

The man she was to meet was said not to be unfriendly to those like her. Lady Mary would have liked to believe this, but kept on her guard: she was not so naive as to instinctively trust the great and powerful. Yet, if anybody could do anything for her in her sad plight it was him, old Henry Howard, Earl of Northampton. A younger son of what had once been the most powerful family in the kingdom, he had lived the typical life of the Court, with its ups and downs, falling like lead in the sea only to rise high in the sky and then fall low, only to rise again; now, though, he had apparently reached what looked like final splendour and greatness. Lady Mary half smiled to herself: someone, perhaps from some pulpit, could well have said that success in life was a clear sign of divine predilection. And the other way round, of course.

In his youth, a long time ago, Howard himself had almost been brought to the scaffold for high treason, like his father the Earl of Surrey before him, and like Sir Everard; differently from them, though – nobody knew exactly why – at the very last moment he had escaped the block and the head that rolled had been his great and powerful elder brother's, the Duke of Norfolk. Just another weird family history, that was. The Government, of course, well knew how to reward reasonable people.

Then, always under the old queen, Howard had once again bitten the dust, but once again Fortune had smiled on him, and he had risen even higher than before when Elizabeth had been succeeded by King James. So high, in fact, as to become the right-hand man of the great Robert Cecil, Earl of Salisbury, His Majesty's most trusted servant: actually, Cecil was the man who held the reins of the country, thus leaving the Sovereign free to go hunting whenever he pleased – which meant always.

Yea, the Wheel of Fortune kept turning and turning. Others, besides the Howards, who had been universally considered almost unassailable, had been cast down so violently and unexpectedly as to leave the whole country speechless. In the last months, following the gunpowder treason, this had been the lot of Henry Percy, the all-powerful Earl of Northumberland, the "Wizard Earl", as he was called. He had fallen together with the plotters (apparently, he was a blood relation of the notorious Thomas Percy) and was now kicking his heels in the Tower awaiting judgment: maybe they would have him beheaded, as had been the lot of so many other noblemen before him.

Howard, on the other hand, working as he did for Cecil, not only had been made Earl of Northampton (a title created especially for him), but also Lord Privy Seal. Accordingly, he had just built himself a sumptuous palace, Northampton House, on the Strand, outside the City walls: this was where Lady Mary was heading.

The two women walked westwards, past Paul's ancient cathedral with its pinnacles, its saints, its gargoyles, and went on towards

Ludgate, whose legendary stone kings looked down from the arch. On the other side of the gate, Lady Mary knew well, the wooden statue of the old queen was frowning down, as if looking for potential traitors, on those who dared enter her city. Here, at least, no human remains were hanging. She looked up and saw that Elizabeth's face had been disfigured: now, nobody showed any interest in having it restored.

As soon as they were outside the walls, she sent Ellen away. Once alone, a sense of anguish, almost of panic, seized her; but she wanted to appear before the great man as if she were a poor commoner. She tried not to think, and walked on without turning back. She had only seen him a couple of times before: surely, he would not remember her now. She felt exactly like a beggar, in this way, going to plead for mercy. Not for herself, of course: if the King chose to do so, he could throw her into the Tower and then send her to the scaffold without getting one sound of complaint out of her. It was for her children, who were still so young and helpless.

As she plodded her way in the snow down Fleet Street, she gazed at the great grey river running on her left, its chilly waters almost completely frozen, and hungry seagulls screeching for food. Further away, one of the few ferrymen left was warming his hands over an almost invisible little fire.

She started to tremble at the thought that she would soon learn about her fate. The King might marry her off to one of his courtiers. And she saw her children being sent away to "sound" families who would raise them as good subjects and teach them unconditional obedience. Perhaps they would be scattered to the four corners of the country and she would see them no more; perhaps she would only meet them as young adults, when they would be perfect strangers to her. Perhaps some of them would end up as far as Scotland among barren moors, in a foreign country where it was so cold and windy, and the people were so warlike and backward and oddly spoken. And they still so young... Muriel was not yet five, while Robin had just turned two... he was always uncovering himself at night, and she was aways rising to cover him up. Who would do this from now on? Maybe Meg would, provided they were sent away together: she was almost eight and might well do this... Or maybe Kit, who was already ten, or else Jack, who she tended to treat as a grown-up but wasn't.

There: at least, she would ask for them not to be sent alone but rather in twos or even threes... Where? And who would take care of them if they got ill? They might not be looked after properly and just die of a common fever...

As for her, she would rather die than marry again and, maybe, have more children; someone else's children, not Everard's... She did not even dare think of this. Rather, she would throw herself into those freezing waters. She kept walking, pushed on by despair; she passed almost all the grand palaces of the Strand housing their *nouveau riches*.

She finally reached the beautiful red brick building, not far from the royal palace of Whitehall; she mounted the steps, walked past the front door and gave her name. The main entrance was crowded with commoners asking for favours: one had a goose to give, another a rabbit, another a chicken and they might well be left waiting all day. Lady Mary, in her cloak and hood, laid down her basket, ready to wait her turn.

Howard, however, seemed to be expecting her, for he had given orders for her to be led to his private study at once. To her amazement, he even stood up from the desk at which he was sitting and walked to meet her. He was a thickset man with a short, well-kept beard and a slight limp. He had grown much older, she noticed: he could be about seventy, but looked older.

"My dear, unfortunate Lady Digby!"

He took both her hands into his and looked at her intensely. Lady Mary was bewildered: what she had expected was an arrogant or patronising attitude. She then took off her cloak and appeared as she was, a true lady. Even in his own fine elegance, he looked at her with admiration.

She wasn't asked to sit at the broad desk full of paper, inkhorns, quills and sealing wax: he led her to the great fireplace, instead, and invited her to sit in a little padded armchair; he then took a seat opposite her and gave orders for a big silver cup of a strange hot drink coming from the Indies to be served to her; its strong spiced flavour remained engraved in her memory for life as a reminder of those days. The warmth of the fire and of the drink restored her: she had already almost forgotten that the higher classes never felt the cold. She did not know what to think, but kept her watch.

He spoke to her softly about the tragedies that at times can hit families, added: "You will have to think of your children, now."

"I will, my Lord. This is why I am here: they are innocent." She lowered her eyes. "And, as for Gayhurst…"

"The King is magnanimous, Lady Mary. Not without my direct intervention, 'tis true, but… I have here ready an act of restitution of the manor-house and all its lands. The title, of course, is forfeit, but the property will be handed down through the maternal line, the Mulshaws, almost as if nothing had happened."

Nothing? The magnificent manor-house turned into a ruin, the horses gone, the cattle pillaged, the seeds stolen. Jack, her firstborn, would inherit that bare ruin, together with the ravaged land, and nothing would be left for the others. But she did not care right now: all she wanted was to learn what would become of her children. She had not dared bring up the matter directly: this is why she had first asked about the manor. So she replied, her voice trembling:

"Gayhurst. In exchange for…?"

"In exchange for nothing, Lady Mary. The King has orders for you, not conditions." Northampton kept gazing at her understandingly, but what he said did not admit objections.

"Of course, Milord." She lowered her eyes into the brown drink, the cup gleaming in the firelight, and waited for the verdict in an agony which she concealed under apparent coolness.

"Your firstborn, Milady. How old is he?"

"He is in his thirteenth year, Milord." She tried hard to control her trembling voice, but to no avail.

"Only? I thought him older…" Northampton went on. "Not exactly the right age to start university… Well, well, this means that he will begin slightly earlier. His Majesty has entrusted him to a most worthy guardian, Lord Robert of Salisbury himself, who has enrolled him at Cambridge. At about sixteen, if he works well, he will take his bachelor's degree. He will also take the Supremacy Oath and the Allegiance Oath, of course, which will open every possible career to him."

Lady Mary lowered her eyes again and stared into the almost empty but still warm cup and was silent. She had nothing to say. She knew perfectly well that this was not a proposal, nor was her opinion requested. Besides, this was more or less what she had expected. Why, then, did she feel that boulder sitting on her stomach? And that would be but the first blow. But her voice had to be firm, this time.

"When?"

"At once, My Lady: in a few days. You will be allowed to go back to Gayhurst with all your other children, whereas Master John will remain in London. Just the time to have him measured and new clothes made, then he will be escorted to Christ's by a trusted man of Sir Robert's. Do not fear, we shall take good care of him."

Lady Mary was silent again. "With all your other children", he had said. No scattering, then, and for this she would have fallen to her knees. She would see them grow up, after all. But the price to pay was Jack. Surely, they would take good care of him: they would tame him like a little dog. But she knew she had no power to refuse and ought to thank Northampton, instead, for leaving all the others with her so that, maybe, she could educate them at home.

Northampton went on: "I know 'tis very hard, Milady: I've been through all this too. After my father's execution, my family went to pieces too. I was only six, then. Later on, in far more recent times, the same lot befell my brother." He sighed and looked down, and his face darkened but for only a second. Then he smiled again, showing a row of yellowish teeth. "But now, you see, time heals all things! Paradoxically, the King holds me dear for the very reason my brother went to the scaffold."

'Twas so. Time, yes, together with much else, she thought. She feared Northampton would try to trick her into a false step, like: "our family too will have to wait for the next reign to get back into favour". Thus, she was very careful to ponder her every single word and not to let her guard down. An imprudent statement, impulsively seeking some understanding, could give her more trouble than she already had.

"I know, Milord. The closer one is to Court, the more uncertain one's lot is, subjected to the whips and scorns of Fortune. I thank you for everything you've done for us. Keep an eye on my boy, I beg you, in the name of…" In the name of what would have once united us if you hadn't sold yourself to Salisbury, she would have liked to say. She said, instead: "… In the name of God."

"I will, My Lady." Northampton smiled reassuringly.

Lady Mary thanked him again, said farewell and, no, she did not want any escort. She put back on her drab cloak and set off alone, under the snow that had begun to fall again in large flakes, towards the bustle of the City, which now was fully awake. Now she would have to tell Jack and she did not know how. She wiped a tear from her cheek with her sleeve and sniffled: first thing, no one must see her cry. She entered the walls and walked through the lanes until the cold had dulled her senses; then, half frozen, her feet soaked, towards noon she went back to the inn.

That same evening, a young man came to the *Mermaid* with a letter of introduction from Northampton: he himself, John Fletcher, gentleman, would take care of Master John Kenelm Digby on behalf of his powerful guardian the Earl of Salisbury. He was a short, plump, beaming man with regular, almost feminine features, a Greek nose and smallish lips, surrounded by a short and rather thin moustache and a correspondingly pointed thin beard; he was fashionably dressed in a big plumed hat and a short red-rimmed cloak lined with fur. As he greeted Lady Mary, he bowed deep and uncovered his head, showing an abundant crop of curly auburn hair. Jack felt relieved, for this man inspired everything but awe: when he had first learnt about his lot, he had expected to be entrusted to a sort of sadistic, vicious knave who would beat him to a pulp at his every little blunder.

Fletcher stayed over for dinner. He had just taken his M.A. at Cambridge and he liked to show off his culture. He ate abundantly, drank accordingly, talked loudly, laughed often. On introducing himself to Jack, even before he heard his voice, he gave him a rakish look, as one who knew every corner of his soul, and, bursting into a hearty laugh, slapped him on the back: "So we're called the same, Master John! Let's make it this way: you'll be Little John, just like Robin Hood's, and I'll be Big John. What d'you say to it?" Jack looked at his mother, then nodded half-heartedly.

Another "Little John" from more recent times had come to his mind: the humble, brave hero who had built hiding places for those who were wanted by the authorities, mainly priests. The pursuivants had taken him and now he was certainly being tortured, down in the Tower dungeons. That little man too, like Robin Hood's, used to be often seen with a friend who had been similarly nicknamed and who was still being hunted down by the authorities. There were hopes that he would manage to run away, because he was so much cleverer than they were. He was Jack's godfather, as well as a great friend of the Digbies. They didn't call him "Big John", which was ridiculous, but rather "Long John", because he was tall and strong, and Jack was happy he had been named after him. Long John and Little John were legend, among their people. Long John was far taller and stronger than this Big John; and also, Jack bet his soul upon it, immensely more skilled in horse-riding and falconry. And he was even more learned, though he hadn't been in Cambridge and never showed off. Jack often wondered where Long John was hiding. At times he thought that sooner or later they would catch him too, because pursuivants and priest-hunters always got what they wanted and the arrest of all those they were after was only a matter of time. At such moments, the future appeared to him as a large black pall which, sooner or later, would extend and cover everything he had ever loved.

"Thou'lt see, we'll have plenty of good time!" Big John later said, winking at him, as soon as they were left alone for a moment. "London is full of entertainments and thy guardian is rich and tolerant: he won't say no to a bit of amusement from time to time. I know every hole of this dirty old town: we'll tour it far and wide!" This sounded like an exciting proposal, but Jack was too miserable to appreciate Big John's good will. Furthermore, from the way his mother was looking at him, he had understood that she didn't like this young graduate and that he'd better never trust him completely.

As had been established, Lady Mary and the children went back to Gayhurst. Jack, who had already had to move to Big John's lodgings in Little East Cheap on that very first evening, went with him to see them off. He didn't know when or whether he would see his family again; he had understood, though, that if he ever wanted to, he had better behave.

He was strong when he embraced them for the last time, just before they stepped onto the cart: he didn't cry and, instead, soothed Kit, Meg, Muriel and Robin who were all tears. He told them that they would soon meet again; which, he knew perfectly well, was a blatant lie. The sorrow of not being able to go with them was a stab in his heart; the more so now that, fully conscious of his new role as head of the family, he feared lest something should befall them in his absence. Was this an irrational fear? Not really. But, as his mother had told him, there was no point in despairing, for there was no choice.

While saying farewell, Lady Mary quickly whispered in his ear: "Resist! Don't let thyself be corrupted. Don't risk thy life for nothing." Then the big rickety cart took them away.

As Jack watched them head towards Aldersgate, he felt the dagger going deeper and deeper into his heart. And what did she mean by "for nothing"? That their cause had become nothing? That Father had died for nothing and so it was for nothing that he was now being wrenched from his family? That, from now on, he should only think about how best to save his skin and that was all? No: he was sure Mother didn't mean this. Then, maybe, she meant "Don't risk thy life for things of secondary importance: do risk it, but only for something worth dying for." Yes, it might be just so: like this, at least, he chose to interpret it.

He would have liked to ask her for explanations by letter, but he very soon realised, in the following weeks and months, that not even his correspondence was free – just like the rest of his life. Big John invariably helped him formulate his sentences whenever he wrote to anyone: it was a matter of style, he said; and then, before sealing it, he gave the letter a final check. The same happened for the letters Jack received: Big John always read them together with him, criticising their lapses of style and sometimes even improvising the Latin translation of one or two sentences. Meanwhile he had had Jack measured for a new set of clothes.

They were in no hurry to leave for Cambridge, Jack was soon informed: so many were the things to sort out in the capital and, apparently, to see and learn as well.

All in all, Big John was not so bad: he was an agreeable companion, besides being an adviser, a mentor and a warden. Things could certainly have been worse: he was no martinet, treated him as if they were the same age and took him along almost everywhere.

In the few months he spent in London, Jack became first of all a regular sermon-goer: both in churches during services and, weather permitting, round the many open-air pulpits. The most ancient and beautifully carved was St Paul's Cross, in the backyard of the great cathedral, just behind its left transept: there the most renowned preachers in the Kingdom alternated, especially on Sundays, almost all day long. Jack soon learnt to tell between the thundering voice of George Abbott, Dean of Winchester and Vice-Chancellor of Oxford university, and the fervent tones of Lancelot Andrewes, Bishop of Chichester and His Majesty's High Almoner. Actually, the two preachers heartily loathed each other, for one was a Puritan and the other was not, but at present they had formed an alliance to defend their King and extol the miracle of his delivery from the fiendish trap of the Powder Treason. They were the two most notable Church authorities of the moment, Big John said to him, and they had recently been commissioned, by His Majesty himself and under the royal patronage, to begin a new, accurate, modern translation of the whole Holy Scripture.

It was unbelievable, Jack remarked angrily, how every single preacher invariably managed, regardless of the Scripture chapter he had started from, to bring his sermon to the recently foiled plot, to the plotters' hellish figures and to the providential preservation of the royal family: it was as if everybody knew that he, John Digby, was sitting in the congregation. They didn't know, Big John explained, but the event had been so devastating as to deserve proper emphasis. Jack envied the other well-dressed boys sitting on benches or in pews all round: they could take the liberty of not listening to a single word

and fiddle with a penknife from their pockets, their waistcoat laces or
the feather in their hats. He too tried to think of something else, but
to no avail: those hammering words about ingratitude, treason,
subversion of natural law, divine wrath and eternal fire invariably
rebounded in his mind for the rest of the day after the sermon, and
sometimes even at night. During the sermons he just sat still and
looked down, his stomach churning, while the preachers thundered
on and, for the hundredth time, he couldn't but listen to all the
horrors of high treason.

Big John – who was certainly no plaster saint of the kind Papists
put on their mantlepieces – also thought about entertaining him, as
he said: since he had to grow up quickly, 'twas well for Little John to
see the world turn. Jack didn't mind, every now and then, putting a
stop to his brooding and losing himself among the various
amusements, down in Southwark, on the Southern bank of the
Thames. He soon learnt to identify all the taverns and alehouses in
that suburb, where they usually went after sermons; he learnt to tell
between the different beer and ale qualities, to detect the water in his
wine, to build himself a man's vocabulary, to bet on cockfighting, to
sing vulgar songs and ballads, to go to the bearpit where, among
encouraging cheers, a bear chained to a pole disembowelled famished
dogs trying to tear it to pieces. All in all, he kept telling himself, things
could have gone far worse.

Escorted by two halberdiers and a young clerk, William Waad, lieutenant of the Tower, strode down the steep steps leading to the dungeons. It grew colder and damper with every step. The others were waiting for him, ready to begin the session, in the chamber below the White Tower, which was dismally lit by several torches. Today's prisoner was a beardless, middle-aged man, as small and thin as an elf, and had already been stretched on the floor, his hands and feet tied to the ropes and pulleys. He was staring at the vaulted ceiling, his lips slightly moving on his expressionless face. One of the men in charge of the pulleys looked worried; he approached Waad and whispered: "I would feel far more at ease, Sir, if we had His Majesty's warrant."

Waad knew this was not possible, for Common Law forbade the racking of the cripple and maimed.

"The matter is too serious, my good fellow. Don't you worry, I'll answer for it." He raised his voice: "Let us begin!"

He addressed the prisoner: "Nicholas Owen, commoner, otherwise known as 'Little John', carpenter, plotter, builder of traitor-holes, arrested along with Henry Garnet, arch-plotter of this devilish plot, I charge you to reveal to me, the King's servant, and to the here-present witnesses, how long you have known him and the nature of your relationship."

The prisoner seemed not to have heard, for he did not change expression. Waad knew well that this here was a tough one: he had already been arrested and tortured, several years before, but had disclosed nothing. Well, circumstances had changed, since then: Owen had once been but a small fish, while now he was the biggest, tastiest prey a skilled hunter as he was could ever hope for. If this man spilled his beans, a whole world would crumble before the Government's feet: the slithering world of hidden subversion, of mental treason, of potential terrorism. It was therefore necessary to handle the matter with extreme calm and caution, for this small fish had grown as big as the Leviathan.

He raised his voice: "Owen, can you hear me?"

"Yes, Sir," answered the prisoner respectfully, without turning his eyes away from the ceiling.

"You know that we shall now proceed to obtain the information we need, for the sake of the whole Kingdom, with the means at our disposal. Do you choose to answer of your own free will?"

"I don't, Sir."

"Then, stretch the ropes!"

Owen was lifted from the floor, his tense limbs making his body look like a wooden tablet. He closed his eyes without uttering a sound.

"What is your relationship with Garnet, alias Farmer, alias Whalley, alias the devil knows how many more names?"

Silence.

"Pull!"

The prisoner moaned.

"Leave it like this," said Waad to the pulley-men.

"Your pain might end now, Owen. Who is Garnet to you?"

"I've served him... for ... four years."

The clerk wrote this down. Waad went on: "Very well, Owen. Tell me now where you were on the fifth of November, when the Powder Treason was to have started."

Owen was silent again, his lips tight, sweaty beads on his forehead.

"Pull!" said Waad. Owen's hands and feet had turned purplish; his wrists and ankles, cut by the ropes, started to bleed. He moaned again.

"Leave it like this. Owen, where were you?"

"In... the country. Garnet is innocent!"

"Where?"

Silence.

"Where?"

Silence.

"Where?"

"He.. is innocent..."

"Pull!!"

Owen moaned out louder.

"Were you at Coughton Court with Lady Digby? Answer, Owen, or we shall tear you to pieces!"

Silence, the blood from his wrists and ankles quietly trickling down.

"Leave it like this. We know how to wait, Owen."

Some minutes went by in total silence, and every minute was as slow as a century.

"Were you at Coughton?"

"Ay."

"This is better, Owen. Who else was with you?"

"I shall... never tell you... never."

"Won't you? Pull!" Owen let out a harrowing, blood-curdling yell. Waad nodded. The pulley-men exchanged worried looks.

"When did Garnet start talking about the plot?"

"Never!"

"Who else was at Coughton?"

"No one!"

"This is no good, Owen. Who else?"

Silence. Waad was furious. "Pull! Pull!"

"'Tis risky, Sir," said one of the men.

"Then leave it as it is. See if he won't speak."

Owen was all in a sweat and trembling. The bones of his limbs were clearly already out of joint: this little despicable cripple was a tough one indeed.

"Pull!"

Owen let out a sort of hushed scream which sounded like a rattle. Waad and the others waited again. Nothing happened.

"Who was with you?"

Silence. Then the prisoner screamed again, louder. Waad opened his mouth to ask another question but stopped short, for blood had appeared on the prisoner's chest too, under his white shirt. The pulley-men started.

"Let go!" shouted Waad. The pulleys turned the opposite way. With one more rattle, Owen lay back on the chilly stone floor, his eyes staring blankly from his ashen face. As they uncovered his chest to see, Waad had already realised that this big fish had slipped from his hands and had fled where no one could ever catch him again. In a fit of temper, he tore off his hat and flung it to the ground.

Big John woke Jack up in the early morning and had him washed and scrubbed from head to toe by Wat, the servant, who then dressed him in his best garments.

"Where are we going, Big John?"

"'Tis a surprise, little one!"

Jack opened his eyes wide: "Maybe to Court? Shall we see the King? And the Prince?"

"Well, wouldn't that be a little too much, seeing thy blood is 'tainted?'"

"And what can I do to clean it up?"

"Why, thou wilt have to turn into a good, exemplary British subject. Thy King will have to be proud of thee; and thy Prince too. This way, sooner or later, thou mightst meet him in the flesh." Big John winked at him, as he had soon realised Jack's fascination with Prince Henry.

They walked downhill towards the river, to the so-called Old Swan's stairs, while the sun shone behind white clouds, and they called out to a wherryman who rowed them upstream, towards the Western walls.

Big John pointed at a glamorous three-storied palace on their right, whose reflection on the water made it look like a great tower. "Baynard Castle, that is, my dear, the London residence of the Herberts, Earls of Pembroke. They've remained in great favour, thou knowst, with the new dynasty."

"How nice," Jack replied. But he was far more interested in the snow-white swans quietly swimming against the green-and-yellow background of the first daffodils running along the bank.

Once outside the walls, they kept upstream along green garden hedgerows till they got to the Strand, with its long row of luxury palaces, each mirrored in the grey river waters, each provided with a private little pier, each with large and low steps leading up to the lodgings. They berthed at the most elegant of all, Salisbury House, whose recent whitewash was almost dazzling. Once up the steps, they approached a wide-open gate which was watched by two liveried guards wearing the rose-and-thistle badge on their breasts and sleeves.

A lackey was ready to escort them across wide corridors and halls all decked with fine tapestry; past mirrors, statues, pictures, the most beautiful Jack had ever seen. They also went past the open door of a magnificent library which seemed to be bursting with books.

Jack's thought went back to his beloved Gayhurst library: what had become of it? It had surely been pillaged and plundered by the government's patrols. He imagined his mother and the children walking in and finding in dismay the torn pages of his favourite books scattered everywhere. They might have put those by for him for a time to come… but when?

They went further on, treading on oriental carpets, walking past snow-white marble statues seemingly alive, artfully carved pieces of furniture, candle-holders of bright silver, under coffered ceilings full of gilt stucco, until they came to an equally lavish private office dominated by a huge portrait of the King in his ermine mantle, looking at them from above a beautifully carved mahogany desk. There they were offered a seat on velvet-soft, red-upholstered chairs and waited. There Jack would soon meet his guardian, the man in charge for what was left of their property; the man who was to decide about his whole future – Sir Robert Cecil, Earl of Salisbury, the most powerful man in the Kingdom. Therefore, he did his best to look clever and mature: he adjusted his ruff, smoothed down his brown shoulder-long hair, put his forelock aside, away from his eyes, and looked at Big John, who nodded at him in approval.

While waiting, his look lingered on a large gilt-framed picture hanging opposite him, behind Big John. It showed scenes from the *Iliad*: the Greek Sinon who, pretending to betray his own people out of personal grudge, was convincing the Trojans to open a breach in the city walls to let in the wooden horse, looming large in the right-hand bottom corner, while Cassandra, on the opposite side, tore out her hair in despair. Jack could also make out, next to the horse, the profile of Laocoon preparing to hit the horse with his lance while, below him, the sea was already ominously churning, ready to spit forth the monsters who would kill him and his little sons. Laocoon was a good man, and a lover of his country, brutally run over and destroyed by outrageous Fate together with his two innocent children, who, utterly unaware of what was to come, were playing on the beach next to him.

Jack would have liked to watch the picture more closely, only, he started on hearing approaching footsteps. But these were too light and quick to be a great man's steps. He was right: they belonged to a young girl, more or less his age, who, walking down the corridor, peeped into the room from the door frame and, on meeting Jack's eyes, uttered a stifled chuckling sound and immediately drew back. Jack had just the time to spot two brown long-lashed eyes and a dark curly lock. He smiled at that unexpected burst of youth and life in such a formal, refined place. The young damsel had apparently been caught up by her governess, for he heard a grown-up voice telling her off from the other end of the corridor: "Lady Mildred, I told you not to!"

"Why, I know, Miss Bridget, but I just wanted so much to see what the face of a traitor's son was like!"

"Stupid, feather-headed hen!", thought Jack in fury, his smile frozen on his lips.

The governess went on: "Well: let us go, now that you have, otherwise your father will be cross."

"Wait! Now that I'm here, I'll just take another quick look and then off we go!"

Jack stood up and got closer to the door; her lively round eyes popped out again. The girl screamed out louder, this time, on finding herself face to face with him. Then she burst into an uproar of laughter and ran away. Not fast enough, though, for, as she got to the end of the corridor, she bumped into someone. Jack could hear the governess' voice apologising for not managing to hold her back, since the little Lady was stubborn beyond measure. Now the girl spoke, her bold little voice ringing clearly: "Forgive me, Father, but I've done nothing so very wrong, have I? I only wanted to see what his face was like."

"And what is it like?" The male voice was sweet, indulging, apparently amused.

"Oh, Father, 'tis terrible! Not ugly, in truth, but so much more terrible for this! At times Satan disguises himself as an angel of light to eat us all up, doesn't he? Like a goblin! Now that he's seen me, do you think he can hurt me? May he come at night to put some gunpowder under my bed?" She could not stay serious and burst into laughter again.

"Don't talk nonsense, dear child. Go, now; I'll see thee at luncheon."

Contrary to what Jack would have liked (and half expected), Sir Robert had not reproached her for disobeying; nor, strangely enough, for her stupidity. Maybe, after all, he too, like Big John, was not a bad man.

He came to them alone, quietly, without having himself announced, in a very simple way considering who he was; Jack, who was still standing by the door, suddenly found himself face to face with him. He was a singularly short man, and as thin, crippled and hunchbacked as he was said to be, but his skin was as rosy as his daughter's. The likeness between them ended here, though: he too had watchful eyes, but immensely sharper; bulging, lashless eyes, like a toad's, especially when he blinked. Not dark eyes but amber-like; not round but slightly slanting, surmounted by arched eyebrows and an excessively large forehead. The squint which afflicted him made his left eye divergent, which gave the impression that he could see and control everything.

He was still smiling, after the meeting with his daughter, his thin upper lip slightly creasing on the left; his grizzled pointed beard was quite thin but well-kept and perfumed, and so was his pomaded hair, which was combed backwards on his large forehead and his long thin face. The finery he wore seemed to increase his height, which was not actually superior to Jack's; but his silken hose mercilessly revealed all the deformity of his short bony legs. This was, then, the man whom His Majesty trusted blindly and called "my little beagle", just as the old queen had called him "my elf". Neither of them could do without him: that large forehead clearly encased a large brain.

Big John, who was still sitting, and grinning for what he had just seen and heard, dropped his grin, jumped to his feet and bowed low, waving the plumed hat he was holding in his right hand; Jack did the same.

"Your Excellency!"

"Hallo, Fletcher."

"Here is young John Kenelm Digby, the late Sir Everard's eldest son."

Cecil looked at him without saying a word. Jack tried to hold that icy, enigmatic stare, but couldn't. He felt he was being examined, analysed, anatomised. When he shyly looked up again, he saw the thin upper lip crease in a new half-smile, slightly uncovering a few crooked front teeth.

"My pleasure, Master John. Please, forgive my child, who surely didn't mean to hurt you"

Jack blushed deeply and didn't know what to say, his heart pounding. He bowed again and muttered a vague "It doesn't matter," which wasn't true, of course: it mattered a lot. And, surely, she *did* mean to hurt him, that accursed little viper. Her light-hearted laughter had hurt him nearly as badly as the cheers of the mobs, there, under the scaffold.

Following his mentor's instructions, he heartily thanked Sir Robert for taking care of him, for lifting him up from the dust of ignominy, for offering him an opportunity to redeem himself and his family: he promised that he would not disappoint him, that he would never stray from the right path. As soon as he had done with his little oration, and had noticed Big John's satisfaction, he regretted every single word he had said: 'twas but a ready-made, fawning speech full of lies. The great man, however, the King's Secreatry of State, lay his hand on his arm. Jack shuddered.

"You see, Master Digby, I believe 'tis possible for *every* man to affirm and redeem himself." His voice was suave, velvety, persuading. "'Tis not fair for children always to pay for their fathers' faults. From now, 'twill all be up to you." This time Jack held his stare. "As for your father…" Cecil sighed. "Alas, he was esteemed and held very dear at Court. I still can't believe his fall. Yet, you heard him yourself, did you not? He broke the law in the most tragic possible way." Jack nodded. "But God, who pulls dark secrets out of their darkness and brings all murky things to light, has foiled Satan's plan, availing himself of His Majesty's sacred person and enlightened mind, thanks be to Him forever!" (who was "Him"? God or His Majesty?) "Since, things being as they were, Master Digby, none of us had realised the great danger which was threatening us all." He sighed again "And, as for the laws…" To Jack's amazement, his amber eyes seemed to get watery "I did not write them myself, unfortunately. Your father and his friends dug a pit before the King and then fell into it themselves. Of course, their crime being as serious as it was, even the King's pardon was absolutely unthinkable."

Cecil started to waddle to and fro across the room, the point of his right splay-foot obstinately sticking out.

"Now, what I would like to do is salvage what I can, Master Digby. Show everybody that one rotten apple does not mean we must chop down the whole tree." He smiled, now. "This said, let's consider your course of studies at Cambridge. I am told you are a clever young man. You will keep me informed on your progress there."

Sir Robert and Big John went on to talk about his curriculum, university life and the future it would offer; and about the necessity of serving the King and Kingdom, and about how very rare true, loyal, disinterested men were, and how needed; and about bribery and corruption reigning everywhere. Jack silently listened, more than to their words, to the sound of that voice, soft and authoritative at the same time; he just nodded every now and then, trying to understand exactly how he felt towards this man who certainly knew what he was about and who, even more certainly, it was not easy to contradict or oppose. While Cecil was speaking, and gave minute details of his future life, it was as if everything would come naturally, as if there were no other possible way. Everything made sense, put that way. What a clever man! Not malicious, not cruel: he had almost cried thinking of Sir Everard. Had he also truly been among his friends? Had the only problem really been that Fate had put them on opposite sides?

In the end, when His Lordship asked him, Jack confirmed that, yes, he would do his best to serve King, Prince and Country. He would have liked to add that his father too had passionately loved his country, but he didn't, because he would never manage to explain Sir Everard's desperate act.

Both Cecil and Big John looked satisfied. The great man dismissed them, reminding Jack to write to him often. Escorted by the same lackey, they soon found themselves on the pier and on the wherry; the whole thing had not lasted more than half an hour.

"And so, little one, are you happy?" Big John asked him while they were being rowed back to their lodging. Jack nodded absent-mindedly, without knowing whether he was or not: he was mainly amazed and confused. And dazed, too, by all that wealth.

Jack remained in London for several more weeks, during which Big John kept teaching him and taking him wherever he went.

"What wilt thou do for a living when I am in Cambridge?" he asked him one night before falling asleep, while Big John, sitting at a small table, was writing in the candlelight.

"I don't yet know, Little John. I wouldn't say no to a career at Court, of course, although 'twouldn't be easy at all. No, no, I wouldn't! Meanwhile, I'll keep doing favours for important people, like this one of looking after thee: thus, I hope His Lordship will have some more little jobs for me. And then, when I can, like now, I write."

"What, poems?"

"That's it! Poems, sonnets, plays... I've just started one for the Children of Blackfriars. 'Tis not a useless thing, knowst thou, in order to avoid starvation!" He laughed.

"Thou'lt never starve, Big John. Thy father was the Bishop of London, not an unimportant man."

"No... how strict he was, poor man, as the good clergyman he was! And then, in his last years he was quite broke: the old shrew sitting on the throne had got quite furious when he remarried. She couldn't stand weddings, knowst thou, Little John; neither for herself, nor for all those surrounding her. Didst know that some were thrown into the Tower for this mere offence? As for my poor father, he left only debts..." He sighed. "Now go to sleep, little man, as thou'rt tired and I'm busy."

One afternoon, as, after being at Paul's Cross, they were waiting for a wherry to row them to Southwark, Jack asked him: "Big John, why art thou so keen on my seeing everything and having a good time?"

"Why, little one, let's say that 'tis good for me too!" He laughed. "And thou'lt see that as soon as the theatres open again after Lent I'll take thee there too, yea, many times. 'Tis also useful to me to watch other dramatist's plays and understand how they're built, so what we'll be doing is combine business with pleasure! And then, of course, thy education's always in my heart; which, they tell me, has been quite neglected up to now. Life, remember, is a great teacher."

"Ay, 'tis", Jack thought. "A teacher who, in order to teach you how the world goes, flogs thee till thou bleedst". Then he thought about the lessons of Religion, Italian and Latin he had had at Gayhurst, together with other gentlemen's children of the county. Secret lessons they had been, for their tutors didn't have a licence and it was better not to tell. Yes, sometimes they were boring, but, even when they were very young, his tutors had been first-class scholars. Upright men too, who looked him straight in the eyes when talking to him and never treated him as their peer or backslapped him, nor did they burst into laughter or wink at him in complicity. Nor did they beat him, though, because they followed the new Continental pedagogy; and then, Jack had always been quite a hard-working little boy. Those tutors never lasted long, however, for sooner or later they suddenly had to pack up and disappear, so that weeks or even months might go by before the children could start new lessons with someone else. Jack's Latin learning might not have been of the most regular but, he wondered, what would his old tutors have thought, had they seen him wandering round all the London alehouses with a man who lived by his wits and took the liberty of correcting everything they had taught him? But, surely, Big John was a little weird because he was an artist. Anyway, how could his mentor know that Jack had changed so many different tutors at Gayhurst? Meanwhile, the wherry had just got to the southern bank and they were now treading a rickety walkway to the wharf.

"Why, Big John, sayst thou my education was neglected?"

"Ah, dear me, how innocent thou art! Thou seest, thy family is certainly all made up of wonderful people: that's what they used to be, at least. The problem is, they were even too good and let themselves be taken in by superstition, especially by a perverted, evil race of people who say they preach the true faith and instead are only trying to give our country away to the Spaniards and the Bishop of Rome. Thy loved ones fell into their net and gave you teachers who've filled your head with devious and dangerous thoughts. Wrong thoughts! Now, what we'll do with thee is, very calmly and patiently, let thee become what they prevented thee from becoming: a true, loyal, faithful Englishman, to whom the future shines bright."

Jack thought of all the sweat he had shed over Lily's Latin grammar: were those the wrong things he had learnt? He really hoped not, with all his hard work. He smiled to himself. Of course it wasn't that, he knew this very well: it was the religion.

"Are the Jesuit Fathers superstitious, Big John?" And he felt a bit toady, for he knew this was exactly what his mentor had wanted him to ask.

Big John nodded enthusiastically: "That's it, Li'l John, they are: 'tis just like that! And 'tis their fault if thy father and his friends strayed from the right path in such a horrifying way."

"What knowst thou about Guy Fawkes, Big John?"

"Ah, he was a devil, that one! Thou knowst what he had in mind, dostn't thou?"

Jack nodded. "But thinkst thou not that he was also very brave?"

"Worse than brave, Little John: absolutely crazy! And cruel too: how could he plan to murder the whole royal family, together with all the noblemen and Churchmen of the Lords? This is just one of the details that came out later: no human being, however perverted, could concoct such a thing by himself. Being a fiendish plan, my little one, it was suggested by fiendish minds. Because now they've found out that behind all this there were thy very friends the Jesuits, the devil's agents! Nay, knowst thou what I tell thee? That in my humble opinion Fawkes was a Jesuit in disguise!" Jack gaped. "Dostn't believe thine ears, dost thou? Yet, thou shouldst know this: at times the wolf disguises himself as a sheep in order to slaughter all the lambs!"

Slaughter: this was what had been on the plotters' minds. Tear to pieces so many great noblemen and the royal family. Turn them all into pulp so they would have to be scraped off the ground with spoons. Jack then asked Big John the question he had never dared ask anyone: "Big John, is my father in Hell?"

"Ay, my dear, I am really afraid he is. So much can be done by those seducers' deceit and equivocation. For, thou seest, being in good faith is not enough: one should also trust the right people. And who on earth is more reliable and just than our King, I say? But we'll have more chances to talk about all this, and then, thou'lt see, thou'lt understand better and better."

They didn't talk much more, actually — facts spoke in Big John's stead; since the hangings were not yet over. Was it really possible for the whole plot to have been contrived by the Jesuit fathers, just as Big John had told him? And for one of its main masterminds to have been his very godfather, Long John Gerard, the one who didn't look like a priest but rather like a gentleman, and knew how to ride, and run, and wrestle better than everybody else, and had taught Jack so many little tricks to be the best hawker in the world? Lady Mary had explained to him that he behaved like that in order not to let himself be taken: he was a gentleman by day and a priest by night. Long John was his hero. Once they had taken him, after all, and thrown him into the deepest Tower dungeons, and tortured him almost to death, hanging him by his wrists for hours on end until blood spurted from the tips of his fingers, and not only had he revealed nothing, but he had also managed to break away: one of the very few who had escaped from the Tower. And, still now, he couldn't be found anywhere. He was as strong as a lion and as sly as a fox. Jack would have given anything to run away to Europe with him and serve him till death.

Little John, instead, the true one, the short, crippled Nicholas Owen, had not made it. Jack remembered his quiet eyes and kind smile: he never spoke much but worked really hard. They had taken him at the end of January and had made him disappear, swallowed by the maw of the Tower dungeons. Jack learnt later from Big John that the little joiner had... killed himself in his cell for fear of further tortures: this was just incredible. Later on, however, Jack had overheard two housemaids talking at the market, saying that, actually, his belly had burst open while they were racking him.

Together with Little John Owen, the Worcestershire Sheriff's men had taken the superior of all English Jesuits, Father Henry Garnet. That one was less well-known to Jack, but he had been their guest at Coughton when the plot had been exposed, and Jack had been struck by the man's holiness. That one was clearly a priest, not a gentleman: he never went hunting and he was quite unlikely ever to have handled a sword; on the other hand, he sang beautifully. When Big John told him that the plot had actually been contrived by Garnet himself, Jack found it not only hard to believe, but outright ludicrous. Could that meek man have cold-bloodedly planned that horrible massacre? That was impossible! And then, Sir Everard had declared from the scaffold, swearing it on his soul's salvation, that the Jesuits had had no hand in it at all.

Jack would have liked to know what his mother thought of all this, up there, at home – provided the news had reached those parts of the country – and whether she believed this. He wondered how they all really were, beyond the conventional letters he got, which invariably said that everything was all right or, at most, that Muriel or Robin had had a temperature or the worms but had now recovered. And he felt guilty because, after all, he was not suffering so much in the company of this peculiar young graduate. Above all, he felt guilty because his powerful guardian, Robert Cecil, Earl of Salisbury, had made a good impression on him: not only did he seem extremely clever, but also kind and understanding.

Jack knew he was at a crossroads. On one side he could see sorrow, poverty, fear, persecution, death. On the other, wealth, finery, friendship, pleasures, life. And, deep within, he had a desperate wish to live.

Spring had bloomed in all her splendour when Big John took Jack to see Father Garnet's execution, the last of the long series which had started roughly three months before with Sir Everard. Once again, the chosen place was not the usual, infamous Tyburn Tree, outside the city walls, but rather Paul's yard, where Sir Everard and his friends had also suffered. This crowd, however, was more curious than enraged. Back then, it had been in a sort of mass hysteria; now, perhaps, not everybody was convinced that the prisoner was really the mind behind the plot. The place was the same, but it couldn't have been more different from the day Jack's father had been executed. Then, it had been all grey and cold, and Jack had been penniless, frostbitten and distraught, while now he was comfortably sitting, together with Big John, on one of the several wooden stands that had been put up; he was fashionably dressed, amidst equally fashionable people. Twelve pence each, it had cost... How much must they have earned from it? He felt out of place.

He looked round: the square itself seemed different, flooded as it was by the light and warmth of the newly risen sun, while the two big plane-trees on either side of the scaffold were covered in strong lush leaves dancing lightly in the breeze. Better to die on such a day, Jack told himself: at least, when you're dragged on your hurdle, you're not cold, nor covered in mud. Was it not better? Maybe it wasn't: maybe dying today, when life looked so beautiful, would be even more painful.

A wasp lighted on his arm. He chose not to kill it and, instead, blew it away. Its buzz already sounded like summer. He spotted, across the square, the little window he had looked out on that distant day, now crammed with faces once again. Surely, as the resourceful young fellow he was, Tim Rice had found new customers: paying guests wishing to enjoy the show from a privileged spot. Of course he had paid too, that day, but for quite a different reason.

Once again, his mind went to his hero, Long John of the little beard: where was he hiding? He might be right here in London, and even right here in the crowd, to say farewell to his beloved superior. He screwed up his eyes, although he well knew that he could never hope to identify him: even if he was there, he was surely in disguise and might look like a blacksmith, a merchant, a gentleman. Just then, Big John looked at him and grinned. Jack feared he could read his mind. Unable to grin back, he looked away from the throng round the scaffold and stopped seeking Long John.

The prisoner finally came, tied to the usual hurdle of rushes and dragged by as many as three horses. Once untied, he slowly mounted the scaffold by himself. He couldn't have been more different from the man Jack remembered: far thinner and so pale, owing to his long imprisonment, that he no longer seemed to belong to this world. Dr George Abbott, Dean of Westminster, whose sermons were so familiar to Jack, offered him spiritual assistance, which Father Garnet kindly refused. Then he gave his last speech to the crowd: as he spoke, he really looked like a holy man. Jack could not hear all the words, for his voice was low and a bit drawling and tired, but what he understood was that Father Garnet simply wanted to pray for his country and for his King. No debating, no politics, no theology; no self-defence, either. Neither did he reply to a few saucy, dirty jokes from the crowd.

They took off his black cloak and hat, then hanged him in the white robe he was wearing under his clothes. Then, while he swung, his mouth open, the hangman approached him to cut the rope and disembowel him alive just like Sir Everard. Jack covered his eyes, still hardly believing this could be done to a man of the Church. But then the crowd started to clamour. Jack opened his fingers just a little and saw some youths come between the hangman and the gallows, while others grabbed Father Henry's feet and pulled hard. There, they had given him a quick death. It was a disgruntled hangman who proceeded to draw and quarter the body, moving fast and roughly, as if he wanted to hurt him as much as possible, now that he no longer could.

"So they ruined his party," Jack thought, "Serves him right!"

When the bleeding – but not beating – heart was held up high, the hangman's triumphant exclamation requiring its ritual choral answer was instead received by general silence. The last thing Jack half saw, before he managed to draw his eyes away, was one of the victim's white shoulder-joints against the red of his sinews, while they were ending the quartering.

In the following days, at home, Big John showed Jack the
transcripts of Garnet's trial and other hot-of-the-press essays and
treatises. He told him he must hate those incredible schemers and
equivocators who had officially legitimised lying and had stopped at
nothing to achieve their vile ends.

"I don't know, Big John: they seemed so good…"

"Remember this always, little one: appearances are deceptive. And
think that, had it not been for them, thy father would now be safe,
sound and happy with you all."

Jack sighed, hardly holding back his tears, for this was certainly
true: in the end, he really didn't know what to think. Maybe, after all,
Big John was right. He would have liked to stop thinking, stop
wondering, but he couldn't: his mind invariably went back there,
continually asking always the same questions. His mind, split from his
heart as if on the rack, was teaching him that all he had loved and
cherished, all that had been sacred to him in the world, had been
wrong. His father had made a mistake which had destroyed both his
earthly and his eternal life, dragging them all into a bottomless pit.

Everywhere, in those months, people talked about little else than
the Powder Treason, and the inhuman audacity and wickedness of
the plotters, their diabolical minds and their adeptness at storing as
many as thirty-six (thirty-six!) barrels of gunpowder beneath the
House of Lords, and the underground tunnel they had managed to
dig to carry out their plan, working at night, shielded by darkness and
by Satan himself, the prince of darkness. Pulpits thundered against
them, libels proclaimed their depravity, passers-by clustered to
whisper, and even children playing in the streets had invented a new,
wicked gunpowder attack game.

The playing companies had also been very active in this field. Big
John now took Jack to popular theatres more often; there seemed to
be no play which, in one way or another, did not refer to dark plots,
intriguing Jesuits, mysterious subterranean passages, murky murders,
threatening dangers foiled at the last minute, or, alternatively, hideous,
heart-rending bloodbaths.

"I'll tell thee," Big John had told him one day as, after lunching at
the *Duck and Drake*, they strolled towards London Bridge and
Southwark for the last time before Jack set off for Cambridge.
"Differently from what the puritans say, the theatre is not immoral at

all!" He chuckled. "And this, I'm afraid, was one matter of disagreement between me and my father."

Big John's voice became a distant hum to Jack as, once they had got near the bridge, his senses filled, as always, with shapes, colours, sounds, smells. It might well be the last time for him to look at this ancient, strong structure whose thick stone arches had resisted the currents of the great river for so many centuries. He looked at the people walking to and fro. Men, women, young, old, from all walks of life, all of them equally busy. He watched the little gaily-coloured houses that had been crammed on the bridge itself along the ages, each of them with its little stall in the front selling their goods; he watched the smaller boats rowing below, and the screaming gulls winging above, and the clouds which, running across the sky, kept on covering and uncovering the sun while the wind carried about a mixture of smells, food, people, fish and salty, stagnant water from the sea.

"Little John, 'rt thou listening to me?"

"What? 'Course I am."

"The theatre, as I was saying, faithfully mirrors the ancient way of teaching, and far better than any other form of art. If what thou wantst to teach appears tough, or boring, or in any way not agreeable, thou must, so to say, spread some honey on the rim of thy bitter chalice: so that, when the sick child tastes the sweetness of the honey, he will swallow the bitter medicine as well, and profit by it, and be healed. 'Tis the same with the theatre: it teaches you lots of things while entertaining thee. So much better than sermons!"

Jack couldn't say he didn't agree on this; but today he was still less eager than usual to see common strutting players put on stage yet another story of conspiracy, treason and murder clearly referring to the Powder Plot, as Big John had already told him it would be. Alright then: he had learnt his lesson, and felt himself sag, out of shame and confusion, each time he heard players loudly proclaim how far human wickedness and cruelty could go.

Meanwhile, they had already crossed the bridge and had reached its ghastly Southern gate, which was haunted by huge black ravens and bristled with human heads, each, to a greater or lesser degree, in a state of decay, impaled on an iron spike. Jack knew very well whose heads they were; after all that time in London, he still hadn't got used to them. The latest they had put up, Father Garnet's, had then had to be turned face upward, for the populace superstitiously claimed that some ot those who had looked it in the eyes had already obtained miraculous healings.

As he always did, he avoided looking up. He wanted to go home. Not even the clear, windy, half-sunny day, not even the beautiful playhouse – the best in London – could lift the dark mood into which he had fallen. Maybe the solution to all his problems was just not taking sides. Maybe he wasn't really being asked to choose between his faith and his country: maybe the apparently unsolvable question would be solved, or rather dissolved, in a portion of roasted fish and a pint of beer bought in the street; in eating and drinking, laughing and joking among other people, and listening to a street minstrel in a public square. Life was so short and sometimes it was so easy to go wrong, to step out of line... it was already complicated enough to think for oneself: why should one always have a good cause to serve, to live for, to die for?

The Globe was the only playhouse where Big John hadn't yet taken him: *dulcis in fundo*, he said. Already from the outside it was really beautiful, a thatched, many-sided polygon. Quite a new building, it was, not more than ten years old, its walls still a goodly homogeneous creamy white, in nice contrast with the dark wooden beams of the main frame. On top of the turret over the main stage one could see from quite far away a small flag, flapping and snapping in the wind. A black flag, today, meaning that the play would be a tragedy. Surprise surprise, Jack thought.

They walked through the entrance under a wooden arch; Big John greeted the woman at the box office, put some coins into the clay jar she was holding and led Jack to the galleries. Two shillings and two pence had given them the right to seat on soft cushions, sheltered from the elements, above the crowd of the groundlings. The inside was made entirely of wood as well, and even more splendid: three tiers of galleries went all round the roofless pit. In its middle, and higher than any head, stood the main stage, jutting out into the noisy, standing spectators, all commoners, already pushing and shoving impatiently. Fortunately it wasn't raining, otherwise they would have been even more impatient, and someone may even start throwing things at the players even if the performance was good.

The stage was, of course, the most lavishly decorated part of all. The elegant canopy sheltering it was a true work of art: it was beautifully gilt and supported by two slender columns painted perfectly to reproduce delicate, rosy-veined marble. While walking past it to reach his seat, Jack saw that its ceiling reproduced the vault of heaven, its blue sky in beautiful contrast to its golden stars, all of which was surrounded with the zodiac signs. Clearly these players had spared no expense: to them it was a matter of earning their living. Just as clearly, moreover, this was quite a profitable business. Heaven, earth, Hell, which could be entered through a trapdoor in the centre of the stage: there was really everything in a theatre. It was like a little world: this is why it had been named The Globe.

At the very top, just below the little black flag on the turret, Jack could see a goodly gilt wooden statue of Atlas (or maybe Hercules?) bearing the world on his shoulders; at his feet, a sign was nailed with the same writing as that engraved on the entrance archway: *totus mundus agit histrionem*. Big John pointed out to him, for his personal culture, that, broadly speaking, this sentence meaning "the whole world plays a player" could also be translated as "All the world is a stage"; and it was the latter meaning, actually the less accurate, which had become dominant in people's heads. Jack nodded and thought about how much he would have preferred being at Gayhurst sweating over Lily's grammar, rather than finding himself forced to watch another dreary parody of the Gunpowder Plot.

When he had taken his seat, however, and when the musicians started to play from their balcony overlooking the stage, and the play began, and the groundlings themselves fell silent all round, Jack realised that this play was different from all others. While watching and listening, he simply stopped being himself and became one with what he could see and hear on stage. It opened with three witches who told mysterious prophecies and proclaimed that fair is foul and foul is fair, which was exactly what he was feeling in the deepest corner of his heart. Then, the good King of Scotland was slaughtered by a treacherous thane who had a fiendish wife, and confusion made "*his masterpiece.*" This was precisely what was happening in Jack's head.

There was, luckily, a comic scene as well: soon after the murder, the drunk (and hunchbacked) porter of the castle thought he was the porter of Hell-gate letting in the damned. This meant that the castle where they had killed the King had become Hell: its inhabitants, therefore, were devils. Jack remembered how, many years before, a company of travelling players had stopped at Gayhurst and (illegally) performed a Mystery play for them, full of angels and devils, which had both frightened and fascinated him; especially when Christ had come to knock on Hell-gate and had torn it away forever. *The Harrowing of Hell,* it was called. This was why his favourite Italian poet, one Dante, had imagined that the gates of Hell had never been closed again.

But, contrary to what Jack had expected, the murderer was not unmasked and instead was crowned king. He looked at Big John and saw that he was so taken up by the play as almost to have forgotten him.

Now the crowned usurper had to cover up his murderous crimes, subsequently turning into a hateful tyrant, killing his former friends.

"What will they do now? Kill him?"

"Dunno'," Big John replied. "Thou knowst that an anointed and crowned king can never be killed: rememberst thou not Dr Andrewes' sermon at Paul's Cross, the other day?"

"'Course I do: that's why I'm asking. Right, no one can kill a king; this king, though, has murdered the previous king and usurped the throne. And he's evil. Can't even evil usurpers be killed?"

"We'll talk 'bout that later, Little John. Now be quiet and watch."

Jack was quiet and watched, but didn't stop thinking. He saw good, gentle people being accused of treason, just like his father. Only, unfortunately, his father had not been innocent. He had declared it on the scaffold: he knew he had given mortal offense and had asked for everybody's forgiveness.

The lines spoken by a Scottish thane struck Jack deeply: *"I dare not speak much further; but cruel are the times when we are traitors and do not know ourselves."* Incredible: this was exactly how he felt. It was as if his heart was breaking because he had to hold his tongue. He tried to concentrate as best as he could on the scene he now had before his eyes: a gentlewoman talking to her little son.

Suddenly, with a mixture of surprise and joy, he recognised that little boy: Tim Rice. He had made it, then! A big smile of satisfaction distracted him, but only fleetingly. For Tim's words made him bounce back onto the stage with his whole being:

"Was my father a traitor, mother?"

And the "mother", who actually was another, not much older boy, said: *"Ay, that he was."*

"What is a traitor?"

"Why, one who swears and lies."

"And be all traitors that do so?"

"Everyone that does so is a traitor, and must be hanged."

"And must they all be hanged that swear and lie?"

"Every one!"

What a stupid woman, Jack thought, talking like this about her husband. Lady Mary certainly had not, nor would ever say anything like that. It was absolutely crazy, though: for the "child" played by Tim had asked his mother exactly what Meg had asked hers, that evening, at the inn. Jack decided not to think about it for the time being, for now he didn't want to miss a single word.

"Little" Tim Rice went on:

"Who must hang them?"

"Why, the honest men."

"Then the liars and swearers are fools, for there are liars and swearers enough to beat the honest men and hang up them!" Tim moved his hands and tongue in a very eloquent way among general laughter. Jack clapped his hands like everyone else. That "boy" was surely not wrong... And then the amusing pun on swearing: everybody, especially the groundlings, must have felt they were all swearers, liars and, thus, traitors. Treason was not so serious, then?

But events suddenly came to a head: in came three murderers, sent by the tyrant, who killed the child and chased the mother backstage, where they killed her too. Even that short comic respite had turned into tragedy in the twinkling of an eye. Tim had remained onstage, alone in a sea of (sheep) blood. His had been a very small part but a really good one. His "corpse" was covered from above by a dark cloth, so that now he might stand for a hill, and in came two other characters who engaged in quite a boring conversation.

"Big John, I know that young player, the one they've just killed. Can I go and greet him when 'tis over?"

"And where canst thou have met a young commoner, Little John?"

"That's when I was staying at the *Mermaid*: I was bored and started to play with him."

"All right, I'll take thee to see him later. Wouldst like a nut?"

"Ay, please."

Jack could no longer concentrate on the play and didn't even recognise Tim, who had appeared and disappeared again as one of the soldiers on their way to besiege the evil usurper's castle.

He kept thinking of the questions Meg had asked that evening, over supper, at the inn. This could not be mere coincidence: Tim had used the very same words. What did all this mean? Was Meg in danger, after all? He longed for fresh – and authentic – news from his loved ones.

He was burning to see the end of the play: It was obvious, by now, that the tyrant would be killed off. There: the little boy's father came and dispatched him, so that peace and prosperity could come back to Scotland. Justice was done, the time was free. How good it would have been if Sir Everard too had stayed alive (or had come back from the dead) to defend him and Lady Mary and the children from villains. He was an orphan, instead, one whose cry reaches Heaven, but also one who had no defence on earth whatsoever.

"Dost understand how the prophecy is fulfilled?" Big John asked him.

"I do, I do," Jack answered absent-mindedly. "Hast seen, Macduff has finally done away with him."

"Yea… Good. But it doesn't fall in with the canons of a true tragedy."

"Why so?"

"Because in classical tragedies the hero is destroyed due to a fatal mistake he has committed, and also because he is pursued by Fate; however, he is always good. The audience, that is us, must suffer for his death, not rejoice."

"My hero is Macduff, so this is a heroic play to me, not a tragedy."

"Of course… Thou'rt not yet thirteen… Wilt understand later the complexity of the human soul." Big John gave him a strange, enigmatic grin.

The show closed with a skilful exhibition of music and dances, while the groundlings' alcoholic intake was soaring sky-high. Now people kept the time clapping their hands, all of them: from the galleries to the pit, from the nobleman to the apprentice. The aristocrats sitting in the balconies waited for the noisy, smelly commoners to go and then they quietly began stepping down the painted wooden stairs. Jack couldn't wait for his turn to come: he only hoped Tim hadn't left!

As soon as he could, he threw himself down the stairs, and was so nimble that Big John, who was neither thin nor fast, lost him for some minutes; he shot into the *tiring house,* where the players changed their garments and makeup.

He found himself in the dark, till his eyes got used to the half-light. A mixed smell of face paint, sweat and resinous wood invaded his nostrils, while everybody, in that crowded place, seemed to have something very urgent to do: put away a costume or a piece of armour, take off a wig or some makeup, get changed. A young man went about barefooted asking loudly if anybody had seen his shoes, but no one seemed to heed him: some laughed out loud, some were chatting, and Jack almost bumped into a lad-servant carrying beer jugs. He couldn't find Tim anywhere, in that hurly-burly: maybe he had gone, after all. Then he finally saw him, alone in a corner, sitting on a low stool, fiddling with a shoe.

"Tim! Tim Rice!"

The lad looked up in astonishment.

"'Tis me, Tim. Dost remember me?"

He smiled and got up. "'Course I do! Welcome hither, Master John!"

"Thou've been so good a player!" Jack held Tim's hand in both his: "Congratulations: thou'st made it!"

Tim blushed with pleasure. "Thank you, Master John... Me ma' 's let me come also 'cause you had told her to do so..."

"Jack, I tell thee: just call me Jack and 'thou' me! 'Twas a terrific show." Jack looked behind his shoulders and spotted the outline of Big John's large shape darkening the doorstep. He stood aside and introduced him to Tim. But the noise was so great that Big John, who kept looking round in curiosity, was not able to catch every word they exchanged.

"How did they hire thee?"

"'Twas a real stroke of good luck. I'd been after them for a while, asking them for a very small part, just to try me. They laughed, apparently at me, and said nothing. Then one day one of 'em, thou seest, the white-haired one down there, his name's Heminges, waves at me. Come here, he says. And he asks me to try a speech, 'cause their youngest player's ill; and they liked me, and so they told me they may keep me, but they still don't know. Now I'll just go to the box office to see what they give me for today."

"Thou'rt happy, aren't thou?"

"Very happy indeed, Master... Jack, that is! What about thee? What'lt thou do?"

"I'll tell thee when we get a chance to be alone." Jack discreetly pointed at Big John, who was admiring some gaudy costumes hanging on the wall. "Now I've got one thing to ask thee before he gets close again, 'tis very important to me: whence comes thy line, where thou asked whether thy father was a traitor?"

"Who knows? 'Twas written in my part. I'll show thee, I've got it in my pocket... Seest?"

Jack considered the creased little paper strip attentively.

"Why dost thou want to know?" Tim asked.

The big room was less crowded, now. Jack lowered his voice: "I'll tell thee later. Who wrote it?"

"Will Shakspere, the poet: 'tis he wrote the whole play, like nearly all those performed by this company. Come, I'll take 'ee to 'im if I can find 'im!"

Jack begged Big John to let him go and meet the great dramatist. Big John nodded patronisingly, satisfied at his pupil's showing some artistic and literary taste. The three of them then went out into the pit, where two servants were picking up rubbish.

"There he is, talking to the leading actor. Come!"

Jack looked at him and suddenly understood everything: that was the man who had been taking notes, that evening at the *Mermaid,* whom he had mistaken for an informer. A great weight was instantly lifted from his heart. That's why he had been writing: he was looking for things to put into his tragedy. And where should he look for them, if not near the family of one who had just been executed? At this point, meeting him had become superfluous.

"Let be: he's talking..."

"What, suddenly dostn't want to meet him any more? He's a fine man, thou'lt see, and never boasts, though he is as rich as a king and as famous as the moon... and then thou'rt a gentleman, he can't ignore thee. Come!"

Surely Tim liked to let the acting world know that he had posh friends. Jack looked behind and saw that Big John too had met an old aquaintance and had started talking.

"Fine," he said to Tim, and walked with him towards the two men. The leading player, Richard Burbage, a stately, large-shouldered man, was the first to notice them and called out to Tim in his powerful stage-like voice: "Hey, Master Rice! Going to collect what's thine? Thou'st been good, just keep on like this. Nay, come on here, I'll give thee thy due myself." He fumbled in his pockets and took out two coins which he laid on the lad's open hand. Tim was beaming. "Thank you, Sir. Me ma' 'll be happy. D'you mean I can continue with you?"

"Why not? When we've got parts for thee, of course."

"Thank you! Master Burbage, Master Shakspere, this is me friend, John Kenelm Digby."

"Honoured." Burbage spoke for both and looked at him with some interest. "Is there any connection with.. ?"

"Sir Everard was my father, Master Burbage," Jack said unflinchingly. "Now I've got a guardian, Sir Robert Cecil, Earl of Salisbury."

"Of course... So we are colleagues!" said Shakspere, the poet, smiling at him. "We're all His Majesty's servants: we, his playing company, and you, his most faithful servant's ward."

"Ay... Congartulations for the play, I liked it a lot!"

"We're happy you approved of it, Sir," said Burbage, "For, you know, we will soon take it to Court!" Then he turned to Shakspere: "After a good *labor limae*, Will, of course, as we were just saying..."

"'Course, Dick: who dost thou take me for?"

Jack smiled. "I am happy you have offered Tim this chance. I realised at once that he was made of the right stuff."

"He's very good at getting himself killed! I believe we'll need him again: our audience loves carnal, bloody, and unnatural acts."

"I just wanted to ask you something, Master Shakspere."

"Tell me, Master Digby."

Jack lowered his voice, so much that the playwright had to bend down and get his ear closer. "You were at the *Mermaid,* one evening, a few days after my father's death, were you not? And you were taking notes..."

"There's a smart youth: you noticed me! I always take notes, wherever I go. Do you see? I have my inkhorn hanging from my belt; for a well-written play must throb with real life."

"And you liked what that little girl said... That's my sister Meg."

"I remember, Master John, I remember. Ay, 'twas a scene that struck me. And a lively little girl with large fawn's eyes."

"Did you know my father?"

"He was a regular customer at the *Mermaid* together with his friends: of course I did."

Jack was enthralled. "Was he a good man?"

"Ay, that he was." Shakspere lowered his voice still more. "You mustn't be ashamed to be his son."

Those words were like balm on an open, bleeding wound. Jack would have liked to ask a thousand more questions of this man who was so understanding with traitors and who had talked to his father so often, but this was certainly not the right place, nor the right moment, in front of Tim and Burbage. Above all, Big John too was slowly approaching. For some strange reason, Jack chose not to introduce him to the men of theatre; so, he said farewell to them and to Tim.

"Good bye, Tim. Coming here to the play has been wonderful."

"Wilt thou come again shortly?"

"I must to Cambridge, at university; I'm leaving London the day after tomorrow. Write to me at Christ College and let me know how thy career proceeds. May I write to thee here at the Globe?"

"Ay! I'll be here every day, if not to act at least to look after horses or clean up: they always give me aught to do. As for writing to thee... I can read whatever hand perfectly, but writing is a different matter... I'll work hard at that!" They both smiled.

"May I ask thee for a favour, Tim?"

"'Course!"

"If thou getst the chance, but be very careful, ask Shakspere what he knows about my father and the Powder Plot."

"I will, Jack. I know what it means..."

"Can I trust thee?"

"Thou must. I shan't disappoint thee."

"I'm glad I've met thee."

"Me too!"

They shook hands, then Jack walked towards the main gate with Big John. He only turned once, on the threshold under the archway, and he saw Tim proudly waving at him, while he stood next to the two most famous men of the theatre.

"So thou'st met the great poet, hast thou not?" said Big John lackadaisically as they were leaving.

"Ay… why didn't thou come thyself? I was ready to introduce thee."

"I know him already, Little John. He's good, sure, and very lucky too. Even if he lacks a bit of discipline…"

"Dost mean he doesn't follow Aristotle's rules? Time, Place, Action? Neither does he follow the unity of style, as for that."

"That's it. Not even those, I would say! Ha, ha, ha, ha!" And without more ado he quickened his pace down the street, to the wharf and the wherry which was to row them back to the respectable bank of the Thames.

Two days later, on the feast of SS Peter and Paul, Big John and his pupil rode North to Cambridge university. Jack would never forget that ride: Big John waking him up before sunrise, the cool morning breeze, the glorious dawn and the blue sky, swallows soaring in circles high above; and his horse galloping, his own fatigue, the peasants' sheep-shearing feasts, the fiery sunset; at last, looming against the sky, the silent dark citadel. So quiet it was that the bustling of London already seemed to belong to another world. This was how quickly life could change. Among these sullen walls, maybe it wouldn't be so hard to forget sorrow and heartache: maybe he could start from scratch, here, and build himself a future. Jack was tempted to think that it might even be better for him to spend some years in Cambridge, rather than going straight back to Gayhurst and having to live day by day with the desolation and misery of the place, continually recalling a splendour and a joy which could no longer be. This was but a fleeting thought which vanished at a wink: how could he ever be so selfish? Living close to his loved ones would surely soothe any sorrow. This way, instead, they would have to go through their new woe all alone, as if the pain of leaving him behind hadn't been enough.

The clatter of their horses' hoofs rebounded against the vaulted ceiling of a majestic stone porch, then was lost again in a wide courtyard. Four or five grooms popped out of nowhere to tend to their animals. Across the courtyard, the lit-up windows of a vast pinnacled building seemed to invite them in. They were met by the pleasant warmth of a great hall where everybody, pupils and teachers alike, was still sitting after that day's feast. Everything in it was definitely reassuring: the large log crackling in the huge blackened fireplace, the torches stuck in brackets on the polished panelled walls, the large tables round which boys of different ages were sitting – all of them older than Jack, all wearing black robes: the whole scene conveyed both order and cordiality. On the other side of the room was the teachers' table; elevated by a dais, it ran from wall to wall. After Jack had officially introduced himself, Big John paid tuppence and a boy in charge of the table service led them to the seats awaiting them. Jack felt all eyes upon him, which was probably normal seeing that, besides being new, he was the youngest of all; therefore, he thought lightly of it.

Big John stayed over for a couple of days, sharing a little room with his young former pupil; then, once the necessary arrangements were made, he said farewell and went back to London. A little bewildered, Jack watched him cantering off. He didn't know whether he was feeling sad and lonely without him, or rather relieved, and freer than he had been for months: actually, since the fifth of November, when hell had begun for all of them.

That afternoon, Jack was escorted by a servant carrying his trunk to the dormitory he was to share with three other students, all of them much taller and sturdier than he was. The big room, though sober and austere, was furnished with everything they needed: two big beds hosting two boys each, a washstand with basin, pitcher and towel, while several painted cloths, mostly showing mythical scenes, were hanging on the walls. At the foot of each bed there was room enough for both students' trunks, while each of the two wide windows hosted a studying space: on one side, a thin long desk furnished with paper, ink, pens, and a stool underneath; on the other, behind a heavy curtain, a comfortable reading seat. A tall bookcase, mainly stacked with religious books, completed the furnishings.

As soon as he crossed the threshold, however, Jack understood the real reason all eyes had been fixed on him on that first night: because everybody knew who he was. His room-mates welcomed him with malicious leer, none of them talking to him. He watched their stupid, calf-like expressions; he wanted to offend them, then bit his tongue thinking that, if he was lucky, these chaps were the ones he would have to live with for the next three of four years. He then said, a little too solemnly, his own words echoing emptily in the hostile silence of the room: "The King is magnanimous and is not of the opinion that children should pay for their fathers' faults." Their only answer was more silence and sly leers. Furious, Jack started to take his things out of his trunk. A carbuncular, fat, flaxen-headed fellow called Nugent, the one who was supposed to share his bed, seemed to be the most hostile of all. As soon as the servant had gone, he said to the others: "Hey boys! D'you think it fair for this scum to be in our room?"

"Not in the least: disgusting!" answered Watson, an ugly watery-eyed brute. "Why haven't they sent him to the stables?" The others

laughed. "But in *our* company, of course, he'll soon learn 'bout life…
Hey, thou worm, how come thou'rt not ashamed to be seen among
honest people?"

The third one, Powell, whose oily red hair bristled like a pine
forest, was even more explicit: "Traitors should be with other
criminals, and their families too: all of them in the Tower, all of them
to the scaffold!" More laughter followed this.

Both frightened and infuriated, Jack threw down the shirt he was
holding and ran out into the courtyard. "So, they don't want me!" he
thought. "Nay, 'tis me not wanting *them*! And, oh, I'll let them
understand this, but in an elegant way. I don't need anyone; I certainly
don't!" He wandered round the cloister, not knowing what to do or
where else to go, his soul in turmoil, and saw that everybody avoided
him.

Life at Christ's soon proved increasingly hard for him; also, and
especially, outside his dormitory. No one wanted to be near him. Not
even during lessons; not even at table, where, if he did not literally
hold his food close, they made it disappear before his very eyes. One
of the younger students once tried to spit into his soup, and failed
simply because he was quick enough to move his bowl away, thus
spilling half its content on the table; another time someone switched
his bread roll with a stale one covered in greenish mould.

It became harder and harder to bear all those wicked jokes, those
little thefts, those little acts of sabotage, and people tripping him up,
sniggering at him, or whispering in small groups: "Traitor! Traitor!"
This happened everywhere: down the corridors, on the stairs, in the
cloisters. But the persecution vanished into thin air, and the chanting
came to a halt instantly, at the arrival of a grown-up.

Sir Everard's crime had apparently been so foul as to leave an
indelible mark on him too: did he also have to pay? Was there no way
to shake off that stain, to wash it away? He had hoped he would be
given a chance to turn a new leaf… Far from it. Jack realised that his
fellow Christ's students were but a cross-section of the whole
Kingdom and that all His Majesty's good subjects hated him just
because he was who he was: given his father's crime, he was guilty of
being born. He would have liked to explain to everybody once and
for all that he was not his father; that, if his father had been wrong,
he would show them, instead, that not all his family members were

traitors. This was why he was here, as Sir Robert had told him. If only they would give him a chance to show it! But no one was willing to listen to his explanations, nor would they care a whit about his rehabilitation. Thus, while the teachers seemed to ignore completely who he was – ignoring, at times, his very existence – the students seemed to know him even better than he knew himself. Jack felt his determination faltering, his inner strength crumbling each day a little more, while the emptiness he felt within, and the desperate need to be accepted, became an abyss threatening to swallow him up. Thus, he tried not to think, to make his face as hard as stone, and basically threw himself into compulsive, scrupulous, almost maniacal study in every discipline.

Fearing lest the bad jokes might get even worse, he tried to stay as close as possible to teachers and supervisors, which wasn't of much help but at least could spare him some of the nastier tricks. Like the morning when he had found his shoes full of excrement and, so as not to be late for prayer, had had to go barefoot along the corridor just outside his room, which someone had covered in dry thorn twigs. It went on like this for months: the whole world appeared to have united against him.

The worst of it, of course, came on the first anniversary of the fatal discovery, on that accursed fifth of November in that accursed cellar. That day had been proclaimed a national holiday even as Sir Everard and his wretched friends were still riding like mad through the country, after the capture of Guy Fawkes. Now, as a result, people throughout the land were all set to light bonfires and burn the effigies of those fierce murderers and regicides. As if their horrible, shameful, disgusting death hadn't been enough: as if they had to die again every year, forever paying, even in this world, for something they had not even managed to carry out. A special thanksgiving service had been set up in every church of the Kingdom for the miraculous preservation of His Majesty and the Royal Family. Jack knew perfectly well that bonfires would be lit at Christ's too, each burning its own straw puppet, its little Guy Fawkes standing for what was commonly identified with Popery, the murderers' murderous faith.

Envisaging a very bad day, that morning he rose before dawn. He slipped into the kitchen to steal some food, then ran to seek shelter in the great study room, where a supervisor kept the silence and watched over the students' good behaviour. Since it was so early, and a holiday, the dark room was chilly and almost empty. Jack, who didn't have the money to buy himself a candle, looked on every table for a stump that was long enough to enable him to read till day came; then he sat down at one of the tables, near a big window which would let in a lot of light, and, opening a big and heavy volume, started to study his favourite subject, ancient history. As he read, trying to learn by heart the names of men and battles, he continually blew on his cold fingers. He was really fond of Plutarch's *Lives*: poring over the feats of those giants of mankind, his everyday life appeared less miserable and unbearable to him, peopled as it was with hypocrites, pigmies, opportunists, cowards, who persecuted him simply because he was weak and helpless but – he had no doubt – would run away in terror with their tails between their legs if only they had had to fight seriously and on even ground.

At the sound of bells, the whole college would soon flow into chapel for the special thanksgiving service. Jack wanted to stay away, but how could he? The supervisor would surely lock the hall and force him to go. Once there, they would all leer at him and snigger and tell the usual jokes, only louder and more insistent, so that, as usual, he would be their laughing stock, only with more people noticing and taking part. Maybe, on that particular day, even some teacher would treat himself to some banter about Guy Fawkes, Papists, or, worse still, Sir Everard.

It was a frosty day and the grass in the cloister, beyond the icy windowpane, was all powdered in white. Every now and then Jack raised his head from his big book to watch the cloudless autumn sky being slowly flooded with golden light. He could already hear some students cackling excitedly: of course they were happy they had been granted one more holiday. Presently, everybody was running to and fro with things to burn: they all wanted to add something to the bonfire. A stake was soon built and lit right in the centre of that cloister, while a dreary chant spread as fast as wildfire; its obsessive, hammering rhythm made Jack's blood curdle: "*Remember, remember the fifth of November. Remember, remember the fifth of November. Remember, remember the fifth of November…*" It was all taking place just before his eyes. Terror paralysed him. He wanted to shrink on the spot and become a fly on the window, so that no one would see him.

At that point the supervisor, who was, as usual, one of the poorer students supporting themselves by working for the university, did something he should never have done: he left the room to go and see the bonfire and, maybe, to warm himself a little; so that Jack found himself utterly alone. Suddenly, as if waiting for nothing else, four grinning sixteen-year-olds broke in and headed straight for him. Jack's heart sank: how could they know he was here?

Before he could stand up or even think of running away, they had grabbed him. "Come on, Digby: thou wert not thinking thou'dst miss the celebrations, wert thou? Today is your day!" They lifted him kicking and screaming, and, as they carried him outside, the mesmerised crowd that had already gathered in the cloister covered his yells with their hammering, obsessive chant. Jack desperately tried to wriggle out of their clutch but could hardly move a muscle, as at least a dozen hands took possession of him. They tied him with a rope, which they had clearly prepared in advance, then hoisted him on their shoulders and took him closer to the fire, which was now roaring furiously, as if requiring more fuel. Meanwhile, the chapel bells had started to clang, in case some student had managed to deceive the wake-up caller and stayed in bed. There was not one adult to see what they were doing to him. The refrain sounded like an ancient, primordial magic spell, louder and louder, faster and faster: "*Remember, remember the fifth of November. Remember, remember the fifth of November!*" None of those around him seemed to have an ounce of rationality left: it was a sort of collective delirium, echoing primitive times, pagan rituals, human sacrifice.

When they reached the fire, they started dancing, maenad-like, round it. There were more and more of them, all drunk with cruelty, while Jack could only see bright eyes, open mouths, grinding teeth… and the roaring fire. This was pure madness: would they throw him into the flames without anyone moving a finger to help him? He tried still harder and more desperately to make himself heard, move, squirm away, but all his efforts only seemed to increase the general euphoria. Would he then have to die today, right now? Would he never see his mother, his siblings, Gayhurst Manor again? Pure, instinctive, animal terror took possession of him; a terror he had not experienced even on the day of his father's death. This was worse than his worst nightmares.

Just then, amid the cruel laughter, the four thugs carrying him laid him down, face downwards, in the mud produced by the heat of the fire and the trodden frost. A silence fell. They forced him to repeat everything they said – and he did, hoarse with shouting as he was until his lungs had nearly burst. Every statement was received by a general cheer. "Long live His Majesty, King James I!"; "Death to all bloody traitors!"; "Death to all bloody Papists!" ("This louder, Digby!"); "Death to the Bishop of Rome!"; "Burn, Guy Fawkes, damned murderer!" He was kicked rolling in the mud; then he was untied and kicked into chapel, all muddy, trembling, crying, his nose bleeding, his lip broken, to take part in the thanksgiving service. No grown-up had seen: no teacher, no servant, no supervisor, no one on earth had taken the trouble to save him from their clutches; consistently, no one now seemed to notice his pitiful state. Now more than ever did Jack realise he was utterly, dangerously alone. He wanted the earth to open under his feet and swallow him up, thus ending all his suffering, all his shame.

It couldn't go on like this. The following day, aching all over and full of bruises, bent over the same historic volume, bathed in tears, he took paper, ink and pen and wrote about it all to his guardian, Sir Robert Cecil, who was also Chancellor of Cambridge University. He wrote that he couldn't bear it any longer, that everybody resented him for something he had not done, that in these circumstances it was impossible for him to study with any profit – nay, it was even impossible to live. He felt tremendous guilt because – contrary to what he had vowed, and to what both his mother and the famous poet of the King's Men had said to him – he was now ashamed of his very own name.

Cecil's reply was brief, concise and not long in coming. Sir Robert was surprised at the ill-treatment his ward had been subjected to and would soon look into it. Jack should, on the other hand, show his own worth, his love for his studies and, above all, for his country. Everybody had to see how different from his father he actually was. Sir Robert did not doubt that all his problems would then be solved in a short time. He wished him a good and fruitful continuation of his studies.

Jack understood that being the best at Latin and Greek would never be enough: what he would have to do was take a clear position in religious matters and publicly state his political allegiance, distance himself from his family and from the faith he had been raised in. He tried this – out of sheer curiosity at first – just to see whether it was really what was expected of him: he feebly answered several questions about which religion was the true one and why. Almost overnight, the persecution against him decreased until it vanished altogether. His room-mates were the last ones to speak to him; but, at last, Nugent too stopped tearing off his blankets and hiding his clothes.

From that moment on, time began to flow, if not smoothly or quickly, at least at a tolerable pace. His very life at Christ's College became tolerable. The weight crushing his heart was lightened, the days followed one another somewhat more tranquilly, all of them more or less the same. Jack wasn't sure he had acted for the best when he had publicly conformed, but he preferred not to know: he had acted in the only possible way to survive.

Meanwhile, he grew accustomed to many things. He grew accustomed to marking the time of day to the sound of the bell that led all students, as if by the hand, from morning prayer to breakfast to their lessons of logic, Greek, rhetoric. He was led through Cicero's orations and epistles, Aristotle's *Ethics, Problems*, and sophistic refutations. He also learnt to grow fond of the rhetoric wars which older students waged against one another. He admired their ability of persuasion, the rationality of their arguments, the clarity of their reasoning: those were real titanic struggles. One of the teachers would propose a topic for discussion and the best students always managed to justify even the craziest of positions, no matter how difficult to defend. He learnt to adopt one perspective at a time, then split it into several opinions, one opposed to the other. He also learnt, of course, the subtle distinction between a virtual opinion and a real one; above all, he learnt to stop short once he went near the slender boundary between tolerable opinions and suspicious or downright unlawful ones. He started to hang out with a small group of four or five fellows who were not very hard-working, not very bright, whose ideas were not very clear: although he often got bored in their company, he felt safer. This way, his Cambridge life became more or less bearable. He soon started to emerge as one of the most promising students of his year.

Sherwin, he was called: Ralph Sherwin. He was about fifteen. He stood out immediately, because he was always on his own and spoke very little, seemingly in contempt of human company. Despite his coming from Yorkshire, up there in the wild North, he didn't look like an ancient Viking at all, for he had a dark complexion and dark hair. His eyes were often lowered, not out of shyness but rather out of spite, or, at most, as if he were lost in his thoughts; as if no one there deserved the effort to raise his eyelids. Then, suddenly, unexpectedly, he would give you such a piercing look like he wanted to knife you.

His collar strings were always undone, his robe awry, just like one who flouted all rules. At times, when debating, he managed to checkmate the teachers. Like when the Scripture Master, Dr Edwards, had extolled the liberation attained by Martin Luther from the yoke of the Roman Anti-Christ: thanks to *Sola scriptura,* he said, the whole false apparel of mediation between God and Man had been pulled down like a prison wall. Well, Sherwin had objected, some go-between was necessary, otherwise it wouldn't even be possible to establish with any certainty which books of the Scripture were canonical and which were not; unless, of course, God had spoken directly to Luther as he had to Moses, and as the angel had spoken to Mahomet. The class had burst into laughter and Sherwin had been punished; from that moment, he had isolated himself even more. He always lowered his eyes, but not his pride. As for the teachers, they were said to be ready to expel him and just waiting for the next time he put a toe out of line. But, after that episode, Sherwin just refused to speak and stayed away from academic debate as much as he could: he would just look at the teachers with a mixture of pity and hatred. If looks could kill, all teachers would have dropped dead at his feet. They certainly couldn't expel him for his look, could they? They all wondered how he could ever take his B.A: debate was compulsory, there. Despite all his queerness, no one played tricks on him, for everybody feared him.

One day, in the heart of winter, Jack was sitting in the common room alone, bent over a thick book of chronicles, busy memorising as much as he could both of its style and its content. He liked history even when it lingered over minute details of sieges and battles by land and by sea, which he then tried to reproduce on the beaten earth of the courtyard in his many lonely moments, using pebbles and twigs to represent Roman ships and legions.

Someone came in; Jack saw out of the corner of his eye that it was Sherwin. He didn't want to seem like a swot to this rule-hating older boy whom, deep down, he admired: he would have liked to appear a bit transgressive like him. So, also in order to have something to say to him, he snorted noisily. "Enough. I'm fed up with it!" Sherwin stopped and looked down on him. It worked: he had noticed him. Jack went on: "And then, what's the use of all this Greek and Roman history, and all these names, Alexander, Caesar and Pompey, and Themistocles and Alcibiades, and who are they to us? What we want is to understand the problems of *our* times. The trouble is, we are not allowed to talk about modern problems! Nor do they teach us modern history, here at university: all we do is sweat over these dead, mouldy languages!"

Sherwin glared at him with his cruel, morose eyes full of spite. "What's the use of ancient history? Thou'rt joking! 'Tis of more use than modern history, which they will never let us study. 'Tis right for that reason, seest thou not? Thou just dostn't bloody get it, dost thou, Digby?" And, without waiting for his answer nor for any other reaction, he turned his back on him and walked away. Jack had never felt so stupid in all his life. That was his first and last exchange of words with the dark hero of Christ's College.

Thus, in a relatively acceptable atmosphere, John Kenelm Digby completed his education. Time ran faster, now. Months and years went by. He soon had trouble recognising his own voice or face: his feet looked huge, his nose as long as a stork's beak. He suddenly found himself very tall, with outsized arms and legs. He felt awkward, clumsy, ugly, even unable to manage his own body: how on earth could he come to terms with the complex reality of his immediate circumstances, how could he give a reason for everything he was, for everything he did? His hard university work, as well as the anxiety of trying to make himself accepted, left him very little time to reflect calmly by himself, to sort out the maelstrom of his thoughts and memories. If, on the other hand, he just obeyed and did what was expected of him, everything turned out to be, if not easy, at least less exhausting.

He tried not to bend too low, though, especially when recalling that last day in London and his mother's parting words: "Resist! Don't let thyself be corrupted. Don't risk thy life for nothing." Well, he *was* resisting, but only in the sense that all he managed to do, as a last bulwark, was to keep his thoughts to himself. Only in his head did he have something exclusively his; the problem was that he couldn't even make it out clearly. When he thought of his father, now, he was horrified to find that he could no longer visualise the features of his face. He saw him once again standing on the scaffold, but all he could recall was his sad smile, and then the blood, all that blood gushing and streaming, blurring Jack's vision. How could he possibly give him satisfaction? Just by showing the world he was different? Was this the way he could restore his father's good name? What would Mother say? What would Big John? And his guardian, Sir Robert? How could he act so as not to disappoint any of them? For the time being, he put off the whole matter: all the big questions of life melted down to the little everyday tasks which made him feel safe. Having people respect him for his culture and competence surely also meant having them respect his name and, therefore, his father's too. All this was quite easy to think out, but a totally different thing to live: for instance, every single year he was officially requested by the university authorities to be an altar boy during the special thanksgiving service for the fifth of November.

He soon entered a different circle of friends: those who, like him, came from dissenting families – either actually or potentially so – from which they had duly been taken away. They were not rebels: far from it. But they belonged to the external, most sceptical circle round the general conformism which was universally called loyalty and integrity. They were, like him, those who remained at Christ's during the holidays as well, both in summer and in winter, because they were still not allowed to go back to their loved ones. Like him, they couldn't seal their letters, nor receive anything that was not unsealed. Anyway, a letter from home full of commonplaces and maybe lies was always better than nothing at all, like a drop of water on a parched tongue, to soothe the heart-rending homesickness they all had within.

PART II

The whole university was a beehive of activity, for the great day was fast approaching: Oath Day, just before the final disputes, for all the B.A. candidates. The Great Hall had been scrubbed squeaky-clean and the back gate bustled with people coming and going: cartloads of cheese, vegetables, hay, straw; peasants riding horses or mules, or walking among geese, sheep, pigs. Pedlars with their laces, ribbons and perfumes doing a roaring trade; busy servants running here and there to find tailors, shoemakers, blacksmiths and jewellers, for on that day their young masters would have to excel all others as to grace and elegance.

Even the Doctors of Divinity, those professors whose fame resounded throughout Europe, had quivered with emotion, thrilled to learn that the royal representative for this year's ceremony would be no other than the Prince of Scotland and England, Henry Frederick Stuart. Jack was at least equally thrilled at the thought of seeing his childhood idol again. He wondered whether the Prince had grown as tall as he had.

The various inns of the town had already opened their doors to the many relatives and guardians who had started flowing in; among them was also Big John, whom Jack hadn't seen for almost four years. As he went down to greet him, he happily realised that he had grown much taller than his former mentor.

"Hey, Big John, thou'st grown small by now!" The shorter man, who had, instead, grown considerably fatter – so much that Jack had almost thought of calling him "Fat John" – looked him up and down, pretending to be offended.

"Watch your tongue, young man! I am always big, or better, great: now even greater than before, 'cause I've become a true poet. Always Big John to thee, therefore; nay, weren't I so modest as I am, I would have thee call me 'John the Great'!"

"Art serious? Dost mean thy poems are being printed and sold? Art thou famous already?"

"Well, well, let's say I've made a good start. But let's talk of more important things: tomorrow, then, is the day when thou wilt definitely leave the straying paths, the stones over which thy family tripped and fell, and wilt be welcomed back into the right fold. These are tears of joy, my boy!" He hugged him again slapping him on the back. "How many things will they have taught thee, how many things wilt thou've learnt since thou wert a little, ignorant, beardless boy all wrapped up in superstition!"

"What, art thou pulling my leg?"

"'Course I am! Ha ha ha ha!"

Jack didn't feel at ease: he knew that swearing loyalty to the King and his Church against everything and everyone else was not exactly the right thing to do. Sure enough, this was what was expected of him: and anyway, did he have any choice? Then, as if it were a prize, he would finally be allowed to spend some days at Gayhurst and meet his family again. After that, he was to go back to London along with Big John: Sir Robert had formed a plan for him, in which an M.A. would not be needed. He was, therefore, to leave Cambridge and all its sad memories forever.

The whole town had been cleaned, spruced up and renovated for the Prince's arrival. The university authorities had organised a grand parade in the streets, with music, flowery wreaths, allegorical floats, tumblers and jugglers, while some of the best and most loyal students would recite Latin and Greek orations. Luckily it wasn't raining, although insistent gusts of wind had begun blowing and the sky was little by little clouding over. All the inhabitants had poured into the main street, waiting for the heir to the throne and his large retinue. People were everywhere: at all windows, on roofs, some even with babes in their arms. Jack was so tall that he could see quite well above the crowd. It was from a roof, though, that the cry came: "They're coming!!!" Instantly, unmistakably, the sound of bagpipes and drums was heard.

The prince's cortege too was a full-scale parade. First came the pipers and drummers in his ducal red-and-green tartan; following them, a troop of liveried foot soldiers, carrying splendid parade halberds. On their chests they bore the Scottish red lion rampant on a yellow field, while their sleeves displayed the Prince's fifteen Cornish bezants on a black field. Then came the horses, led by the Gentlemen of the Prince's Chamber, also clad in the ducal tartan: those among whom Sir Everard had once dreamt he might introduce his eldest son. At the tail-end of the parade were foot soldiers. There, amid his Gentlemen but absolutely unmistakable, Jack saw Harry Stuart.

He was riding the most beautiful white Andalusian anyone had ever seen, tall, majestic, with a curving neck and a floating mane, adorned in green and gold: a truly royal mount. The Prince was beaming at the crowd and sitting very straight in his saddle, his left hand holding the reins, his right one waving at the people, every now and then taking off his beautiful crimson plumed hat and waving that too, showing his short dark-blond hair. Under the crimson, silk-lined mantle that he had thrown elegantly over his shoulders, he was wearing a snow-white waistcoat all embroidered in gold, on which a black velvet ribbon stood out with his golden St George medallion; His ruff of Flemish lace was also white, while his red hose, along the flanks of his white steed, showed off both the dark Garter on his left calf and his long sinewy thighs; his golden-spurred high riding boots looked as soft as cheveril.

This was their spotless King-to-be: this pure, upright youth would hold the reins of the Country just as he was now holding those of his fine steed: with ease and mastery. He was said to be the right opposite of his father, with whom he often argued; Some said that he really wanted to call back into fashion, as he had said he would do since he was a child, the ancient chivalric ideals; and that he would not only reign but also rule directly, and not delegate everything to others in order to do what he pleased. Above all, he was said to hate the vice, favouritism, and corruption reigning at Court. He loved bravery and elegance, arts and virtue. Jack felt at one with the exultant crowd; his loud welcoming cheer, joined to theirs, came straight from his heart.

The whole university could speak of nothing else and even the least conforming students – that is, the restricted circle Jack was friends with – shared the general enthusiastic atmosphere.

"A goodly lusty youth; and a clever one!"

"D'ye know what he's done? This is true, on my soul, not unjustified rumour, ask whoever you please. He's put a little alms-box at the entrance of St James' Palace, whereby he fines all courtiers who speak even one coarse word in his presence."

"Why, this must be called exaggeration! 'Tis Puritan-like and bodes no good."

"What? With all that goes on at Court? Let be, I really hope that, once he succeeds to the throne, he'll clean up all that rubbish."

"We certainly couldn't wish for anyone better, after that sour old spinster and this buffoon king who spends all his days hunting."

"And maybe, who knows? This promising youth will also bring tolerance."

"Ay, who knows? King James, anyway, is said to be negotiating his son's marriage to the Spanish Infanta."

"That'd be good, marry! but don't hope too much: I'm afraid such a plan will never meet success at Court, not to mention Parliament."

That evening, the Prince and his gentlemen dined in the Banqueting Hall together with the teachers and the B.A. students. Jack, who could hardly swallow a morsel, felt a sudden desire to get close to him in some way. He asked the teacher mastering the ceremony to be allowed to serve a dish or a chalice to the Prince. As he expected, he was told that all roles had already been assigned. Jack begged him: "I pray you, Dr Anderson, remember who I am!" Anderson looked surprised: "Your identity does not entitle you to any privilege, Master Digby: far from it."

"I know: 'tis just that I would like... as if to make up for... my father's madness, his wrong company, and swear my absolute loyalty to the Prince. Look, Sir, I've written about it all on this piece of paper."

And so he had. Acknowledging that this might be identified as a good result for Christ's, Anderson made an exception and granted Jack permission to approach the Prince and serve him a dainty dish of candied fruits. Beforehand, however, for security reasons – as one never knows -, he was searched from head to foot. When the moment came, almost at the end of the meal, Jack went up to him very slowly, and far more nervous than he had been for years; he put the dish before him and fell to his knees with imploring eyes. The Prince looked at him in surprise. Jack glanced at the little note he had put under the dish, looked at him again, then got up, bowed and walked away. He couldn't remember when he had last felt this happy. It would be a joy to swear loyalty to such a youth. Tomorrow, during the Oath Ceremony, when he was to declare his complete agreement to the Government's lines, Jack would only think of him, not of the King, not of the corrupted Court, not of the penal laws, not of the ongoing persecution.

In the afternoon, on the eve of the great day, the graduates-to-be were allowed to go to town and have some fun: fortunately, on this occasion, the new Rector, Reverend Carey, was broad-minded and anti-puritan enough to turn a blind eye, and even two blind eyes, on the licit and illicit pastimes of his students. Big John had met several old acquaintances of his old days and had gone out with them, thus leaving his protégé free to celebrate his degree with his fellow students.

John Kenelm Digby, therefore, left Christ's with them, for once without any tiresome adult watch, through the narrow, mysterious Cambridge lanes. They went past the shambles, where the blood of butchered beasts flowed in special little sewers; they visited several alehouses; they ate and drank plentily, bought trish-trash from street stalls, bet on fighting cocks, sang loud goliardic ballads in the streets. Then, towards dusk, Ned Whiman, the wiliest of them all, winked at the others: "Now, boys, I know where to go, so that we can have a real party!" He led the way to a suburban street and a worm-eaten wooden sign where a clumsy hand had painted a now faded red rose.

Ned knocked as one acquainted with the place. The woman who opened the door was different from any other woman Jack had ever seen: she looked young but wasn't, her neckline very low, her face all painted, her yellowish hair artificially curled and her smile too wide for the total strangers she was admitting. A bit tipsy, she was holding a pewter tankard.

"There we 'ave four more, my turtle doves. Let's make room!" she squealed to other women sitting at a round table in a crowded, poorly-lit room, who were drinking with other students among whom Jack recognised some fellows from Christ's. More students were standing on a large staircase, chatting with a few scantily dressed girls. The woman stood aside and held out her hand: "'Tis tuppence to get in and then it depends on what you want, he he! Please come in, little lords, and let's drink to your Oath! Long live the King!" She laughed out loud and lifted her tankard. Jack paid his due and stepped into a noisy, warm, rather stifling room smelling of alcohol, perfume, sweat, excrement – there must be, in some corner, a chamber pot that hadn't been emptied – and withered trodden herbs strewn all over the floor.

Ned exchanged a few more words with the woman, who laughed again, then the "little lords" were at once escorted upstairs, to a very large room hosting many beds, each secluded by heavy drapery which might once have been lavish but was now as worn out, dusty and colourless as the rest of the room.

Pulling aside the drapes at the point indicated, Jack found himself close to an untidy bed, its linen all crumpled. He perceived the outline of a woman sitting at the foot of the bed. Her face was also painted, but her hair was as untidy as the bed and her bodice partly undone, as if not worth doing up every time. In a barely audible whisper, she told him to put one shilling into a little box. Jack fumbled for a coin in his pocket with the tips of his fingers and looked round: the box lay on a little bedside table next to a dim lamp which only lit a part of the woman's white-painted face; all the rest was hidden in shadow. He tried to have a better look at her. Seeing him hesitating, the woman repeated her request a little louder, in a somewhat singsong, decidedly lower-class accent. Jack started. That voice was different from the others: not coarse, not vulgar, not hoarse with drink... and not even a woman's voice. It was thin, trembling, feeble: a child's voice. Jack looked at her again in astonishment; he met two frightened eyes, which ran down at once to her almost completely bare breast. He saw a delicate forehead, a small nose and nothing more. He looked at the hands she held clasped in her lap: they reminded him of Meg's hands. He wondered how long this girl had been in this place: she might even have been born here. And what had previously looked partly like boyish knavery, partly like some rite of initiation, suddenly appeared to him under a different light. A sense of unutterable disgust took hold of him. He would have liked to save her, although she might already be marked by syphilis: he would have liked to take her by the hand and lead her out, in the open air, far from this foul-smelling, sickly perfumed, suffocating place; take her home to Gayhurst, and let her play carefree with Meg, maybe with dolls. He did nothing of the sort, of course: he just dropped his coin into the box, grabbed the cloak he had cast into a corner, turned his back on her and without a word, as if in flight, he was down in the street in an instant.

He walked hurriedly towards Christ's, his nausea mounting, partly due to what he had eaten and drunk, partly to what he had seen and smelt, but above all to what he had been on the point of doing. Never again, he told himself; never again! He felt foul, filthy, old and corrupt, merely for having been in that place.

The fresh evening air and the rather long walk gradually made his headache go away and cleared his mind. "This is what happens to those who follow the herd like sheep," he told himself, "I should have thought it out better." The whole incident also seemed a bad omen for the ceremony of the following day.

"'Tis wrong," he started repeating to himself, "'Tis all wrong!"

His university life, all the time he had wasted, his sophistic studies, his prospective career at Court, his degree, the Oath. His silly pastimes, the company of such as Whiman, the hypocrisy that made him smile complacently after unbearably long, bombastic sermons, his bowing to courtiers and other prominent people who everybody knew were rotten to the bone. He would have liked to run away, but whither?

As he came to the front gate, he found it ajar. No guard was there to identify him. They had probably all gone to have a drink, taking advantage of the building being almost completely empty. "Ye idiots," he thought. "This very night, nobody being here, thieves could break in. And how on earth would you explain it? But here, of course, no one gives a damn for anything." He walked through the porch and across the yard into the main hall; he angrily grabbed a light and headed for his room. His footsteps echoed on the stone slabs of the deserted corridor; there seemed to be not one soul in the whole College. He shivered: what if some knave had really broken in? What if they were still there?

As he was walking past the great kitchen door, deep in thought, he was sure a figure moved in the shadows and quickly squatted behind the big oven. His heart sank. Then he tried to be rational: if someone was stealing food, it was surely none of his business. This served the guards well. He felt relieved too, because such a petty thief couldn't really frighten anyone; provided, of course, that this hadn't been an illusion produced by the swaying of his lamp. He moved some steps further, but in the end gave in to curiosity: he turned back, braced himself and walked into the kitchen. "Let's see, John Digby, if thou canst at least be brave with little sneak thieves", he said to himself. He approached the oven and projected his light into the corner.

It wasn't a common thief. It was Sherwin. Jack could well have imagined this: the misfit, the only one who hadn't joined the group of carousers. Yet, he thought he had seen Sherwin going out with the others: like him, he must have come back earlier. What Jack had never dreamt was Sherwin going round stealing food and provisions at night! Maybe he was broke and sold the College food to some town shop. This Sherwin chap, then, looked down on everybody and then stooped to this. His, therefore, was just an attitude: he was all pretence and, deep down, he was just as much of a hypocrite as everybody else.

Instead of feeling guilty at being caught red-handed, Sherwin glared at him with his usual scorn and showed him what he was concealing under his robe: a bare bodkin, its blade shining dismally in the light of Jack's lamp.

"Thou'rt not going to report me, art thou, Digby? 'Cause if I suspected thee I'd have to slit thy throat."

"What, art mad? All for a chunk of bread and cheese?"

"Dostn't get it, as usual: I need 'em for the trip."

"Wilt not take the Oath?"

"Art crazy? Never, on my life and soul! My course of studies stops here. I've got a ship waiting for me at dawn on the coast of Norfolk, then away to Flanders. Thou hast not seen me, hast thou, Digby?"

"'Course not. Art thou bound to Douay?"

"I am, right now; then I'll see. Wouldst like to come along?"

"How could I, as sudden as this? I can't; and then, in two days, I'll finally be allowed to go home to my family after four years. No, I'll stay."

"And take the Oath?"

"How couldn't I? But of course I admire thee. Art thou not afraid of reprisals 'gainst thy loved ones, though?"

"Only got an old uncle, up in York. I don't think they'll hold him responsible for my choices: haven't seen him or written to him for ages. C'mon, let's to my room; help me carry this stuff." This sounded more like an order than an invitation.

Jack walked before him, holding the light, ready to warn him in case he saw a mouse stir. They walked through more deserted corridors without meeting a living soul, up to Sherwin's equally deserted dormitory, where he had everything almost ready.

"Thou knowst what'll happen if they take thee, dost thou not, Sherwin?"

"'Course I do. But we all owe a life, sooner or later. And, anyway, I'm fed up with this bloody country. Life may be very short in any case: 'tis better to do the right thing and not regret it. But art thou not disgusted at thyself for tomorrow's ceremony?"

"I'm not, 'cause 'tis not in my power to refuse: my guardian holds my family under his thumb. And then, I'll cross my fingers as I swear."

"Don't be ridiculous... knowst thou why the world is such a bloody mess? Because of weaklings and lily-livered blokes like thee bending before the course of history. Those who abide evil are as guilty as those who actively promote it."

"We *are* too weak, Sherwin. There's nothing we can any longer do."

"Maybe there isn't; but I'll die before I bend my head. I want to leave a mark, even a blood mark: like an insect swatted on a wall. Always better than nothing at all."

"And what if someone from overseas were to wage war against thy country to dethrone the King? Wouldst thou join them?"

"Ay, I wouldn't mind that. But, as it is, no one will do anything of the kind, to be sure. Those times are over now."

"We've never been friends, Sherwin: why'rt thou so frank to me and dost speak treason and tell me things that may cost thee thy life?"

"'Tis like my will, Digby. My last spiritual will, let's say, and my true words, in case they take me, kill me off and spread the usual ignominious confession bearing my signature. Remember this: once a man ends up in the Tower, nothing is certain any more."

"Wilt thou become a priest?"

"I won't. I'm angry with God, I don't want to serve him. Why doesn't he make himself heard? Why doesn't he do aught?"

Jack was silent and then said: "Maybe because we acted wrongly as well."

"Art thinking of thy father?"

"Ay."

"Then thou still hast not understood! They were heroes, not traitors. They knew perfectly well what they'd do to them, had they failed; which, of course, was most likely. But they didn't let themselves be discouraged: they gave their lives for a good cause. For the Enterprise of England! Fawkes is a hero, and thy father with him. Fawkes was from my town, York, and up there none of our people speaks ill of him."

"Sherwin, 'twould've been a mass slaughter. So many innocent people killed... And surely our King..."

"... Our King is a shameful figure and I would kiss anybody's feet who did away with him for the good of mankind! 'Tis as Catesby said: desperate remedies for desperate diseases. I myself wouldn't say no, were I told that, unluckily, I've got to blow myself up to put an end to this accursed tyranny. Guy Fawkes for ever! Who knows? I may really do it, one day." He bared his teeth in an unsettling grin.

Jack was horrified. One thing was a military attack, a regular invasion preceded by a declaration of war; another was treason, regicide, or, still worse, a surprise suicide attack and mass murder.

Sherwin went on: "And anyway, this is not the whole of the story. Dost thou really think everything went as we were told?"

"The Plot, meanst thou?"

"Ay, ay, with the secret oath involving the Jesuits, the underground "mine" right in the middle of Westminster without anybody noticing it, and Fawkes like a crazy nitwit going to check the powder right when they were coming for him, and all this government crap... Come on!"

Jack's face darkened. "But then how...?"

"Thou'rt a fool, Jack Digby. Ay, Fawkes was an extraordinary man, a hero of our times, who resisted unspeakable torments for as long as three days; but, in the end, he was a man like us and told them everything they wanted to hear... Or rather, he is said to have."

"Ay, but the other plotters, including my father, confessed from the scaffold."

"There's no limit to blackmail: not even death. Now, thou wilt stay because of thy family, wilt thou not?"

Jack nodded. Actually, he would stay because he was not brave or strong enough to act differently; because things were not so bad for him; because both Big John and Sir Robert had promised him complete rehabilitation for his whole family; because, if he behaved, life wouldn't be so hard for him and everything would be so much easier and painless. He had never seriously considered possible alternatives to the path traced out for him from the outset. But now the thought that there might be more to learn – that there might be hope of shedding some light on such a disturbing aspect of his father's personality – overshadowed everything else.

"But how did things really go, then?"

"Good question. Hast thou investigated a little, at least, on who the other plotters were?"

"Not much, actually. How could I?" Jack was ashamed to tell him that he had not investigated at all: partly because he hadn't had the time, partly because he didn't know where to begin, but most especially because his dominant thought, since his arrival at Cambridge, had been how to survive in a hostile world.

"Well done! Go and see how many of them had been close to Essex."

Jack was even more bewildered: what was Essex? A county or a person? He dared not ask. Meanwhile, Sherwin had finished his packing and, while fastening the clasp of his cloak, pointed with his chin to a sheaf of papers he had left on the floor:

"I meant to burn those, but if thou wantst'em thou canst keep'em. 'Tis only important for them not to be found here. Wait, one of them is surely to be burnt: too compromising."

He bent down, took a certain thin, unbound libel out of the stack and threw it into the fireplace, where the embers came back to life and licked all round it. On the front page, Jack had just the time to read the title, *Challenge to the Privy Council*. He couldn't make out the author's name, which might not even be there. He picked up the rest of the documents; then, after putting out the light, he walked with Sherwin to a little back door, making sure, as he had done on their way there, that the way was free. Now Sherwin turned to him.

"Fawkes was a hero," he repeated. He made to go, then turned back and looked him in the eyes: "Don't let'em transform thee into a deferential nodding puppet: 'twould be their greatest victory. Wake up, Digby!" Then he tapped him on one arm. "Farewell!" and was lost in darkness.

"Good luck to thee, Sherwin," Jack whispered.

He bolted the little door, then took a tinderbox from his pocket, lit his lamp in the moonlight and slowly walked to his own dormitory, the papers under his arm. A weird chap, that Sherwin. He still couldn't

understand whether he liked him or not; of course he was flattered
by the secrets he had revealed to him, but he wasn't sure he believed
him. A hothead, he was, and dangerous. Though a brave one too, for
sure...

Wake up, he had told him. Wake up, wake up! Those simple words,
which Sherwin might have uttered out of sheer irritation, made him
feel different. It was suddenly as if he had really been asleep for all
those years; as if only now were he emerging from a lethargy he had
inflicted upon himself so as not to feel the pain. But sometimes it
might be more important to stay awake, and accept suffering, rather
than numb one's senses trying to survive life's blows unscathed.

And who knew what sort of papers were these he had left to him:
secret, treasonous documents, maybe? Where had he found them?
And now, were the papers found in his room, would he be thrown
into the Tower? Was this Sherwin's last bitter joke? A bit paradoxical,
that would be: Sherwin – a potential traitor and murderer – at liberty
overseas, and he in jail without knowing why. But such was life,
sometimes: he had always known that all the London prisons, and
especially some of them, such as the Clink, were crammed with
honest people whose only guilt was their wrong religious persuasion.

Once in his room, he was glad to find that Watson, Nugent and
Powell were not yet in. He shuddered as he thought of them in the
brothel. He laid the light on his trunk, spread the papers fan-like on
the bed and started to examine them. He was both disappointed and
relieved to find that not one of them seemed to be compromising:
they were mostly literary works, some famous, some not, some of
value, some quite cheap, some in prose, some in poetry, together with
a few short historical works and even two or three plays. Why, then,
didn't Sherwin want them to be found? "They mustn't be found here,"
he had said. That youth was a total enigma. He flipped through some
pages, looking for some strange note between them, or maybe some
coded message scrawled on the margins. He saw some handwritten
words, but they looked liked a student's ordinary notes. "I'll have a
better look tomorrow in the daylight," he told himself. The lamp was
nearly out, now, and started to gutter. Jack shoved the papers among
his own notes, then undressed and went to bed. But he stayed awake
for hours on end, racking his brain about the Plot: how could Sherwin
be so self-assured? Where did the truth lie? How reliable could

confessions wrung under torture be? Might trial transcripts be lying? And who was the Government? The King? The Privy Council? The Parliament? Who took important decisions? Which were the Court factions? And what was Essex?

He suddenly felt like a real fool and as clueless as Sherwin had said he was. He decided that, starting from tomorrow, he would try as hard as he could to learn more; even if he was afraid that, by now, the entire affair of the Powder Plot had turned into such a tangled web, practically impossible to unravel. But it would be such a good thing to clear his father's memory! If he found even the thinnest of threads, he would cling to that. And tomorrow, maybe, when Prince Harry became King Henry the Ninth of that name, Jack could finally hope to be welcomed among his Gentlemen. The Prince had surely read his short little note, by now. Maybe he had already forgotten about it; maybe, instead, in a few years this curious episode would come to his mind: who knew, one day they may even laugh about this together.

It was almost morning when his three room-mates came back, dead drunk. They kicked him once or twice and mocked him because he had been scared to bed a woman. But what did he care about them? He pulled his blanket over his head and tried to go to sleep despite the noise and the teasing.

The great day had come. All the bachelors-to-be were washed, shaved, scrubbed and perfumed by their servants, who then put their best robes over their best clothes. Sherwin's flight was discovered only at the last moment, for, on finding his bed empty, his room-mates had thought he had been spending the whole night revelling and had imagined he would turn up (drunk, possibly) directly at the ceremony, being the oddball he was. But when he did not answer the roll call, a great turmoil ensued. All corners were searched thoroughly – as the rascal might have hidden just for fun – until the university authorities sent out a patrol of younger students eager for preferment to look for clues, first to other colleges and then into town. No trace of him was found. Jack told everyone he had come back before the others, the previous night, owing to a strong pain in his belly; that he had run to the privy, then straight to bed and hadn't seen him.

When breakfast was over, all the students thronged into the College chapel; in the pews behind them sat their friends. The ceremony started with prayers and sung psalms; then Dr Carey preached his sermon, extolling – as usual – the virtues of a loyal subject and condemning any form of dissent. Obeying the Sovereign meant obeying God, who had appointed his deputy on earth to have him rule in His name. Jack only listened to the beginning and was soon lost in his thoughts: if every sovereign was God's representative, how could wars be explained? Might God have different wills continually clashing against one another?

He wondered where Sherwin was: after all, he might have made it. Jack was looking forward to examining more closely those papers he had left him. He also wondered whether, by now, Sherwin had started to esteem him a little. Most likely he hadn't: he only despised him, just as he despised everyone else there, and had left that apparently dangerous material with him just because he was sorry to burn it. He, on the other hand, had done nothing to deserve that fearless dissident's esteem.

After the sermon, the great moment finally arrived: one by one, they were all called to the wooden altar-table, before a small throne where the Prince was sitting, to take their Oath and to swear, their right hand on the Bible, their loyalty to His Royal Majesty James, the first of his name, and their readiness to defend him from whatsoever attack and whatsoever foreign power, first of all from the Bishop of Rome, who did not have any jurisdiction or authority in Britain. The Oath was followed by the signing of a large, specially-made university register.

On hearing his name called out, Jack looked back in hesitation, but Big John's ruddy face was smiling encouragingly. He thought of Sherwin, who perhaps at that very moment was running in the forest, pursued by the town patrols, or, perhaps, already on the big ship sailing to Flanders. Then he looked in front of him, at the throne where the good future King sat. He wondered if, when he saw him taking the Oath, the Prince would recognise him as the boy of the note. He stood up and did his duty, looking at him straight in the eye, smiling, forgetting even to cross his fingers. When he returned to the pew, he was a true and loyal British subject.

There followed one more banquet for all of them: a great feast where wine flowed freely and which went on even after the Prince had withdrawn to his rooms. In the general euphoria, it was not difficult for Jack to simulate a new onset of stomach-ache, which was surely due to the food and wine, and to seek the intimacy of his room. Once there, he took Sherwin's papers out of his trunk and started to turn the pages. Some were printed, some were barely legible manuscripts. Again, he was seized by a sense of disappointment and relief at the same time: definitely, nothing dangerous or compromising.

He even found a tragedy. The front page had been torn away, but someone had scrawled its title on the first available page, on top of the text, and had also added: "*As it hath beene diverse times acted by His Highnesse Servants.*" The company he had seen perform at the Globe just before he had left London: the players who had hired young Tim Rice. This play, surely, could not be compromising at all: still less so than the others. It might contain a coded message, though. Jack's mind ran back to the strange performance which had made him feel so deeply involved, that time at the Globe. *Macbeth*, it was called. He would really have liked to find it in print: he had tried to get it through colleagues, teachers and other acquaintances, but it had been impossible to find: strangely enough, it appeared not to have been printed yet. He thought back on his friend – if he could be defined as such – the young commoner, Tim, whom he had not written to at all; he also thought of the strange playwright of the King's Men who, in order to give life to his art, wandered through the streets of London jotting down notes about the joys and sorrows of its people.

He put back all the other documents into his trunk, concealing them as well as he could among the folds of his clothes, and went to sit by the window, behind the coarse brown curtain, on the seat that had been excavated into the thick wall, the tragedy in his hands. He read it all through quite quickly, impatient to find secret notes, forbidden statements or at least some little clue about why Sherwin considered this specific work so important. He was even more disappointed: it was the usual revenge tragedy dealing with a young prince who sought revenge for his father's murder, took up the whole play to carry it out, spoke too much, pretended he was mad, killed several people by mistake and in the end was killed in his turn. What kind of a story was this? Jack's only consolation in reading through that seemingly never-ending play was that he found a handwritten note on the margin of one page, next to a long soliloquy. It consisted of one only word: *Essex*. What did this mean? Had Sherwin written it?

While he was brooding over the play, and kept turning its pages back and forth in bewilderment, Big John came to seek him out and see how he felt.

"I'm here, Big John, in the window seat. I've thrown it all up, slept a little, and now am better, I thank thee."

"Too many emotions, he he he! What dost thou read, my dear?"

Jack answered with the cleverest line he had found in the play: "Words, words, words."

Big John grasped the reference at once: "Ah-ah, *Hamlet*! I see that thou'rt now keen on plays, just as I am. And how is it possible for thee never to have been taken to see one performed in all these years? Fortunately, I had already seen to that myself. Ha ha ha ha ha!" His loud, slightly strained laughter filled the room. "Let me see..." He took the booklet from Jack's hands before he could stop him. "'Tis right him – the Prince of Denmark."

"Dost know this play?"

"And who does not, Little John? It stormed the theatres, in its time. Like all the great poet's plays, for that matter."

"'Tis by Shakspere, then." For some reason, Jack pretended not to know.

"'Course 'tis: didn't thou catch his style?"

"I didn't, but only because I've read it quickly: I just wanted to see the end. But now I'll read it over again."

"Not that 'tis worth it, mind thee! 'Tis nothing more than the remake of an older play, which in its turn looked back to Kyd's famous *Spanish Tragedy* that's more than thirty years old. He's never been so very original, Master Shakspere: he likes to copycat here and there... Although, I must say, now and then one can find a good line or two among his many second-rate ones."

"Hey, look at the airs and graces thou putst on! Dost believe thou canst write any better?" Jack, who had stood up and taken back his little book, now looked down on him.

"Well, modestly... There are things thou still knowst not, Little John. Recently, as I told thee, I've been discreetly successful."

"As successful as that? Dost write plays? And are they performed at the Globe?"

Big John was clearly pleased with Jack's amazement; he looked nonchalantly at the big stone on the ring he wore on his left finger. "Ay, there too. Although, to tell the truth, I don't much like popular theatres: I prefer private ones, and boys' companies over men's. But if one wants to emerge, one has to follow the wind a little, doesn't he?"

"When I come to London, wilt thou take me to see aught?"

"'Course. Now thy re-education is almost complete, I can well introduce thee into society. Ha ha ha ha ha!"

Jack smiled along with him, this time. But from then on, every moment he had on his own, no matter how short, would be good to examine this very famous play in depth, written as it was by the man who had aroused so much curiosity in him at the time of his great personal tragedy.

Nature had started to blossom all over once again when Jack, his heart pounding with almost irresistible joy, finally set off for the great manor-house where he had been born. Those four years away from home had been like one long, painful winter to him. Not being allowed to meet his loved ones, not even for the holidays – not even for the Twelve Days of Christmas, when Christ's was left empty and all the rooms echoed hollowly and despondently – had been hard to bear. But now, at last, the day had come. Big John was with him, of course, together with Wat and Dave, the two servants Sir Robert had given them.

His chaperon was now droning on and on about Ovid's *Metamorphoses*, his voice like the tedious background buzz of a bluebottle, while Jack's senses were all bent on breathing the air and scent of home. By now, he was used to this young intellectual following him everywhere outside the safe walls of Christ's College. He had more or less learnt to manage Big John and play his game, talking about what *he* liked the way *he* wanted, in this peculiar friendship imposed on him from above, leaving him with no choice possible.

The pastures were still of the same rich green that always followed thaw; the trees as tall, the brooks as clear. He spurred his horse to a canter, running past the ruins of Snelshall priory: just another heap of stones. The country was peppered with them, grey wrecks slipping away into legend. Jack had been told that these treasures, at one time, had lain scattered throughout England, as if it were a fine jewel-studded garment.

Where was all that beauty, now? All that could be plundered had ended up in the royal coffers, forever taken away from common people: people who couldn't understand the long scholarly sermons of the royal preachers; people who couldn't or wouldn't read either the Bible or Foxe's renowned *Book of Martyrs;* people who, once left to themselves, had inevitably drifted back into barbarism. What, instead, could not be stolen had just been left there to die slowly, inexorably, vanishing from history.

Jack was still deeply buried in his thoughts when he saw, yonder, emerging from the horizon, the high top-boughs of the oaks lining the Gayhurst parkway, all dotted as they were with little buds. He spurred his horse again, which broke into full gallop, leaving his fellow-travellers behind.

This would only be a short visit, after so long, but he would enjoy it from first to last. Once again he breathed deep, and the air smelled with spring and fresh earth, while a scared wild bunny dashed across his path; he looked up at the clouds running after each other against the bright blue sky, and the sun appearing and disappearing. He tried to guess what his loved ones looked like, now. He realised that he himself had changed a lot: he hoped they would recognise him, and that the younger children wouldn't shy away from him, thinking him even uglier than he actually felt. Little Meg was already twelve and must be quite the well-bred, well-educated young lady by now: he wondered whether she had learnt to watch her tongue or still tended to speak too much. Kit must be really big, now he was fourteen; but, as Jack had learnt from their mother's letters, he hadn't yet started university, nor would he in the short term. Then there were Muriel and Robin, who must be nine and seven: he wondered how much they had changed, too, and how they all spent their days. Were they as poor as Jack believed them to be, or had they managed to put by a small fortune? What was Gayhurst's income? In his letters to his mother, Jack had not dared bring up financial matters. He wondered how their old manor looked, now, shuddering at the thought that they might have hidden something from him: maybe they had had to sell everything, maybe they actually lived in the village, among the commoners who had once served them. Maybe one of them was ill, or even dying… dead… Jack was now galloping faster and faster, spurring his horse on and on, each minute seeming like an hour.

He rode past the old mill where he had played as a child, cutting up little bark-boats and launching them into the brook, while he dreamt of becoming a famous admiral; past the great oak in whose branches he used to climb and under which he had once taken shelter from a violent thunderstorm. That time Sir Everard had punished him for going out alone without even telling Adam, and he and Lady Mary so worried…

Now that he was closer to home, his father's face came to his memory much more clearly. Jack could see his long hair, his well-trimmed moustache, his ash-blond beard, and his deep eyes, as bright and blue as the sky that was now above him. Sir Everard had always been handsome: the heroes of yore must have looked at least a bit like him. Jack rode through the open gate and shot, arrow-like, down the oak-lined parkway, branches rustling in the wind, a flight of turtle-doves rising like a vapour cloud at his gallop.

He saw Lady Mary run out to the main yard as soon as she heard approaching hoofs. So she, at least, thank God, was still there; apparently, things were not (or not yet) beyond repair. Provided that the children too... Jack dismounted and ran to her. She looked more delicate than before: the skin on her face, which was still so fair, had got thinner and even whiter, almost transparent, while a few thin silver threads had appeared in her raven-black hair. Her clothes were much plainer, now: always neat and clean, but made of humbler texture. His heart ached as he recalled the gorgeous dresses and jewels she had worn when he was a child.

"Mother!" She was far smaller, now, and so frail he feared his hug might somehow break her.

"Jack, how thou lookst like thy father! Thou'rt already nearly as tall as he was. Thou'rt beautiful!" Lady Mary stepped back to have a better look at him, tears in her eyes. Then she took his hand, brought it close to her face and started to sob: "These were his hands, Jack!"

Just then, Adam and Ellen had shyly appeared behind her. Bending the rules of etiquette, Jack embraced them warmly. Big John and the two servants presently caught up with him; still sitting in his saddle, Jack's chaperon stayed a short distance away, a silly grin on his face, waiting to pay his respects to Milady.

Lady Mary glanced at the newcomers, then hugged her son again; this time, to whisper to him: "Hast taken the Oath?"

"I have, mother. Was it very wrong?"

"Nay, what else couldst thou do?"

They loosened the embrace and Lady Mary dried her eyes with a coarse cotton kerchief. Meanwhile the children had run out as well: Kit, Meg, Muriel, Robin, all clustered joyfully round him. Jack was happy to find that everything was well with them, and that they had grown so much. Little Robin had lost his blond curls; he was thinner and had taken on a serious, adult-like expression. He looked slightly embarrassed, too, for he didn't remember him very well. Meg, who was not taller than Lady Mary, had not cut her hair since then, and a long thick brown braid dangled between her shoulders; her dark fairy-like eyes had remained the same, only they had longer lashes. Muriel, instead, who kept jumping with joy, had recently cut her hair herself, without her mother's permission, and now had a short slanting fringe that looked like a little Highland pony's black mane; she had ruddy cheeks and dark lively eyes, not unlike Meg's, though not as big. She was carrying a white kitten in her arms, which she had saved from the river at birth and now followed her everywhere, even to bed. Kit was almost as tall as him, but had wider shoulders; his large smile showed fine white teeth and a simplicity of heart that Jack feared he himself had lost forever.

He sadly noticed that the girls' skirts were too short, and the boys' sleeves and trousers had repeatedly been mended on their elbows and knees. He felt ashamed of the elegant clothes of silk, velvet and fur that he was wearing. But they admired him, instead, and were happy for him, and the girls couldn't stop fingering his cloak and the lace of his shirt, while Robin overcame his shyness and asked to try on his plumed hat. They told him he had turned beautiful and were all joy at the sight of the simple candied fruits in an embroidered little cloth bag which Jack had bought at a stall, down in Cambridge, for a penny.

He asked them to have a tour of the old manor all together. The painful memory of the day he had left it, not knowing why, or whether he would ever come back, made his stomach turn again. He thought back to the hurry, the broken sentences between his mother and the servants, the feeling, soon to be confirmed, that something devastating had taken place. Why did they have to leave everything behind? Where was Father? Why didn't he come back as he had promised? Why did they have to run away like this, without him? And why on earth didn't anybody explain anything to him?

They went up what had been the grand staircase. As he had guessed, everything, now, tasted of poverty and bleakness: not a tapestry, not a picture, not one ornament on the walls, while the windows shut the sun off through simple, colourless curtains. As Lady Mary had told him, the pursuivants had even taken away the fine panelling of polished carved wood, which had left a light-coloured stone streak all along the bare walls.

Jack smiled to himself as he remembered a specific low-relief carved image, in the lounge leading to his room, before which he used to linger in awe, frightened and charmed at once. It showed a satyr who, grinning in a way he then found horrible, stuck out a realistically long, protruding tongue. That was the devil, to him. It was exactly like this that he appeared in his childish nightmares, ready to grab him and take him to Hell, which gaped like a huge monster, there, right at the foot of his bed, ready to swallow him. That devilish satyr popped up beside him, especially when he was ill, if he turned on his left side; but then, fortunately, on his right, to save him, out popped the rosy-winged angel from the fresco reproducing Heaven on his parents' bedroom ceiling.

Now, however, everything was either brown or grey and even the angel was faded and scraped so you couldn't see his face, and voices echoed sadly in those now too large rooms. Many had been locked up, to avoid heating them in winter, and their walls already smelt musty. The dead hearths in the big fireplaces looked like black, hungry mouths: not an ornament on their mantlepieces, not a log between the firedogs.

"It looks so desolate to thee because thou rememberst it as it was in its golden days," Lady Mary told him as she noticed his miserable look. "We've got used to it, and it's not so bad. This life is only a bit more sober, but none of us is in want of anything... as to material goods, of course." They often even managed to give a bowl of soup to some pauper. A simple wooden or tin bowl, though, for not only had the silverware and china been taken, but even the kitchen crockery had been either smashed or stolen.

Jack soon learnt from Meg that they had a new tutor, who taught all four of them, both boys and girls, and who would keep well away until Big John had gone: as far as possible, life went on as before, albeit stripped down to the bare necessities. Lady Mary personally ran the kitchen and held the pantry keys; she had learnt to make bread, bake sweet and savoury pies, roast meat, and make butter and cheese, some of which was sold by Adam at the Milton Keynes market. Although not one of Sir Everard's magnificent horses had been left, one of the stables was occupied by two young, silken-flanked brown

cows, who responded with a 'moo' to Kit's hollo at milking time. And
then there were the chickens all scratching about everywhere, along
with a few geese. Besides Adam and Ellen, who had renounced their
pay, they also had a young kitchen maid for the heavier jobs and a
woman coming from the village on laundry days. The kids now played
in the park barefooted, so as not to wear out their shoes, and went to
the forest every day to pick up wood to burn in the great kitchen
fireplace. They truly looked healthy and comparatively happy: Jack
was relieved by all this.

That night, he would try to have a secret talk with his mother. He
waited for Big John to fall asleep, but couldn't help the creaking door.
Dave, the servant, who had put up his couch just beyond it, started
and sleepily asked him whether he needed anything.

"'Tis nothing," Jack replied. "Just looking for a chamber pot: I've
found it, now." He angrily shut the door: little did he think he was
being so closely watched, a prisoner in his own home.

Big John was always with them during the day as well, with his
Latin quotations and unbridled laughter. Lady Mary would look
daggers at him. "I can't stand him!" she whispered one day in Jack's
ear. He just smiled sadly.

As soon as he was alone, which mainly happened at night, by
candlelight, Jack went back to Sherwin's papers, about which he would
have liked to talk to Lady Mary, if only Big John had left them alone
for one moment. A few of them were in Latin, but the vast majority
were in English; some of the poems, besides, were decidedly second-
rate. There were two tragedies, the one by Shakspere and a Roman
play by one Jonson dealing with Sejanus, Emperor Tiberius' right-
hand man: a most depressing work, which made you cry in disgust at
human cruelty. Some of the historical works were, instead, about
Julius Caesar, while others were about some ancient English kings.
Jack also read *Hamlet* over again, trying to make out how it must have
been performed at the Globe.

He started to like this Danish prince who was both foolish and
wise, hesitant and rash. To begin with, his father too had been killed.
True, Hamlet's father was a great king murdered by a villain, whereas
his own had been executed as a traitor: that, therefore, was the end
of their likeness. But he felt he shared things with this prince: the
sense of disinheritance, of mourning, of bewilderment, even of

injustice. For, deep down, despite his crime, Sir Everard hadn't killed anyone. Hamlet attended university, like he himself, and a Protestant one, like his: he might have felt as confused as he did, therefore, from the doctrinal point of view as well. One night, as he was staring in perplexity at the thickly printed words and wondering whether they might mean more than they showed, some lines of his favourite Italian poet came to his mind:

> *O voi ch'avete li 'ntelletti sani,*
> *mirate la dottrina che s'asconde*
> *sotto 'l velame de li versi strani*[1].

That was it: read between the lines. This he must do. The Prince's father, for example... That father, or better, that ghost, came from a place of atonement and mortification, fast and fire, where he was "purging" the sins he had committed in life. From Purgatory, of course. But Jack's Cambridge professors, Doctors in divinity, had always taught that Purgatory was anathema, part of a backward doctrine which only superstitious Papists could believe: a doctrine which, surely, none of the King's true subjects could follow. The ghost of King Hamlet, then, couldn't but stand for exactly that forbidden world, those ancient times which had been officially banned by the Government. A lost world which Jack hadn't known personally but which was now regretted by so many. How could the Master of Revels, down there in London, have let the King's Men perform such stuff? Yet it was written, though by hand, on the first page, and so many people had seen it performed. On the other hand, however, all this had happened under the old Queen, when things might have been different.

The ghost, besides, cried out for revenge. Surely in real life, and in Jack's own case in particular, it was impossible even to think about taking revenge for Sir Everard's death. But, utterly hypothetically, if he had chosen to do so... who would he have to kill? That revolting hangman who had torn open his father's body – if he could even find out who he was? Edward Coke and the other long-tongued lawyers

---

[1] Dante: "You whose intellect is healthy, / Look at the doctrine concealed / under the veil of strange lines" (Dante, Inf. IX, 61-63).

who had tried him? Waad, the lieutenant of the Tower, who might have had him tortured? Or would he have to do away with the Secretary of State, his own guardian, Sir Robert Cecil, Earl of Salisbury? Or else... like Hamlet... and as Sherwin too had said... the King himself?

"The world may well be a playhouse", he thought, "But once you get off stage onto the beaten earth of the pit, amidst real dust and real mud, your heroism fades into the light of common day". Real life was different. Seen in this light, what might have appeared as a heroic deed, if performed in a play, seemed to him mere folly. Or, rather, wasn't it that he was a coward, and much more so than Prince Hamlet?

Among talks and walks, tales and laughter, the handful of days of his Gayhurst visit ran past very quickly, like grains of sand in an all-too-small hourglass, till the last night came. Jack stayed up late, sitting at the old scrubbed table of the great kitchen with Lady Mary after the children and servants had all retired. As usual, Big John didn't feel unwanted and, nay, was happy to keep them company. Jack felt furious at the thought of not having been able to exchange even a couple of words with his mother in private. Hoping to bore his mentor to death, then, he started to ask her for news from all the blood relations he could remember, and all their families, and who they had given their children in marriage to, and who had been godmother to whose baby, and how much jam they had made that summer, and so on. Big John followed the conversation for a while; then, sitting as he was on a bench against the wall, he soon started to lose control of his head, which went swinging to and fro, till his eyes slammed shut, he fell forwards and started to snore loudly, head on the table.

"Have you seen, Mother, how boring topics do their job?"

Lady Mary smiled. "Don't be naive, Jack, this man has the endurance of an elephant. Tomorrow I'll ask Ellen what exactly she has put in his beer."

They talked about everything, all night long. Jack told her about his university life, only leaving out the most painful episodes – both out of shame and in order not to grieve her. He told her it was all true: the fifth of November was really being celebrated throughout the kingdom as the day of national salvation and, in Cambridge too, bonfires were lit every year, burning Guy Fawkes, the cruel murderer, in the effigy of a monstrous puppet. Lady Mary was silent and only shook her head. She told him about the difficulties of keeping their recusancy, hinted at (but playing them down) their money problems, and how she managed to have the children educated despite the penal laws; didn't they look quite happy, and wasn't all her hard labour to keep the family together slowly bearing fruit? Then they talked about Jack's future; about how Cecil would soon find him something to do at Court, or he might even ask him to take holy orders; he would find him a good wife as well… They laughed.

"Seriously, Mother, so far I can't but speak well of him. He's always kind and understanding, as busy as he is."

"Sure… until one doesn't object. In good time, though, we'll see who's right."

"He's generous, too."

"Why, thinkst thou he's using his own money to keep thee at university? That's our fortune, my dowry, that is, for that was taken away as well, after the trial."

"Mother, who was Essex?" he asked later, while telling her about Sherwin: he showed her the marginal handwritten note on *Hamlet*'s page, which he had run up to fetch from his room.

"The Earl of Essex, Robert Devereux. The old queen's last favourite; stepson, or maybe even natural son, to Robert Dudley, Earl of Leicester. Young, handsome, strong, noble, brave, rich, powerful. He ended up on the block about ten years ago… Nine: I was expecting Muriel, then. He'd fallen from grace and thus tried a coup to free the Queen from those he believed were her bad advisers… Guess the first and foremost of them."

"My guardian, perhaps, Sir Robert Cecil of Salisbury?"

"That's him. Back then, though, he was no nobleman, and not half as powerful as he is now. The two of them bitterly hated each other and, in the end, with his aristocratic parentage and his good looks, Essex wasn't the one to prevail. Now, let me see this booklet… 'Tis a very famous tragedy. Ay, many people, back then, tried to compare Prince Hamlet to poor Essex. Wait, there's even a part where… Here it is, I remember seeing it performed some time later, in London, with thy father. For it was staged right in that year. Dost see, here the King's counsellor hides behind an arras."

"Ay. He's an intriguer."

"Didst know that's exactly what thy guardian had done during Essex's trial?"

"No!"

"Ay! Everybody knows that. And this peculiar tragedy had a certain level of interpretation which seemed to have been specially written for all the unsatisfied: that's why thy father wanted me to see it performed, in my state."

"Unbelieve! But didn't the King's Men get into trouble for this?"

"I don't know... Not that I know, I mean. They're astute people. They were the Lord Chamberlain's Men, back then, and already famous."

Then, Jack told her about how Meg's words on that memorable evening had also reached the stage; she was pleased. "A nice man, this Shakspere," she said. "He's careful of people's sufferings. Thou knowst, he's got a powerful patron, the Earl of Southampton, who's also from a recusant family. Well, Southampton was Essex's right-hand man in the plot, and was sentenced to death with him, but was then pardoned by the Queen."

"How interesting! And was Essex a Papist, too?"

"He wasn't at all; but he had promised to obtain us tolerance: this is why some of us had supported him. And, anyhow, he'd gathered round himself all the politically unsatisfied, for whatever reason."

Apparently, then, Shakspere himself was in touch with dissident circles, and more closely so than Jack had thought. How could he learn more?

The tallow candle on the table burnt lower and lower, then started to gutter ever more frantically and fitfully, as if in panic against the approaching darkness, till it went off in a swirl of smoke, its heavy pungent odour lingering in the room; but neither the mother nor the son budged. They just lowered their voices still more, in case Big John woke up, and went back to talk about Sir Everard. Lady Mary told Jack everything she knew about the Plot: her husband had only entered it at the very last stage, when everything had already been thoroughly planned.

"All he said was that something was to be done with Catesby and Tresham, and he had offered to find war horses and ammunition, to gather all his friends (he had many, thou knowst) and to meet them in a certain place on a certain day. Then, it all went so fast... He never told me more; partly because he didn't have the time, and partly, as I told thee, so as to keep me out of it and not force me to lie. He went out at five in the morning, on the fifth of November, telling me he had to meet up with the others. We were expecting him for dinner, and instead he arrives home – much earlier – in a great rush, tells me that all is lost, that he must flee – and he never came back. I only saw him one more time, a month later, in the Tower. Dost understand? He was already a dead man, then. And only for a few minutes did they let me see him, just the time for a last farewell. I've been thinking a lot, thou knowst, all these years, but I can't come up with an explanation. To put things simply, the man who could enter such a plot is not the man I married and loved. From the day Fawkes was taken, 'twas as if they had all gone mad. Mad with fear, perhaps... The matter is, they all took to horse and, all together, began running here and there all over the county, with the idea of urging all the recusants in the area to rise up in revolt. They soon became like the spreaders of the plague: all the houses they touched were later implicated into the Plot and ruined. During their flight, thy father, in secret, left them – for the others would have killed him, had they found out: he ran away from those who were running away and gave himself up to the authorities. But 'twas too late: that crime had already left a permanent mark on him, as on everybody else. He was not among the main plotters, as I told thee."

"Why didn't he tell his questioners?"

"Of course he will have told them: I told them myself, when they questioned me, but that changed nothing. As for the records they later published, they didn't relate the real facts. For instance: Cecil learnt about the plot thanks to an anonymous letter sent to Lord Mounteagle: this is universally known, for Mounteagle was publicly covered with glory as his Country's saviour. But Mounteagle was brother-in-law to Tresham, one of the plotters: his is a strange role... Just think that, with all the instruments of persuasion of which the Government can dispose, no one ever found who wrote that letter."

"Ay... as if 'twere no longer important. And, anyway, Mounteagle was found out to be innocent: is it possible, then, for Father to be innocent too?"

"It isn't. Not in their sense, at least. They certainly broke the law. The King is certainly legitimate and all the plotters had sworn loyalty to him. The problem is, of course, and I often heard thy father talk about all this with Long John and the others, the problem is when laws are unjust. Robin Hood was an outlaw too, wasn't he?"

"Ay, mother." Jack smiled faintly. The conversation had become a barely audible whisper, although neither of them doubted about Big John being fast asleep.

"And what about Guy Fawkes?"

"I know nothing of him, I've told thee. His family wasn't from this county, nor from Warwickshire like Catesby's, Grant's and Rookwood's. He was a Northerner, I believe…"

"He came from York, Mother, as I was told by that student who ran away from Cambridge."

"That's it. I only know what everybody else knows, that he had fought for the Spaniards in Flanders before the peace treaty, and that was enough to make him an outlaw: that's why he used a different name, like Long John and the other Fathers. Long John was never taken, though, and this makes me really happy."

"But they killed Little John under torture, Mother, then they hanged Father Garnet as the mind behind the plot: I witnessed his execution too."

"I know… Just imagine, the mind behind the plot: this is a lie! I know this is what everybody says, but 'tis not true. He was our guest, right here, in those days, and I know he had tried in all possible ways to prevent them from resorting to violence, as soon as he had an inkling that Catesby had something weird and dangerous in mind. And when he was told about Fawkes' arrest, he was just astounded. I was there, Jack, at Coughton: it was as clear as daylight that he knew nothing at all about it. He merely cried: 'We are all utterly undone!' I burst into tears, then, for I realised what he meant. He was right, of course: we *are* undone. And all those like us know not only that he was innocent, but that he is a saint. Long John, instead, as I was telling thee, managed to find a place on a ship right on the day of Father Garnet's execution; and, from the Continent, he continues proclaiming his own innocence and that of all the other Fathers. The Government doesn't believe him, of course, but we all know that they are totally innocent of the plot. Their sheer acquaintance with Catesby was enough to destroy them all."

Jack listened as if mesmerised, his emotions heaping upon one another, rising and falling like a tide, then surging and overflowing like waves in a stormy sea. His mind in a whirlwind, he sensed that the deep-rooted shame that had lain deep in his heart for so long was now being transformed into pride. It was like feeling he had always known such things.

"I really wish I could do aught, mother!"

"Do not even think of it. Like thy father before thee, thou wouldst only get matters still worse for all of us. Action has become impossible, Jack. Remember, each and every one of us is held responsible for all the others. This is what Catesby failed to consider, or refused to, and what ruined us all."

"But they can never read my thoughts, mother."

"Exactly: what matters is the way thou art inside. 'Tis what thou'lt have to hand down to thy children. Thy thoughts belong to thee, they are only thine and no one on earth has the right to pluck them from thee. What's important is for thee to keep loyal to thy father's memory and to the memory of those like him. They were not evil, thou seest."

"I've never believed that, mother. You know, I don't want a career at Court. As soon as I can, I'll come back to Gayhurst forever."

"They'll never allow thee, Jack." Lady Mary smiled bitterly. "They'll find thee a bride to their taste, one who will raise thy children according to their lines. Just look at the De Veres and so many others…"

"We'll see! Were't only for myself, not for your sake, they would first have to drown me in a sea of blood! So that everybody would see. And anyway, what with their bloody penal laws, they will soon destroy us all."

"Methinks not, Jack. Their game is not to create new martyrs but rather obedient subjects: if we are not, our children and grandchildren will be. They're in no hurry, thou knowst. Our cause has been defeated, not so much by prison, torture or the scaffold, as by fines and expropriations. Defy a man openly, humiliate him before the people, insult him, tread over his face, trample him underfoot, and he will rise, showing a bravery he himself didn't know he possessed: he'll fight to the death against thee. On the other hand, make laws against him, make him a criminal in people's eyes, mar his reputation, touch him in his goods and chattels, expropriate him, persecute his children and all his loved ones, make him feel the poor hero of a lost cause, wear him out. Then, pay him compliments, offer him unhoped-for favours if only he will forsake his stubbornness: he'll give in without clamour and, in the end, thou wilt triumph."

"Therefore, 'tis wrong to bend one's head."

"Sometimes one gets nowhere by fighting in the open field. If we want to survive in this country, we must perforce bend our head, but then raise it again at once. We mustn't let them destroy us: we have the duty to survive, to tell the whole world about what is happening. For what's written and published down in London is false, we all know that. Our only hope lies in our children and in our children's children to justify our ways."

They went on talking like this, sitting at the old table in the dark, their heads almost touching, Big John snoring loudly beside them, until the break of day. Then Lady Mary helped her son pack. They parted, satisfied that they had at least managed to have their longed-for talk in spite of everything.

"Farewell, Jack. Don't be sad. Think about what we've told each other. Not that there is anything to be done: please, promise me that thou wilt do absolutely nothing. 'Tis only to let thee understand that good and evil hardly ever stand on one side only, and that things are seldom as they appear. As for the penal laws, all we can do is pray." She looked at him straight in the eyes. "Pray and nothing else, hast thou got me?" The tone of her voice left no room for objections: surely losing a husband had been enough for her.

"What else could I do, mother? Even if I wanted to do aught, I would never get the chance: that one," and he nodded towards Big John who was instructing the servants "clings on me like a mussel on a rock!"

While riding to London, Jack's mind was wide awake despite the sleepless night. He thought of the past, and, consequently, of the future. He would soon speak to His Lordship and find the way to tell him that, no, thanks, he was no longer interested in the plan he had devised for him; that he didn't want honour and riches, that he would serve the King in his heart (especially the next King, which was not strictly necessary to underline), but he wanted to go back home, where – he vowed – he would never trouble a soul. Of course, he would thank Sir Robert for all he had done for him, he would be grateful to him throughout his life, but he just wasn't fit for London, since he was not ambitious. Surely, if he accurately prepared a good speech in these lines, especially now he had acquired a few rhetoric skills, he was confident that the great man would listen to him: what could he care, after all, about such a green, poor, unimportant youth as him?

Once home, he would learn to till the land. He would get his hands dirty, breeding his own livestock and trading his own goods, so that he would soon make the property prosper again. He would marry a girl from a family like theirs and would get Gayhurst to swarm with life again. There would be room enough for all his siblings, with everybody's husbands and wives, should they like it. Or else, Meg and Muriel would marry young neighbouring gentlemen, and his brothers and himself would often visit them, then they would go hunting all together.

He began again to think about young Prince Hamlet. He felt closer and closer to him. Hamlet, like him, lived in a hostile environment, which, to boot, was full of spies. This was the prince's dilemma: if he killed the murderous usurper, he would be guilty of *lèse majesté*. He was well aware of this, of course, and in the famous soliloquy, which even appeared in poetic anthologies, the real problem was: *am I ready to give up my life for what I mean to do?*

This was exactly what set Hamlet apart from the fearless heroes handed down by tradition: he was afraid of death. How did he manage to overcome his fear? By preparing himself. In the end, the readiness was all. Life was but a long preparation in view of the last act. The Meeting with Eternity. This was what Jack too had been taught by his clandestine tutors. At the end of the play, however, while he lay dying in his friend's arms, what did the young prince worry about? Not any longer about what expected him beyond death, but about his own good name. "*Report me and my cause aright to the unsatisfied*," he told his friend Horatio. Which meant, of course, that Hamlet didn't trust official records, nor historical works, nor acts of Court and trial transcripts like the ones he himself had been shown by Big John. As if the true version of events could only be told by voice, or, at most, only performed on stage...

His mind went to all the libels about the Powder Treason divulged by the London printing shops, all of them rigorously approved by the Government. They couldn't be telling the whole truth: they were never allowed to. As soon as he could, he would read them all, though he felt sick just thinking about it. They must all be inflamed by hatred, ranting about the fiendish Plot and the hellish minds of the plotters.

Things couldn't really have been like that. If they hadn't, then, how had they really been? If, as Sherwin said, Guy Fawkes was no fool, how could he have let himself be taken with his hands in the jam pot at the very right (or wrong) moment? Jack resolved, now he was going back to London, to try at all costs to learn more. There might be another way to rehabilitate his family's name, other than by showing himself to be a true and loyal subject. This might be what Sir Everard had wished more than anything else: for him, his son, to tell the world his story as it had really been, thus healing the tremendous wound inflicted upon his name. Shakspere, therefore, had unwittingly represented him, Jack, in the character of Horatio, and Sir Everard in Hamlet, and all this before their time. Amazing.

Anyway, he now had to investigate. And, when he found out, he wouldn't thwart the truth: he would report it, however uncomfortable it might be. For no one must be afraid of the truth.

In the distance, the City of London finally emerged from the green pastures, enveloped in a bluish haze. The red sunset was dimly mirrored in the great, slow, meandering river, which lost itself into a throng of little houses and belfries. As he got closer, Jack made out the strong, ancient walls, almost completely concealed from sight by a crop of little buildings leaning against them like breeding mushrooms on a tree stump. It was so crammed, inside the walls, that more houses had scuttled out in all directions forming small country suburbs.

"Art thou still living in thine old Little East Cheap lodging, Big John?", Jack asked him.

"Ay, still there, Little John, and 'tis ready for thee too!"

The City gates were already being closed for the night curfew: the riders had just the time to get inside the walls, while all shops were closing as well. They headed for the great cathedral, and thence eastwards, to the room Jack remembered so well.

For a while, then, Jack went back to his London excursions and the various kinds of entertainment – plays, animal fights, taverns and alehouses. He started to wonder what Sir Robert had in mind for him. They would soon meet him again, Big John told him, and that was when they would get more detailed instructions. His mentor seemed happy of this little holiday; quite surprisingly, though, he led him to church even more often than before. They toured almost all the parishes of the City and listened to an impressive number of sermons.

On one Sunday morning they went to Paul's Cross, where they had another opportunity to listen to Dr George Abbott, recently appointed Bishop of London. That day, for once, the main theme was not the blind obedience which was due to a sovereign, but the subtle corruption of the soul which traps the careless. From a life of virtue to mortal sin, it was such a short step! God, of course, would never allow his chosen ones to perish in everlasting fire; but why should one try God's patience? We should never underestimate the tricks of the devil, who, like a roaring lion, was always looking for someone to devour. Now, as everybody knew, sloth was the father of all vice. It led to laziness and to seeking vain pleasures. The quest for pleasure led away from churches: to alehouses, brothels, playhouses, where the poor souls were exposed to every sort of temptation. And, the devil being notoriously far cleverer than us, his best strategy to lead us to sin lay in persuading us there was nothing wrong in what we did. But a good Christian, the Bishop went on, must be as wise as a serpent, along with being as innocent as a dove, and always to be on guard, when not at work or in church: if the spiritual life was not progressing and improving, this meant it was declining and withering. Instead of seeking distractions, therefore, a good Christian should spend six days working, as God did when he made the world, and the seventh resting in a licit way: that was, edifying his soul through sermons and reading and meditating on the Word of God.

In contrast to what he would have done a few years before, Big John was all looks and nods.

"Dost like this Abbott, Big John?" Jack asked him as they walked out.

"Bah! He's a bloody Puritan, boy, but I'll grant'ee he *can* speak, though I'm usually for the more moderate ones. Not that there isn't a part of personal interest on my part, mind me: just now, when I'm starting to be a bit successful as a playwright, this bloke would have all the playhouses closed down, nay, pulled down!"

"Why wert thou noddin' thy head, then?"

"Well, that's because, right then, I felt I was a bloody sinner. Hell frightens all of us, doesn't it, and who can ever be certain of salvation? But don't worry, Little John, I've already moved on by now! Ha, ha, ha!"

One day, as they were walking out of St Saviour, Southwark, where Dr Andrewes had been preaching on the Ten Commandments, and about how they could be all summed up in one – obedience to the King – and while Big John was explaining to him how right he was, Jack said: "I didn't remember thee as such a conformist, knowst thou, Big John."

"'Tis not conformism at all, little one: 'tis sheer common sense. The older one grows, the wiser he gets. Meself, by now, am already one-and-thirty and, in the end, I can but agree that our pastors' line – which, more or less, was also my father's line, ha, ha! – is the best of all: there is no other. Thou knowst well that I'm not made for Puritan extremes: too sad! Not that they ain't right, mind me: Dr Abbott, for instance, is *most* learned. But the flesh is weak, as thou mayst know: I really can't give up the theatre! As to the other extreme, Popish superstition, thank God it received a mortal blow with this very Powder Plot. Now, with all due respect for thy father, 'tis universally clear to everybody that, as King David says, the wicked have fallen into their own pit, since all their plotting has turned against them and their desperate cause, because…"

Big John's voice suddenly sank into a loud bleating coming from the street: it was a herd of sheep obstructing the way. People flattened against the walls while a baker's apprentice, whose basket had been knocked over, was now swearing like mad and having much ado recovering the loaves scattered down the street. Jack saw a little lad of six or seven, all dirty and in rags, grab one and disappear into the crowd. Big John went on undisturbed with his speech, only raising his voice. Jack snorted.

"No one now, Little John, trusts Papists any longer, of course; and they're right! I find, instead, that His Majesty's way is the just middle way. I'm relieved to think that I don't have to rack my brains to find the right path, for the great discerning job has already been done by someone else. And, mark my word, this king knows his theology. As thou wilt've been told in Cambridge, he's had a new translation started of the whole Holy Scripture, which will mend every single mistake and misunderstanding. What can I do before such competence? Only take off my hat!" Big John was serious, which rarely happened. "My salvation is in my King's hands, both in this life and in the life to come: everything holds together." He clenched his fist.

"Actually, though, Andrewes' sermons hardly ever deal with salvation, but rather with obedience, exactly like the ones I used to hear in Cambridge."

"Ah, 'tis all one, boy: just obey, and thou'lt be saved. For the King takes my obedience upon himself, as well as thine, and is ready to be held responsible for't before God. Even if thou be full of vices. Isn't this a consoling thought? Doesn't it give thee peace?"

"Sure. What shall we do now, Big John, go and have a drink? Or hast become too virtuous for that?"

"Come on, don't worry, I am the usual vicious sinner! I'll only be converted on my death-bed, ha, ha, ha! Shall we to the *Duck and Drake*?"

"I'd rather go to the *Mermaid*: thou knowst, I'm fond of it, and 'tis also closer. And then, I'd like to greet old Bill Thomson, who was so kind to me and mine at that terrible time."

"Let's go, then!"

Bill Thomson was still there, running to and fro between the kitchen and the tables, continually cleaning his thick short fingers on the filthy apron that he could hardly do up round his big belly. He was still the same, only slightly balder. At first he didn't recognise Jack; then he covered him in compliments and offered the first round of beer. Then Big John was soon called over by some acquaintances, who invited them both to sit at their table. It was not difficult for Jack to find a pretext to go back to the counter, where the ostler was putting clean jugs away.

"So I look like my father, don't I, Bill?"

"You're his spitting image, Master John! He was blond, but your features are exactly the same." He shook his head. "Ah, poor man!"

"Tell me something about him, Bill. One day, I'd like to write the story of his life, despite his being a traitor. If there's something good to say about him, I will." He hadn't thought of this previously, but he realised it was just another of the things he wanted to do. "Tell me something I don't know: I already know he was kind and gentle, and such a good Lord, and that he had many friends, even at Court. What did he do when he came here?"

"The same as everybody else did, Master John. They drank, talked, laughed together. He was always with Catesby, clearly very fond of him. Sir Ev'rard was one as loved bein' cheerful, but I've never seen him drunk. Neither was he a womaniser, and I don't say this out of respect to you who are 's son, but because 'tis the truth. Even though one was never short of temptation, up there at Court, and 'specially one like him, but he didn't like such things. As for th'others, I must say that they were somewhat rakish, at times, skirt-chasing, you know... Their group used to meet in that little room down there, you see, which they asked me to keep specially for them. They were all generous, but your father was the most generous of all and always paid for th'others, too! Only, Catesby and Percy, and Tresham as well, and some of th'others, were raving mad without anybody realising that! That was the problem!" He looked at Jack seriously, his bulging little eyes twinkling, his big blue-veined nose a few inches from his. "Because one must be utterly gone round the bend to throw onesel' headlong into a new plot after 'scaping by the skin of one's teeth from the previous one. Mustn't one? Am I right?" He raised the jug in the air to check its cleanliness and screwed his eyes.

"What meanst thou, Bill?"

"Why, I thought you knew, Master John. They were all steeped in the Essex conspiracy up to their ears, but the King pardoned them, yea, and their foot already on the scaffold. They got away with a goodly fine and saved their skin. Forewarned is forearmed... No more than three years had gone by. Let me think... Ay, they started the new plot soon after peace was made with Spain, and the City swarming with Spanish soldiers of the delegation coming here for their glass of sack... Everybody knows this, from the records that were published later... What sane man would behave like that? And, of course, a madman will do anything; but 'tis hard to believe they all went mad together! Yet, 'tis so."

Jack gaped. Now he understood what Sherwin had meant, on that last night. He didn't hear Big John calling out to him from his table on the other side of the room.

"But... were they into it with Essex, like the Earl of Southampton?"

"Why, they were. That one, though, once he had escaped by a whiff, was wise enough not to go asking for trouble again and, instead, is now quite close to the King. Those fools, on th'other hand... Raving mad, I tell you! What I'll never understand is, why the hell your father decided to trust 'em. How could he?"

"I don't understand either, Bill."

Jack stared off in the distance, always oblivious to the cries of Big John and the noise of other customers. Nor did he even hear the ballad sung by a minstrel in a corner.

Together with Big John, Jack was finally summoned to Salisbury House, where he would meet his guardian in the flesh for the second time in his life. At first he thought he could take this opportunity to tell him that he had decided to give up his rehabilitation plan; but then, he felt that he had better not face them both together, Sir Robert and Big John, therefore he put off this weighty matter to a more appropriate moment.

They found the great man sitting in an elegant little lounge, in a queer, high-backed, oriental-looking little chair; he was reading some papers and smoking tobacco from a long, carved pipe supported by a special attachment on the floor. Very smartly dressed in his usual costly garments, as if he were on the point of going out, he looked tense and seemed to have lost his rosy complexion. He remained seated before their deep bows and smiled slightly, his right lashless eye, as usual, looking at them, his left one seeming to embrace the whole room.

"Hallo, Fletcher. Morning, Master Digby. We haven't met for some time, have we? I'm pleased to see you have grown up so, in body and, I hope, in mind." He looked down on the documents in his hands: "Papers, papers, always papers! As soon as I lift up my head, another stack is ready for me thicker than the former." He sighed. "I have not much time for you… Unless you care to go to Hatfield with me, which is still far from finished."

"As Your Lordship thinks fit: 'twould be a great pleasure to us!" Big John was quick to reply.

"Let's go, then. My carriage is already waiting at the front gate, on the Strand. Only one minute, though. Will you please wait for me here, as I've got some orders to give." When Cecil stood up Jack was in pain for him, for he was still shorter and more crooked than he remembered him, his lavish clothes and high-heeled shoes only making his deformity stand out, with that hump on his back that didn't seem part of his body, his right foot sticking out as badly as ever.

On leaving the room, Cecil met two women, who Jack had heard chatting in the passageway.

"Papa, where are you going with the carriage?"

"To see the building site at Hatfield, dear."

"Can I come?"

"Not this time, Milly: I'm in a hurry. Come on, don't pout: I'll take thee next time."

"What a pity… As you wish, Papa."

"Ah Milly!" he said, as if forgetting. "Wilt thou please keep company to my guests: I'll be back in a moment."

"Of course I will, Papa."

"Oh no", Jack thought, "Not again that pin-headed harpy!". All the resentment of his first meeting with Cecil's daughter, which had been buried deep within himself during those years, welled up again. He would have preferred, and by far, Nugent's teasing.

Thus Jack saw again, emerging from a doorway, the round dark eyes that had so spitefully offended him on that far away day, and those dark curls, and those rosy cheeks. Fortunately her eyes were modestly lowered, this time, as it became an honest maiden. The girl was followed by a woman whose voice might well belong to the same governess as four years ago, as far as Jack could remember it – an elegant, blondish, middle-aged gentlewoman all ribbons, lace and curls. Big John bowed low, waving his hat, and Jack did the same.

"My respects, Lady Mildred. A good day to you, Mademoiselle Barrett. Let me introduce to you Master John Kenelm Digby!"

"*Enchantées*," said the girl, speaking for both and slightly curtseying.

"Pretty", Jack thought. "Not a beauty but, compared to her father, she is surely a miracle of Nature. Her mother must be a fairy, to make up for him!". She had a small nose, a shapely mouth and a large forehead, not very different from her father's. Though not tall, she was already taller than Sir Robert; her voice was gentle and unexpectedly low for such a young woman.

"Please be seated, I pray you," she said. She moved easily and naturally as a good lady of the house. "Methinks I've already met Master Digby once, on an occasion in which, I'm afraid, my behaviour was all but disgraceful." She looked in his eyes smiling a little: "Will you please forgive a naughty little girl, Master Digby?"

"Don't even mention it, Lady Mildred: I had practically forgotten about that!" lied Jack.

She probably was still stupid; fortunately, however, she had at least learnt her manners. She asked him some circumstantial questions about his Cambridge studies and then, maybe to show off a culture she didn't have, started talking literature with Big John, who went on to tell everybody about the latest poems and plays he had written. Miss Barrett, too, looked deeply interested: "You are the author of *Philaster,* aren't you? I *really* liked it and I'm sure that, thanks to you, tragicomedy will become *very* fashionable."

"You are flattering me, Madam! Ay, I must admit *that* one was discreetly successful, far more than any of my previous plays. Not that it was *my* fault if my first one, to make an example, was not so well received: the matter is, the audience expected something different, like murder, revenge and such hackneyed stuff, always the same." Big John had started moving his hands. "But they didn't *understand* what a tragicomedy is. It must get *close* to a tragedy without *being* a true tragedy: thus, a murder must be threatened, not performed, and, wherever possible, it must be crowned by a happy ending. It must be serious, though, not funny, not ridiculous, and not even commonplace or concerning everyday life, which makes it clearly different from a comedy. Let's say that I'm trying to... re-educate people's taste. It was all the old playwrights' fault: I mean, those of the previous generation. They chose to mix up all genres and reduce them to a huge, coarse hodgepodge, just to entertain the mob and put more money in their pockets. But the Ancients weren't a gang of fools, I say, and if Aristotle gave some rules he must have had his very good reasons."

"You have a co-writer, haven't you?"

"Ay, Milady, that's Frankie, a young friend of mine. We do great team work together! Among the Moderns, our model is the famous Ben Jonson."

"The Papist?"

"Well, Papist... I wouldn't say so nowadays... One must acknowledge that he writes good things, and even Queen Anne much admires him. After all, he's made himself useful, lately, and has helped the course of justice, even working for His Lordship your father, in the aftermath of the Powder Treason." He turned to Jack: "Sorry, Little John, but this ugly little story keeps turning up everywhere, he he he!"

"I've noticed this, Big John, and I'm grateful to thee!"

"Come on, Master Fletcher, don't be indelicate."

"I'm not, Your Ladyship: young Digby here can take a joke now… and then, a lot of water has flowed under the bridge since then, has it not, my dear?" Big John tapped him on one shoulder. "And, 'tis true, blood is blood, but Master John has learnt a lot since the time he was all wrapped up in superstition and sedition! We cannot choose the family we wish to be born in, can we?"

Jack grinned in embarrassment. He couldn't tell whether Big John was cheerfully teasing him, as he seemed to be, or rather heavily offending his family. In the latter case, what should he do, unsheathe his rapier and run it through his chest, there on the Persian carpet, before the two gentlewomen, in the home of the King's right-hand man? Slay him as Hamlet had done with the hypocritical, flattering courtier? Come on, life was different. He therefore kept on smiling like an idiot and said nothing.

A footman soon came to announce that Sir Robert was waiting for them below. They took their leave from the two women and went down a great marble staircase, followed by three more liveried footmen. Beyond the guarded front gate, a beautiful coach was waiting, attached to four white stallions – and who knew what they were worth! Its polished dark wood was all inlaid with glistening mother-of pearl; its windowpanes shone like transparent crystal. Sir Robert was already seated inside. They were invited to sit in front of him on soft leather seats, while two of the footmen mounted the back footboards. The coachman cracked his whip and off they went.

"It will take a couple of hours at most, with these horses: meanwhile, we can talk."

"So, Your Lordship, the building works are going fast, I've heard."

"They might be faster, but I don't complain, Fletcher. The problem is, I must see to it personally, if I want things well done. I didn't believe my ears when the King proposed swapping our family home with his old palace. For historical reasons, mainly: as you will know, Hatfield was the palace where Her Late Majesty, God rest her, spent her youth and, therefore, it is an unexpected honour for me to be its owner. His Majesty, on the other hand, had an interest in Theobalds, our place, owing to the vast hunting land surrounding it."

"So you are refurbishing the ancient dwelling…"

"Not at all: it was practically falling apart, so I had two thirds of it pulled down and had the remaining part, the so-called Great Hall, reduced to stables, he, he, he… To think that the Queen held her very first Council of State there… an old crumbling ruin. Now, what I want is a new, modern dwelling worthy of the best Continental palaces, and Hatfield is ideal as to territory and distance from London. I would've been sorry to pull Theobalds down: my father, to whom I owe everything, had put all himself into it. But now I'm sparing no expense: 'tis there I will retire when God and the King allow me."

"Your Lordship, the King will never give up such an experienced counsellor as you are. I'm afraid you will meet the same lot your father met under the Queen, plodding through his job to his very last day."

"We'll see, Fletcher, we'll see." Sir Robert smiled, his upper left lip slightly creasing. "Now, let's come to our Master Digby here. You have completed your course of studies young man: there's no need for you, as I wrote, to go on to an M.A. *"For in the multitude of wisdom is much grief"*, saith the prophet; *"He that increaseth knowledge, increaseth sorrow"*. But I'm glad you excelled in your studies. They tell me you are a bright, quick-witted youth…"

To make sure, however, Sir Robert questioned him about several articles of the university curriculum. Jack answered readily and unflinchingly, without even having the time to wonder what it was best to say: as if mesmerised by the peculiar gaze of that amber eye, he invariably, automatically gave him the answer he knew Cecil was expecting from him. They went through philosophy, rhetoric, logic, theology, until his guardian appeared to be satisfied and confirmed the judgment that had been expressed by Jack's Cambridge teachers. Then he changed subject. "I mean to be frank with you: as you know, your fortune was forfeit to the Crown following your late father Sir Everard's high treason; you were supported at university with what was left of your mother's dowry, Lady Mary, *née* Mulshaw. Those funds have by now run out: which means that, apart from your family seat and its surrounding estate, you are left with nothing at all."

Jack nodded. "I'm not afraid of material poverty, Your Lordship."

As if he hadn't heard, Sir Robert went on: "Therefore, we will have to find you a bride of good family and tolerable income. It will take some time, I fear, since you have absolutely nothing, apart from your good looks and your erudition. A wealthy widow maybe…" Jack shuddered. "But if you had some little income, of course, that would help."

"Your Lordship, I can't say I am interested in marriage as yet."

Sir Robert smiled as if he were joking: "But *I* am, my dear lad. You will do exactly as I tell you; or else, as a small refund for the expenses I've met to support you, I'll see myself compelled to take possession of what is left of your family seat."

"But Gayhurst is a ruin, Your Lordship!"

"It is… A ruin with a vast park, a ruin which may well be pulled down, if one is fond of hunting, to build a nice little summer residence. Do you understand me?" Cecil was still wearing his strange smile, his right eye fixed on Jack.

"I do, Your Lordship." Jack would never manage to tell him that all he wanted was go back home and be left alone. "What must I do?"

"For the time being, you will remain with Fletcher, who is in my employment; next, I'll let you know. We need someone at the censorship and someone at the Chancery, I believe." He closed the conversation as if he had been talking of chicken breeding and turned to Big John, ignoring Jack completely: "So, Fletcher, how is your work going on?"

"Very well, Your Lordship, I thank you for asking! They were in need of one just like me in the Bishop's and Archbishop's offices: there's an increasing amount of manuscripts to be overseen for publication and not even Bancroft's chaplain, that Harsnett, can make it alone: not any longer! They need learned people, and astute ones as well, able to see what a document is getting at. Apart from that, as you may have had the chance to notice, in my free time I amuse myself with some writings that can set an example, both in literature and in morals."

"Very good, Fletcher, very good. You, therefore, will teach young Digby what to do and how to move."

Jack thought that it would be more and more difficult to untie the knots binding him to this elegant, shining carriage. Sherwin made it so simple, but it wasn't at all. Would he then spend his whole life in Sir Robert's employment? Would he marry a horrid rich old widow, if Cecil should think it advisable for him to do so? The white stallions raced; the wheels creaked slightly; the landscape fled away behind him exactly as the events in his life: it was impossible to get off.

Hatfield was really a magnificent estate, surrounded by a huge park soon to be peopled with deer, pheasants and other wild beasts. "What for?", Jack wondered. He strongly doubted that his guardian, as crippled and crooked as he was, could ride a horse, to say nothing about hunting. Yet, he appeared to be very fond of it.

Sir Robert had deliberately exaggerated when he had said it was still a building site: the walls were all up and formed a most stately structure, with a central body and two wings, the roofs surmounted by elegant turrets. Myriads of builders, joiners, sculptors, carvers, decorators, marble cutters were struggling against time to complete the interiors, while furniture and ornaments were already on their way. "We'll try to finish it up before summer, including the Italian and French gardens."

Jack and Big John met the main men in charge: Lemynge, the famous architect, one Basil, the Surveyor of the King's Works, Tradescant, the head gardener who had introduced many new plants, and Rowland Bucket, the famous decorator.

"Next month we're expecting a renowned Italian sculptor, Torrigiani, and the great Inigo Jones: then, perhaps, I can say I'm satisfied."

They walked down what was to become an Italian loggia, to find a long gallery and a grand staircase, its banister skilfully carved and polished, till they came to a huge chamber – the Marble Hall, with its tiled black and white chequered floor and wall-panelling of bas-relief decoration. It was almost finished. Only one of the walls was still bare – Sir Robert explained – because it would host the *Rainbow*, the most beautiful of the old Queen's portraits. On either side of her, as if waiting for the great Queen, the portraits of Sir Robert and of his late father, William Cecil, Lord Burghley, had already been hung.

Jack got closer to them. Sir Robert had been portrayed several years before, for the picture bore the date "1602": he must have been quite a young man, then. Not young enough, however, Jack thought, as to justify the alterations worked by the painter, who had decidedly softened his features. In the picture, Cecil's forehead was not so wide, while his squint had almost completely disappeared. The calm, serious expression on his face was likely to have been carefully studied so as not to leave space to his asymmetric, disquieting smile: like this, his lips had quite a harmonious line. Sir Robert's pointed beard, now grey, was thick and reddish in the picture, singularly reminding Jack of the carved wooden satyr which used to frighten him so much as a child, persecuting him in his moments of weakness and discomfort. That was also why he could have contemplated that portrait for hours, attracted as he was by its strange magnetism.

In the top left-hand corner, the simple writing *Sero sed serio*, Sir Robert's motto, was clearly visible. Those words weren't new to him, but Jack couldn't remember where he could have heard or read them. *Late but seriously*. What did they exactly mean? That he had come late to the Queen's service, when she was already old? Or else, more likely, that the Cecil family had come too late to the Crown's service to receive one of the most powerful titles of nobility? If so, did it mean that a great title, and a great name, were actually only a matter of who came first? For Sir William's grandfather, everybody knew, had been an inn-keeper, and the high nobility had always despised him for this. But, as the English peasants had invariably said each time they had risen against their masters, "*When Adam delved and Eve span, who was then the gentleman?*" Sir Robert's motto, therefore, could be read in a seditious key: everybody had been equal, in the beginning, and those who first came to serve the victorious party were rewarded with a good title carved in marble. It had been so, in fact, for all the great families of yore: the Howards, the Percies, the Wriothesleys, respectively Dukes of Norfolk, Earls of Northumberland, Earls of Southampton. But they had all been eclipsed, now, by Cecil's "late" star, rising higher and higher in the sphere of Fortune.

In the portrait, Sir Robert was dressed in black, in reference to his humble, hard-working sobriety, as well as to his Calvinistic inclination. Beside him, however, were some unmistakable symbols of power: a bell to call his servants, an embroidered case containing the Great Seal, and a couple of folded letters, one showing Cecil's list of titles, the other maybe containing secret instructions for his men; among whom, of course, was Big John.

The others had walked past long ago; Big John called out to Jack and he had to leave his contemplation of the picture. Sir Robert showed them King James's room, for which a life-size statue of the King was being prepared to be set above the princely fireplace, as Sir Robert expected His Majesty to visit Hatfield quite often. That was who the deer park was meant for, Jack thought. At that point, however, there was something unclear. He picked up the necessary courage and asked his guardian: "Pardon me, Your Lordship, but this park seems very large and beautiful to me: how come the King gave it to you instead of Theobalds? Is the hunting land still better there?"

"Of course it isn't, boy. But Hatfield was *not* like this when we made the exchange." The two men smirked, Big John's plump chin shaking his pointed little beard, Sir Robert's left lip creasing.

"Does this mean you have bought more land?"

"Let's say I have, lad; only, there was no one to pay the land to, so I just enclosed it and that was the end of it."

"That's it! The King hadn't thought of it, had he?"

"Apparently not, Digby. Or maybe he didn't like the labour to get it… His Majesty is as active in his sports as lazy in practicalities."

"Now I get it," lied Jack.

They went out again into the Italian garden, just as the servants started to unload several carts full of ornaments. For the time being, everything was to be taken into the Great Marble Hall; the precious objects would then be carefully unpacked as the rooms, passages and wings were finished: Sir Robert was clearly in a hurry. "Who knows?", Jack wondered. "Some of all those works of art, of all those precious pieces, may come right from my home. Here everything is brimming with beauty, while Gayhurst is languishing in grim misery".

Sir Robert wanted one of his latest purchases to be already set up into a specially made glass case: it was a priceless set of rock crystal pieces of purest Bohemian quartz, each carved out of one block. It was made up of four vases, four possets and ten spoons, all of them finely carved, all of them perfectly transparent. Sir Robert took a golden-rimmed chalice and showed it to his guests: "Pretty, isn't it?" Moving in his hands, the crystal sent out little flashes of shining white from the thousand facets the craftsman had skilfully chiselled one by one.

"What a beauty, Your Lordship!" cried Big John.

Sir Robert laid it down carefully. "Let's go and have a better look at the gardens," he said.

This abode was clearly the great passion of Cecil's life, his creature. He was happy to show it to everybody, including the two of them, an obscure poet and a ward of his from a seditious family. Jack wondered how many people he had brought there: maybe even the King, even the Prince had already walked down those garden paths. Didn't His Lordship have a friend to show all this to, apart from his daughter, who, being so stupid, and a girl, could never understand? Sir Robert also had an eighteen-year-old son, Big John had told him, who, however, was abroad, studying and experiencing the world. Who else did he have? This man, who was universally respected and dreaded, this most clever of men to whom Nature seemed to have been so merciless, this man – who was so ugly but loved to surround himself with beauty – now appeared to him, from a human point of view, pitifully poor.

As soon as he had the chance, Jack asked Big John: "Sir Robert seems to be very lonely, thinkst thou not? He's a widower, isn't he?"

Big John slapped his back and laughed out loud: "He is, but he found consolation in no time!" He winked at him. "One would never tell, but he has a couple of pretty women round him... Not one, two! And among the prettiest that can be seen at Court!"

Jack gaped. "Thou'rt joking! But if he's so ugly... uh... respectfully speaking, of course."

"Ha, ha, ha, ha, my lad, thou'st got a long way to go... The two gentlewomen, who are both married, must have their good reasons!" He lowered his voice. "No, Little John, seriously, 'tis really dangerous to contradict Sir Robert. To put this simply, he just takes everything he wants, 'cause he knows he can. I suggest thou never set thyself against him!"

"And who are these two... gentlewomen?"

"One is Lady Walsingham; the other, none other than the Countess of Suffolk, one of his dearest friends' wife. Don't be in pain for him, lad: Sir Robert is never alone when he chooses not to!"

"But what about their husbands?"

"Ha, ha, ha, ha! They are lonelier than he is, to be sure!"

Seeing that Big John was in a confidential mood, Jack asked him one more question. "Listen: When I told Sir Robert I had understood, I actually had not: why did the King ask him to exchange the estates, rather than simply enlarge Hatfield?"

"Thou seest, boy, I believe that was a matter of popularity... Or, maybe, His Majesty simply had not thought about it. But Sir Robert always does!"

"Does what?"

"He exploits occasions for the best."

"And how could he acquire all this land for free?"

"He did what everybody else does: he enclosed the village common land."

"He didn't!"

"He did. For, sooner or later, someone would: so, better he than someone else, thinkst thou not?"

"But, this way, the village folk've been left without any forest to get wood from, and trap small game in, and without pasture for their livestock. He's broken the law of the land!" Jack was shocked: Sir Everard would never even have thought of anything like that.

"'Tis nothing *that* serious, little one, no one died for this. The villagers grumbled and muttered for a while but, by now, the dust has settled. I believe that, in the end, that land was not *that* necessary for them, otherwise they would really have risen in rebellion. Knowst thou, Little John, there's also lots of folks acting the poor-mouth but then, in the end, they always manage to get by; many of 'em through illegal activities, too, which never come to light. And then, what's an acre of forest or a field to them? The King, on th'other hand, will be amazed when he sees the transformation of this place, and, once again, he'll have to acknowledge his Secretary of State's genius."

"Ay, he will." Jack was silent for some seconds, then spoke again: "Listen, Big John, dost thou think it absolutely necessary for me, in order to prove my loyalty to the Crown and to Sir Robert, to marry the woman he chooses? Can't I, for instance, just tell him that I thank him with all my heart for the pain he's taken, but that I am just not interested in marriage?"

"Thou'rt joking, Little John: thou'st seen that, as soon as thou tried to, he got cross. Remember, lad, never cross him! Besides, Sir Robert is not only the King's minister, but also thy guardian, and his wardship is ruled by law. Thou mightst need to know how it went with the Earl of Southampton, who was once a promising, idealistic youth from an ambiguous family as thou art. Only, he was far wealthier, for his father died before he could be tried and therefore his property was not forfeit. Well, many years ago he was so daring as to unceremoniously refuse the bride chosen for him by his guardian, Lord Burghley, Sir Robert's father. And she was not just *any* bride: young, rich, famous…" Big John lowered his voice: "She was no less than Lord Burghley's grand-daughter, Sir Robert's niece! But Southampton was after one of the Queen's ladies-in-waiting: forbidden game, of course, from a forbidden hunting ground, ha, ha, ha! Well, he jilted the poor girl just like that, and, for this liberty, he accepted to pay an exorbitant fine: five thousand pounds!" Jack started. "And thou, boy," Big John went on, slightly winking, "Where wouldst thou find all that money, thou who hast not two pennies to rub together?"

"But, Big John, may that man be the same Earl of Southampton to whom Shakspere's narrative poems were dedicated?"

"Right him, little John! Why?"

"For no particular reason: I thought I had already heard about him."

"Then thou'lt have also heard that, like many others, he slipped into the dirty little vice of sedition and spent some two years in the Tower."

"Ay, methinks I've heard something like that…"

"'Cause, thou seest, boy, loyalty is a virtue one learns in one's youth! That one, instead, had been seditious ever since the beginning… But the Tower has cured him, now, and he has mended his ways, Ha, ha, ha, ha!"

Jack, then, went back to Little East Cheap with Big John, who was now all taken up by his flourishing literary activity and had him run all sorts of errands, thus adding up to the work he had to do directly for Sir Robert: the days of his merry wanderings through the City streets were over and now he barely had time for himself.

Ordinarily, his task was to help the King's censors, who had originally been all clergymen but now, overburdened with work, often entrusted to other people apparently innocent manuscripts which were in any case to be looked through. They kept to themselves, instead, and to their close and trusted servants, the more suspicious books, which, not surprisingly, were also the most interesting: works about history, philosophy, science and, of course, religion. What was left for Jack and other young graduates in search of employment was treatises on gardening, zoology, art, good manners. Jack usually went to fetch the manuscripts he had to examine from the palace of George Abbott, Bishop of London; he took them home, then read and underlined in red ink the sentences or even words he found inappropriate. The most interesting work he had happened to read so far was a treatise on falconry, which reminded him of his happy childhood, and also of the family friend who had escaped execution.

The only alternative he had was translating – from and into Latin – dull legal and commercial documents which he had to fetch from Sir Robert's clerks, at Salisbury House, several times a week.

He often walked past his guardian's huge library, its high vaulted ceiling supported by slender, elegant columns, which had captivated him ever since he first set his foot in the Cecil household. He invariably stopped a few seconds on its threshold. From the entrance, he couldn't see the end of that maze of ceiling-high shelves. Each time that he eagerly glanced at the rows of books arranged in good order, he repeated to himself that he was an idiot, a hopeless dawdler, who already some weeks ago should have asked Sir Robert permission to use the library for his personal recreation. In there, he was sure to find answers to at least some of the questions tormenting him. He kept justifying himself to himself by saying that he practically never came across Sir Robert; that, had he asked him for audience on such apparently trivial grounds, his guardian would become suspicious; that an opportunity would certainly soon materialise and all he had to do was prepare a convincing enough speech. He felt exactly as Prince Hamlet would have felt, whose story he had by now almost learnt by heart. Like him halfway through the play, up to now he had done absolutely nothing. But, as days ran so quickly, he didn't even have the time to think, let alone seek information about the Plot.

Until, one day, continually repeating to himself that "the readiness was all", he picked up all his courage and asked a servant to tell Sir Robert that he wished to ask him a quick question of little importance. He would first speak about something else, informing him about how his work was progressing, and finally, as if the thought had just come to his mind, he would ask him for permission to use the huge library. As soon as he stepped over the daunting threshold of Cecil's office, however, and met Sir Robert's inquisitive look, that lashless right eye of his piercing him from behind his paper-encumbered desk, he began to stumble on words, realising all of a sudden that none of the fake reasons he had rehearsed in his mind was really consistent, so he went straight to the point.

Sir Robert, who had no more than a couple of minutes for him, smiled his usual, lip-creasing, thin smile. "And when wouldst thou think thou couldst ever go there, my dear boy? Thou art up to thine ears between books to censor, documents to translate and other little chores, I'm told."

"I don't know, Sir Robert… 'Tis true, Sir Robert; 'Tis so beautiful, though, that each time I walk past it I have the impulse to walk in…"

Sir Robert looked at him inquisitively, probably amused both by the youth's embarrassment and by his curious request. He granted him permission, provided that he didn't let it interfere with his job. Jack couldn't make out whether he suspected anything. He thanked him with a low bow and left the office quite satisfied with himself: he had taken the first step.

He decided to work longer hours in the evenings and to spend at least one hour each morning in the library, looking for the true roots of the past. Maybe he wouldn't discover anything: but, at least, he would never regret not doing everything within his power. His father's ghost needn't come back to reproach him.

Jack remembered forever the day he first stepped into that great labyrinth of paper and parchment. The young sun dimly lit only some spots of the great towering shelves reaching up to the high ceiling, crammed with volumes of every size. Precious leather bindings, titles engraved in gold, rested next to stacks of folios tied together with strings or ribbons, bright colours fresh from print side by side with ancient codexes whose original colours could only be guessed. Everything smelt of paper, sealing wax, ink, wood, dust. The shelves, all bent with weight, leant as if too tired against the columns of the rib-vault and had been arranged so as to exploit all the available space, so that they formed corners, curves, nooks, crannies, some of which, even in full daylight, could only be illumined with the help of one of the lamps on the great central table. Fascinated, Jack lit one and started to walk through a narrow passage between shelves. First of all, he must make out how the materials had been catalogued.

Round the first corner, however, he was surprised to find that he was not alone: a few steps away from him, a man was standing still, a lamp in his hand, completely absorbed in the contemplation of a wall of books. Of course: several people each day must use such a well-furnished library. The man was rubbing his grey goatee beard and scanning those volumes behind small round spectacles, getting both his face and his lamp dangerously close to the inflammable books. He was all dressed in black, his hatless head completely bald. He must be quite old, judging from his bent shoulders and the snow-white ruff that had been very fashionable in the previous reign but was now obsolete. The old man turned reluctantly, on hearing Jack's steps. Jack greeted him kindly and introduced himself; he answered as kindly and a bit patronisingly, speaking both very clearly and very slowly:

"John Speed, son, a scholar. I've got several works going to press and I wanted to check a quotation about which I am no longer sure, but I cannot recall where I had read it. Thou knowst, I am exceedingly untidy: I always take notes on tiny pieces of paper and then lose them... I'm hopeless, I fear. And with my sight failing me ... But my publications are absolutely flawless!"

"What do you deal with, Sir?"

"History and geography – cartography, to be precise. And exegesis too: I'm on the point of publishing a biblical genealogy which has taken up a lot of my time; I believe it was worth it, though. And what art thou doing here? Couldst kindly repeat thy name to me?"

"John Kenelm Digby, Sir. I am one of Sir Robert's wards. I studied at Cambridge and now work for him."

"Digby, Digby,… let me think… Ah, Digby!" He opened wide, behind small spectacles, small sharp eyes which ran away at once.

"Sir Everard was my father, Sir."

"Yes, yes, I remember: a most unfortunate affair… But 'twas not thy fault, was it? And Sir Robert is magnanimous." Jack nodded. "Come here, closer, and give me a hand, wilt thou, for thou seest better than me in this scanty light: look, what I'm trying to find ought to be round here. The author's name is Norden."

"This one here?" said Jack, bending towards the lower shelf and taking out a big volume.

"Right this one. Good boy, thou'rt quick-witted! Come, I'll show thee what exactly I was looking for. Let's hope 'tis there: put it here on the table, please."

Jack took the book and sighed: it was almost time to go and, for that day, his research work would end there.

He came back on the following morning, before dawn, to make sure not to meet anyone else. It wasn't difficult to find a whole shelf dedicated to the Powder Treason, not far from the entrance. It was all there, both in print and in manuscript: the trial transcripts, the prisoners' confessions, the libels for the popular press, the official reports written for foreign embassies, the sermons, and even some of the plays that had sprung up all over London during those months. Sir Robert clearly wished for them to be widely seen and read. There was also a beautiful print portraying the main plotters. Not that it was realistic, for the unknown artist had given each of them the same face and the same idiotic happy expression; it was very evocative, though. Above the faces were the names: "Robert Catesby", "Guido Fawkes", "Thomas Percy", "Tom Wright", "Christopher Wright" (the two brothers that had been killed together with Catesby and Percy during the siege) and finally "Robert Winter" (a wrong spelling for "Wintour") handing a note to "Bates", Catesby's servant. Jack remembered Bates, whose face was actually quite different: he had been the first prisoner, on that day, to pass through the crowd; the one whose young wife was called Martha. He hadn't been the first, however, to get to the scaffold: that honour had fallen on Sir Everard.

Jack wondered whether more documents existed, reporting something different and quickly hidden away: there might be some, but such a prudent and wise man like Sir Robert would have been more likely to destroy them. He started, therefore, slowly and carefully, ploughing through the several official versions, moving very cautiously because his interest in the library must seem of a general nature. He wouldn't squat down in a secluded corner: he wanted people to get used to his presence there. He chose a big volume, not very different from the one he had taken from the shelf for Speed; he laid it open on the big central table and put the booklet he had started reading over it. It seemed to work, for two men, one after the other, walked hurriedly in and out without noticing him or speaking to him. But, he soon said to himself, they were unlikely to notice him regardless: nobody was interested in what he read. As long as Sir Robert, or, maybe, for some strange reason, Big John didn't come in… but no one did. He sank deeper and deeper into his reading.

All documents seemed to agree on the essential points, apart from the Jesuits' involvement, which only appeared later and became increasingly important till it dominated the whole plot. Of course: the government maintained it had been discovered later. But Lady Mary had told him, and he felt this to be true, that the Jesuits were not involved at all and that, instead, as soon as they had realised that something strange was in the air and that Catesby and his mates were up to no good, they had tried all they could to prevent them from resorting to violence. The problem was that, according to the law, even mere suspicion of ongoing treason, and failure to report it, was already a crime. In this sense, therefore, those who had even an inkling that the law was about to be broken and did not immediately denounce it would be as guilty as the plotters. All of them: wives, children, servants. Lady Mary had been guilty too and, therefore, so had the Jesuit Fathers. Father Garnet had been arrested on the twenty-seventh of January: no accident, then, that all the plotters had been executed quickly on the thirtieth and thirty-first, ahead of his transfer from Worcestershire to London; before they could give evidence for or against him. This was why Sir Everard had chosen to protest the Fathers' innocence loudly from the scaffold.

This, therefore was the Government's version of events, which Jack managed to put together after several days' work: soon after the failure of the Essex Conspiracy, in 1601, a group of Papists, "obstinate in their superstition and impatient of the just penal laws," sent envoys to Spain to organise yet another armed invasion which would conquer England to Popery. Their efforts didn't reach their end, however, because in 1603 the Queen died and King James started peace negotiations with Spain; peace was concluded, at last, in August 1604. Differently from what many had thought, the final treaty did not mention any toleration for English Papists, who now suddenly found themselves without their powerful patron, Spain. "Egged on by the Jesuits," then, a small group of gentlemen started to plan the wicked deed of blowing up that Parliament which they believed was sure to issue new penal laws, thus adding to the already grievous persecution. The original group was made of Robert Catesby, Thomas Percy and Thomas Wintour. After swearing secrecy on a sacred book, they gradually involved a few trusted relatives and friends, especially to finance the enterprise. The notorious Guy Fawkes, the one who ought to have lit the fuse, was hired as Percy's servant.

They were to dig a mine under the House of Lords and store into it an amazing amount of gunpowder. Meanwhile, they would put armed forces in the Midlands, near Coombe Abbey, the manor where the nine-year-old second royal child, Princess Elizabeth, dwelt with her little court. The London plotters would then set fire to the powder during the ceremony of the opening of Parliament, where the King, Queen and Prince were sure to be present. At exactly the same time, the Midlands group would storm Coombe Abbey and kidnap the little princess, who, at that point, would be the heir to the throne (would she?). They would then crown her Queen and put her under the custody of some high-born Papist (who? This was not clear), give her a Papist husband and thus bring England back under the Roman yoke.

This plan was absolutely crazy, impossible to carry out, Jack thought. To begin with, how would the two groups keep in touch, so as to work in synchrony? Would those in the Midlands proceed to kidnap the Princess without knowing whether the powder had gone off? Or, rather, would they have to wait for a signal from London? This was most unlikely as, in the meantime, the princess' wardens might be warned as well, and would have time to move her out of their reach. Unless they had set a horseman just outside the City walls, ready to run as soon as he heard the blast; but no document mentioned such a messenger. They might have thought of a carrier pigeon, then... but what if it had fallen prey to a hawk? Jack's mind had begun to wander beyond plausibility; but was there anything plausible in the whole matter? He went back to reading.

The explosion would have claimed, besides the lives of the Royal family, those of many pro-Papist noblemen, all friends and even relatives of the plotters. The plotters, however, would address this problem, according to all the documents Jack had perused, by just warning "some of them," whatever that might mean, not to go to that parliamentary session. As for the others... desperate remedies for desperate diseases, Catesby had solemnly stated. It was true, Jack thought: those were not men but brute beasts.

As time went by, always according to official sources, they ran out of money, so they involved wealthy Ambrose Rookwood, Everard Digby and others in the plot. They were all asked to take the secrecy oath and were quick (too quick, Jack thought) to pass from revulsion to consent. Now, there was no problem believing this for those who thought Papists were capable of anything, but Jack was unable to believe that things had really gone this way and that his father would so light-heartedly enter such a crazy plot. Sir Everard was bound to have known that, seeing the very high likelihood of failure, he was so recklessly jeopardising his wife's and his five children's lives, all of them still so young.

Catesby, Percy and friends, besides, seemed singularly idiotic, as they had been digging their infamous "mine" – a tunnel, that was – for months on end (in the centre of Westminster? Without anyone hearing them?) before they collided with the very thick foundation walls of the House of Parliament. At that point, they decided to change their plans, because they came up with a new idea (but couldn't they have thought of it before?), which turned out to be far more practical: there was a cellar, just below the House of Lords, that they could rent. And so they did, therefore, in Percy's name, and began to hoard (always without being seen or heard) the famous thirty-six barrels of gunpowder. The fools: they had spent months breaking their backs digging for nothing! So they put the powder in place and took off, leaving former mercenary Guy Fawkes to guard the premises in Percy's name.

Divine Providence wanted it so that at the end of October one of the Crypto-Papist noblemen who were to attend Parliament, Lord Mounteagle, was warned in an anonymous letter not to go, for *"God and man hath concurred to punish the wickedness of this time,"* so that on that day (the fifth of November) they would receive *"a terrible blow."* Bewildered, for, despite his religious doubts, he was a loyal subject, Mounteagle ran to report the incident, and the letter, to His Majesty's Privy Council, who read the letter, didn't know what to make of it, but didn't think too much about it. Not even Sir Robert Cecil, the cleverest man in the Kingdom, worried exceedingly or racked his brains over it; he decided to show it to the King in good time, however, once His Majesty came back from his hunting party.

The news of the letter being discovered soon reached the plotters (maybe because Mounteagle was their friend: his wife was even sister to one of them, thought Jack), but they went on as if nothing had happened, just hoping that the Government wouldn't make much of it (but how could this be?), or that those cryptic words would be too difficult for them to interpret. Yet the letter's entire transcript was given in several of the documents Jack had right in front of him and was quite clear: *"They shall receive a terrible blow this Parliament; and yet they shall not see who hurts them."*

In the end, it was none other than the King himself who recognised the terrible threat. Partly due to his all but divine cleverness, therefore, and partly thanks to the aid of Providence, His Majesty understood that gunpowder was somehow involved and thus graciously supplied the key to the enigma just in time to foil the plot. The cellar under the Lords was then searched for the first time: Guy Fawkes was already there, guarding the powder. Without suspecting anything, the royal guards asked him who he was (but he gave a false name) and let him go. A few hours later, on the very night before the opening of Parliament, they searched the cellar again: and again was Guy Fawkes found, in the very same spot, with a light and a fuse. So they searched the cellar more thoroughly and, lo and behold! Under a heap of wood and iron bars, they found the powder.

Among the documents, Jack also found a note written in the King's own hand, dated 6 November 1605, authorising the torture of *"that wretch"* Fawkes, recommending lighter tortures to begin with, gradually going on to the most excruciating: *"et sic per gradus ad ima tenditur."* In three days of such torture, about which no details were given, all the names that the Government wanted came to light.

On the evening of that fateful fifth of November, meanwhile, Catesby, Percy and the others, who had left London on the previous night heading for Warwickshire to meet with the other plotters, learned about Fawkes' arrest. They understood that their plans had been thwarted and that the Government would very shortly learn all their names. What did they do then? They rallied anyway in the established spot, Dunchurch. "There we are!", Jack thought: here, and from here only, did Sir Everard actively enter the game. From Dunchurch, instead of fleeing to the woods and into hiding, all in different directions, they took to horse and began a desperate, mad flight to as many Papist manor-houses as they could reach. Totally insane, as Bill Thomson had said: all their plans failed, they tried to raise an army to resist both the Government's forces and local patrols. Not unexpectedly, no one opened their doors to them. As Lady Mary had said, they had become anathema: all those having any contact at all with them were later arrested and many of them ended up on the block.

The plotters even broke into Warwick Castle and Hewell Grange and stole a dozen war horses from one, and weapons, more gunpowder and money from the other, thus adding common theft to high treason. At that point, what had been a compact group of rebels of about eighty strong had gradually thinned and, as many of them tried to flee, had turned itself into a larger group of prisoners guarded by a smaller group, the main plotters.

Hunted down by the pursuivants, by county patrols and by all His Majesty's faithful subjects, they eventually barricaded themselves in Holbeach House, Staffordshire, owned by one of them, ready to fight to the death. Before this, Sir Everard had secretly left them and given himself up. While waiting for their pursuers, and realising that the powder stolen at Hewell had gotten wet – for they had carried it in the rain in an open cart – they decided to spread it out to dry near the fire (*near the fire??*). No surprise that it caught a spark and went off, blinding one of them and wounding several others. Served them right; for they had fallen into their own snare, as the psalmist said. Holbeach was soon surrounded; a gunfight followed in which the two arch-plotters, Catesby and Percy, fighting back to back, were finally brought down by one bullet. The Wright brothers were also shot to death. The others, more or less seriously injured, were sent to London and thrown into the Tower.

Jack saw that one of the libels gave the details of Sir Everard's trial, and reported his declarations to the Court (and the answers by Coke and Northampton): he had joined the plot, he said, out of friendship, love of Popery and fear of further persecution, and he didn't much care if his wife and children paid for it too. Jack laid the libel down. Whatever this was, this was not his father.

The prisoners' torture-wrung declarations unveiled an astounding amount of other names, among which, not surprisingly, were those of the best known and most esteemed Jesuit Fathers, whom the Government had been after for ages. Several of them were found and arrested, hiding as they were in friendly homes. Jack found pages and pages relating in minute detail their and their supposed accomplices' questioning – especially Father Henry Garnet's. Meanwhile, however, as Jack already knew, all the plotters had been executed and could no longer either confirm or deny what had been written down. He read Coke's speech against Garnet's devilish equivocation, plus the report of Little John Owen's "suicide". Lastly, the documents confirmed that Long John Gerard and Father Tesimond were still at large, hunted down by the Law. Jack knew for certain that they had managed to sail to the Continent, one disguised as a Spanish soldier on board a Spanish ship, the other hidden among butchered swine on a merchant ship.

Jack's reconstruction of events was accurate and painful. First he read the smaller, thinner libels, much more easily concealed among the pages of any big volume resting on the table, and then he passed on to the bigger ones; always very carefully but encouraged by the early hour, when the library was almost always deserted.

One day he took out a book which was quite thick, though not very large. It was a valuable edition, bound in what was clearly a peculiar, costly kind of leather smelling of oilskin. No writings were on the cover, apart from an apparently handwritten Latin inscription: *Carnem severa paenitentia castigavit.* He opened it: it was yet another solemn Government book entitled *A True and Perfect Relation of the Whole Proceedings against the late most Barbarous Traitors, Garnet, a Jesuit, and his confederates,* containing, once again, records of questionings and trials, especially concerning the Jesuit superior. The usual vicious contents in luxurious version.

"May I? Am I bothering you?" said a female voice.

Jack started, yet tried to remain perfectly still. It came from the entrance, next to the door he could not close. He slowly looked up to find his guardian's spoilt, obtuse daughter. Why the hell was she already up? This one, he thought, is the living proof that intelligence doesn't necessarily run in the family. So much the better: he was in no danger of being discovered.

"Surely, Milady." He had closed the book, now, but there was no hope of putting it back on its shelf without her noticing it: never undervalue dimwits! He put on a brave face.

"I meant no, you are not... I was admiring your father's splendid volumes."

She came closer. "*Were* you?"

She utterly ignored Ovid's *Metamorphoses* lying open on the table and went straight to the book he had just closed. "And *that* one just fell into your hands, didn't it?"

"Is't forbidden by the law? I happen to have your father's permission to consult all the books I want." He couldn't help his angry tone, though he regretted it at once.

"Ay, Ay, 'tis the same thing as I do to conceal poetry books. I don't know why, but Papa doesn't want me to read them. I just *love* sonnets... I'm not sure, however, that he cares what *you* read; but I might tell him regardless: at least, he would be amused!" She chuckled and took the book from his hands, looking at the cover. "Ah, the *True and Perfect Relation*! It can't but enlighten you on how filthy traitors end up."

"Why, is there anything I do not already know about such filthy traitors as my father?"

She narrowed her eyes. "There may be: for instance, that their skin makes splendid book covers!"

"What??"

"Aha, thou knewst not! Well, I'll tell thee: this comely little book is bound in human skin, your arch-traitor Garnet's. A relic, would you say?"

She smiled triumphantly, addressing him thus, as if he were a servant. Jack was at a loss for words. "Let's not stand on ceremony", he said to himself, and sat down. He took a deep breath.

"We? We who? I have conformed to the Church now established."

"Who meanst thou to deceive? Thou'rt only a Church Papist: that is, a still worse time-server. My father knows perfectly well what lies at the bottom of thy heart."

Jack lowered his defence. "He can't know: I know it not myself… seest thou all thy prejudice? Thou'rt not changed since thou sawst me as a sort of circus entertainment." Now, she would tell her father horrible things about him, maybe adding some lies, such as that he had tried to seduce her. He didn't care.

She, however, perhaps out of pity for him and his miserable expression, sat down beside him, without much noticing the confidential tone he had also used, for which alone he could have been punished.

"All right, I may have over-reacted: in fact, my father cannot but speak well of thee. The fact is, I can't brook Papists."

"Of course thou canst not: thou'st been taught to hate them since thou wert a child. 'Tis sweet and rewarding to always side with the good, the strong, the rightful."

"Thou'st forgotten 'the clever'."

"Ay, 'cause we're all twits."

"'Tis enough to see how cleverly they organised this plot that never held water."

"So, thou'st noticed? That's why I'm trying to understand more: I assure thee that Papists are not a bunch of imbeciles. And then, you've got many at Court too, haven't you?"

"We might, before the Plot: now, thank God, we no longer have!"

"But wasn't Queen Anne converted some years ago?"

"Ay, and look at the idiot she is: cleverness dwells elsewhere."

"Hear, o hear: thou hast something for everyone, thou who knowst nothing at all about the world. Here, in thy princely palace, thou dost not even imagine what life's like for us who grow up in fear, persecution and terror. Thou'lt never know what it means to watch thy loved ones being disembowelled to entertain the mob."

"Well, quarterings quite upset me."

"Don't tortures?"

"Torture is made necessary when one who is a proven criminal will not contribute to save innocent people."

"Thou speakst as if quoting from memory. Thou'st been taught this too: 'tis only natural. I believe we shouldn't even start arguing, thou knowst, for the two of us will never meet. At most, thou mayst feel a bit of pity, as if a dog or a cat or a fighting bear were killed, but nothing more."

She was thoughtful for a moment.

"Thou'rt right. I'll never understand Jesuitical equivocation, which is nothing but a justification of lying. I'll never understand your superstition, nor your blind obedience to a foreign power, nor, decidedly, the macabre inclination that urges you to dip your kerchiefs into your martyrs' blood while, their belly open, they are breathing their last, or else to try to lay your hands on parts of their bodies to take home with you; and even less will I understand your gullibility, which makes you see miracles everywhere." She was finally silent, but he would have let her go on: it wasn't worth the effort to contradict her. She was apparently disappointed by his silence, and went on: "In this book, however, something troubles me."

"What's that?"

"I'll show thee." She got up, took the book, moved a few steps back holding it waist-high, the front cover facing him. "What seest thou?"

On the golden-brown leather, hit by the early sunlight filtering through the window, Jack could notice lighter spots forming a sort of pattern. He took some seconds to make it out: it was a human face. "My God! 'Tis Father Garnet!" Instinctively, Jack fell to his knees and crossed himself.

"Is it really him? Art sure? Aren't thou being deceived by thine own superstition?"

"'Tis him, I swear! He was a guest in our house. I didn't know him very well, but I remember his face perfectly. How dost thou explain this?"

"I don't know, but there must be a rational explanation: miracles are ceased. 'Tis surely disquieting, though," she said, turning the book towards herself. "It wasn't so clear only a few weeks ago." She laid it back on the table, instinctively rubbing her little hands in her precious light-blue taffeta dress embroidered in gold. "Witchcraft, I guess… It gives me goosebumps!"

"I may be asking too much of thee, but just try to be rational: if Jesuits really had such powers, couldn't they just have jinxed the King without risking their skin?"

"How can I know? Not always do criminals follow logic. Perhaps they wanted to do something sensational, something that had never been tried before, that would leave a mark on history. Utterly insane! Because your religion is surely *not* for rational people. How can you think that one can be freed from pain, in the life to come, by the offers I give your priests?"

"And how can you believe that God damned some people before he even created the world? And all this because an obscure German monk woke up one day and thought he had suddenly understood things that *everybody* else had got wrong for a thousand years. What he wanted was actually the Church's goods: that's why our great obese king broke up with Rome."

She looked straight into his eyes; then narrowed hers and spoke slowly, her voice suddenly lowered.

"Church-Papist my foot! All thy Cambridge studies have been absolutely fruitless."

Jack froze in horror. And now? What if the little Countess had been sent by her father to test whether his re-education had actually succeeded? He had fallen into the trap like a chicken. He looked back at her and whispered: "How canst thou know? What wantst of me?"

She giggled carelessly. "Nothing: I was looking for something amusing to do and I've found it!"

"Wert thou not sent?"

"What thinkst thou? Thou'rt not so important as to bother the Earl of Salisbury's daughter!"

Just then, they heard a female voice, presumably her governess, calling her from the hall.

"I must go," she said, "Playtime's over. I'm going to complete my culture."

"And thy prejudices."

"Look who's talking!" said she, poking out her tongue. "Adieu." And out she ran, without leaving him the time to reply.

She was strange and capricious, thought Jack. Though she'd been filled to the ears with rubbish, one couldn't say she was stupid, after all. Very slowly, with reverential dread, he shoved Father Garnet's book back on its shelf; then he put Ovid back too and walked out.

On his way home, he felt his heart thumping against his ribs: what if, after all, this spoilt little girl – even granting she really hadn't been sent – had run to denounce him, like this, just out of spite? He bit his lips angrily: how could he have been so rash and let himself go with this stranger who despised everyone like him and had all possible instruments to ruin him? She might be the whip hand in Cecil's coach. Anyway, what could he do now? What's done is done and what's said is said, he thought. He was no longer in Cambridge, where one step out of line or saying the wrong thing meant a good beating. He was a man, now, and had to make his own decisions. So, what if the little shrew had run to blabber everything to her dear daddy-o? What did he care, deep down? Might Sir Robert throw him into the Tower? Might he confiscate Gayhurst and cast his family into the street like this, all for a casual conversation?

He tried not to think too much about it and, as soon as he got to the Little East Cheap lodging, he sank as deep as he could into the treatise on dancing he was examining. He could not really understand what he was reading, however, because Father Garnet's face, which, God knew why, had been impressed on the book cover made from his very skin, kept emerging – as if by magic – from the thickly written pages of the manuscript. He felt, by the same strange sort of magic, as if he were in the Tower dungeons with him, just before they butchered him.

Fortunately, though, in the following days he did not sense anything different from usual: no one asked him to confirm the orthodoxy of his opinions, or how he spent his time inside the Salisbury House library. Maybe, after all, Sir Robert's daughter had not reported him and life could go on as it always did, from one dull job to another. Or, maybe, his rash words had only been written into his file to be used later to ruin him.

Jack was on his way to the Bishop's palace to deliver some books – which, in truth, he had not read very carefully, skipping a page here and there – when he suddenly thought of calling on his player friend, Tim, whom he had no longer heard from. He was ashamed he had not once written to him. Might the young commoner have remembered to collect some information for him? Perhaps he had not, but he was the only person Jack knew, in London, who was not somehow connected to his guardian.

As he walked, he kept thinking about the Plot: it was all really weird, to begin with Catesby's and Percy's extraordinary cruelty. Catesby had apparently declared that murdering innocent people was justified in view of a greater end: he hadn't even stopped at the thought that his own relations and friends would be among the victims. It looked like a suicide mission, for both himself and the others. Was the hatred of those men towards the King so great, then, after His Majesty disappointed their expectations of tolerance? How heavily had they been oppressed by the penal laws? Of course, many families had been reduced to poverty by the recusancy fines. Jack remembered overhearing Long John tell Sir Everard that each law contributed to creating culture: that was why, by now, people felt they were entitled to hate Papists more than the devil himself. Was there, then, really no way out, other than slow, painful extinction? How could their bitter exasperation alone, though, lead to such an absurd bloody act?

And then, there was the strange magnetism Catesby had worked on all the others: even Sir Everard had apparently declared he had joined the group, first of all, out of love and trust for Catesby. Ay, what a reliable one this Catesby was! On learning that the plot had been betrayed by the anonymous Mounteagle letter, he said nothing and sent Fawkes to inspect the powder, just to see whether or not he would be arrested. Then, seeing that he hadn't been, Catesby thought the letter hadn't been noticed and gave orders to proceed. He was really insane, playing so recklessly with the lives of his acquaintances, his friends, his relatives. A cynical man.

As for poor Fawkes, he had clearly never learnt about the letter, and had gone on as quiet as a lamb to the slaughter. Jack had held Fawkes' last confession in his hands. He remembered the shaky signature revealing grievous tortures, unspeakable suffering. Who, then, could be sure he had really said what he was reported to have said? A tortured man will declare, and subscribe, whatever he is told.

Jack shuddered. If that ever happened, how would *he* behave under torture? Heroically, like the true Little John, who had let himself be dismembered rather than betray his friends? Or else, would he not bear the torments and break down at once, revealing even what he didn't know? Bend, step aside, get up again just to survive: this was all very well for women and children. But, when the time came, a true man must be able to suffer and die. How nonchalantly, up there in Cambridge, Sherwin had said that we all owe a life! And who knew what had become of him: had he really managed to reach Flanders, and thence Spain, France, or maybe even Italy?

He caught sight of the apse of the great cathedral emerging from among the houses, not more than twenty steps forward. He walked on.

The figure of Catesby, then, was a mixture of bravery and recklessness, cunning and ingenuousness. As for Thomas Percy, his story was still more incredible: a poor relation of great Henry Percy, Earl of Northumberland – the greatest magnate in the Kingdom –, he had asked him for a job and had become the superintendent of his estates, specialising in collecting taxes in whatever way he might deem necessary. He must have been a very resolute man, one who could be extremely persuasive. Northumberland had even had him admitted among the King's Gentlemen Pensioners, a special body of fifty guards Sir Everard too was part of. But then, if they wanted to kill the King, why not take advantage of their privileged position and simply stab him, as the French could do so well? Percy, instead, had started this mad, most expensive plot, involving a hundred people in a crazy enterprise doomed from the very start.

As if all this hadn't been enough, what had Percy done, on the morning of the fourth of November? He had gone to visit his powerful patron at his London residence of Syon, allegedly to talk to him – what about it was not clear, probably just trivialities; which was learnt at once, of course, by the Government. Thus, Northumberland fell from grace, was fined as no man had ever been before and ended up in the Tower, whence he had not yet emerged.

What Catesby and Percy really had in mind was unclear. What would they have done if, against all odds, the plot *had* been carried off after all? Did they really mean to put little Elizabeth on the throne and use her as a poor puppet in their hands? Would they have her appoint them regents to the throne together with the unknown nobleman (maybe Northumberland) who had already accepted that office? What a pity not to have even an extorted confession from either of them: what a shame they had been killed before they could speak. But hadn't Sir Robert recommended they be taken alive? What need to shoot them, seeing Holbeach House was surrounded by the Government's forces? And what a coincidence, both killed with one bullet: two birds with one stone, really... But who would have dared disobey Sir Robert's orders? Jack wondered how angry his guardian might have been, not being able to question the two men who knew more than all the others put together.

Meanwhile, he had walked round the cathedral and had reached the poor house he remembered, the small window looking right onto where the scaffold had been. Only, now, the door was bolted and nailed, its interiors clearly empty. Where had little Tim Rice gone? Next time the King's Men went onstage, he would try to go: some of them might remember the boy who used to look after their customers' horses and once had even performed with them, and they might know his whereabouts.

Tim had probably found something else to do, after all: if they hadn't kept him, he might have opted for the less exciting but safer printer's job. As soon as he had a free moment, Jack would try Fleet Street too, then, just outside the walls, and also the printing shops nearby, around the cathedral.

It was true, times were getting really tough, tougher then ever for playing companies; especially now that this sort of Episcopal Puritan, George Abbott, had been made Bishop of London. Jack had often heard him thunder from his pulpit against the immorality of playhouses and all other entertainments, and with such fervour as to upset even Big John: one nation, one belief! It was time to put an end to the popish remnants the country was riddled with, the theatre being one. England would never be like France, whose king, in ignorance, weakness, or both, tolerated different religions, thus signing his own country's death warrant in a very near future.

It was getting dark; it had started to rain, and all the shops were closed now; swallowing his bitterness and disappointment, Jack soon found himself in front of Abbott's door and knocked.

That night, over dinner, Big John told him that John Speed, the scholar Jack had met in the library, had formally requested Sir Robert's permission to have young Digby as a secretary, at least until he delivered the three big volumes he was finishing to the printer. Jack was glad of this: he could go to the library more often and skip for some days, or even weeks, the boredom of translating the usual dull stuff for those obscure clerks, or of nit-picking wearisome treatises no one would ever read.

"How come thou knowst Speed?" Big John asked.

"I met him one day in the library as I was looking round. Thou knowst that Sir Robert has kindly granted me permission to use it, as long as it doesn't hinder my work; thou also knowst my love for books, dost thou not?"

"I know it well, little one: one day I wouldn't be surprised if thou too started to climb the high peaks of Helicon, just like me! *Talis magister, talis discipulus*: such is life!"

Jack smiled silently as he bit into a chicken leg. "I'm not the little one, between thou and me," he said, his mouth full. "Pass the stewed turnips, please. Are they still warm? Anyway, I like those new apples better, thou knowst, those coming from the Indies and growing underground."

Jack started, therefore, to work on John Speed's proofs, between Sir Robert's library and the old scholar's lodgings. That was to be his *annus mirabilis,* Speed said, for, as he had already told him, he had as many as three masterpieces on his hands: besides the Bible genealogy he had mentioned, he was finishing a *Historie of Great Britaine* ("Britain": this was the name by which the King loved to call his kingdom, after he had united England and Scotland under his rule) and also a great, precious atlas, which he had entitled *The Theatre of the Empire of Great Britaine.*

Jack had never in his life seen such beautiful, detailed maps of every single county. The pictures were literally covered in captions, drawings, heraldic shields, which thronged all round the actual map, every county bound inside colourful borders all cobwebbed with rivers, forests, villages whose names, written in tiny letters, were all to be revised: with his failing sight, Speed would never have managed that.

As he worked, Jack lingered on the Midlands maps. Just below them, he stopped to contemplate Buckinghamshire, where Gayhurst and his dear ones were, while a violent pang of homesickness stabbed his heart. He reluctantly turned the page, ranged it exactly where it should be and passed on to Warwickshire. Here was Coughton Court, the manor-house his father had rented from the Throckmortons, at Catesby's suggestion, to carry out what he had called the "enterprise". Here were several other houses belonging to other plotters and their accomplices, especially north-west of a little town, Stratford, through which ran the Avon river; while to the East was Dunchurch, the village where the plotters had gathered before starting their mad dash across the country in search of support.

He closed his eyes and saw Sir Everard galloping on the magnificent horse he had loved so much, surrounded with servants, friends, relations, all of them involved in the same crazy Powder Plot, all of them possessed by the same madness. He imagined his father's fine features, his resolute expression, his blond hair floating in the wind under his black felt hat, his cloak fluttering, his deep voice now imperious. He could almost perceive the smell of the sweating horses, the sound of their breath, the trampling of their hoofs on the ground. He could almost hear the frantic orders that the main plotters gave to the rest of the group, leading them first here, then there, and finally up to Holbeach House (still further north-west, appearing on the same page but in the next county), until the predictable, inevitable final catastrophe. In those burning-hot days, the scaffold awaited those who merely stopped to talk to one of them, or handed them a · piece of bread, a flask of water. They had brought death and desolation to everything they had touched. Jack turned that leaf too, tears in his eyes.

With the help of a big magnifying glass, meanwhile, Speed was scrupulously, painstakingly going over the already printed pages, every now and then asking him a question. Jack was sure the old scholar had chosen him not because he lacked potential helpers, but rather out of curiosity about his personal life. Thus, between one page and another, Jack had told him about his mother, his brothers and sisters, Gayhurst, and then – trying as much as he could not to talk about his father – about his life in Cambridge and London.

"Thou'rt a bright lad, Digby. Wert good at Cambridge?"

"Quite good, Master Speed."

"One of the best?"

"Ay, Master Speed."

"Good boy: modesty is also important. What wilt thou do, now, in London?"

"I'll wait for Sir Robert to find me a position, Sir; meanwhile, I'm trying to be helpful as I may."

"And dost thou get along well with that Fletcher?"

"I do, Sir. 'Tis him introduced me to the theatre world, which I much like. He himself is becoming quite a renowned dramatist."

Speed frowned, his small eyes almost disappearing, behind his thick little spectacles, between his bushy eyebrows and the swollen bags filling the circles under his eyes. "A bad world, Digby, a bad world. Pleasure-loving, dissolute, licentious, immoral, bordering on the illegal. Keep on thy guard, lad, or they will corrupt and ruin thee."

This made Jack absolutely certain that Speed was a Puritan. He was careful not to contradict him and said nothing. But Speed went on: "Well, wantst thou not to know why?"

Jack was finishing to arrange his pages. "I believe I already know, Sir. 'Tis not dissimilar from what our Bishop of London, Dr Abbott, keeps saying. The theatre deters people from going to Church, besides anarchically mingling all social classes, and men and women; moreover, its farces are immoral. And then, the playhouses are full of pickpockets and harlots looking for customers. But I am very careful, Sir, and, above all, I only go there for literary reasons, to listen both to fine poetry and to the good patriotic speeches they give every now and then."

"Do they? And knowst thou what players usually do after their performances? They go round the City in their garish costumes, despite the law forbidding it, and eat for free, pretending they are this or that great nobleman. Just put it on my tab, they say, I'll pay it all together. And the ostlers, of course, daren't say no. And what sayst thou about their boys, nay, little children, who they force to dress up as women? The Bible is very clear on this. And why is Holy Scripture so peremptory about this? Because it leads to sodomy! Upon my soul, I'll bet they're all sodomites as well."

Jack choked a hearty laughter: that was probably what the players would also do, could they hear the old man pass his judgment on them. Players had always loved teasing those like Speed and parodying them on stage. But now Jack did not want to argue, and even less to arouse suspicion. "You're right, Master Speed."

But Speed was inflamed, by now, and went on: "As for patriotic speeches, I guess thou art referring to their history plays: those are actually the worst! Fortunately, and oftentimes, the Bishops themselves have seen to those, starting at least ten years ago. Because 'tis from them that our ignorant, illiterate commoners learn our country's history, ignoring that there is nothing falser!"

"Are you serious, Master Speed?"

"Thou hast studied, Digby, and oughtst to know. Never heard about Sir John Oldcastle?"

"I have, Master Speed, in Foxe's *Book of Martyrs*."

"That's it. Well, this holy man, this morning star of religious Reform, the players turned into a drunkard, a foolish, dishonest glutton! Canst thou imagine?"

"I vow I've never seen anything like that performed, Master Speed."

"That's because censorship works, at times, God be praised! But, the fact is, thou'rt too young: this was a shameful event of some years ago. The players thought they'd get away with it by simply changing their character's name... But they didn't. And then, they are blasphemous! Luckily, quite recently, the Government has forbidden them to pronounce God's name in their shows, otherwise we would soon have seen public blasphemy put on stage, and wholly unpunished. Knowst thou how blasphemers were punished in the Ancient Testament? By being stoned to death! Keep thy guard, lad, for youngsters like thee tend not to see the snares set for you by those cunning foxes!"

"I thank you for warning me, Master Speed: I will watch out and try not to keep company with them. There, the maps of the counties are all right. What else shall I check?"

There were several reasons why Jack was actually looking forward to stealing away from his many errands to go to the theatre once again.

Jack was braving the wind through the suburban lanes he knew so well. He remembered promising Big John that they'd go together to see the King's Men as soon as they performed a Shaksperean play. In fact, he was very careful to avoid him: he went alone and secretly, even considering dressing up as a commoner so that no one they knew could tell Big John they had seen him there. Then he thought better of it, for he wanted to appear as his true self to the players; in the end, he just donned the largest cloak he had, covering his face almost completely as he walked. At the end of the show he would approach the players in their *tiring house* and try to talk to Shakspere. He had many questions for him. He was the King's dramatist, but Jack couldn't see his plays bursting with loyalty: they couldn't have been more different from what was being preached from the King's pulpits. Whose side was he on? And how could he keep his balance, with all the ambiguities he put into his plays? Moreover, while he was about it, he might even ask Shakspere what he thought about the Plot: did he trust official records? Did he happen to know anything more, or anything different? And then, of course, he wanted to ask him what he remembered about Sir Everard.

Despite the uncertain weather, many people were queuing before the box office. Above them, and above the stage, the little black flag flapped like mad in the blowing gale. Jack paid his six pence, took his seat next to two *Inns of Court* students and waited for the play to begin. He noticed that, since he had last been here, the stage had lost some of its fine golden paint, and that the blue "sky" of the ceiling under the canopy was duller. Here and there the galleries had been fixed perfunctorily, with a couple of nails and the first piece of wood at hand. Might the company be short of money?

He bought an orange from a woman and focussed his eyes on the stage, as the pit was shaken by a loud flourish and the first two characters appeared. Despite the little black flag, the first scene was decidedly comic: not even today had Master Shakspere abided by Aristotle's rules. But then a whole Royal Court entered, with an old king (Jack recognised Richard Burbage) who had decided to split his British kingdom into three parts, one for each of his three daughters.

Quite an old story, Jack thought. The best of all openings remained the one in *Macbeth,* with its three witches and their chant: what a shame he hadn't been able to find it in print!

He wondered whether Shakspere remembered him; if he did, and if he managed to talk to him, the King's playwright might let him go through his papers; he might lend him the manuscript of that famous, tremendous tragedy. Shakspere could trust him: he would handle it with utmost care and give it back to him as soon as he had read it. He might even let him keep it for some days, long enough to copy it down.

Now the old king wanted to know which of his three daughters loved him most, so that he could distribute his lands according to their love.

"Old idiot, what does he expect? The truth, maybe?" one of the two students sitting beside him jibed. But Jack had understood, by now, that this poet's – and this company's – plays were never commonplace, never to be read at face value. Following *Hamlet*'s pattern, therefore, he started to look behind every speech for interesting references to contemporary events. To begin with, the division of Britain could not be after King James's taste, who had busied himself a lot in the opposite direction and even now seemed to have little else on his mind other than uniting his two kingdoms legally and permanently.

And then, this absurd request to show their love… following which, two of the daughters swore hyperboles of unconditional devotion whereas the third one refused to lie and fell into disgrace… This was a typical fairy tale theme. From the political point of view, however, it was not dissimilar from another pledge of absolute loyalty, the Oath of Allegiance, which King James claimed from all his subjects and which he too had just taken, up there in Cambridge. Could the youngest daughter, then – the one who, refusing hypocrisy, had also refused to declare her love – stand for King James' political and religious dissidents?

But it was probably all in his mind, a castle in the air, Jack thought, and this was just a fairy tale with an unhappy ending. And lo, the old king, blinded by pride, banished from Court all those who were truly faithful to him, those who preferred telling him uncomfortable truths rather than covering him in flattering lies: now he practically delivered himself up into the hands of his evil daughters. Meanwhile, an aged nobleman, the Earl of Gloucester, went through all sorts of misadventures due to his bastard son, who spread slanders and treachery both against him and against his own half-brother, Gloucester's legitimate son. The poor youth, Edgar, was forced to flee, and to roam the country with nowhere to go, owing to... an anonymous letter? What a coincidence: it reminded Jack of the letter sent to Mounteagle, which, just like the one in the play, might well be false. Or was it rather his obsessed, diseased mind which saw references to the Plot and to his own father everywhere?

He tried to stop that, and to enjoy the play without asking himself too many questions. There: good Edgar, unjustly banished and hunted down, disguised himself as a mad beggar and went under the name of "Tom o' Bedlam", just as if he had escaped from the asylum outside the London City walls (and which would certainly not have been there in King Lear's time). He even had to crawl into a hollow tree-trunk to escape capture and execution. There was nothing to be done: the most obvious connection in Jack's mind was with Sir Everard and his fellow plotters as, on that accursed fifth of November, the most relentless man-hunt that their generation could remember had been unleashed. But surely, and maybe even more so for those who were not directly involved in the Powder Treason, Edgar brought to mind Father Garnet, who had spent years hiding in the secret "holes" prepared by the humble carpenter recently torn to pieces in the Tower dungeons.

Now, the theme of madness surfaced again: just as in *Hamlet*. Because of their folly, foolish people were allowed to speak, even to tell uncomfortable truths. The King's jester, his Fool, was both amusing and moving: though he suffered together with his master, he tried to cheer him up without fawning over him. Instead, he tried to make him see that he had dug a pit for himself. This jester was at once tender and funny in his motley clothes, his colourful fool's cap, his sad expression. That part, one of the students sitting beside Jack told him, was usually played by the best comic actor of the moment, the famous Robert Armin, who also had a beautiful singing voice. Today, however, the Fool part had been given to someone else, a younger boy, who, although very expressive, couldn't sing as well. Jack wondered whether Armin was sick. He wasn't, the student told him:

Armin had fallen into disgrace and no one knew whether he would ever come back to the stage.

The old King was now shut out of a castle, left alone with his Fool and two beggars, one sane, the other allegedly insane; as the King was going mad too, there were now three fools on stage, none of them really or completely mad. Moreover, a storm was approaching: Jack heard the usual rumble produced by a cannon ball sent rolling on a special metal track. Meanwhile, quite curiously, the London sky had actually turned darker, and that artificial metallic sound was echoed by real distant thunder. The players started to hold their garments tight round them, for the wind was growing stronger.

This was a wonderful scene, at least for those sitting in the galleries and sheltered by the roof: while Lear shouted at the storm, there was no need for the players to use their fireworks, for real lightning arrived. Who were these men? – Jack wondered in amusement. Could they command the elements? The two students were also amazed by the coincidence, and probably so was everybody else inside the Globe. It now began to pour with very real rain: it was just beautiful. The groundlings covered their heads as best as they could and many of them left, cursing; but the players seemed to draw new strength from this natural encouragement. The performance, which before this had not been very convincing, now really took off, until Jack entirely forgot the main reason he was there. As had happened that day long ago, he totally identified himself with the play.

The old Earl of Gloucester, the one who had been betrayed by his bastard son, had tried to help his poor king, and for this alone he was now tied to a chair by the evil Duke of Cornwall, who then – horrible to see! – plucked out one of his eyes barehanded.

It was here Jack shook himself and managed to separate fact from fiction: one of the servants on stage, the one who just now was rebelling against the fiendish Duke, seemed… Ay, he *was* Tim Rice! He had stayed on, then, to become a true professional! In the duel which followed, Jack saw that Tim had also become a remarkable swordsman. Very shortly, though, Tim confirmed what must have remained his greatest skill, the ability to get himself killed; for, just as he was about to have the upper hand over the Duke, he was stabbed in the back by the hellish Duchess. Now the Duke, however mortally wounded by Tim, was free to pluck out poor Gloucester's other eye.

What followed was the triumph of Evil and the defeat of Good: the two old men were one blind, the other mad, while their good children and other faithful characters were treated as traitors and outlaws. Exactly as in *Macbeth,* traitors were good. Decidedly, Jack had to speak to Master Shakspere.

Meanwhile, a civil war had broken out on stage and good Cordelia had put herself at the head of the French army to invade Britain and free her father the old King from his oppressors. So, not only were traitors good, but invaders might be good as well: unbelievable!

Unfortunately, however, nothing seemed to stop the *mysterium iniquitatis.* Now defeated, Cordelia said in resignation: *"We're not the first who with best meaning have incurred the worst."* Was this a sort of justification for treason? Sir Everard and his fellow plotters too had deemed their meaning good, obviously: which villain, in real life, really believed himself to be such? Who was ever totally aware of their own evil? Who didn't have some justification always ready, both for themselves and for others?

But, lo and behold: just when Jack had lost all hopes, Good triumphed once again. Gloucester's banished good son, Edgar, whose name had been *"lost by treason's tooth bare gnawn and canker bit,"* recovered his honour and his identity and killed his evil brother in a duel, while the old king's two cruel daughters were done away with by their own cruelty and lust. Old Gloucester had died of joy, but King Lear recovered his senses and was reconciled to his good, unjustly banished Cordelia. Good triumphed and Jack felt, along with the rest of the audience, that it had been worth so much suffering. The tension was loosened, and a wave of pure relief swept both pit and galleries. Not unlike *Macbeth,* then, even this one wasn't a true tragedy.

But no, it wasn't over yet… Lear came back onstage with his daughter in his arms… Was she dead? Why? What idiots: they had forgotten to save her. This was both vulgar and trivial… The groundlings who had not been scattered by the storm were all eyes and ears. Her old desperate father, in great lament, held her in his arms as if she were the dead Christ, echoing an icon of grief. It all looked like a new Golgotha, exactly as when Sir Everard had been killed. Surely there couldn't have been more blood, on Calvary; not to mention that that sort of table to which they had tied his father looked so much like a cross. It had been like a crucifixion: the most painful and infamous death men could think of. Was this blasphemy?

He focussed back on the tragedy of this old king on stage, who still couldn't grasp what had happened and wanted to see whether his daughter was really dead, until his heart burst when he saw what looked to him like a spark of life… But he was wrong. Everything was catastrophe: a mass slaughter, as in *Hamlet*. What for? Jack had identified himself so much with what was taking place on stage that he had almost wanted to run down and save Cordelia. There, this was the real end of the play. Now Edgar advanced towards the groundlings and gave a short speech in rhyming couplets: *"The weight of this sad time we must obey, speak what we feel, not what we ought to say."* (What did he mean? Who was he speaking to?) *"The oldest have borne most: we that are young shall never see so much, nor live so long."*

The rain had stopped some minutes before, but no one had noticed. And now a strong wind was clearing the afternoon sky. The groundlings, though drenched to the skin, started to clap their hands like mad, followed by the audience in the galleries. Before the final dance was over, Jack dashed impatiently down the steps and through the pit towards the *tiring house*, just as he had done that day, as a child.

Again was he surrounded by half-darkness, and by the mixed smell of makeup and sweat, art and life, which he had forgotten. The players spotted him at once, this time, either owing to his smart clothes or to his height. A middle-aged man asked him what he was looking for and, as soon as he learnt, started calling out aloud: "Tim! Tim Rice! There's visits for thee!" Tim emerged from that small busy crowd. He advanced in slight alarm, since he hadn't recognised him, so tall he was; the same couldn't be said about him, who had remained quite short and slim, while his longish blond hair was still more ruffled. The questioning look on his clever face, which was still sprinkled with freckles, broke into a smile of joy as soon as he understood who was before him. They shook hands vigorously: of course he remembered him!

Jack briefly told him what had happened to him since their last meeting; he apologised for not being in touch in all those years. "Well, I didn't write either, did I? Though I can now write really well." Tim smiled again. "But I've often thought about thee, thou knowst."

"I have as well. The other day I went to seek thee in thy place, but I saw it was deserted. Fortunately I've found thee here. So, thou'rt a professional now!"

"The house was empty 'cause I can now afford something a little better. I live not far from here: come, I'll take 'ee to greet me ma', so we can talk in peace."

"Before we go, couldst thou take me to Shakspere again?"

"Today he had to run off, he's gone already: thou'lt find him tomorrow."

They stopped on their way to buy a loaf of bread and some salted fish, which Jack insisted on paying for; then Tim led him home to his mother, who could now see and hear very little and could no longer embroider or even sew: fortunately, her son brought home enough for both. She looked really old, now. She was happy the young Lord had come to see them; her expert hands fingered the texture of Jack's clothes and she smiled her faded smile in approbation: prime quality stuff which only a true Lord could wear. He was *not* a Lord, Jack kept telling her, but to no avail.

"You'll see, Mistress Rice, that your Tim will soon become a gentleman: he's such a good player as to buy himself a title from the College of Arms!" Jack said, hoping he was speaking loudly enough. The woman laughed in satisfaction, showing her missing front tooth.

They now had two rooms overlooking a sunny, well-aired backyard, and enough money to heat them in winter. On the walls, Jack saw the same prints which had previously hung directly on nails, now framed; he noticed, though, that the little wooden rosary was gone. He and Tim sat down at the only table, covered in a fresh white cloth, in front of a mug of beer, while Tim's mother came and went about tidying things up.

Jack told him more in detail about Cambridge, starting from his initial difficulties, and then about how he lived now, again with Big John, and then at the Bishop's palace, Salisbury House and Speed's office.

Tim spoke about his life with the playing company: "They usually give me several minor parts."

"Dost mean thou played someone else, apart from that servant?"

"'Course I did: who thinkst thou devious sneaky Oswald was? I was only wearing a wig."

"But the voice was different! And he was fatter, too."

"Well, I'm a player, am I not?"

"And have you been to Court?"

"We have, and several times too."

"Even before the Prince?"

"Before him and all th'others. The best time to be there is during the Twelve Days of Christmas; but this year it looks as if the best is still to come, for the King is negotiating to marry off his two elder children, both Prince Harry and Princess Elizabeth. So that, if everything goes well, we'll have as many as two royal weddings in a couple of years, with all the feasts and celebrations following. 'Twill be exhausting... But also a lot of money!"

"If so, then you could have afforded some little maintenance jobs in that poor playhouse."

"'Tis not for lack of money, Jack: 'tis that the main sharers are not sure 'tis still a good investment. Thou seest, at Court things are always all right, and, more or less, the same happens in private theatres – by the way, we now play at the Blackfriars too, a real luxury. 'Tis popular theatres, like the Globe, whose future is uncertain. This Bishop is like a plague for us: sooner or later, he may well succeed in having all of them closed down, together with the bearpit and the bullpit, on grounds of immorality and corruption of His Majesty's good subjects, like this, throwing out the baby with the bathwater. As happened under the old queen, the Court still protects us, and so do the wealthy. For the rest, I know not..." He took a swig of beer and dried his lips with the back of his hand.

"Anyway, I must really congratulate you all: once again, the play was wonderful!"

"Didst not already know it? 'Tis quite an old tragedy Shakspere wrote even before the one thou sawst; 'tis always rather successful."

Jack looked straight into his eyes. "Listen Tim, I *must* speak to Shakspere. First of all, I need to ask him what he remembers about my father; and then I'd like to understand what his plays are really about. I've found the text of *Hamlet,* which, I see, can be interpreted in different ways." Tim was earnest, listening in silence, almost worried. "Thinkst thou not there's a thread of dissidence there? Whose side is Shakspere on? But this, maybe, thou canst tell me thyself, for the rest of the company must side where he does. Why are his 'traitors' always good people who take their country's destiny into their hands? Just look at this young princess, Cordelia: she isn't afraid to invade her own country for a greater good. Seest thou not? And then, I'm interested in the problem of one's good name, which we can find both here and in *Hamlet:* how can one be rehabilitated? I know not how to explain it, but I feel Shakspere's tragedies sort of carved into my flesh, as if they were always speaking about me, right about me, and about my father too, each time in a different way. I would like to read his other plays: I've been looking for *Macbeth,* 'cause I wanted to examine closely the way he deals with treason: methinks I remember that the hero, Macduff, flees abroad and comes back at the head of foreign forces. The tyrant had had his family slaughtered, hadn't he? He'd sent killers to slay that child who was thy first part, the one who first proclaimed before an audience my sister Meg's words. I'd like to watch that play again, I was saying, or at least read it, but *Macbeth*'s script can't be found anywhere. Thinkst thou Shakspere would let me have a look at his papers? He can rest easy, of course, he can trust me: I'll never sell them to a printer. I thought that maybe thou couldst put in a good word for me…"

Tim looked down and was silent. He sipped some more beer, wiped his lips slowly, then said: "Thou'rt a good subject, Jack, ain't thou?"

"What meanst thou? Ay, in *that* sense. A conforming subject."

"And in close touch with Cecil."

"And in close touch with Cecil." Jack stared blankly into the void. "He holds my family in his hands, dost understand? But I'm also the son of a recusant who was everything but cruel, bloody and crazy. I want to learn how it all really went, Tim, and I believe Shakspere can help me. And thou, what knowst thou?"

Tim was still silent, avoiding his look, fiddling with the dark bread crumbs that had fallen on the snow-white cloth. Jack went on: "I see thou trusts me not. I'm sorry to hear this, for I trust thee and I need thy help, because there's clearly something amiss in the official records of the Powder Treason. Things can't have been as they say: 'tis practically impossible."

"I don't know thee so well, Jack, after all. Thou lookst honest, but speaking of dissidence means risking one's skin. And, as long as 'tis *my* skin, 'tis not worth much, thou knowst, 'tis not such a valuable good; but I would never ever put Will Shakspere's life at stake. Not only is he a poetic and dramatic genius: he's also an extraordinary man. Such cleverness, such generosity... 'Tis actually thanks to him that I've joined the company at all effects: 'tis he as guaranteed for me, he as did me the honour of formally taking me on as his 'prentice. Every now and then he allows me to serve him. And I'm so proud, Jack, so proud I can work shoulder to shoulder with him... I've learnt so much from him... I believe his name will be remembered by posterity." He had tears in his eyes, exactly as if he were reciting a dramatic soliloquy.

"I'm no spy, Tim. 'Twasn't true, I guess, that Shakspere was in a hurry and had to go: thou simply didst not want me to meet him." Tim was silent again. "How can I persuade thee?"

Tim shook his head and looked down again at his crumbs. "I'm sorry, Jack! Thou seest, the Gov'ment's agents never look like knaves: far from it. They seem, and they often are, good people, who were wont to hang out with other good people, but at some point or other they can't help carrying out certain orders, for their lives, or their loved ones' lives, are hanging by a thread. Up to now, maybe, Cecil and his cronies have asked nothing much of thee; but, when the moment comes, art thou sure thou'lt manage to say no? How many things couldst thou not have ever refused up to now, even hadst thou tried?"

Jack closed his eyes: he knew all too well that Tim was right. Was he then riding a trotting horse that could start galloping at any moment, not responding to his command? He suddenly felt as he had felt on his way to Hatfield, locked up in Cecil's luxury coach. It was like this: he had taken the Supremacy Oath and the Oath of Allegiance without even blinking and was now taking orders from Big John, Speed, Cecil. Had he ever tried to disobey even the smallest of their directions, or at least to discuss it? Was this then his life? Up to which point could he keep his independence, at least within himself, as his mother had recommended he should do? How much of himself, instead, would they take? Would they send him on some dangerous mission and then throw him away like a rag? Or, still worse, would they ask him to betray his own people?

Tim went on: "Thou canst not imagine how many men I've seen selling their friends, even their own kin. Take thy friend Big John: what thinkst thou his main activity is?"

"As for that, he's not my friend. That is, I've never chosen him. Friends are often the only ones we can choose, in this life."

"I like, thee, Jack, and I'd like to trust 'ee. But these are cruel times... as we always proclaim from the stage, for that matter."

"I'm not holding this against thee, Tim. I understand. We'll talk about Shakspere another time, when and if thou understandst beyond any reasonable doubt that I've got no double ends."

"I don't doubt this, Jack. The matter is, the less thou knowst, the less thou canst be forced to tell."

"All right. What about talking about the Plot, then? 'Tis an old story, by now, almost for everybody. And about my father? Just try to understand how important this is to me."

"Ay. 'Tis not a problem as long as I risk my own life, I've told thee: I can choose this. And then, I'm small fry, no one is interested in me. On that day, while thou wert watching thy father die, I wished I could do something for thee." Jack's heart sank as the most blood-curdling of his recurring nightmares materialised once again in his mind.

Tim went on: "And I also remember well what thou asked me before thou leftst for Cambridge. I've tried to investigate, also because 'twas an intriguing story, but haven't discovered much. To begin with, I went to Westminster to see the famous 'mine' or tunnel under the Parliament, but the House was surrounded with pikemen who let no one get close. I could clearly see, though, a big mound of fresh earth in the garden. I let things settle for a while, I waited for the guards to be removed and then went back there: it will have been September or October. I could only see the mound, by then all overgrown, but no trace of digging. 'Twas too late to be sure, but I think the story of the mine isn't true and the earth in the garden came from somewhere else. I've also been to see the place where the plotters had placed the powder: 'tis not a dungeon or a cellar, but rather a chamber on the ground floor with several entrance doors. I don't know what this means, but 'tis not as we imagine it. And how could they have brought all that gunpowder and kept it hidden, there, among the Westminster crowd?"

"'Tis very strange. Why on earth would the Government have invented such a useless detail as the mine? Weren't my father and his friends already guilty enough?"

"Dunno'. Of course, 'tis more effective like this: 'tis theatrical to plot so darkly, demon-like, in the earth's entrails."

"Ay… The other blatant lie is that the plot had been 'hatched', as they say, by the Jesuits: people know they were not involved."

"For the time being, people only know they did not contrive it, not that they were not involved. Because the Government *has* involved them."

"What meanst thou, 'for the time being'? Why so?"

"Because our children, and our grandchildren after them, won't know this for certain, not having witnessed any of the events. Maybe thou'st not yet seen how the propaganda machine works. I was told that, in those first times, many libels went round, together with some ballads, giving a completely different image of the Plot; but they were all found, one by one, and destroyed. The only surviving documents tell the official version. Thou'lt know that the players too had to do and say certain things, in those months. We too, obviously, as we're the King's Men. But I'd just arrived, back then, and I was a child: I couldn't understand."

"Was *Macbeth* among the plays that had been commissioned?"

"'Twas. But other companies were much more explicit in denouncing terroristic Popery from the stage."

"I've seen them all: Big John took me. And I believe I've also read all the official records, in Cecil's library. I'll tell thee what I discovered: that the main plotters, Catesby and Percy, and some of their friends, had just been pardoned for taking part in another plot."

"That was…?"

"The Essex conspiracy, in 1601."

"I know everything about Essex."

"Who told thee? Thy fellow players?"

Tim shut his mouth tight and shook his head, hinting at a smile, and did not answer. "But I didn't know 'bout this," he went on. "Pardoned, thou sayst?"

"First sentenced to death; then fined, reduced to poverty and reprieved. They got away with a few months' imprisonment. Why weren't they executed along with Essex?"

"Hard to say. Of course there must've been a reason: Cecil's hardly the one who gives for free."

"This Essex was no Papist, right?"

"Never in 's life; but he was supported by several Papists 'cause, as usual, he promised toleration."

"One of those who got away was the Earl of Southampton, right? Great friend and supporter of the Earl of Essex, as well as of Shakspere."

Tim completely ignored Jack's reference to the playwright. "His mother, the Dowager Countess of Southampton, is said to've thrown herself at the little-great man's feet, who got him the old Queen's pardon, so his sentence was commuted to life imprisonment. 'Twas King James, then, after not more than a couple o' years, as pulled him out of the Tower with his apologies." Tim lowered his voice. "'Cause our King too, when he was only King of Scotland, was in with Essex, although this can't be said aloud. Because the official reason for Essex's rising was that he wanted to get back his free access to the Queen and get rid of Cecil; the true goal was to throw her off the throne and swap her with this king before his time: no one knew she was going to kick the bucket in two years, nor that he'd manage to get the crown so smoothly. Of course, Cecil's head would've been the first to roll, had the coup been carried off... And with no one complaining, so hated he is by the people."

"Shakspere dedicated to Southampton as many as two long narrative poems..."

"Ay, 'tis universally known. But I can't tell thee more."

"Well, thou needn't: 'tis quite clear to me that Shakspere was also leaning in that direction." Tim raised one brow and said nothing.

Lady Mary's words about Essex, on that last night at Gayhurst, came to his mind and he said: "Many, back then, identified prince Hamlet with the earl of Essex. That Cambridge student I told thee about even scribbled his name on the margin of the famous main soliloquy."

"*To be or not to be?*" Tim smiled enigmatically. "To bear or to fight and, maybe, die?"

"That's it! So, my interpretation is coherent."

"Enough, I've already spoken too much. Wait, one more thing I'll tell 'ee, Jack."

"Well?"

"Dost remember when thou camest to see me and I recited that soliloquy for thee alone and thy servant, in that hole of a room where I lived?"

"I perfectly remember both that man predestined to Hell and thy impeccable performance."

"Its author died before he was thirty, Jack. Knowst why?"

"I don't... Wait! Because he was an adventurer, thou toldst me."

"Not exactly. He was actually a Government double agent who knew too much. Maybe he wanted to cross over to the enemy, or he wanted to put a stop to it all and get out. He got killed off by a group of fellow agents in a tavern, down in Deptford. 'Twas said to 've been a row for the reck'ning, but what thinkst thou? I wonder how much he could still have written, and we could have performed..."

"Well, one less rival for thy poet!"

"Shakspere is unrivalled anyway. But 'tis not this..."

"I was joking. Art thou afraid he might get killed as well?"

"Ay, Jack. Even if he's trying to keep out of it. And even if we try to protect him. 'Tis not always easy, though; what's more, one must be able to tell between prudence and cowardice, courage and folly. Now that I think of it, I'm also afraid for thee. Be careful, when accepting Cecil's tasks."

"As if I had any choice. Luckily, those libels about the Plot have already been destroyed: if one of them slipped into my hands, I'd have to report it! But first I would read it and copy it, of course."

"Dost understand, then, how they work? Dost see thou can't draw back? Keep thy guard."

"I'll try. I'd better go, by the way, in hope Big John's literary commitments have kept him busy for the whole afternoon: I could never tell him I've been to the play without him. Thanks for everything, Tim. I promise I won't try to get in touch with Shakspere without telling thee first."

He took his leave from Tim and his mother and set off towards Little East Cheap, beyond the river, first walking over the bridge and then up the little sloping street, speeding up as he got closer. So, apparently, the tunnel might never have been there, and the cellar was not a cellar. Moreover, after the Plot had been foiled, many clandestine libels had begun circulating, telling a different story: how he wished he could lay his hands on even one of them! But, even if Cecil had kept some, he would never have left them in the library. It would be a very interesting thing to do, then, if he could enter Sir Robert's private office – but that was really out of the question: being found in there would be like signing his own death warrant amid unspeakable torments. Besides, the chances to get in were practically nil. Nay, Cecil must have destroyed all unofficial documents. As for Shakspere, Jack was very sorry not to be able to approach him, but he would patiently wait for Tim to allow him: he was a man of honour and Tim was his friend.

Big John was already at home and, somewhat innocently, asked him where he had been.

"To the Inns of Court, outside the walls: I've learnt that a former fellow student of mine is now studying there, so I went to seek him out."

"Who?"

"Nugent." Which was highly unlikely, seeing that Jack couldn't brook that pimply fat-ass, but this was the first name that came to mind and he hoped Big John wouldn't remember him. Fortunately, he made no comments. Jack went on: "But he wasn't there. Then the storm came, so I took shelter in a tavern and had dinner there. Then I walked back, which took me far longer than I thought. I hope 'tis not a problem, Big John."

"No problem whatsoever, Little John! I had dinner all alone as well, but there was nothing to be done. Problems? None!"

Was this his way of telling him he hadn't approved of his solitary excursion? Jack preferred not to ask. He shrugged slightly, as one who could do nothing about it, then readied himself for bed.

Early the following morning he went back to the Salisbury House library, as he did almost every day, for he had to go through some final checks on Speed's behalf. When he had done, he started to cast his eyes about. The relic-book was there, seemingly inviting him to take it out of the shelf; but he preferred not to touch it, to say nothing of the risk of being caught leafing through it again. He gazed at all those big volumes, wondering which further step to take in his investigation. He started taking out a large illustrated book on gardening and placing it open on the table. Then he looked round again and, seeing no one came in, went up a ladder and reached what looked like a row of identical books, their golden-lettered backs glistening in the rising sun. They were the transcripts of State trials. "Will the Essex one be here too?", he wondered. He took out the 1601 volume but dared not take it down, so he remained standing on the ladder, the book in his hands. How easy: there it was. One of the most notorious trials of the previous reign: how many pages it took up! Jack turned the leaves impatiently to the end, where he found several lists of those who had been condemned. *Persons executed... Persons attainted and fit to be executed... Persons indicted and fit to be arraigned... Persons already indicted and to be forborne to be arraigned but yet fined....* Here he found Robert Catesby, together with the Wright brothers, who had then been killed together with him and Thomas Percy. *Persons fit to be forborne from being indicted, but yet to be fined....* They were legion: Jack couldn't believe Essex's plot had involved so many. *Those that are fined and reserved to Her Majesty's use...* What did this mean? Robert Catesby's name appeared in this list too, together with Thomas Tresham's, Mounteagle's brother-in-law, who had been into the Powder Plot to his ears and had then died in the Tower awaiting trial.

Up to now, more or less, the names were those Bill Thomson had mentioned at the *Mermaid*. Bill's words now echoed in his brain: "Of course, a madman will do anything; but 'tis hard to believe they all went mad together!" He was suddenly covered in cold sweat. There, on top of the ladder, he began to feel dizzy. But he braced himself, breathed hard and went on reading.

He now found a wholly unexpected name: William Parker, Lord Mounteagle, fined an amazing four thousand pounds. How could this be? Mounteagle, a nobleman and a peer, his country's saviour; the one who, on receiving the cryptic anonymous letter, had run to show it to Cecil, thus foiling the whole Plot. This showed, instead, that he had been a dissident, a potential traitor, years before the Powder Treason. Come to think of it, none of the trial transcripts reported any enquiry on the author of that letter, and, apparently, Mounteagle had never even been questioned. His name appeared out of nowhere when he got the letter, then disappeared again, like a pike in a lake coming to surface just to catch an insect. Well, this man's name now popped up again from the past *and* from another plot he had survived: fined and "reprieved". In exchange for what? Could Mounteagle have deceived Catesby and Percy? Might he have learnt about the Powder Plot from his brother-in-law, Francis Tresham, and then, at the right time, written the letter himself? Or rather, were they all in the same boat, as they had been in 1601 with Essex? Which boat was it and why?

As a new wave of panic seized him, he closed the volume, shoved it back in its place and climbed down the ladder a fast as he could, his knees trembling. He began to flip through the big gardening book; he watched the beautiful, harmless drawings for some minutes, fascinated by the Latin plant names, each with its own properties, until he had calmed down. Then he bent down to the lower shelves and took out one of the official records about the Plot that he had previously read. He remembered that, here and there, among the lists of those involved, some words had been erased, either by being scraped away or by having thin slips of paper glued over them. He checked again: and so it was. He tried to read the names, but to no avail. Maybe Mounteagle's name was one of those that had been removed. Decidedly, something was rotten in the State of Denmark.

He put that book back as well and buried his nose in the gardening book, his heart pounding. His time in the library was almost over when he heard some light steps approaching. "Let's hope 'tis not the nosey little Countess", he told himself, "I'm not in the mood, today. Now I've discovered she's not total nuts, she scares me a little".

It wasn't Mildred. It was Cecil himself. Informally dressed, this time, with no ruff and in his slippers. "Good morning, boy. We haven't met for a while, I believe."

Jack jumped to his feet and bowed as low as he could: "Your Lordship, what an honour!" He thanked Heaven he had no compromising material in his hands. How stupid he had been so far: Cecil might have caught him red-handed anytime looking into the Powder Plot. What would he have done, then?

"How does thy work proceed?"

"Quite well, Your Lordship. I've analysed about twenty books, marking down the sentences I believed to be ambiguous or dangerous. Not that I found many, in truth. As for my translation of Chancery documents, it proceeds smoothly. At present, though, as I was ordered, I am working for Master John Speed. The job is almost done: today I've taken my last references," he showed him the piece of paper on which he had noted them down, "and then we can go to print."

"These must all be such tiresome chores, mustn't they? So that yesterday afternoon thou decidedst to take a little time off and amuse thyself."

Jack's heart sank. "I... I apologise if I have offended by this... I... I..."

Cecil smiled his asymmetric smile. "More than me, 'tis Fletcher that feels offended: I wonder why thou didn't ask him to go with thee! And Speed too, we may say: he had only just warned thee against those that, to him, are the dangers of those places. Mark me, one may not agree with him; however, thou toldst him thou didst, didst thou not?"

Of course, Sir Robert was in close contact with Speed too. "I'm so sorry, Your Lordship! 'Twas a sudden decision taken lightly, as I walked. I really meant to go to the Inns of Court, then then I heard the play proclaimed and changed my mind. Big John, that is, Fletcher, wasn't with me and, had I gone back to invite him, I would have missed the beginning... And when I got back I was afraid he might get offended, as I said, that's why I lied to him. As for Speed, actually, I didn't mean to go at first, but then I yielded to temptation... Because I like plays so much, even if I know them to be morally dangerous..."

Cecil waved slightly, as if underscoring Speed's being but an old-fashioned visionary haunted by apocalyptic fears. "Remember, boy, that cheaters never prosper! Didst thou talk to anyone inside the playhouse?"

"I exchanged a few words with two law students sitting next to me." Scared to death as he was, Jack was adamant not to reveal anything about Tim, and still less about his ideas concerning Shakspere. He only hoped he hadn't been followed after the play.

"'Tis nothing for this time, boy. But, from now on, be sure to tell Fletcher about everywhere thou goest. If he's not with thee send him a servant, if thou hast one, otherwise do not go."

"I will, Your Lordship, that is, I won't. Please, forgive me!"

Cecil waved again, as if to say: "Don't mention it again!" and waddled to the door while Jack breathed a slow sigh of relief. On the threshold, Cecil turned round, as if suddenly remembering something. "Ah, Digby, now that I think of it: what dost thou say to going on with thy work at the theatre? How wouldst thou like that?"

"I beg your pardon, Your Lordship?"

Cecil moved a few steps back. "Thou seest, boy, the Government's control over the playhouses has been losing its grip, lately. Plays are ever increasing while Tilney, the Master of Revels, is old and sick. We have already flanked him, of course, but we are aware that one thing is reading and approving a script; another is seeing it performed. Thou wilt well understand that a speech may look harmless or neutral on paper, but once it's put on stage it may take on an offensive, even seditious meaning: a gesture, an emphasis, a particular intonation may be enough... As, I'm told, such things happen daily, I want several of you to attend popular playhouses and report about what goes on there. The Bishop of London, Dr Abbott, is extremely worried."

Jack felt a new chill run down his back. He didn't want to be a Government agent. That was where Cecil and Big John had had in mind to take him ever since the beginning. Tim was right. And neither could he simply go to a play without ever reporting anything, for among the audience there would always be more agents, unknown to him, so that one who wouldn't report what was to be reported would become an accomplice in sedition.

"Don't be scared, 'tis not that difficult: Thou'lt start working with Fletcher, who will teach thee. I understand thou mayst be frightened: players can be nasty beasts at times... Take care!" And, once again turning his back on Jack, his splay foot pointing outwards, Cecil left.

Jack could feel a new terror surging from his toes to his hair. What was to be done now? Of course he had to tell Tim and the King's Men at once, but how? From now on, he would have to spy on his only London friend and, if necessary, betray both him and what was dearest to him in the world. Tim had been right in everything. Might he also be right in fearing for Shakspere? Was the great poet in danger? Did Cecil mean him, when he said that seditious words were spoken everyday on stage? What should he do, how could he decide how to move? He felt like an insect in a box under a magnifying glass, observed and recorded in its smallest move. Flight was utterly impossible. Cecil's beautiful carriage had started to gallop like mad.

Yet another tragedy was over, in the usual bloodbath, and all the bodies had been removed from stage. It hadn't been a great performance: far worse than Henry Howard, Earl of Northampton, had expected; considerably below their usual standard. Maybe the thin, constant drizzle was partly to blame, which had accompanied the play almost since the beginning, as if the sky too were crying too feebly. The luxurious lodge where he was sitting with his guest was fortunately dry, although uncomfortable, but the dampness was seeping through his skin to his bones, which would surely not help his nasty backache. The commoners standing in the pit were restless, wet and cold, and had ill withstood the longer monologues – a few of them had even thrown rotten fruits. Below his wide plumed hat, as he nervously bit the end of his now cold pipe, Howard glanced at his Spanish guest, the Duke of Frìas, and sighed. The Spaniard didn't notice: he seemed to have enjoyed the show, after all. Funny foreigner, with that stiff old-fashioned ruff, that absurdly pointed moustache, those jet-black eyes. Frìas had been trying hard to learn their language ever since he'd come to London, several years before, but his speech was still utterly ridiculous, his "R" absolutely irritating. He seemed satisfied, though – even if Howard had no doubt that he hadn't understood much of the play – and kept his eyes fixed on stage, resting both hands on the carved wooden railing.

How strange it was, after all this time, to be at peace with Spain: yet, this was already the sixth year. Once, his guest and himself might have killed each other; now, here they were together, in this forced fellowship, he and the man who had defied great Francis Drake, "El Draque," as the Spaniards called him back then, God rest his soul.

Frìas didn't even appear to have noticed the obvious dissatisfaction of the crowd, down there. But lo! As usual, a couple of players advanced on the still bloody stage; from their high balcony, the musicians started a lively jig and the audience went clapping their hands following its rhythm. Two more couples joined in, spinning round the stage in their gaudy costumes. In a young player's fine dress, Howard thought he recognised one that had belonged to an old aunt of his: if not that one, it was certainly very similar. She had probably left it to one of her house maids, who, never hoping to wear it, had sold it to the King's Men.

As soon as the dance was over, the players bowed ceremoniously to the two of them, the aristocratic audience of the lodge, and the crowd looked up and applauded them. Howard slightly waved his gloved hand and smiled. It was also for this reason, after all, that people of his rank chose a popular theatre: in order for the commoners to see them. That was why he had dressed, on that day, all in green, so as to make his clothes stand up against the glittering golden paint of the wooden lodge. He smiled at his guest too, smoothing his well-trimmed grey moustache. The main reason why he was there, of course, was to make everybody sure that all performances were watched by the Government. Among his many tasks, this was certainly one of the least disagreeable, had it not been for the stiff seat and the dampness.

The music and dance, together with beer flowing river-like, had stirred the spirits. The gate was eventually opened, and the crowd started streaming out; the two noblemen and their servants waited for the playhouse to be almost empty, then calmly stepped down the steep narrow stairs.

Several of the poorer folks were waiting for them beyond the gate. Howard, who knew well how much the Government objected to alms-giving, in that it encouraged sloth in the idle, had nevertheless given orders for some groats to be handed out to young apprentices in order to gain their esteem. Others presented written petitions to him, little cheap favours, which his servants gathered into a leather purse while keeping him and his Spanish guest well sheltered from the foul-smelling plebeians. Just for precaution, though, Howard took from his pocket a perfumed little lace kerchief and held it under his nose.

Escorted by their servants, the two noblemen started to walk towards the Thames, whence Northampton's private barge would row them back to the Northern bank and to the City.

"What a wonderrful perrforrmance!" cried Frìas grinning enthusiastically. Howard nodded, although he didn't agree at all; but then, Spain was known to be an uncouth, backward country where the only popular entertainments were bull fights.

"Our people love plays, as you have had the chance to see. Some come surreptitiously to watch them, without their masters' permission, thus risking their jobs. And we must say the King's Men are the best players in the whole country. This way, Your Excellency."

Walking through crooked narrow lanes, lined on both sides with wooden houses that at times seemed to knock into one another above their heads, they went past the most popular brothel of Southwark, with its white "Rose" sign, and their voices blended in the loud arguments of men walking out of the bearpit. The annoying drizzle had ceased, at last. While they descended the steps leading to the wharf, the setting sun showed its face from below a leaden cloudy slate and shrouded everything in golden light, whitening the trunks of the poplars bordering the river, making their silver and green leaves brighter, as they were ruffled by a slight breeze. The wide grey river, swarming with boats and wherries, ran as slow as ever and went to throw itself, on their right, under the big arches of the stone bridge surmounted by its throng of little houses. The small procession, a colourful spot in the grey and brown dusk, boarded the luxury barge on which the Howard golden eagle emblem was clearly visible even at a distance; they pushed off and were soon lost amidst the river traffic.

The leading player, the famous Richard Burbage, had just washed and changed and was now walking out of the packed tiring house. He had a sore throat and was well aware that he hadn't been at the top of his skill. He walked among the servants picking rubbish in the pit and reached the other shareholders in the box office.

"Don't say anything, boys."

Heminges, the company accountant, was not really dissatisfied because the day's profits were as good as ever, so he told him cheerfully: "I'll only say thou'rt getting old, Dick."

"Look who's talking, thou white-haired Nestor!" roared Burbage. "But 'tis not a fault, is it?"

"Don't be tragic: it happens," said Will Shakspere soothingly. "And the others were a bit low-key too: it happens and that's all. Thou'rt always the best: however things turn, people love thee!"

"Thou knowst it too, Will, we're all getting old. 'Tis no longer as it used to be. Sometimes I wonder how long we'll go on tumbling on stage: we're too old for that! We'll shortly need crutches. The last time I fell, while rehearsing the duel scene, I thought I'd broken my back, so much did it hurt…"

"I think of it too, every now and then: withdrawing from the stage. I'm even older than thee, Dick, look, my hair's all gone. Hey!" he went on, addressing the other shareholders, "Have you seen the paint on the right column is starting to peel off too? We've got to tell young fairy-handed Tim to fix it as soon as he can."

Tim Rice came in just then, carrying a casket of beer. "I've ordered the sausages, they'll bring 'em in a minute."

Old Heminges took some bread and a long knife from a cabinet "Clear the table: some more, some less, we've all deserved this!"

The sun was almost down when they went out, after finally locking the gate, and found themselves in a small opening, among suburban lanes, where the grass had been trodden away by the feet of thousands. They said good-bye and scattered, to meet again in the morning for the rehearsals of the next play.

"Goin' home by river, Will?" asked Heminges and Condell, who were heading for the wharf.

"Nay," he answered. "I'll breathe some fresh air and walk some way with Dick. Goodnight, gentlemen. Come with us, Tim, we'll walk thee home."

The three of them set off together towards the bridge. Burbage was still melancholy.

"Cheer up, man!" Shakspere told him. "Once home, tell thy missus to make thee a mug of hot milk, brandy and honey: thou'lt see, tomorrow thou'lt be thyself again and they'll clap their hands till they bleed."

"Maybe they will. But milk and honey won't give me back my lost years. I'd need the elixir of life for that: a sip of ambrosia and off I go! 'Tis as thou always sayst, Will: time's devouring us. 'Tis not so easy. Today, for the first time, I feel really old. 'Tis true, we're all mortally ill, 'tis only a matter of time. And poor Austin's come to my mind, and I'd like him to be still here with us… I know, people think I'm really as they see me on stage, a hero, and instead I'm a poor little man just as they are. And my throat hurts so!"

His friend laughed. "Well, we've walked a long way together: thou couldst as well be glad and thank Heaven. Rememberst how we were twenty years ago?"

"Ah, we could have cleft the world in two, back then! It's all been beautiful, Will."

Burbage's mind went back to the old rickety theatre in the disreputable Northern district where they had started and where he still lived. They had been young and naive, bold, rash, unaware of the dangers surrounding them. He remembered the first time that people's cheers had made him dizzy; the first times his audience had hailed him with an enthusiasm that, before then, they had only shown to the absolute best. Tarlton for comedy, Alleyn for tragedy. Then someone had said that he himself, Richard Burbage, the joiner's son, had outstripped them both because he excelled in both kinds. It was not really so: he knew perfectly well that he had a flair for tragedy.

He remembered the twists of fate, the laughter, the blows of good and bad fortune, their hard work as players, carpenters, dustmen and everything they managed to do. The exhausting rehearsals from dawn to dusk and even later, at times, in the dark, lit by tallow candlelight giving bad light and a worse smell. He remembered the hard times when London had been decimated by the plague, and the wearisome summer tours through towns and country. There the strong bond uniting them had been forged, tightened with the sweat of their brows, this bond which still kept them together, as different as they were from one another. They, the survivors. They, the band of brothers. And how they had mocked their Puritan enemies from the stage, and how they had been covered in applause by amused crowds, amazed at their daring. So that, as tiring as it all was, it had been real fun, and rewarding from every possible perspective. And when that Puritan landowner of theirs had thrown them out of his land hoping to make them close down, they had hired skilled carpenters, instead, and had dismantled the old Theatre in one night, secretly, from below his nose, to rebuild it anew in Southwark: that had been the rise of the Globe. Ay, they had taken their risks, but they had always had the best of times. What with fear and laughter, their friendship had grown like a tender plant but was now as tough as a full-grown tree. And how the city authorities had it against them, and how the Master of Revels had always sided with them, and how even the frigid old Queen had enjoyed their plays. He remembered the thrill of their first Court performance, so many years ago, and the terror not to be up to it; above all, the terror to offend; so much that Will had even written about it in his epilogue, that they didn't mean to offend anybody.

"Thou knowst, Will," he went on, "At times I think that the illusions, the jokes that we put on stage, will be remembered after us."

"Illusions, thou'rt right. Will they, as thou sayst, despite the Puritans doing all they can in order for them not to?"

"Of course they will! Nay, the more they insist, the more people will come to see us, and then buy thy plays and read them. As long as they are printed, for sure. Like that pinhead who's come out with thy sonnets."

"Let be, don't remind me! Call him pinhead... He's made a lot of money." Shakspere got thoughtful. "Seriously, Dick, thinkst thou I should retire and be a country gentleman?"

"Of course not! Thou knowst well enough thy place's here."

"Not really: my place is at home, with my wife, my daughters, my relations. I've always been a country boy and now I've become an old country man. At times, I play with the idea of going back home forever..."

Tim, who was all ears, shuddered at the thought.

"But thou won't," Burbage said.

"I won't, as long as I've got things to say. Thou knowst, I'm planning a new fairy tale."

"Poring on thy books again, Will?"

"That always, till I die! But what I would actually like to write, this time, is something totally, exclusively mine. Thou knowst, life's magic, and the theatre's magic, the relationship between fact and fiction, art and life. I'm not sure, I'm just thinking about it... Ay, 'illusion' is a good word."

"What I'd like thee to write is a good tragedy, Will. As thou didst of yore, a play people can feel belongs to them. So that they can understand how bad our time is, how serious the situation. Then I believe I could go back in time and be again the great Burbage I used to be, storm the theatre and carry their hearts away."

"The times have changed, my dear chap, as thou knowst better than me. People no longer side with us; they fail to understand. Or maybe they don't want to."

"Dost mean the Powder Plot?"

"Sure I do. The Government's done an extraordinary propaganda job, people don't dare any more. Only now have we really lost, thou knowst."

"What... happened with the Powder Plot, Master Shakspere?" Tim asked shyly.

"I'll explain this to thee some other time, lad: 'tis a complicated story."

"Therefore, art thou finished with tragedies?" Burbage went on.

"Ay. I'm finished with heroic deeds, and heroes giving up their lives for an ideal. Maybe we shouldn't even have ever started... Too much blood, too many misunderstandings... The only space left is to beg some tolerance for a thinning group increasingly scared, bent, crushed. In a little while, we'll utterly disappear from this country. All's left for me to tell is fairy tales, since no one is any longer willing to spill their blood for a noble cause. But fairy tales can also be interesting, Dick: methinks the first ones I wrote captured the Prince's heart."

"Dost say so?"

"'Tis only an impression: we'll see whether I'm right or not. Actually, though, there is one last tragedy I'd like to write. Not a heroic play, not a revenge tragedy, but rather a heart-rending drama, full of intimate suffering, which may deal with our past... I can't say, I'll let thee know."

They had reached Tim's lodging, who would have given his right arm to walk on and listen to them talking about theatre and life. But there was no excuse for that, and it was even later than usual. They said goodbye and Tim vanished into the dark porch.

The two of them sped up, in order for Burbage to reach Bishopsgate before they closed it for the night. Shakspere was about to resume the conversation but was struck dumb by heavy approaching steps behind them, in the dusk, down the deserted street. They turned in fear, their hands on their daggers, because they had their part of the box office takings in their pockets. Then someone called out to them. "Masters Shakspere and Burbage, gentlemen?" It was a royal messenger, followed by two Palace guards.

"Ay," answered Dick.

"How the hell...", thought Will. They had clearly been following them ever since they had left the theatre, waiting for them to be alone. The messenger had a letter of instant summon to the Royal Palace of Whitehall for each of them. They set off, therefore, without a word, as if in a small procession, down the Southwark lanes, the messenger leading, the two guards following them, their halberds reflecting the last rays of the setting sun, as the bells of all churches sounded the curfew and the shops, inns and alehouses began to close for the night.

Shakspere tried to keep calm. This was surely not the first time they had been summoned to the Palace, though never at such a time of day: after all, weren't they the King's Men? They might be invited to Court even ten times, in the winter season. They were famous, by now, and reasonably wealthy. It was only normal for the Government to ask them for something in exchange, every now and then. "Every now and then? Let's say that!", he thought. Provided it was not to question them again: what could the authorities say, this time, against them? Nothing, nothing at all. They were only a troupe of tumblers, and not even young at that, good at entertaining people. Had they trespassed again? Since the King had been on the throne and had welcomed them under his own protecting wings, they had tried to find a balance between what they would have liked to put on stage and what they must: Shakspere knew well he was unrivalled in this. Even when they had really meddled in politics, shortly before the old Queen's death, they had managed to get away with it. But now, old Austin was dead and could no longer save them from trouble. As long as they didn't suspect the existence of a play that had never been performed... No, this was impossible.

Where was this messenger leading them? Surely to some important man working for Cecil. Probably the Earl of Northampton, who had been at the Globe that very afternoon and might have seen or heard something he didn't like. Ay, it must be that way; even if, thinking it all over again, he wasn't aware of anything that may have sounded disagreeable. Idiots, they would have been, to speak ambiguous words with him so clearly visible in his bright lavish clothes.

By the way, was he decently clothed, in his working garments? Without a ruff, in his everyday shirt, darned hose and worn-out waistcoat? Well, that couldn't be helped. His short light cloak, at least, was quite new and fashionable.

They had reached London Bridge. Will and Dick walked past its Southern Gate without looking up: they knew perfectly well what was above them, what they didn't want to look at. People were strange: at times they followed you, interpreting to perfection what you meant, apparently even willing to give their lives for the dream you were enacting for them. Other times, however, most times, the mob was a raving, bloodthirsty beast, regardless where truth stood. There wasn't much difference, then, between the bearpit and the Tyburn Tree. How many innocent men had been sacrificed among people's cheers, without anyone wondering whether or not they deserved death? Executions could be like puppet shows, with someone moving their strings.

Some hangings, it was true, had produced indignation; like Rob Southwell's. And then, the mass madness at the discovery of the Powder Treason… Blood they had wanted; and blood they'd had. He shuddered. Already five years had passed, but that blood was still fresh.

Their heavy, regular pace was the only sound in that ghastly silence. The messenger led them to a small boat moored just below the bridge; thence, it wouldn't be a long trip. Night fell. The light of the small lantern fixed on stern showed apparently calm, untroubled faces.

The majestic royal palace slowly emerged from the black horizon, its many windows all alight, getting closer at every row. They shortly moored at the wharf of what, more than a Court, was a little town in itself. Meanwhile, London rested peacefully: apart from them, not a soul was walking outdoors.

After being introduced into the main wing through an almost invisible back door, they were led through many passageways up to a great hall ablaze with lamplight and, thence, to a little room where one only candle was burning, its walls all covered in magnificent tapestry. Here they were, in the beating heart of Britain. The messenger left them. Will and Dick remained standing, their hats in their hands, looking in each other's eyes. They didn't dare say a word, though, and hardly budged. They knew all too well that the tapestry could conceal secret informers and that every word they said, even half a word, could later be used against them. Just as in Dick's favourite tragedy, whose sneaky meddler ended up with a rapier through his heart. But real life wasn't like that.

In the half darkness, Shakspere looked at his old friend, the great actor adored by the crowds, the powerful hero who managed to bring even rocks and stones to tears. He looked at him and saw a simple plain man like many others, weary, pale, lost. In the candlelight, his beard even seemed to tremble a little, every now and then, as if choking back a sob. He tried to smile, but he was frightened as well. Had he played too much? Had he pushed the game too far? Had he underestimated other people's cleverness? Had he put his friends' and colleagues' lives at stake for a stupid battle of wits? No. One thing was certain: this was *not* a mere battle of wits. But, at least as certainly, Cecil was not to be underestimated.

For the little great man it had been a child's play to get rid of all his enemies. To put it simply, every time he had smelt danger he had attacked first; and his attacks never forgave. The memory of the young Earl of Essex was still fresh in everybody's minds. The Queen's champion, people's beloved nobleman, the comet of England. He'd been a shooting star, rather... A shiver slithered down the playwright's back: he remembered all too well how the Earl of Southampton had agreed to support his friend Essex, who had found himself on the scaffold before he could say "ay", without even managing to say a word to the Queen, and Southampton too had been at a tooth's skin from death. Even their company, back then, had entangled itself in that groundless dream; and it had been so humiliating to have to play a comedy at Court so soon after Essex's beheading, and to have to laugh – and make people laugh – as loud as they could, only to show their total non-involvement in the whole matter.

They were kept waiting for ages, till weariness and anguish became unbearable. At last, a servant appeared who escorted them, always in complete silence, through more halls and passages, up to a totally dark room, only lit by the moonlight entering through the half-opened window and drawn curtains. Against it, they could make out the profile of a crooked little man sitting at a desk.

"What an honour!", thought Shakspere, who, before then, had only dealt directly with His Excellency a couple of times. What an interesting paradox for this slim, deformed body, to encase such an alert, skilful mind. Fit for a play. Already seen, already exploited years ago: a horrible toad whose skull contains a priceless jewel. An earth-bound, bow-backed boar, his bloody crooked tusks in the shape of deathly scythes. Time's lackey.

"Our deepest respects, Your Lordship," Dick said in a ceremonious yet firm tone, as they both bowed low.

A servant came in with a light, together with a young scrivener with his quills who sat at a little table, near the desk, to put down on paper every word that would be said. Their inquisitor's face then emerged from darkness, ghastly in the candlelight. Like them, he had also grown old since they last met, four years before. His face was ashen, his huge forehead even larger as the hair round it had receded, his beard thinner, his mouth surrounded with small wrinkles conferring to it an even sterner expression.

"Shakspere and Burbage, King's Men?" his cold, subtle voice filled the room.

"The same, Your Lordship."

"You know, don't you, that the King of France has been murdered?"

Will and Dick exchanged looks. "When?"

"Three days ago. Stabbed to death by a Papist."

"So what?", they would have liked to say, "What is that to us?".

Dick said, instead: "We are deeply sorry to hear that, Your Lordship."

The voice went on drily: "No need to over-react: peace to his ashes. The fact is, His Majesty fears for his own life."

Silence fell.

"Don't you have anything to say?"

"We are sorry about that too, of course. But…"

"But you can't see the connection with you and your company."

"We honestly can't, Your Lordship."

"'Tis simple: 'tis a matter of loyalty."

"Do you mean… the Oath?"

"Ay, that too. But not only."

To the two players' dismay, more figures had silently emerged from the shadows – it was hard to say how many – and were now standing behind them.

"His Majesty demands absolute loyalty to himself, his Government, his Church. From now on, there will be no more fidgeting: either with him or against him. Therefore, ay, the Oath. The

Bishop of Rome, of course, as meddling and abusive as ever, has forbidden his followers to take it. But the Bishop of London, Dr Abbott, has been rather clear: the Oath of Allegiance will become law for everybody, through a royal proclamation, starting from June. What about you? Whose side are you on?"

"We are obviously on His Majesty's side, Your Lordship, with England and St George. We are the King's Men!" Dick readily declared.

"Let's try to be serious and stop playing. Everybody knows that the last Papists of the Kingdom have taken shelter right at Court and round it. But now, thanks to the new royal proclamation, we'll get rid of them all. As for you and your activity, a certain play you performed was not to our taste."

The little man stood up and walked round the desk, slowly advancing towards them. He was still more crooked than he had been in his youth. Will and Dick knew very well that he had never liked their playing company, ever since they had put on stage the worst villain of history, a cruel, devious murderer, who was as crooked and hunchbacked as he was. In those times, almost twenty years ago, it hadn't been so difficult to convince the authorities that their villain was simply Richard III and *not* Robert Cecil, and that the timing of the plays' first performance, just as young Cecil officially emerged from the shadows as Secretary of State, had been pure coincidence. That position had been harder to uphold more recently, when Rob Armin, that damned fool, had put a hump on his own back to play the part of the drunk Porter in *Macbeth* and then, as First Witch, had said those forbidden lines. People had split their sides with laughter, of course, but Armin had gone through a tough time and spent two days in jail. "I didn't know 'twas forbidden to put on a fake hump on stage!" he had said in his defence. And now he would probably never be allowed on stage again, whereas they would never be allowed to perform their *Macbeth* as they had performed it back then.

"Which play? Today's one, which saw the presence of my Lord of Northampton?"

"Not that one."

"Then might it be the tragicomedy I set in ancient Britain, *Cymbeline*?" Shakspere asked. "I took it from ancient chronicles, as I almost always do, and…"

"That one, ay, that one. It deals with the relationship between Britain and Rome: 'tis no good." The great man's narrowed eyes had an undefinable colour. "You must at least change the end: Britain has *never* owed any tribute to Rome, nor has it ever acknowledged any empire other than its own."

"If we have offended we are sorry about it, Your Lordship, and we shall amend. As we have always done, we shall. But, this time too, the Master of Revels had approved it…"

"Ay, ay, we will soon discover why. All in good time. He's become short-sighted, Tilney has, besides being old; that's why we've put Buck beside him. We'll see whether, with Tilney no longer there, Buck will be as generous with you. Ah, Wilson," he added, "Escort Master Burbage to the Earl of Northampton: he will have a further chat with him."

A man came out of the shadow and beckoned Dick towards the door. As he walked out followed by two of them, Dick turned back to his friend in anguish and fear. It was a request for help which Will couldn't meet. He only said, while they were leading him out:

"Your Lordship, we have always been His Majesty's loyal subjects, and the Queen's before him, God rest her soul."

"Loyal? Everyone has '*Secret thoughts, in the depth of his heart.*' Holy Scripture, my good man, Holy Scripture: what would we be without it? You see, not always is it possible to bring to light what is hidden in the depth of one's heart. Although there are usually no secrets to us. And you know as well as I do that our deep thoughts may betray us."

"But, Your Lordship, no man can be incriminated for his thoughts alone." The playwright lowered his eyes, as if fearing that Cecil might read his mind by just looking into them.

"Maybe not yet for his thoughts alone, Master Shakspere, even if we're getting there … Even if we are. And, anyway, the heart of a traitor is to be torn out! His Majesty will no longer be surrounded with potential murderers." Cecil was getting closer, his voice lowered to a hiss.

"Your Lordship, why on earth should anybody even think about treason? Now that our foes have become our friends and Spain will not support any plot… And Persons, the Jesuit, is also said to be dead. These might be just rumours, of course, but…"

A chilly, disquieting, asymmetric smile creased the great man's thin lips. "Since when can a common player claim to deal in high politics? Let such things to experts and mind your job, Master Playwright. I do not believe it would be hard, for instance, to collect evidence against you." Cecil looked straight at him with his bulging right eye, his left one lost in darkness. "They tell me that several of your scripts have been published: I wonder whether, by putting them together and having them analysed…"

"But those are corrupted, pirated texts, Your Lordship. Last year, for instance, as you may happen to know, some sonnets came out with my name on the front page, but they are *not* mine."

"It would be interesting, anyway, to collect all your works and search them for seditious statements. It might even be a child's game." Cecil kept smiling threateningly, his eyes narrowing to thin slits. "What if I now ordered you to hand over all the manuscripts in your possession? I have someone endowed with the right competence who has already offered to do the job."

"A malicious eye may find traces of sedition even in the street cobbles. What for, Your Lordship? For the ruin of honest, loyal subjects who earn their bread with the sweat of their brows? Look, rather, at the love for our Country we have aroused among the commoners with our Histories. Don't you think *that* has been good service to the Government too? And how often have we carried out the Privy Council's orders? In your late father's time, Sir William, may God rest him, do you remember how we brought on stage a Jewish villain just when he wished us to do so?"

His thought went back to those heinous circumstances, to the evil blow that the Earl of Essex, however noble and honest, had dealt against the Portuguese Jew Ruy Lopez, one of the Queen's doctors. Why had he done that? After so many years (how many? More than fifteen) and as much reasoning, and after many attempts to justify that anti-Cecilian champion, Shakspere couldn't find a different explanation: Essex had made that man suffer a traitor's death only to show Cecil that he too was skilled at unmasking secret plots. This was the way of the world: rich and powerful people were all alike and, in the end, human life wasn't worth a groat. At Lopez's ruinous fall, the Lord Chamberlain's Men had bent, as always, to Sir William, Lord Burghley's will. Shakspere had only made his own Jewish villain a little more human as a homage to that poor man, but that had been all. Because heroism is good and glorious and makes you immortal, but fear is a monster which grips your throat and paralyses your body and soul. He now felt it again, right in this moment, cold, ruthless fear. He gulped, trying not to leave space to his insidious questioner, and went on: "More recently, then, it was Queen Anne herself who asked us for a Moorish hero, and there he was, in a goodly tragedy of love and jealousy. Just think, Your Lordship, how useful we may still be to you"

"Useful, useless, harmful: that's unclear. What do you say to this?" he handed him a rolled document.

"A Star Chamber decree?"

"Exactly. In which a Sir John Yorke is fined four thousand pounds for allowing the private performance, in his manor, of some openly seditious plays. Two of which, read you well, were yours."

"I see. But mine are not seditious, and I've never heard of this Yorke. You know quite well that, unfortunately, many of my plays circulate freely beyond any possibility of control: they can be performed, and altered, by anyone."

"You remember that this King Lear here mentioned was not to His Majesty's taste, do you not? Yet you performed it once again, and not before yesterday."

"But only for popular audiences, Your Lordship, who, on the contrary, like it much. The box office, you know… We'll certainly never take it to Court again. And then, one thing is disliking a play; another is finding seditious elements in it. What's wrong with an old king who leaves his throne, has two ungrateful daughters, goes mad with sorrow and dies? Here, too, moreover, I have invented nothing: I've but revisited for modern tastes an older, quite poor play. I don't know how other companies performed it; we've put it on stage *exactly* in the form approved by Tilney, without adding or taking one line."

"Ay! With the good, banished daughter leading a foreign invasion against her own country: this is looking for trouble indeed."

"Your Lordship, we performed the cut version, as was recommended to us. We did not think we would offend…"

"Pity that scene was still there. Don't play with me, Mr Player: my men are always there. Your *Lear* must disappear from popular theatres too, is it understood?"

"It is, Your Lordship."

Shakspere bent his head, then looked up again to listen to the next question.

"This appears to be a singularly unfortunate time to you, as your production has been singularly disliked: what has become of the original text of the Scottish play?"

"*Macbeth* was burnt, Your Lordship, and before witnesses."

"As if I didn't know that you can write it again from one day to the other, digging into your players' memories."

"You will also know, My Lord, that, differently from *Lear*, *Macbeth* was never printed: this way, it will give you no further problems."

"Let's rather say it will give *you* no further problems."

"All right. There too, however, the original source was historical…"

"Master Shakspere, your constant, most irritating insistence on the absolute reliability of your sources is a game that won't hold: so much the less since you yourselves have put this little game on stage, showing it off as a clear device for a character who wants to put his nose into dangerous State matters."

Ay, that had been in *Hamlet*, under the old Queen: it had been really stupid of them. But it had been carried off so well… A murder performed before the murderer so as to frame him. A well-known, apparently innocent story used in a specifically allegorical sense. It had been decidedly imprudent of him: writing that scene had been a little like exposing himself and his ways. But, back then, he had been too sorrowful, too outraged for Essex, and for Southampton, and for all they had stood for.

The scratching of the scrivener's quill on paper became to Shakspere like the noise of pulleys dislocating bones from their joints, down in the dungeons of the White Tower. He wondered whether this cheap underling had written what he had really heard or whether he'd been ordered to add something against him.

Cecil went on: "Let's say I do not like your playing with words, nor your forcing one word to open up like a magic box whence you can pull out a thousand different meanings, even opposed to one another. This is equivocation, my dear poet, and, as such, 'tis already a crime in itself. What do you say to this?"

Shakspere was silent.

"But, God willing, we'll soon leave this nasty vice behind. Francis Bacon, my dear cousin, is working in this sense, as you may have had occasion to notice, towards the *scientification* of our language. Crystal transparency: one word, one meaning. This is the style of the future, my dear playwright."

"I must say I feel a bit old for the present times…"

"Don't start again playing with words. Do you think one could be a pure artist?"

"Do you, Your Lordship?"

"'Tis for me to ask questions, if you don't mind, Master Shakspere."

"Of course: I apologise. Actually, I believe that art should always have a moral aim, otherwise 'tis nothing but a jumble of lies and becomes utterly unjustifiable."

"Good boy, you've given me a perfect summary of the Puritans' arguments against your profession. On the other hand, you are also a good player, besides being a discreet poet. But I'm not as stupid as that, man. And neither as bigoted, actually. I can't say I know what God wants or wants not from us. God surely has no need either of us or of our poor works. He could crush us all in one move like wearisome ants, but he has saved us, instead, through his inscrutable, mysterious justice. That is, he has saved some of us – the lesser part, as it is. You, for instance; do you believe you know what is good, what is evil? Would you be so proud as to arrogate to yourself this exquisitely divine faculty? I would not. *My only knowledge is Christ,* as the Apostle saith. What is a sin, Master Shakspere? And what is a crime? And the difference between them? Can there ever be a worse sin than sedition? Than dismembering the mystical body of a sovereign State which was instituted by God himself? Here we are no longer talking about little personal matters, Master Poet, but about the future of whole nations. Who am I, and who are you, to decide on such important matters? Who can ever be saved, after rising against God's settled order?" Sir Robert's fervour was increasing. "Why should one cut oneself off from His Majesty's good vine? Why not delegate our soul's salvation to those who know better? Why commit this execrable sin of pride?"

"I'm only a poor dramatist, Your Lordship, not a theologian. However that may be, we are not rebels. And we also seek to educate our people through our art. Teaching them, for instance, to love our country. I would say we've been discreetly successful so far, as I was saying before…"

"Too successful, my dear poet, too successful. To say nothing of preachers, who keep complaining about their empty churches and your packed playhouses. 'Tis only your kind, besides them, who gets into such close contact with the mob. One of the two is potentially dangerous: guess who. 'Tis time you fell back into line." He paused.

"Your other seditious play, of the two that were performed in Yorke's manor, was about an evil incestuous king who, if I'm not wrong, would behead all his daughter's young suitors."

"I was told at once about the Court's disapproval, despite Tilney's approval: I've burnt that script as well."

"And what do you say about your latest play?"

"The one about the lost and found daughter, *The Winter's Tale*?"

"Ay, that one. With a poor queen unjustly accused by an evil king who wants to repudiate her, and so she is put on trial… Where? Lo and behold, in Blackfriars! She appeals to a foreign power, which declares the marriage good and says she is right. Haven't we already heard such a story? Haven't we heard it in Papist circles?"

"Do you mean to refer to His Late Majesty Henry the Eighth, God bless his soul, and the Dowager Princess Katherine? Actually, I believe, the comparison is a little bit far-fetched: I've taken the plot from a tale written by an old friend of mine, the late Robert Greene. I can produce its printed copy, if you wish, it must go back to at least twenty years ago. Clearly, if we begin to reason on the level of analogy or even allegory, there is enough to incriminate the whole world."

"Ay, there is. *If thou, O Lord, Straightly markest iniquities, O Lord, who shall stand?* Isn't it like this, Master Shakspere? But you mean to redeem yourself and live, don't you? You don't mean to die as many others did." Cecil shook his head. "You don't court death, dear poet. You well know that God does not want the sinner to die but to be converted and live. Besides, choosing death would require much more courage than you have."

"'Tis probably true, Your Lordship. Actually, the story of the Dowager Princess has always thrilled me, but from a merely artistic point of view, if you see what I mean. Nay, 'tis the other way round to what you guessed. 'Tis Greene's character of the wronged queen that has recalled that unfortunate former English queen to my mind: the commoners are ready to shed tears for her and to applaud us, Your Lordship. So much that I… I have already started to write her tragedy. But I won't even touch politics, be sure of that."

"You will leave alone poor Katherine's tragedy: 'tis still a burning-hot topic. Unless it is to celebrate her virtuous husband…"

"Henry VIII?"

"Of course. The founder of the true Church, the one who was so brave as to free us all from the ancient, abominable yoke. Why not? I am surprised, rather, at your Histories dealing with almost all English kings, from the thirteenth century to the sixteenth, and stopping right at the rise of the Tudors. Why not Henry VIII?"

"Your Lordship, this would be a wonderful idea, but I am afraid I haven't got the talent or the energy to do it, by now." Shakspere felt he had gone red in the face, but not out of shame.

"Just as I thought. That's why His Majesty and I have thought to give you a young helper."

As the dramatist was still silent, Cecil went on: "That's the idea. We are looking for a promising young poet to put beside you. What do you think, Master Shakspere?"

"I think… I think that, for the time being, my strength is still enough. And that I will surely abandon the idea of writing a tragedy about Katherine of Aragon: no problem whatsoever about that. But, certain as I am that you'll manage to find a young dramatist endowed with great energy and terrific talent, beyond all doubts superior to mine, I would still rather work alone. That's because I have a way of working that is all mine, you understand what I mean: I don't follow the plot point by point. I may wake up at night, instead, to write one only line… I don't think I can explain myself as well as I should: I may be a decent writer, but I'm definitely a poor speaker. The fact is, I already experienced that as a young man: working together takes up so much longer and, seeing the many requests for this period…" He spoke as fast as he could, almost without thinking.

"I believed collaboration rather shortened times." Cecil was still smiling, in the candlelight, his strange smile creasing the right side of his mouth. Shakspere was almost at a loss.

"Actually, it doesn't. Not for the way *I* work, at least. You see, I started my career by contributing to other people's plays, but now 'tis different. Maybe, as I said, I'm too old…"

"Do you mean to say, therefore, that His Majesty and myself have had a very bad idea to improve the company's plots?"

"Not at all. The fault is all mine, for I can no longer work with others." He tried to smile back to him. "Ask my colleagues: 'tis extremely difficult to interfere, that is, to interact with me… Trying to change something I've written. We start arguing and we waste all our time and the players get impatient. You see, ours is a very delicate job, very delicate. 'Tis made of a peculiar balance, since what is also essential is a good relationship with the company, sealed by long years' working side by side, to be successful…"

"I'm dismayed. Because this decision is ours, anyway."

"Of course it is."

"Meanwhile, the Oath is always waiting…"

"I know I'm sort of sorely trying your patience, Your Lordship, but I ask you for some more months to think about it."

"This might be granted: the Earl of Southampton keeps interceding for you before His Majesty. He, however, has promised that he will take it very soon. Why don't you follow him?"

"It will not only be thanks to him that you grant me some more time, Your Lordship."

"Of course not. Our people love you, Master Shakspere. This is the real problem. They love you and your company. Sometimes they even seem ready to die for you. They need to see that you follow the right path, that you really love your King as if he were your father. Should we resort to more persuasive methods, you know this very well, we would already have got what we seek: we always get it. But this would backfire among the commoners, the *mobile vulgus*. And we can certainly wait. They must see you walk into the fold spontaneously and even enthusiastically: this way, they will throng after you. This is why we'll give you some more time. After this, however, if stronger measures are made necessary, we won't refrain from using them: desperate remedies for desperate diseases. As for the commoners, they'll have to live with that."

The thugs standing behind him got still closer, encircling him.

"Does the end justify the means, Your Lordship?"

"Of course it does. And 'tis at least as obvious that God has chosen His Majesty King James to represent Him on earth. We have so few certainties, Master Shakspere, in our miserable life, and this is one of them. Now, listen to me. This is what we want of you: one, a most absolute conformity and a regular, recorded presence to religious services. Of your own free will. Two, a new cycle of Histories, let's say a third cycle of four plays, after the two you wrote in your youth, to extol the new order and the King's paternity to his beloved subjects. 'Twill also very clearly show all people whose side you are on, you and the whole of your company. This is the plan you are to follow. Part one: a play about good old Henry VIII, the breach with Rome, his wedding with Anne Boleyn and Princess Elizabeth's birth. Part two: Elizabeth as a young woman, from her misadventures under her Papist sister to the glory of kingship. Part three: the defeat of the Spanish Armada; anti-Spanish patriotism and cleverness in crushing all Antichrist's plots. Towards the end, let's say in Act Four or Five, the dark plotting of the villain Earl of Essex will out, but in the end Truth, Time's daughter, will triumph. Part four: King James' glorious reign, his subjects' happiness, the providential discovery of the devilish Powder Treason (we'll establish its characters together), prophecies of peace and prosperity under his heirs to begin with Prince Henry. That's all: a very easy thing to do. As for the rest, do as you please. Let it not be said, then, that I wasn't understanding towards you"

Shakspere spoke after a while. "'Twill take a long time, Your Lordship," he said in the end.

"Not more than the King and I are willing to accept, Master Playwright. Six months for the first play, in time for the beginning of the winter season for Court entertainments. Six months for the Oath as well, obviously for the whole company. Otherwise, we'll withdraw permission to play and you'll have to close down. Am I clear?"

"Very clear, Your Lordship."

"Two years from today for the complete four plays. You'd better get down to work at once."

"I will, Your Lordship."

"The interview is over, you can go. I believe you are a clever man, Master Shakspere, after all, despite your devious country origins."

"I thank you, Your Lordship, and I humbly take my leave."

He was escorted to the front gate, which opened and quickly closed as he passed. It was the dead of night and, apart from him and the guards, everything was still and silent, the streets deserted. He walked out of the City of Westminster and slowly headed for the walls of the City of London following the black river. Exhausted, aching all over, he could barely stand on his legs. He wondered whether Dick was still inside or they had already released him. He almost stumbled into a sleeping youth who had nestled on the side of the street. A beggar?

The youth raised his head: it was Tim Rice, who, as soon as he had got into his home courtyard, had heard their names called out and had followed them, running not to lose sight of the boat.

"What's the matter, Master Shakspere?"

"Nothing, Tim. Nothing new. *Cruel are the times when we are traitors and do not know ourselves.* Hast been here all the time?"

"I have, Sir. I feared they would throw you into jail. I would've had to tell th'others, wouldn't I?"

Shakspere tried to smile. "The situation is not so dramatic, Tim. Hast seen Burbage?"

"I haven't, Sir. But I fell asleep, beforehand, and he may've got out without seeing me. What have they done to you?"

"Nothing: we have only talked. About many things: about the company's future and such things. They've given me instructions."

"Bad news, Master Shakspere?"

"So and so. Nothing very surprising: things which, sooner or later, I expected. Don't be afraid, Tim. Let's go, I'll take thee home."

"You won't, Master Shakespeare: Southwark is far away, at night, without wherries. This time, let *me* take you home."

They set off together. Shakspere felt old and tired. He put one hand on Tim's shoulder and they kept walking silently. Tim would have asked him a thousand more questions, but didn't dare. After more than half an hour they got to Ludgate, in front of whose still bolted doors some people were already waiting to get in: a few shepherds, peasants and tradesmen with their carts, barrows and beasts. They wouldn't wait for long, as the horizon was already showing the first light of dawn. Shortly, bells started to toll, and the gate opened. As he walked underneath it among the little crowd, Shakspere looked up at the old Queen's statue, whose noseless face seemed to be watching him threateningly from the realms of death. "My respects, Your Majesty", he thought. "Has my Yorick's message reached you? You've seen: despite all your paintings, after all, now you've really become like him. Have you laughed at this together?"

They walked round the cathedral and headed north. At the crossroads between Silver Street and Monkswell Street, they said goodbye. The playwright smiled wearily. "Don't thou worry, Tim: 'twill all be well. Thanks to thee for waiting for me and walking me home. This morning thou canst skip the rehearsals. Go home and rest: thy mother must be worried out of her wits."

"I'll go to her at once. Thanks to you, Master Shakspere. Good day!"

He watched him walk away. A good boy, this Tim Rice. Shakspere knew how he worshipped him, how he would have given his life for him, and he hoped not to let him down. This youth was also a promising actor: he wished him to get on well in the company, even after he withdrew from the scenes. Because, sooner or later, the moment would clearly come, and might not even be too far away.

It was full day when he caught sight of his lodging. Instead of going in, however, he stopped at the *Talbot*. There wasn't much time to rest, before rehearsals began: better to have some breakfast and regain some strength for the day.

The tavern had just opened and was almost empty. He sat at a table in a corner, staring thoughtfully at his ale pint. The game was over. The vortex of fame which had got hold of him in his youth had taken him far. He longed for the freedom he had enjoyed when, first as a young player and then as an apprentice dramatist, he had been an absolute nobody. He hadn't been anybody's slave, back then, apart from the box office. It had never been hard to fill up the theatres and please the crowds; not with as skilled a leading player as Dick. Now, instead... Now the matter was really complicated. In fact, the game had been getting increasingly dangerous for years, now – he had realised this even more when the King had chosen them as his official company. His Majesty had never been fond of plays: why then, had he wanted them so close to him? Most likely because someone, maybe Cecil himself, had whispered in his ear that they had better be kept under control. Thus, what had started as a little satirical game had turned into a potentially deadly trap.

His sight made misty by want of sleep, his eyes swollen, but his mind too watchful to go to sleep, Shakspere looked at the tiny bubbles emerging from the pewter tankard to the white frothy surface. He didn't know what to do. He felt responsible for all the others. Today he would first talk to Dick, to learn what they had asked him or told him to do, and then to all of them, and decide what was to be done. Then, of course, he would have to bring himself to destroy *that* thing. He seized his tankard and emptied it in a gulp. But, while he was putting it back on the table, he unmistakably felt a cold dagger-blade being softly laid against his throat. His heart sank; he went stiff, perfectly still.

"So I've scared thee, haven't I, Shakescene?" a well-known voice resounded behind him.

"Ben, old strumpet!"

He jumped to his feet, turned and punched the stomach of his pretended attacker, who bent double chuckling. "There's nothing thou canst do: between me and thee, I'm the smarter one. And the one with more hair on's head as well!"

The newcomer was a stout younger man, slightly taller than him, with a brown beard and moustache and a big drinker's belly. He sat down in front of him, ordered two more pints, some more bread, butter, cheese and some sauces.

"Thou lookst quite glum, Will."

"How smart of thee to notice! I didn't sleep a wink last night, to end up with thee trying to cut my throat. But thou'st only caught me by surprise because I was sleepy."

"Aha! Besides being more learned, I'm also more cunning, and I would've surprised thee regardless. What's up?"

"Nothing special: the London hunchback summoned us to Whitehall, me and Dick. He said 'tis time we stopped it, that my plays are seditious, that the boys' performance is seditious, that I must change *Cymbeline*'s end, that we can never put *Lear* on stage again, that we all must take the Oath, which is soon to become law, that neither he nor Abbott will make any exceptions…"

"'Sblood!"

"Wait, I'm not finished. That he will soon provide me with a young, more reliable poet (not thee, I hope!) to help me, and, lastly, that I must write four more histories centred on recent events, a Tudor apotheosis giving way to a Stuart apotheosis. Ah, and that the king of France was murdered, three days ago, maybe four, by a crazy Papist. Is this enough?"

His expression darkened, Ben gave a sad, solemn, huge bite into a chunk of bread he had just dipped into mustard. "Tremendous", he spluttered. Then he seemed to hesitate. "Listen Will, I didn't mean to tell thee," he said, his mouth full, "but a few days ago they called me too. I believe they partly did it to scare *thee* as well, so I deliberately kept this to mesel', so as not to play into their hands. They've given me one month to take the Oath and definitely turn to the State Church. Otherwise I'll end up broke and in jail once again. I'm fed up with it all, Will!"

He grabbed his tankard as if he wanted to dive into it and swallowed the whole of its content, then rubbed his mouth in his sleeve and went on: "Thou knowst, Will, I think I'll take it. I'm weary, absolutely worn out. I might end up directly on the scaffold, seeing I've been sentenced to death before, thou knowst. I'm scared!"

"Wilt thou conform?"

"What else could I do? I'll tell thee one more thing, Will. Me too, once, had to appear before the Hunchback himself. That was four years ago, in the full storm of the Powder Plot. He wanted some names, otherwise he would involve me directly in the plot and have me hanged."

"And didst thou give them to him?"

"Ay, that I did. I know 'tis revolting, but I did. After that, I even wrote poetic praises for that sewer rat. And for Mounteagle too, the despicable great hero of the day. But I saved my skin. At times I wish I hadn't, Will. I wish I'd died, like Garnet. But I'm not brave enough to die, I'm only coward enough to live! Great heroes can only be found in the tragedies we write!"

Ben covered his face and started to sob.

"Thou'rt drunk, Benjamin Jonson."

"'Course I am! Otherwise I'd never've told thee… But 'tis all true!"

"I won't judge thee, Ben. Thou'rt the usual old whore, but I love thee. I know thou'rt not a lionheart, that thou'rt a disgusting sycophant who disgustingly flattered the horrid hag who sat on the throne before this pederast came. How didst thou call her? "Goddess excellently bright"? A vile phrase, "excellently" is a vile phrase: I still don't know how thou couldst think it out! Therefore, come on, don't be sad: I know thou stinkst. I only hope those thou involved have got away as well as thee."

Ben was piqued: "Now I really want to see thee, knowst thou, Shake-tail!"

"Thou wilt," Will sighed. He took his knife and started to slice down the orange skin he had before him. "I was thinking that this is the price of fame. When we were poor and unknown, then we were free. And, to tell the truth, we took extremely imprudent liberties, we did things that could now damage us. But such were we, and thou wert even worse than me, with thy *Isle of Dogs*. Did the two of you – thyself and that rascal Nashe – think you could get away with it? Damned fools, you put all of us into trouble! But then, little by little, we started to get closer to the power sphere, until we now risk being burnt to death, both of us." Shakspere seized the candle from the table and brought it dangerously close to Jonson's face, who withdrew.

"Like Phaeton, Will, who almost burnt the whole Earth. Or like Icarus who, when he dared get too close to the sun, fell down into the sea."

"Like stupid moths, Ben, without bothering the Ancients. Like mean, unimportant beings who have stepped into a bigger game than they can bear. I remember how honoured I felt when the King chose us as his company, at Carey's death. And when he gave us that fine cloth to make garments for the coronation progress, as the true lackeys we had become."

"Thou wert beautiful, Will, all in red!" Jonson grinned ironically, his eyes still wet with tears.

"I'm always beautiful: on that day I was only better dressed than usual. Anyway, those crimson clothes were a bad omen. I even had to bear the canopy... a bad experience: have I ever shown thee the sonnet I wrote for that occasion?"

"No need for that, my dear: thy sonnets are under anybody's eyes for twelve pence."

"Ay, damned Thorpe! Well, there's something else I've never told thee. Listen. On the first night we perform at Court, we see the King never taking his eyes off Tommy and Nick, our two boys, especially when they play women's parts. What do we poor fools think? That he enjoys their playing. Unfortunately, the King doesn't understand a damn thing about drama! After the show, however, he requested them both to go to his royal chamber. Dost understand, now, one of the many reasons why he appointed us Gentlemen of the Chamber?"

"My God!" Ben covered his face. "What did he do to them?"

"Thinkst thou we dared ask, on the following morning? Just imagine the shame, for us who had apprenticed them swearing to their mothers we would take care of them! Of course, poor things, they were distraught. What should we have done, run and stab the King? Or put some powder under his throne?"

"Both! And then crown the Prince, our last hope!"

"Ay, ay. At times thou only speakst 'cause thou'st got a mouth, Ben. But now, thou seest, the same thing is to happen to me," Will sighed. "Only metaphorically, I hope!" and he laughed bitterly.

Ben was sad again. "We've lost, Will, thou knowst."

"I do. We've lost."

"*As flies to wanton boys are we to the Gods,* Will: *they kill us for their sport.* Now I get what thou meant by this line: the 'gods' are our rulers."

"Maybe, Ben, maybe. But I won't give up: 'tis a matter of dignity. Hast thou got a bit left, I wonder? And where is it, maybe there?" He pointed to a purse hanging from Ben's belt.

Ben laughed sadly and pulled out of it paper, ink and pen. "Don't look."

One minute later he handed him the piece of paper: "Here, I've written thee an epigram, all for thee. One day it will appear in my *Complete Works* and will be worth loads of money. Art thou not proud of it?"

"Ay, ay. Thou'lt publish thy *Complete Works* as if thou wert a true poet, not a despicable playwright. And thou'lt even find readers and buyers. Believe it, Ben!"

Will read the few scribbled lines:

> *Playwright, convict of public wrongs to men,*
> *Takes private beatings, and begins again.*
> *Two kinds of valour he doth shew at once;*
> *Active in's brain, and passive in his bones.*

"'Tis not clear: is this me or thee?"

"Both of us, Will: I was beaten in my flesh till they tamed me. Thou, instead, art still like a frisky, skittish colt, despite thy age. Of course, thou shouldst've been more careful of what thou wrote: now, if all chicken come to roost, thou'lt end up in jail."

"Well, for the time being, differently from thee, I've managed to avoid it. Although we've recently got into trouble again for thy fault, when we put thy *Sejanus* on stage. 'Twas too explicit, my dear, too explicit! But, of course, this means I can write better…"

"Nay, it means thou'rt more cowardly! Thou and thy stupid boast, whatsoever thou penn'dst, never to have blotted out one line… But now I would thou hadst blotted at least a thousand!" His tone was one of pathetic begging. "I've gone through my troubles little by little and now 'tis all water under the bridge. Or so I hope, at least…! Thou, instead, riskest paying much dearer for all thy seditious lines heaped upon one other." He laid a hand on his arm. "C'mon, Will, come with me: I'll see thee take thy Oath. Let's take it together."

Shakspere drew his arm away and glared at him: "What, hast thou been promised a reward?"

"'Tis not excluded, Will, 'tis not."

"Thou'rt a real whore!"

Jonson laughed out loud, now, as drunk as ever.

The shrill cry of a fishmonger wheeling her barrow down the street broke their conversation.

"I must go, Ben. I've got rehearsals, first at the Globe and then at the Blackfriars. Leave the reckoning, 'tis on me. Take care."

Shakspere rose, paid the hostess and walked out.

Jack woke with a start, panting, all in a sweat, after the recurring nightmare he still couldn't get used to. He sat up and looked round. Big John was snoring soundly, his chest heaving regularly, his fat profile projected against the wall by the dim moonlight.

A spy, that's what they wanted to make of him: a traitor to his own people. They wanted to entrap him into a far worse kind of betrayal than Sir Everard was said to have committed. All this, paradoxically, was meant to rehabilitate his good name. Should he betray and ruin some people in order to show his loyalty to others? Never! He would keep his mouth sealed about all theatrical activities, and about any seditious word or deed he might notice. He was curious to see what they would do to him, if he didn't report what he was supposed to. Rather, he would pretend he was an idiot, just like Hamlet. As long as they left his loved ones alone, however... His heart was pounding in his chest, in his mouth, in his temples: he could never go back to sleep.

He tried breathing some fresh air. He got up and looked out of the window. He could see the whitening skyline, all bristling with cusps. The great river soon reflected the first light of dawn. He soon heard chirps out of nowhere and saw the first birds on the wing. The street below him was deserted, apart from a couple of cats, which he followed with his eyes until they disappeared round a corner. Then he spotted a human figure wearily plodding towards Fish Street and the bridge. He thought he recognised him — it was Tim Rice. He must have spent the night out of doors, for he looked even more ruffled than usual. He whispered to him. Tim looked up.

"Hey, 'tis me! Must speak to thee now!" Tim beckoned to him to go down. Jack looked at Big John, who hadn't moved. Very slowly, then, he opened the door, trying not to make it creak, and went some steps down, walking past the closed door of the little servant's room. Tim was waiting for him at the front door. Jack let him into the pitch-dark entrance.

"'Tis really as thou toldst me: they're sending me to the playhouses as a spy! And I'm afraid I'll no longer be allowed to hang round all alone. I can't meet thee without them suspecting both me and thee: what shall I do?"

Tim's whisper resounded in the darkness. "Didst talk to Cecil 'bout thy ideas on Shakspere?"

"Never! Who dost take me for?"

"He's been questioning him and Burbage all night long."

"Tim, I swear... Dost really think it's been me?"

"I don't know, Jack, I don't know what to think. Nor do I know what he said to them. Shakspere told me not to worry, that everything'll be alright, but the great man is sure not to waste his time smacking thy shoulder and telling thee to be good."

"I'll try to find that out, if thou wouldst. Listen now, 'tis important: tell Shakspere and the others that the number of government agents in popular theatres is on the increase. I'll no longer manage to talk to thee, because my co-workers, whom I don't even know, would report me. Worst of all, if I never report anything, they'll suspect me too. What shall I do? I thought I'd pretend I'm mad, but I'm not sure it would work: I'm not a player as thou art."

"Take time. We'll shortly close for the summer. Don't report anything before it and then we'll think of something."

"I'll often come to the Globe, from now on, but I can never say a word to thee, I'll even pretend I don't know thee. 'Tis dangerous, dost understand?"

"By the Rood, I perfectly do! And how can we go on investigating 'bout the Powder Plot?"

"Let me think… There! When I come to the Globe, I'll hide a note under the cushion of my seat. But thou must be quick to take it."

"Thou shouldst always take the same seat, which can't be done. And then, 'tis too dangerous and in everybody's reach. Better to shove a note with my name directly into the box office jar, then I'll see how to send my reply to thee. 'Twould be nice to think out a secret code, but there's no time."

"Orange juice! Canst only read it when heated. Not lemon, which gets invisible again when it cools: orange. Then, of course, the notes must be destroyed at once."

"Right."

"I hope I'll manage it without being seen. I'm scared, Tim. Now I must run upstairs, 'cause if Big John wakes up we'll both be in trouble, but thou especially. Thou couldst not believe how he sulked when he found out – I don't know how – that I'd been to see a play without him and that I'd lied to him. Now I must gain back his confidence. I'll see thee, I hope!"

"See thee soon."

"Ah, Tim. I've found one thing about the Plot. Mounteagle appears among those involved in the Essex conspiracy; he bought his freedom with a tremendous fine."

"And, most likely, with some dirty job. Bye!"

Jack felt calmer now: at least, he had warned his friend. He walked back into the room letting the boards of the floor creak: by now, he could say he'd been to empty the chamber pot. Big John didn't wake up, nor, apparently, did Wat and Dave.

He lay down again and slowly went to sleep, thinking back to the Powder Treason and wondering who could have written that anonymous letter. It had probably been Mounteagle himself, in order to step out of the plot in a simple and – for him – painless way. He might even have contrived the plot, to take revenge against the Government for fining him so hard, but then he might have been afraid. Revenge: was this why he had convinced the others? Catesby, Percy, Fawkes?

He thought that, after all, the idea of the paper notes was too dangerous: if he managed, he would only write once to Tim, telling him to abandon that way of communication. They ought to think out something less risky than that.

In the library, Jack was so deep into his reading he didn't hear the light steps approaching. He started, therefore, when he heard the sound of a familiar voice:

"Here is our inveterate Papist all taken up by yet another seditious book."

"Seditious thy sister: look here." It was Francis Bacon's *Advancement of Learning.*

"Ah, my poor unlucky cousin, the King's pet..." Milly smiled maliciously. "He got married last month. Dost know how old he is? Forty-five. And his wife? Fourteen! Younger than me by two years. If that's what she wants..."

Jack didn't feel like wasting his time with this capricious little girl who kept provoking him just for the fun of it, and had resumed his reading. "What wantst thou? I'm busy."

"Nothing. I've come to see a Papist, as I did that time, as a child: to me, 'tis like going to the Tower ménagerie to see fierce beasts and rare monsters." She giggled. "I was bored: my brother's always away and I've got nobody to quarrel with... Miss Barrett is so wearisome, poor thing, with no sense of humour whatsoever: she is so easily offended, then starts sulking until I apologise. With thee, instead, there's no problem!" Jack continued to take no notice of her. "Dost hear me?"

"Ay, ay, thou'rt welcome. That's why we exist: to bear your abuses and line your pockets."

"Well, that's self defence, actually. If you hadn't started from the beginning to plot against the Queen..."

"...You would have destroyed us at once." Jack was starting to lose his patience, which was exactly what she wanted.

"Ay, we would: you and your nice Jesuits, with their little vice of absolving criminals in advance!"

Jack laid the book down and looked at her. "What art thou talking about?"

"They do: I've learnt it from most reliable sources. Your confessional boxes are but nests of vipers to get people to commit crimes. Disguised as spiritual directors, they absolve criminals after giving them directions how to do it, so your murderers and regicides are sure they'll go straight to Heaven."

"I won't even start arguing with thee: 'tis only wasted time! Never heard of Guido da Montefeltro, I suppose, and not even of one Dante Alighieri."

"Thou'rt right, I haven't. Who are they? Disgusting, churlish people, for sure."

"Dante was a friend of Petrarch's, so to say. He wrote the greatest poem of modern times, an epic on the life to come, which I don't think can be of any interest to thee: Popish stuff, thou knowst. Well, Guido da Montefeltro is one of his characters. He's universally believed to be a saint; Dante, instead, has put him in Hell exactly for what thou'st just told me now: because he gave sinful advice presuming he had already been forgiven." (Jack didn't mention that this pretended absolution had been sinfully promised him by a Roman pontiff: better not to add fuel to the fire). "And so, when he died, Guido thought he would go to Heaven, and so did Saint Francis, who came to take him there: that single sin, however, cost him his eternal salvation."

"Second-rate Italian literature, I suppose, steeped in superstition. How come thou knowst it?"

"Silly question: I've read it, of course."

"Was such stuff ever translated into English?"

"What, art thou sleuthing on thy father's behalf, so that it can be found and destroyed? It never was. I read it in Italian, as a child, with my tutor."

"So, thou claimst thou knowst Italian, the poets' language! If thou expectst me to buy this…"

"So, thou thinkst I'm lying. Now I'll show thee," said Jack in irritation. He took out a beautiful little gilt-rimmed volume, opened it casually, read aloud and then translated into English: "'*Voi adunque mi richiedete ch'io scriva qual sia, al parer mio, la forma di cortegiania più conveniente a gentilomo che viva in corte de' príncipi, per la quale egli possa e sappia perfettamente loro servire in ogni cosa ragionevole, acquistandone da essi grazia e dagli altri laude; in somma, di che sorte debba esser colui, che meriti chiamarsi perfetto cortegiano, tanto che cosa alcuna non gli manchi.*[2] This is Sir Castiglione. Art satisfied?"

Milly was silent, hardly concealing her admiration.

("One up! Finally!", Jack thought.)

"Ha. Things being like this… Wouldst thou be willing… To teach me? A little, at least," she added, almost shyly, then changing her mind at once and looking at him defiantly.

"Don't tell me that the richest, most spoilt little lady in England cannot dispose of a petty Italian tutor."

"I do tell thee, instead. My father had me learn French and Latin, but not Italian. My brother did learn it, but I didn't: maybe papa was afraid I'd bury myself among Petrarch's sonnets in the original tongue and turn too frivolous."

"Or too independent, maybe, since thou likest reading: for, thou knowst, some Italians have written really devilish things!"

"I forbid thee to make insinuations on my father! I could as well run and tell everybody that thou art still an arrant Papist and have thee arrested."

"Ay, of course: I'll be sent to the scaffold for quoting Dante!" he laughed. She seemed to be joking, but he couldn't be sure about that. If she hadn't reported him previously, she was unlikely to do it now. He must watch his tongue, though. "Well, it means thou no longer wantst to learn Italian."

"But I do! All right, then, thou mayst stay free, at least until I've learnt to read Petrarch."

"I humbly thank you, my young lady: your generous opportunism is typical of your caste!"

"Thou'rt welcome! Let's make it on Wednesday, in the early morning, when everybody believes I'm sleeping. Thou knowst, dost thou not, that the ancient Romans used to learn Greek from their scholarly slaves?"

---

[2] "You ask me then to write what is to my thinking the form of Courtiership most befitting a gentleman who lives at the court of princes, by which he may have the ability and knowledge perfectly to serve them in every reasonable thing, winning from them favour, and praise from other men; in short, what manner of man he ought to be who may deserve to be called a perfect Courtier without flaw."

"Thou'rt right. More or less, 'tis the same: the Romans were uncouth and ignorant, but stronger than the Greeks, who, however, were endowed with superior intellect."

"The Romans were simple and upright, whereas Greek civilisation had decayed because of the strange sophisms among which they lived and which detached them from reality. Exactly like you and your equivocating Jesuits."

"Come on, the Jesuits yet again! You're all alike: when you run out of topics, you start again with the old story from the beginning."

"No, seriously, John Digby, what sayst thou about the confessional seal? If one is plotting treason and his confessor absolves him and refrains from handing him over to the authorities, 'tis only fair for that priest to be incriminated, is it not?"

"Well: first of all, one goes to a priest not to tell him what he's planning to do, but what he's already done and of which he repents."

"Let's put it like this, then: a Guy Fawkes who has managed to escape and who is being hunted down throughout the Kingdom by order of the King. Such a one repents, goes to confession, and not only does the priest fail to hand him over, thus forswearing his duty as a subject, but gives him absolution and lets him go. What sayst thou to this?"

"One: that Guy Fawkes did *not* blow up Parliament and, therefore, until otherwise proven, he is *not* a murderer. Two: that if thou goest to confession for bad intentions which thou never put into practice and hast now sincerely repented, of course thou getst absolution. Three…"

"No, wait, let's say one like Guy Fawkes who has really blown up Parliament."

"Well, in this case absolution is not certain at all: the repentant must atone for the damage he's done and, if he has offended anyone, he must ask them too for pardon. As far as I know, a confessor may ask him, as penance, to give himself up to the authorities; or else, he could send him barefoot on pilgrimage to the Holy Land, which would rid the Kingdom of him practically forever."

"Sorry, but this is a clear example of your laws blatantly clashing with the laws of the Kingdom."

"Maybe they do; but I believe that, if Fawkes had really blown up the Lords, no confessor would ever've absolved him."

"What art thou talking about? They would've given him their blessing! They would've blessed a slaughter, and a regicide! As happened in France, after the St Bartholomew massacre!"

"This is nonsense, little Countess! Look at this French king's murderer, this Ravaillac, last month: no Papist blessed his act and everybody deplored it, instead. That one was truly a crazy Papist. But, here at home, we wouldn't get mad if you didn't *drive* us mad with fear and persecutions."

"You wouldn't, for you are already mad, all of you. How can you not see your own folly? How can you let yourselves be dismembered for something that is so completely wrong, so completely out of this world?"

"As to dismembering, and disembowelling, just stop a moment to think: my father and his friends suffered the same punishment as this French murderer. A fine example of the equity of your laws! One who has really killed the King and one who may, I say *may* only have planned to do it but then didn't, suffered the very same death: dost realise this? The King of France is dead, the King of England is alive, and think how much blood this Government has spilled for a crime that has *not* been committed!"

"'Tis only because, thanks to our secret services, and to my father, these regicides were stopped in time. But down there, in Hell, they're sure to be suffering the same pain as that Frenchman: so, why not the same earthly sentence?"

"Lucky you, the detainers of truth, you who know in advance who's to be saved and who's to be damned: practically, all your foes will to Hell, while you and your friends will all to Heaven. 'Tis so easy, like that!" Jack lowered his voice. "If Truth is in the King's hands, though, I wouldn't so confidently entrust him with my soul."

He bit his tongue as he realised once again that he had spoken too much and said things he'd better have left unsaid. Again had he fallen into the old trap of talking to her as if she were his equal.

She also noticed this, and smirked: "What if I reported thee for these things thou'st just said?"

"'Twould be most dishonest and just like thee and thine, who first set traps and then throw stones. But something tells me that thou won't."

"Thou'rt right: I won't, because I want to learn Italian."

"And how come thou'rt not afraid to learn it from one like me, a monster's son?"

"Basically, thou seest, I believe those like thee are not evil or malicious, deep down. I mean: this is not the point. It is your ingenuousness, your gullibility that ruins you. Your priests, and the Bishop of Rome, make you believe that fair is foul and foul is fair, and you believe them. They throw you into your enemies' mouths while promising you Heaven, and you, poor fools, go and get yourselves killed. They are using you, dostn't understand? They have their political reasons, while you give yourselves up to be dismembered and die among unspeakable torments only out of superstition."

"Oh, lucky me, as I've got thee to explain to me the way of the world, the way of history! How could I ever have realised anything without thee, without thy high and mighty arrogance? Why is it that there's never anything higher, to those like thee, than political and personal interest? Nothing really worth dying for? Between thou and me, however, I'm not the ignorant one, if thou truly wantst to be tutored by me. So, take back what hast said at once, or I'll have nothing of it!"

Jack was gradually raising his voice. But, now she had managed to infuriate him, she burst into laughter: "Come on, how touchy thou art! 'Tis always so easy to have thee fly into a rage... I'm going: see thee on Wednesday. *Adieu, mon esclave!*"

And, still laughing, she disappeared along the corridors.

Jack was walking along the Thames under a threatening sky of rolling purple clouds, in the company of a pockmarked-face, sinister-looking stranger. It was but yet another mission that had fallen upon him from above. In fact, the job had been given to Big John, who, however, was unwell today and had consequently asked his young apprentice to take his place. Jack had received this unexpected task with a mixture of curiosity and fear, as, for the first time in his life, he would get inside the Tower of London, the unconquerable fortress, the many-towered castle from whose thick walls and deep dungeons so many prisoners had never emerged to see the sun again. He didn't know why they were going there and neither did he know the man's name; what he knew, instead, was that he'd better not ask questions. He hoped it wouldn't be anything against his conscience, but there was no point in worrying in advance: when he learnt what it was, then he would decide what to do.

The Tower was the most notoriously cruel and unbreakable prison, where the enemies of the State were thrown, including those who had committed high treason and *lèse majesté*. But to all those like Jack and his family it was, more than anything else, a sacred memorial, a sort of shrine that had also hosted countless martyrs of the régime, to begin with Thomas More and John Fisher, many years before. Those walls resounded suffering and sacred memories, to them. Its inner walls were said to be covered in crude carvings engraved by the prisoners, during their many idle hours, to fight anxiety, terror, pain, and to leave a tangible trace of their passage there, in their all too often short lives. Jack longed to see whether his father too had left an inscription, a pattern, or even his bare name scraped on stone; but, even had he known the exact spot where Sir Everard had been held, he didn't think they would allow him a quick visit there.

Like everybody else, he knew what lay below the White Tower: the torture chamber. He ardently hoped there had been no need to torture his father as well: by the time he had given himself up, the Government had already learnt – or had got Fawkes to subscribe – everything they were interested in. But he was equally torn at the thought that no one would ever learn the extent of Sir Everard's sufferings, once he had been swallowed up by those stone-cold walls.

If he couldn't retrace his father's steps, he hoped at least to spot some famous prisoner: for not all of those in the Tower were put to ill use. Renowned Sir Walter Ralegh, for instance, another of the old Queen's favourites, was known to dwell in the *Bloody Tower;* more than a prison, the Tower was to him a forced residence where he lived quite well, reading, writing, making scientific experiments and even hosting friends. His wife used to live with him, they said, and one of his sons was known to have been conceived right there. Yet, like Sir Everard, he had also been involved in a plot and, at least theoretically, had been sentenced to death for high treason. Had the King chosen to do so, he could have him executed from one day to the next; at the moment, though, His Majesty didn't seem to be interested. Jack hoped he could catch a glimpse of that famous explorer and courtier of yore, maybe while he was having a walk in the garden.

Another famous and high-born prisoner was the "Wizard Earl", Henry Percy of Northumberland. Extremely cultivated, he dealt in astrology, alchemy and, not unlikely, in occult sciences too. He was there owing to the Powder Treason, of course, and unlikely to be ever set free again, even if he managed to escape capital punishment. Jack wondered whether Nortumberland was really the one the plotters had chosen to sway the Kingdom. Thomas Percy had certainly declared they were related by blood; as certainly, Northumberland had made him a Gentleman Pensioner without having him swear to the Allegiance.

It would be wonderful, thought Jack, to manage to approach Northumberland and ask him what exactly he knew of the Plot, and whether what was being said was all true, and which role Sir Everard had played. This was out of the question, of course, even if the Earl had really known. And, had he managed to ask him, Northumberland would certainly not reveal anything to him, even less so on learning he now worked for Cecil: how many Tower prisoners had then been executed thanks to witness given by spies disguised as visitors? Jack would have given anything to approach him, or to even spot him from a distance. He had seen him, once, as a child, and presumed he was more or less the same: tall and pale, his abundant brown hair like a lion's mane, and his unsettling, piercing eyes. And he must feel just like a caged lion: Jack would have liked to know whether he spent his time studying or walking up and down his cell in long strides.

As for lions, Jack remembered that, as a meagre consolation for not seeing notorious prisoners like Ralegh and Northumberland, he could always visit the royal wing of the Tower, which included the royal *ménagerie* with His Majesty's rare beasts and monsters, including several lions and some white bears, fed on cats, dogs and dead animals by their keepers: perhaps he might see that part at least. Wherever they were bound, he resented being led on like a mule by this stranger who never spoke a word to him.

The Tower loomed against the horizon, a dismal fortress watched by incessant rounds of halberdiers armed to the teeth. A parallel citadel, an ancient moated castle. Against the darkening sky, the King's flags were flapping on the four turrets surmounting the White Tower, their golden lions on a red field quartered with the fleurs-de-lys on a blue one. Jack's anxiety increased as he approached the gate, together with an irrational fear that he was actually being taken there in order to be arrested. What for? Maybe for his secret talk with Tim? Or for having spoken too much before Milly? Impossible. One could never tell, however.

In a mix of relief and dismay, he found that his mission for the day was of a simple bureaucratic nature and didn't in the least concern the part of the Tower that was used as a prison, nor the royal residence, and not even the notorious torture dungeon, but rather the Royal Armoury, where they needed an ordinary clerk who could decipher and copy in fair hand, in good chronological order, a sea of old bills and receipts written in different hands, most of them practically illegible, and then write down all the debit and credit in a big register. The job hadn't been done for months, nay, maybe years, and it wouldn't be easy to find one's way among those heaps of papers.

His colleague left and Jack found himself uninterestingly, prosaically, stupidly sitting at a small desk, quill in hand, compiling a huge volume in high secretary hand (to which he added some flourish here and there), copying entries and numbers from an unspecified amount of small, worn-out notes of different sizes while, all round him, several workers of the Royal Ordnance ranged muskets, pikes and culverins, moved cannons, cleaned the rooms, listed and classified all things. He started to think that Big John had just pretended to be ill, that morning, because he knew what a hard, boring task lay in wait for him. So, maybe, he had taken advantage of the situation to sit at his little table, a goodly jug of sack beside him, to write some amusing comedy. Or maybe he'd gone to a place where he didn't want to take his young apprentice and which he was at least a little ashamed of: where else would he meet the women he bragged about?

While he worked mechanically, with the labourers' voices in the background, his thoughts continually went to his father. He wondered whether the Armoury was far from his cell, and whether he had been treated respectfully, as his being a gentleman deserved, or whether everybody, even the guards, had despised him and even laughed at him.

Out of pure curiosity, he turned back the leaves of the big register he had in his hands to see whether or not it went back to the days of the Plot. Yes, it did. *"Anno MDCV"* His heart jumped at the sight of an entry which bore the date of 7 November 1605, only two days after Guy Fawkes' arrest. On that day, the Royal Ordnance had received *"from out of the vault undernethe the Parliament house corne powder XVIII hundred weighte decaied which was there laide and placed for the blowinge up of the said howse and destruction of the kings Maiestie the nobilitie and commonaltie there assembled. Received as aforesaid Corne powder decayed, crowes of iron with round pommells or heads twoe."*

The powder of the Plot! The powder that had been stored in the notorious thirty-six barrels in the cellar that was not a cellar... So, they had brought it here! Well, of course they had: where else?

Decayed? What could this mean? If there was a fit place in the world to ask, it was right here, in the Royal Ordnance. Jack went back to the page he was writing and carried on working for several minutes, then he asked quite a casual question of one of the men who were going back and forth: "Hey, my good man! Can corn powder decay?" The man, who was in his shirt, laid down a heavy cannonball, sending it rolling into a corner and, all black with soot, came closer, wiping his forehead with a kerchief, glad of that unexpected break.

"'Course it can, what a question! Didn't ye know?"

"I didn't," Jack smiled, almost apologising. "You know, I come directly from university. I can translate beautifully from Latin and Greek, but I've never handled a musket!"

The man displayed a row of yellow teeth. "Marry, I'd 've said that!" he grinned, glancing at the youth's white hands and long thin fingers. "'Tis to be kept dry, corn powder is, 'course, otherwise 'twill decay in no time. But after a while it'll go to Hell nevertheless, 'cause its components fall apart; and then they 've got to be remixed all over again."

"Good to know! And can good powder decay in a short time? I know not, like a couple of days?"

"That never! 'Tis a gradual process: 'twill take a couple o'years, more or less, depending where 'tis stored."

"And what happens if good powder gets wet? It can never be put to dry near the fire, I guess."

"'Course it can: on my soul, 'twill ne'er go off. But ye must spread it out well, to be sure, 'cause e'en good powder can only explode if 'tis well pressed. And dry, 'course."

"Only if well pressed: I got it. 'Tis interesting: I thank you!"

"Are ye plannin' to enlist, young Master?"

"That's it: I wouldn't mind that. For, by now, one is even allowed to go and fight for the Spaniards, isn't he?"

"He is, for sure! If ye need some advice, though, were I in your shoes I'd go under the Archdukes, who're more reliable in their payments. Right now they've patched up a truce, 'tis true, but I know they're still recruiting to help the Emperor, ye know."

"The Archdukes of Flanders, Albert and Isabella: that's a good idea. I thank you!" Jack pretended nonchalance and bent his head on the big book while the man went back to his cannonball. His hand trembling, he dipped his quill into the inkpot but forgot to let it drip and left a row of big black drops on the page. He mechanically took some blotting paper and his penknife to repair the damage, but his hand wouldn't stop trembling and his heart was hammering against his ribs as if it wanted to leap out of his mouth, while beads of cold sweat covered his brow.

Then Meg came to his mind, on one of his last days at Gayhurst, when she was learning from their mother how to make bread. She had kneaded the dough, covered it and left it to prove; then she had gone to play and had clean forgotten about it. On the following day, the proven dough had gone all flat and damp; Meg felt bad as she thought it had to be thrown away, and worried lest Mother would be cross. But Mother had smiled, instead: she had just sprinkled it with some more flour, kneaded it just a little bit, and it had started to rise again. This was exactly how it went with gunpowder, then: just like forgotten dough.

Did this all mean that the powder placed by the plotters under the Parliament was no longer good? And had it been like that for more than a year, maybe two? So that no one, in the end, had ever risked their lives: not even if Guy Fawkes had managed to light the fuse. Nothing of this, of course, appeared in official records or in trial transcripts. The plotters had been brutally tortured, covered in ignominy and sent to their infamous death, and their families ruined, their homes ransacked, their names destroyed, for something that they meant to do but would never have worked. For this and only for this Little John and Father Garnet had also lost their lives. Unbelievable: it just couldn't be true! His father had been taken from his family and quartered alive, his loved ones reduced to poverty – all for nothing!

Owing to some strange twist of fate, Guy Fawkes had become the most notorious of the plotters, a sort of scapegoat. It was in his honour that on the fifth of November every year those horrid, triumphant stakes were lit; his was the name given to those ghoulish straw puppets that people threw into the fire to celebrate the miraculous preservation of King and Parliament: he had become demon number one. But the real Fawkes hadn't planned anything and had just followed Percy's orders. He was probably the only one, in the original nucleus of plotters, not connected by blood or friendship to any of the others.

Fawkes was likely to have been hired, and paid, just as the skilled soldier he was, since he had been a mercenary in Flanders, on the side of Spain, for several years. How could he not know that corn powder might decay? How could he have failed to realise that the powder they had carefully stored could never explode? The plotters' plans, of course, had first been hindered when the opening of Parliament had been twice put off, by nine months in all. But such an expert soldier as Fawkes would never have carried on with the plot – in which, moreover, he was risking far more than all the others, since he was to preside over the premises – had he even slightly suspected that the powder was no good. Nor would he ever have tried to light the fuse, of course.

Besides being tortured more than all the others, and so savagely that he had hardly been able to mount the scaffold, Fawkes was the one who, more than the other plotters, had looked like a real fool, because he had stuck to his instructions even after the plot had been betrayed by the anonymous letter; above all, because the government patrol had found him twice, in only a few hours, in the famous "cellar" below Parliament. The first time, on the afternoon before the explosion was planned, the government officials had let him go; so, what did he do? He went back at night, to check everything was all right for the following morning. What the hell did he have to check, he, a soldier and maybe even an artificer, if he had even failed to realise that the powder had become utterly useless?

As for that other episode, the only real explosion that caught the plotters at Holbeach Manor while they were surrounded by Government forces – what had actually happened there? That powder had just been stolen from Hewell and was clearly good. But, since they had conveyed it in an open cart, it had been drenched by the rain; the plotters had then spread it out in front of the fire, knowing very well that it could *not* go off. However, against all rationality and natural law, it caught a spark and *did* go off. Might it have dried before they had expected or noticed? But how could it explode if, besides being "good" and dry, it also had to be perfectly well pressed?

The whole story reeked of sulphur, and its stench didn't come from the gunpowder in the Tower, nor from the obsolete, old fashioned weapons lying all round him.

Despite the early hour, the sky was already bright. In Cecil's huge library, Jack was waiting for Milly to start their first Italian lesson. As usual, he had taken from a shelf a book he wasn't interested in and had begun flipping through its pages, trying not to look conspicuous but betraying a certain uneasiness. True, at that time of day hardly anyone came in, but it would be really embarrassing to get himself caught while giving forbidden lessons to Sir Robert's daughter. He could as well have refused, of course, so that – maybe for the first time in her life – the little Countess would find someone contradicting her; but that spoilt little brat had got on his nerves, with all her insinuations about people like him being uncouth and ignorant. Now, instead, it would be his turn to ascertain that the richest and most famous aristocratic young lady in the Kingdom after the royal Princess was far more ignorant than he was.

The belfry of St Clement Danes struck seven. Jack wondered whether she would truly come or she had just meant to tease him, to make him feel even more ridiculous than he already felt, to state her own power over him. Maybe, after all, she didn't care at all about learning Italian. This might be but a trick to discredit him in Sir Robert's eyes; maybe, Milly had even told her father that he had started to court her. He had been wrong to accept: maybe he had better go now without making himself noticed. But, now that the guards at the front gate had seen and identified him, how on earth would he justify such a short visit?

The volume he had taken was absolutely harmless. He knew it well: it was a collection of journals of sea voyages, put together and edited by one of Sir Robert's chaplains, Dr Richard Hakluyt. He opened it, laid it on the big table and tried to concentrate. He started when, almost noiselessly, Milly ran in.

"Have I frightened thee, my teacher?"

"Not in the least," lied Jack, relieved by the fact that maybe, after all, she had not betrayed him or tricked him. "Thou'rt late."

"Dear Bridgie'd got up a minute: I had to wait for her to go to sleep again."

"Sit down, then. Hast brought thy tablet?"

"What for, pardon me?"

"To write down the alphabet, of course. I'll teach thee all the new sounds, then we'll try to write some simple words."

"Don't talk nonsense, I'm not a little child. What I want is to read Petrarch."

"'Tis thou who talkst nonsense. One can't feed roast beef to a newborn."

But Milly was adamant, and Jack had to yield: maybe she had even the whole day to argue with him, whereas he never had enough time. Therefore, they started comparing a Petrarchan sonnet with its famous English translation at the hands of Sir Thomas Wyatt. From the verbs of the Italian sonnet they went back to conjugations and, little by little, they analysed every single word of its two quatrains. Jack had to acknowledge that his pupil was not stupid at all: on the contrary, she was a bright, quick-witted learner. Which, very likely, was what made her most similar to her father.

"'Tis beautiful!" she exclaimed after a while. "So much better than Wyatt's version."

"Well, that's not surprising, seeing the poet he is. But dost thou really like such dull love poems?"

"Of course I do! And I can't wait to read the whole *Canzoniere*. And then, this particular poem has always been one of my favourites, because it deals with the contradictions inside the human soul…" Milly became thoughtful, then spoke again: "Thou canst not understand, of course: not that I dreamed of it, ih, ih, ih!"

By now, Jack had got used to her sarcasm and spoke back: "Careful: Petrarch was but another superstitious Papist, like all Italians, wholly steeped in plotting and lying. 'Tis strange thou likest him so much."

"I'm sure he had no alternative: he just had to be!"

"Ay, but in his heart he was a forerunner of Luther, like Wycliffe, the Lollards and Sir John Oldcastle, and like any other remarkable mind that ever was. For nothing good may come from Rome, can it?"

"Thou's taken the words right out of my mouth: 'tis *exactly* what I meant to say!"

"How explainst thou, then, his *Hymn to the Virgin*, maybe the most beautiful poem Petrarch ever wrote?"

"'Tis simple: it will've been written by someone else in imitation of his style. And of course he was a Papist: one had no choice in those dark times, I've told thee!"

"Choice? What meanst thou by "choice"? Dost think thou'rt at the market? If thou dost, now one has even too much choice and 'tis worse than before."

"Anyhow, we are only going to read Petrarch's love poems: the rest is totally irrelevant to me."

"Thou'rt wrong, my dear: we'll read what *I* choose, otherwise I'll back out and thou canst go back and get bored with thy Miss Barrett, embroidering and playing music all day."

"And thou canst go back to crossing out thy treatises of mineralogy and manners: I thought thou foundst teaching me amusing, at least a little."

"Ay, I'm having the best of times, acting as bull's-eye to thy arrows. Thy jokes aren't even funny, as for that."

"Uh, how… touchy thou always art! But then, thou'rt just like the rest of thy kind: no humour at all."

"Ay: that's because life is no laughing matter to us. There's no hope thou canst understand this, apparently. Because, to us, life's a nightmare. Thou walkst thy straight way without any doubt, or even a perplexity, ever crossing thy mind. Thou listenst to Abbott for thy theology, which, then, is but a revisitation of Nowell's ridiculous catechism, the one thou must've been taught as a little girl, where thou findst that loving thy neighbour, nay, even honouring thy father and mother, means nothing else than loving the King."

"Thou'rt speaking high treason, knowst thou not?"

"'Course I do. Come on, then, give me up to the guards. Do!"

"Thou knowst I won't, but don't start taking advantage of it." She chuckled and changed subjects: "Hast ever been to Italy?"

"Of course I haven't! Where do I find a permit to cross the sea, and the money? And then, 'tis so far away, and the journey there so full of dangers… But one should surely go, at least once in life."

Long John Gerard was said to be living in Naples, now. He would so much have wanted to meet him again.

Milly went on: "I wonder whether what they say is true: that it never rains during the day, that the sea is blue and so is the sky, and the sun is golden, and people never starve because the trees give their fruits along the streets: figs, oranges and lemons, grapes, olives,... that one doesn't even get as sick as we do here, and people are cheerful and often dance and sing, both in the streets and at home, and, when they do, thou canst hear their music as their windows are always open..."

"Ay, what's this, the Eldorado? I really don't believe 'tis all true; but, if even half of it is, one should really go. And then, of course, to us 'tis a pilgrimage; but you would also like it, since 'tis full of works of art. Before I die, I want to see Naples and Rome."

"I want to see Florence, and Venice! They say 'tis similar to London, with people travelling by boat: only, 'tis immensely richer and more refined. And then, like London, 'tis always at odds with the bishop of Rome!"

Jack snorted: "Thou'rt really as tiresome as a mosquito: apparently, this is thy only topic of conversation. However, I'll tell thee for thine information that any European country has more works of art than England, because we had the wonderful idea of destroying all ours. *All* of them, together with all the priceless libraries and miniated codexes. This is the superior culture you are so proud of! And where have the few surviving works of art ended up? Locked up in aristocratic homes."

"Including my father's, right?"

"Of course. But the vast majority were destroyed. 'Tis enough for something, or someone, to be accused of superstition to make their destruction lawful. But, as for our national history, hast thou ever wondered how things can really have been? Right here, in thy library, in thy home, a few feet away from thy fine chamber, there must be something that really tells about England's past. Thou shouldst search it high and low, of course, as thou hast time to waste. But has the thought ever crossed thy mind? Hast thou ever taken the trouble to go back directly to the real sources, and not be contented with the lies thou'st been fed with? Thou'rt not a twit, Milly: just wake up!"

Instead of biting back, she stared at him in astonishment. Jack thought of Sherwin, who, rather than swearing unconditional loyalty to this king, had chosen perpetual exile. "Wake up!" he had told him on that night, at Cambridge, before he left: "Wake up!" And it had been like rubbing a dry cloth over a misty mirror.

The King's Men were staging a play that, though already a couple of years old, was always effective: a tragic story of love, war and death whose hero and heroine were far older than childlike Romeo and Juliet.

The great Richard Burbage was ready to enter as Mark Antony, the renowned triumvir who threw away an empire for a woman's sake; beside him, Tim Rice was unrecognisable, dressed up as Cleopatra, black hair long and flowing, his face whitened with paint, his hips wrapped tight by a gorgeous coloured dress, his arms, neck and head covered in gaudy fake jewels. Burbage's wife, Mistress Winifred, who was now standing at the gate to collect the fees with the other women, was really skilled at dressing players: after her treatment, Tim could hardly recognise himself! Still harder to believe, despite the incontrovertible evidence, was for him to have actually been given such an important part: but the boy of the previous year had now developed such big shoulders and such a rough voice that now rendered the role absolutely out of his reach. Sitting on a low bench, waiting for the others to give the last touches to the Egyptian queen's cortege, the two players were looking through the chinks of the closed door at the pit being filled with commoners running in like ants to a drop of honey and noisily crowding round the main stage.

"Looks like we'll do very well today too!" the leading player exclaimed in satisfaction, clearing his voice in his Roman toga. "Luckily, my throat is quite well today. Well Tim, art happy?"

"Very happy, Master Burbage: you know I've never had such an important part before. I hope I won't let you down..." he smiled. "But, I was just thinking, what if my muscles don't swell up like balloons and my voice doesn't turn as coarse as a toad's? Shall I have to play the woman forever?"

"Ha ha ha ha! Let's hope not, my lad, though one never knows... I'm joking: thou'lt see, the moment to play the man will come for thee too. Dost remember thy first time on stage?"

"How could I possibly forget it, Master Burbage? Little Macduff, the precocious pretty child slaughtered on stage. A short, intense part. My only hope lay in playing those few lines impeccably. I remember my anxiety as if it were yesterday… Four years have already gone by, instead."

"What about today's play? Which part wouldst choose, if thou couldst?"

Tim didn't hesitate a second: "Enobarbus! His descriptive speech to his fellow Romans about the Queen of Egypt is peerless: for that short speech I would give a hundred silly lines spoken by Cleopatra."

"I agree, 'tis beautiful."

"That's why 'tis only logical for him to be played by Master Shakspere: spoken by him, those lines are pure magic. But I'm also thinking of Enobarbus' role, this man who betrays his friend and master, then dies of a broken heart on learning that Antony has forgiven him: I like that part madly!"

"Well in this sense we can say 'tis definitely not thy role!"

"'Tis not. But I feel so much pity for him, I don't know whether more for him or for Antony. I also like Cleopatra's character, of course. Her best lines are when, just before she dies, she prophesizes about me, right about me! This has been one of Master Shakspere's strokes of genius: the audience loves it! *"The quick comedians extemporally will stage us… And I shall see some squeaking Cleopatra boy my greatness i'th' posture of a whore."* 'Tis exactly what the Queen of Egypt can't brook; 'tis this, besides her love of Antony and her defeat, that brings her to kill herself: she has foreseen *me*, Tim Rice, playing her part, and she hates me for it! She took her own life, but didn't manage to prevent it! But then, of course, 'tis also beautiful when she tells about her dream of Antony, as great as he could've become, right when they've lost everything… And do you like this play, Master Burbage?"

"I like its lush, decaying superabundance. When I think of it, everything gets wrapped up in silver, gold, ivory and purple: methinks I can even feel Eastern perfumes creeping into my nostrils. Above all, methinks this Antony fits me more and more, as I get older. I like to play this aging hero who fights against time and wants to be divine but fails, and only lives on dreams and memories. I feel like him, by now, if only a little: an old player with a long past and a brief future who every now and then still has to play the youth. Like Hamlet's: that part, I fear, will stick to me till I die! Even if the mere thought makes me laugh, with my grey receding hair… Thinkst thou not *this* part fits me much better?"

"Ay, Master Burbage: I believe you'll be as superb as ever!"

"As for thee, just remember to act coquettish!"

"I'll try, Sir."

"Don't overdo, though. But don't worry: thou didst very well at the rehearsals. Art nervous?"

"A bit, Sir, but as soon as we walk the boards I'll be fine." Tim breathed hard.

Burbage stood up, turned round and, seeing that everything was ready, called out loud: "The progress's ready: let's begin!"

Tim felt a slight shiver run down his back; as he always did when his moment came. The audience went dumb as the short flourish introduced the two first characters and Ostler, in Philo's role, pronounced the introductory speech. Tim revised in his head his first, easy lines. He must attract people's attention without appearing ridiculous, which would be rather difficult in this attire and hairstyle. He should act naturally, as if he had always been a woman. Easy to say. He thought once more about how he would have liked that other part, which – just in case – he had already learned by heart, the one he had just told Burbage about: Enobarbus, the old Roman warrior who is faithful to his master, runs away after defeat and then dies of grief and repentance, asking the Moon to end his life and to throw his heart *"against the flint and hardness of my fault, which, being dried with grief, will break to powder, and finish all foul thoughts."* No. He, Tim Rice, would never betray his master. He'd rather die!

There came the key-line for their entry: *"His heart… is become the bellows and the fan to cool a gypsy's lust!"*

Tim gave his arm to Burbage and, at the next flourish, walked on stage slightly swaying his hips. They were greeted by rapturous applause.

Contrary to what he had hoped, Jack couldn't keep in touch with Tim, as he wasn't sent to the Globe again, but rather to many other minor theatres, often little more than taverns; always together with Big John, obviously, who had explained to him in detail, as if he didn't know already, which attitudes were suspicious and disliked by the Government.

Then, at the end of the month, all playhouses were closed by the municipal authorities, for the plague was said to have started again, killing more than thirty people a week. Coming and going from Salisbury House to the bishop's palace, Jack came across several funeral processions and even some houses that had been quarantined, their doors barred and nailed: there the plague had struck. He thought of the poor souls living there, buried alive like rats: they were most likely to die even if they escaped the contagion. Many people, if they could, offered bribes to the city officers so they would register a different cause for their loved ones' death. This way, the bulletins were never truthful, and the epidemic kept spreading despite the draconian security measures, while, as usual, some grew rich from other people's misery.

As summer went on, it only grew worse. Noblemen, rich citizens and all those who could afford to do so fled to the country; all public places were closed, while the bishops thundered from their pulpits about this new divine punishment; people repented and prayed God to put an end to the plague. Especially among the poor, death bells kept tolling while the city graveyards lacked both room and undertakers. Seeing a meagre theatrical season approaching, the theatre companies started to tour the country, leaving the London playhouses silent and lifeless, awaiting better times.

Sir Robert Cecil had many things to do at Court: now more than ever, the King had made himself scarce and had disappeared into the country, distracting himself from the weighty burden of governance between one hunt and another, and Cecil was the only one who always knew what to look for in the sea of documents and papers. He would remain in London at least until the epidemic touched one of his servants. Only then, maybe, would he withdraw to Hatfield, where the building was now almost completed. Meanwhile, he hoped he was protected enough by the apotropaic power of the glistening sapphire he wore on his left ring finger.

It was important, though, for his young daughter to go at once; His Lordship, therefore, asked Big John and Jack, refined and cultivated enough to offer agreeable conversation, to escort the little Countess and her entourage and make sure she arrived there safe and sound.

They left soon after luncheon. They passed Smithfield and took Aldersgate Street, the large road surrounded by green fields leading north. In the luxuriant countryside, the thick smell of new-mown hay blended with lime tree flowers, so that the air seemed made of honey. Riding alongside Cecil's beautiful carriage, and braving the scattered showers that followed them all the way, the short fat man and the lanky youth pleasantly chatted with the little Countess and her governess about history, literature, religion, drama.

Jack and Milly were both very civil and pretended not to know each other well, their friendly terms only betrayed by a few quick glances they exchanged every now and then. It was really strange to seek an adversary's complicity, unbeknownst to their respective older companions. Seen like that, languidly gazing out of the splendid coach window, Milly really looked like a kind, gentle aristocratic damsel, not the little sharp-tongued termagant she actually was. Jack cast another sidelong glance in her direction and had to acknowledge that, all in all, in her travelling garments, her cheeks flushed by the cool breeze, his pupil was a singular kind of beauty. Even if, as soon as he had a chance to speak to her alone, he would certainly tease her for the ridiculous feather she sported on her ridiculous hat. He couldn't make out the expression on her face while she looked at him from her fine window – all bright with inlaid mother-of-pearl, on whose frame she rested her gloved little hand: scorn or admiration? Once he even caught her gazing at his new dark-green hose, above his spurred boots: maybe she didn't like this colour and would later laugh at him… Or was she looking at the muscles of his thigh?

Now it was finished, Hatfield was a real marvel, with its red bricks and white mouldings. The old wing, the one that had been reduced to stables, was surmounted by short turrets, each with its little elegant Moorish dome, vaguely reminiscent of the dismal ones at the Tower of London. The gardens, now in full bloom, were also finished and they included a green maze of perfectly squared hedges.

Madam Barrett invited the two gentlemen to stay for the night, for it was already late afternoon: they could dine all together, then the two of them could take their time and go back to London on the following morning. Big John was happy to accept: it was not every day one could say one had been a guest in that fabulous palace.

After an impeccable dinner in the Great Chamber, in the West Wing, where the fireplace was dominated by yet another portrait of Sir Robert – it was a glazed mosaic in the purest Venetian crystal, this time – Big John begged Lady Mildred to play something on her fine small Dutch organ. Then, after they had all congratulated such a competent performer, the head architect, Master Lemynge, led his young mistress and her three companions to tour the building and the grounds. They saw everything apart from the Eastern wing, which was not yet finished and would be entirely reserved for His Majesty when he deigned to come and visit. They went through staircases, passageways, porches and lodges, admiring the fine gold, the stucco and fresco works decorating the high ceilings, the huge tapestries on the walls, the life-like statues in smooth white marble, the pictures, the precious furniture in rare exotic wood.

The family chapel was also almost finished, Lemynge explained: only the twelve stained-glass panes were left to be put into their window frames behind the altar, illustrating scenes from the Ancient Testament. Each of them was a little masterpiece in itself and had required the collaboration of three master glaziers, one English, one French, one Flemish. Then they walked out, in the golden light of the sunset, towards the gardens and the terraces. Here too, every detail had been studied to perfection, from the geometric flowerbeds to the paths under rose bowers, next to wonderful fountains whose crossed jets spurted from as many stone creatures' mouths: fish, mermaids, tritons, chimeras.

"It's certainly weird to be here, in this earthly Paradise, while down in London people are dying in scores," Madam Barrett remarked. "Here, the plague simply doesn't seem real."

"'Tis right in this frame of mind that true art can arise, my dear Mademoiselle: in this precarious, fragile balance between anxiety and peace," Big John replied. "Too much involvement in men's woes thwarts the detachment that is necessary to contemplate life, while, on the other hand, excessive isolation makes the artist a sort of stranger to the world, shut up in his ivory tower. Great Boccaccio, to mention but one, envisaged his *Decameron* starting from exactly our situation, with a group of gentlemen and gentlewomen seeking refuge from an epidemic on the beautiful Florentine hills. Like us, they retreated into a villa; which, however, must have been a thing of nothing compared to Hatfield, he he! Nay, tonight we could even emulate them and launch a contest of tales or poems, like this, just to kill time, while down there, in town, the plague appeases its wrath by claiming its victims." Big John clearly meant to show off his writer's skills and already saw himself as the applauded winner.

"Ay, we could, if we weren't exhausted," Milly remarked drily. "Methinks I'll retire very early, tonight."

Big John laughed: "Of course, Lady Mildred. Mine was but an example!"

Milly seemed sort of sullen the entire evening, so much so that she didn't speak to Jack even once. Decidedly, he didn't understand her. But, of course, the point was that she enjoyed taking advantage of her class superiority and today she hadn't had that chance. However, given that in those months she wouldn't need him and his lessons, she ought not to make him feel so superfluous. Aristocrats are all alike, he thought: they pretend to be well-bred, but then they are the rudest of all. Seeing that Milly was unwilling to start a conversation, Jack let her stew in her own juice and began to talk about Italian art with the architect until, after a while, the two women withdrew to their chamber.

The following morning, however, Jack was up and about very early and started wandering in the park alone, breathing the fresh air, under a clear sky announcing a glorious day. He didn't want to admit it even to himself, but he hoped Milly would do the same: he knew her habits, by now; he knew that early morning was her moment of freedom. There she was, in the distance, alone but for a tiny black dog, under a bower of damask roses, intent on gathering a huge bunch. She was wearing a sober white dress which was like a foil for the dark curls cascading on her forehead and shoulders, only held back by a simple white band of the same cloth as the dress.

Jack got closer and, pretending to notice her only at the last moment, simulated surprise: "Thou art having a walk too, I see."

"Ay," said she without turning round. "So that thou couldst not help speaking to me."

"Well, I've got used to it, by now. Wert thou cross last night?"

"Only tired and bored to death. But now it will only get worse: the two of you will go and I'll be left alone with Barrett and the domestics." She turned and gave him the bunch to bind and strip of its leaves. "Hold here a second, please; mind the thorns."

"One would almost say thou dostn't dislike my company... Or rather, in thy fine little gloves, hopest thou I'll prick myself?"

"Ha ha! I hadn't thought of that! Well, I wouldn't go that far: let's rather say thou'rt better than nothing at all. Wait! Turn round a bit, like this, and look at the newly risen sun."

"Why?"

"The colour of thine eyes: I thought they were blue, instead there's some green as well."

"So what?"

"Nothing: they could be yet another work of art decorating this gloomy museum."

If it was a compliment, Jack preferred not to notice it. "Ay, wait, give me those fine little scissors of thine so I can pluck them out and give thee as a present. Dostn't like Hatfield?"

"Nay, 'tis a golden prison."

"*This* a prison? Thou'st never seen a real one, I guess."

"Of course not, what thinkst thou? Why, dost thou like it, instead?"

"There are more works of art here than in all the rest of the kingdom, apart, perhaps, from the royal palaces. Paintings, statues, tapestries and arras, carpets. And then, precious crystals and jewels..."

"Poor papa, 'tis his little obsession. Knowst thou what he told me one day, while showing me a necklace of rubies which had belonged to his mother? My grandma, that is: this is why he named me Mildred. He told me that jewels and works of art are the only thing that lives on, that doesn't die; that one should make sure to hand them on, in families, to make them last till Doom. That human life is but a whiff of wind worth nothing, and so it is with money, offices, honours, fame, even earthly glory. That death is certain, that it gets each day closer without any of us being able to lengthen our lives by one single hour, nor take one conscious step towards Heaven." She suddenly burst into laughter: "I must be really very lonely, for sure, if I tell all this to thee of all people!"

"Maybe thou'st grown fond of me, like of thy little dog."

"Who knows?" she said, instead of speaking back to him in scorn, which left him quite surprised. "At least, thou gavest me lessons and madest thyself useful, somehow; thy lessons were more interesting than all the others put together."

"I'm obliged! Obliged in every sense, of course... But why didst say "gavest", in the past?"

She sighed. "Because I don't know how long papa will leave me in confinement here. To be sure, in town it must really be awful..."

"A disaster, I fear. A massacre of poor people, especially old folks and children. Think how lucky thou art, instead of complaining as usual."

"Thinkst thou I don't consider it? 'Tis right this upsets me: staying here embroidering, and chirping on the harpsichord, just like a canary in its cage, while down there people are dying of sickness and sorrow. Were I a little less important, I don't say a plebeian but maybe a rich merchant's daughter, I'd rather stay in town and help as I can."

"I didn't know thee as a benefactress and friend to the poor."

"And I am not: I don't give alms to the idle, who are too lazy for work. But during a plague 'tis different: I don't believe 'tis divine punishment, as no one can deserve it."

"Dost mean the renowned royal preachers, of the like of Andrewes and Abbott, talk nonsense?"

"Everybody does, every now and then!"

"Even thou?"

"Not I!" She smiled.

"Thou'st just said one of the many thou shootst out, as if from a cannon: that the poor are poor because they *choose* not to work. 'Tis but one of the many silly ideas thy brain's been stuffed with."

"Ay... Luckily I've found thee to explain to me how the world goes!"

"Come on, let's stop quarrelling."

"Thou'rt always the one who starts: I wouldn't."

"Yet more nonsense... Let's leave it as it is. We'd better go: I'll take this huge bunch and thou'lt carry the dog."

"Her name's Tessa."

They set off towards the manor, where a sumptuous breakfast was awaiting them all.

"What wilt thou do in the next months?" she asked him.

"The usual things: carry on with the tasks I'm given and try not to catch the plague. What about thee?"

"I'll play, I'll sing, I'll sew, I'll walk in the park, I'll read, and I'll do my Italian homework: I've taken it with me, thou knowst, together with Florio's dictionary. When I come back, shall we resume our lessons?"

"We'll see: if I have time!" said Jack smiling.

"Thou wilt: I'll tell papa to leave thee some time off, for I've got some errands for thee."

"Humiliating errands, for sure: treating me as an errand-boy to keep me in my place together with all those like me."

"Enough! I thought we would say farewell without any more arguments, for once, but if thou wantst it so I'm always ready to start again!"

"No, let's leave it at that, with our unresolved contrast, since none of us knows when we'll meet again."

They had sighted the white walls of the rear facade, by now, its low marble stairs gently descending into the park. She stopped, put the little dog down, took the roses he gave her and, before anyone could see them from the house or from the terraces, she reached out her gloved hand. "Farewell, then."

"Farewell," he said, and, partly to be gallant, partly as a joke, partly because he didn't know what else to do, he kissed her hand. Then they silently headed for the French windows wide open on the terraces, already flooded with sunlight.

Jack was slowly walking among little stalls and pretending he was interested in the items there exposed, now and then fingering things and asking for prices: musical instruments, dagger sheaths, belts, purses, cooking pots, ornaments... He was actually on a mission, stationed outside Northampton House, waiting for the man with the brown cap he had seen go inside to come out again. He had no idea who he was: simply, Big John had told him to follow this man and report his whereabouts to him. "Watch out, mind me: that one's a real fox!" he had added. Jack was nervous and worried: who was this man? Might he be a "colleague", another Government agent, trying to double-cross his masters? Or, more simply, was he just someone the Government was controlling? What if he had guessed that Jack was waiting for him outside and had made off through another door? Or if he walked out this door Jack was guarding, but then managed to make him lose his track? He would have looked like a clueless idiot to Big John, Northampton and maybe to Sir Robert as well.

Above all, was what he was doing right? It probably wasn't, but, as usual, he was in no position to refuse. He wondered why on earth Big John hadn't done this in person and had sent him, instead, who was too tall not to be noticed in a crowd. But Big John was either too lazy or, on the contrary, too busy with his writing; or else, he had decided it was time to test him. Anyway, Big John had probably grown too important for such simple menial work; like on that time when he had sent him to the Tower in his place... unwittingly doing him such a favour! Maybe it was a bit of everything... It was better to just do it, as usual, and not think it over too much.

Time snailed by. At last he saw the man come out through the front gate and descend the stairs, his hands in his pockets, a nonchalant expression on his face. Differently from usual, the City streets weren't crowded, for people still feared the plague, so that Jack could see him quite well; unfortunately, however, he was also more visible. The man was apparently wandering here and there with no destination, walking to and fro through winding lanes, turning every now and then to look over his shoulders. He made for the bridge, crossed it, made a quick, short stop in a tavern, then went back, crossed the bridge again, turned back, slowed down, then quickened his step omce more. Had Jack followed him more closely, the man couldn't have failed to notice him. Following him at a distance, instead, though he continually risked losing him, he hoped to remain unseen.

He followed him for more than one hour, again wandering without any apparent destination, through all the City streets. In the end, Jack's efforts were rewarded when he saw him knock on the door of the French embassy, near Blackfriars. A servant came to open and let him in; on the threshold, the man turned round for the last time. Jack walked into an alehouse opposite the palace, sat down next to the window and ordered a pint. He sat there for another hour, but the man never came out. He paid the bill and went back to his lodgings to report to Big John.

Three days later, over luncheon, Big John congratulated him: thanks to him, a dangerous double-dealer had been arrested and jailed.

"Will they question him?"

"Well, of course they will! What thinkst thou?"

"And torture him?"

"Only if he refuses to cooperate."

"And sentence him to death?"

"Who knows?" Big John shrugged. He bit into the sausage he was holding in his right hand spiked on his knife, and then into a piece of bread he had in his left hand. "That's none of our business," he said, his mouth full.

"That's what *thou* sayst! 'Tis as if I'd sent him to jail myself; but he's done nothing to me!"

"And is this a problem? That man's broken the law, while *we* serve it. Wouldst let the worst of murderers go free, provided he's done nothing to thee?"

"But that man is no murderer, is he?"

"As far as I know he might well be: but that would change nothing, for I know I've carried out my task and served my King. Wait! 'Sblood, what an itch..." Big John laid down his knife and quickly reached under his clothes, on his left shoulder and down his back, feeling for a flea. "Aha, here it is!" Holding it between his finger and thumb, he looked at it with satisfaction before noisily crushing it and cleaning his blood-smeared thumb nails into his napkin.

Jack had stopped eating and, resting his face on his hands, thought that the Government would crush dissent in the same way as this flea. He didn't want to be a spy, but what could he do? Once again, like on that evening at the brothel up in Cambridge, he felt filthy, foul, both inside and outside. He laid one hand over his eyes.

His ringed fingers full of grease, his thumb nails still stained, Big John now held his sausage high up in the air, peering at him as if studying his reaction. He then smiled encouragingly: "The first time it always burns, Little John; then, the pain fades away. Just have some more wine, wilt thou, and thou'lt feel better in no time!" He filled his goblet to the rim. Jack hadn't moved, his hand still over his eyes, his elbow on the table. "There's only one way to feel better, when thou hast to do something... something thou'rt not used to. The first time, thou'rt revolted at thyself: 'twas the same as happened to me too, thou knowst."

Jack raised his head: "Really, Big John?"

"Oh yes, many and many years ago, when I was still a poor little student, ay, totally broke. 'Tis sad, when thou knowst thou wert born to do great things and there's not a dog offering to employ thee. When thou art the best at university, admired and envied of everybody, and on the very next day thou findst thyself to be a mere nobody who risks starving to death and for whom no one gives a damn. Because no one offered me holy orders, thou knowst, despite my father having been who he'd been. But the times had changed. Thank God, Little John, thank God Sir Robert picked me up from the street and entrusted me with that mission, which was to determine my whole future. It was no less than a mission abroad, snooping among our enemies!"

"And how did it go?"

"Ah, perfectly well! But, exactly as thou dost now, I didn't feel at ease." His lips twisted slightly, as though in pain, if only for half a second. "Then, knowst thou what thou must do?"

"What?"

"Do it again, as soon as possible. And then again, and again, till thou getst used to it. And this is the way it goes, knowst thou: it hurts less and less, till it simply turns into a job. As common folks say, 'tis only a matter of growing a thick skin! Trust one who knows better, boy!"

Big John smiled complacently and winked at him, like one who has found Columbus's egg. Jack said nothing. He just looked at those self-satisfied small hazel eyes sinking into that plump face. Then he suddenly realised something that, deep down, he had always known: with him as well, Big John was merely working, and, had he received orders from Cecil or Northampton, he now wouldn't bat an eyelid cutting his throat in his sleep. Then, with Jack's body still warm in bed, blood trickling on the floor, he would go downstairs to have a goodly breakfast or scrumptious luncheon exactly as he had now. The disgust he then felt – both for his mentor and for himself – was stifled only by uncontrolled, primordial fear.

Although the first spate of cold had caused the death rate to drop, the plague bulletins were still alarming. Differently from what had been anticipated, therefore, the London authorities had not allowed the reopening of the theatres, not even for Michaelmas, and, for that year, even the great Southwark fair had been called off.

Big John was on a mission overseas, but he couldn't, or maybe wouldn't, tell Jack what it was about, and not even where. He was unlikely to have been sent to such far away places as Italy, Spain or Bohemia, seeing that he couldn't understand one word of those languages: Flanders or France were more likely, or maybe some German princedom. It might be malicious, on Jack's part, to think that Big John had taken the first opportunity to sneak away from the plague; one could never know, though. Meanwhile, he enjoyed those few weeks of unhoped-for freedom, well aware that it was but a sort of probation time, since Wat, the servant remaining with him, was watching him like a hawk and would certainly report even his smallest transgression. And, after the *Lear* episode, it was decidedly better not to arouse new suspicion.

Jack was now walking down London Bridge, among the crowd, above the muddy waters of the great river which, despite the Government orders to reduce traffic to the minimum, was teeming with boats and barges of every kind. He was heading towards Southwark on behalf of Abbott, Bishop of London, to see whether any place of entertainment had opened illegally. It was just unbelievable how willing people were to put their lives at stake in order to make money. Actually, however, the situation did not appear to him as tragic as it had been the previous summer: most of the red crosses on doors were old and faded and the marked houses were no longer being guarded by plague watchmen.

Jack would first make for the bear pit: if he had to fine somebody, he would rather that somebody not be a playing company. But someone suddenly jogged him from behind, probably on purpose. It was a short, plump man wearing a wide-brimmed hat and a big moustache. Seized by an absurd but disquieting fear – might he be a plague spreader? -, Jack was quick to look squarely into the stranger's eyes, ready to unsheathe his rapier. He smiled at once, instead.

"Tim! What the hell…?"

"Hallo, Jack. I'm a player, ain't I?"

"The best in the world!" laughed Jack. "But what art thou doing in this attire?"

"Looking for thee, of course. Just keep walking. I've got things to tell 'ee and don't want us to be seen together. I was going towards thy place when I spotted thee in the crowd."

"Who art thou, and whither are we going?"

"Let me see… I'm one thou once metst in a playhouse, before the plague. One whose name thou knowst not and who's now invited thee to have a drink. As for my job… wait… I'm a wherryman. Thou'rt coming with me 'cause thou wantst to see whether thou canst draw important information out of me: who's coming and who's going on the river, who's got a licence and who hasn't. In the end, of course, thou'lt've learnt nothing… Because… I'm too drunk." He started to stagger slightly. "Will that do?"

"Perfectly!" They walked together towards the Southern gate.

"How good to meet thee! Have ye players been touring the country?"

"We have, Jack: we had to. 'Twas just pathetic. There's a chill in the air… some villages clean rejected us without even looking at our faces. 'Tis the end of merry old England, as Burbage says. No more cakes and ale!"

"Was Shakspere with you?"

"He wasn't. That is: he only rode some way with us. Thou knowst, in summer he always goes home, in Warwickshire, for the harvest, since he's a landowner as well. This year, though, he still hasn't come back to London, which worries me a bit. He's sent word that he's some business to see to, but I don't know… However, I was saying I've got news for thee. And how was thy summer, instead?"

"Quite bad: I'm being given increasingly delicate and ugly jobs and I don't know how to get out of them. On the other hand, I've discovered something sensational: the powder of the Plot was decayed."

Tim stopped short in amazement: "Art joking?"

"Not at all: 'tis written in the Royal Ordnance inventory, in the Tower, perfectly clear and visible."

"What means this?"

"It means that, earnestly speaking, no one ever risked their lives. Something is rotten, Tim, in the State of England. Besides, thou wilt know the rest of the story, about the plotters' flight, and their putting more powder to dry near the fire so that it went off, blinding one of them."

"At Holbeach, thou meanst, where they had barricaded waiting for the Government forces?"

"That's it. A man working in the Royal Armoury told me that if the powder is decayed it can never go off. But even good powder won't, if 'tis not well pressed; besides being dry, of course. Well pressed and dry, dost get me? And the Holbeach powder, however good, was spread out and wet. What thinkst thou this means?"

Tim slightly lifted his large hat to scratch his head, ruffling his ruffled hair even more. "Damn me if I know, Jack. 'Tis as a tangled skein whose end's been lost. The powder they had placed to blow up the Lords can't go off, whereas the one which couldn't go off did… 'Tis simply absurd!"

"I've been thinking about it all summer. There can be but one answer."

"That is?"

"'Tis quite simple, actually. At least one of the plotters must've tried to blow up the others, at Holbeach, by setting fire to a barrel of pressed powder which was certainly *not* wet or spread out to dry. It sounded too strange to me, too stupid of them, to dry the powder by the fire risking an explosion!"

"Dost mean there was a hidden traitor? The traitors betrayed? This sounds like the title of a play!"

"There's no other explanation. It probably was someone whose name wasn't recorded in any of the official documents. As for Guy Fawkes, he's a mystery to me. The powder was decayed, Tim, and he was a soldier: he can't have failed to realise that. Maybe he was there just to check it, but he can't have ignored that it could never go off."

"Art saying that Fawkes was innocent? That he might not have had an inkling that the powder they had hoarded was meant to blow up the Parliament?"

"At this point, I believe there is no other possible explanation."

They walked into a dark, low-ceilinged tavern on the river bank, its air thick with tobacco smoke, and sat down at a small secluded table.

"Hey, how many people here! They're certainly not afraid of the plague."

"Everybody knows the epidemic is over, otherwise not even the playing companies would've come back to town. 'Tis just that they've chosen to let people believe the death rate is still high, 'cause they don't want us to come back into activity! So that those, let's say, dying of consumption or in childbirth are written down into the plague bulletins."

"That's why, every now and then, some places reopen illegally."

"Of course! However, let me sum it up," said Tim, his voice hardly hearable in the general din. "Catesby and Percy, who've both escaped by the skin of their teeth from the Essex conspiracy, organise something on which they force all the others to swear secrecy."

"Wait, let's not forget Mounteagle. Official records say that the plotters felt oppressed by the penal laws. Probably, instead, these three, and maybe Tresham as well, had been impoverished by the fines after the Essex affair and were seeking revenge."

"Maybe. Percy, therefore, rents a chamber under Parliament and puts one of his men, Fawkes, to guard it, who never learns there's a plot going on. As for Mounteagle, admitting he was in with the others, sooner or later he's seized with fear, so he writes a letter to himself and runs to show it to Cecil. The others, in the end, all die. Doesn't this sound absurd to thee?"

"'Course it does: not more absurd, however, than the official version. There's something eludes my grasp... Knowst thou what my mother told me? That she thought my father didn't know everything about the Plot. All he'd told her, anyway, was a lie: that things were being prepared to go and fight in Europe, so she had suspected nothing."

"Another one who knew nothing. But was there anyone, among the plotters, who knew something?"

"Thou'rt right: 'tis almost ludicrous."

"Now I'll tell thee my news: last summer we rode through Warwickshire, where Shakspere lives. As I told thee, we travelled together for some of the way, then he went home. We even called at the *Red Lion,* in Dunchurch, the inn that the plotters (including thy father) had gathered in, on that fateful day, with horses, weapons and ammunition, ready to leap into action and kidnap the little Princess. I asked one of the servants whether he remembered what exactly had happened and he told me that, ay, the group had gathered right there – and he showed me the table –, when Robert Catesby in person ran in like one possessed, with Percy and others coming straight from London with him, crying that the King had been blown up, together with the whole Gov'ment, and that the moment had come for quick action."

Jack started: "But 'twas a lie!"

"'Course it was: he must've been deceived. Who'd told him the explosion *had* taken place? This I would like to know! At that point they all rushed out, but many of them tried not to follow Catesby and Percy: all they wanted to do was leave everything behind and go home. But they were forced to stay all together, that servant told me, on pain of death. I'll now add one more piece: try to think. Let's suppose, on a purely hypothetical level, that the gentlemen who had gathered at Dunchurch didn't know anything about the London coup; that they were really preparing something else, such as, as thy father had told thy mother, a mercenary force. Try to make *that* out..."

"Wait, Tim. Right, let's use our brains. So: if I wanted to go to Europe as a mercenary, I could also legally buy some gunpowder to take with me, couldn't I?"

"'Course thou couldst. Seest what I mean? And now, thou sayst that the powder was decayed. But, if it was bound for Europe, so much the better if it was: I could have carried it there by ship in all safety and mix it anew once I got there."

"Guy Fawkes, therefore, might not have been completely out of his mind, after all."

"Exactly."

"Substantially, this would mean that the plotters were deceived."

"This is what I think," Tim concluded. "What we ought to find out now is: who on earth told Catesby that the King was dead? Clearly, someone he trusted: maybe the very one who then made the Holbeach powder explode..."

"This sounds really absurd to me... But, in this perspective, everything changes, does it not? Moreover, we've got to consider Mounteagle's role, which, at this point, doesn't add up at all. For, were it true that there was no ongoing plot, why should he report one to Cecil, involving his own friends and relations and practically delivering them up to an atrocious death? Because, if Catesby and Percy were his friends, Tresham was his sister's husband... 'Tis useless, Tim, too complicated: we haven't got enough elements and I'm afraid we'll never have. Too much time has gone by and the direct witnesses are all dead. Who, for instance, was to keep Fawkes, from London, in contact with the Warwickshire plotters?"

"Probably someone who managed to get away. Someone certainly betrayed them, but I can't make out how it happened. 'Tis all so confused... There must have been a traitor, somewhere, about whom no one suspected. *Fair is foul and foul is fair... Confusion now hath made his masterpiece... Cruel are the times when we are traitors and do not know ourselves.*

Jack's face lit up: *Macbeth.* I remember those lines. Thou knowst not how much I'd give to read it... Is this what Shakspere and the King's Men also think?"

"Shakspere is an artist, Jack. I've quoted these lines just because they fitted our subject. I've got no idea what he thinks."

"Thou liar!" he laughed. "Keepst not trusting me."

Tim smiled too: "Give me time, Jack. Seriously, though: I've never spoken about the Plot to the King's Men. I tried, once, but they didn't give me any answer. And, even if they knew something, they would surely not tell me, of all the world."

"Just tell me one thing: does the *Macbeth* manuscript still exist?"

"It doesn't." Tim gave him an enigmatic look. "It only exists in our players' memories. Knowst thou not that we are the abstract and brief chronicles of the time?"

"Hamlet!"

"Ay. But let's talk about facts, Jack, not theatrical fiction."

"All right. Thou wert the one who started, though. Well, what we've got to do now is: one, find out what exactly happened. Two, understand why. Three, find some evidence. Four, run to tell... who?"

"Even supposing we make out how it all really went, we'll never find any evidence. Besides, who can be interested in it, by now?"

"The whole of our people! I believe the true story of the Plot to have so many extenuating circumstances as to alter people's perception of it. They show, to begin with, that the plotters were *not* bloodthirsty villains. Knowst thou how hated Papists are, now, owing to the Plot?"

"Come on, Jack. Wouldst thou write a proclamation and shout it from the roofs? Or maybe write a play to explain things to people?"

"Not I: Shakspere might!"

"Art joking? He'd have to be crazy!"

"He's already done it, in a sense, long before the Plot, as if prophesizing about it: *You that look pale and tremble at this chance…*"

Tim went on, his eyes alight: "*That are but mutes or audience to this act, had I but time… as this fell sergeant Death is strict in his arrest… O, could I tell you…*"

"What could he tell us, Tim? What? *O God, Horatio, what a wounded name, things standing thus unknown, shall live behind me!* Shakspere had no idea, obviously, but Hamlet is my father and I am Horatio. I must live, and not get myself killed as he did, to tell his story and heal his wounded name. Before the Plot, my father's reputation had always been spotless and even admirable: despite his religious deviance, he had been admitted among the King's Gentlemen Pensioners."

"We've got another tragedy which unwittingly says something about him: *The evil that men do lives after them; the good is oft interred with their bones.* Dost know it? That's *Julius Caesar.*"

"Never heard of it, unfortunately. And, anyway, my father ended up even worse, for he was never buried. They quartered him alive and gave his remains as food to the crows."

"I know, Jack: I was there." Tim got thoughtful. "Seriously, though, whom thinkst thou we should tell our deductions to? I guess Cecil wouldn't know what to do with them."

"As for the King, he is happily persuaded he has foiled a terrible plot with the help of God: he wouldn't give this up even before the evidence we haven't got."

"Who, then? Maybe another powerful man, like Sir Francis Bacon, the man of the moment, or else the Earl of Northampton, who used not to dislike Papists?"

"Forget it, he's sold himself like the others. As for Bacon, his only interest is in his own advancement, 'tis enough to see how he betrayed

Essex, who'd been so good to him... Wait! Who else but Prince Harry? He's bounteous and honest: at least, he would listen to us. He may even remember meeting me before: for when he came to Cambridge, in spring, I managed to personally give him a little note. I wonder whether he's read it and..."

"What did it say?"

"It said that I, a traitor's son, am not guilty of my father's crimes and can't wait to show him in person what loving one's Sovereign means. I regret it, now, because back then I thought my father was really guilty and his sentence fair."

"He may remember thee... One thing thou shouldst do, as the scholar thou art: write a libel, an anonymous one for the time being, dedicated to the Prince, where thou explainst thy version of the story, as soon as we have a convincing one. Above all, thou must show that the official tale doesn't stand to reason."

"Wow, that's most dangerous: if Big John found such a manuscript among my things..."

"Hast got any better ideas?"

"I haven't. Just imagine I write the libel, what do we do then?"

"We let the Prince find it somewhere: we'll work out the details later. It'll have to be something rational, very well balanced, based on facts. Precise, logical, sharp, overpowering. No abuse, no sentimentality, only a touch of pity for those poor persecuted Papists, trampled down and betrayed by someone they trusted. What sayst thou about it?"

"'Tis deadly dangerous, but I like it. Thinkst thou I ought to write it in English or Latin? Latin is better, as everybody in Europe can understand it. And in Spain, of course: after all, they are also to blame if..."

"Who gives a damn about Europe and Spain? Thou must write for thine own people."

"But ours is much too clumsy a language, too poor, I am not sure I'll manage it. 'Tis fluid, thou seest: nothing lasts, if 'tis written in English."

"Not so: 'tis flexible, supple, the language of the future! And anyway, the first thing we need is for thy writing to get its message home here and now; then, we'll see."

"All right. This very night I'll draw a list of contents. But too many pieces of the jigsaw are still missing. We ought to meet more often. I would I had more freedom, but how can I shake off this yoke of Big John and the others?"

"Dunno'."

"Should I run away, Cecil would take revenge on my family. But, somehow, I will have to act: I can no longer go on like this."

"I wish I could help thee, my friend."

They left their table and Jack paid the bill. When they walked out it was already getting dark. In his wide hat and fake moustache, Tim disappeared in the shadows. Jack finally reached the bearpit, which certainly couldn't be open now; but all the same he made sure it was locked and bolted and went back to report the fact.

Already before dawn, people all through the kingdom had started to set fire to the stakes they had carefully built on the previous evening: they would soon begin to throw straw puppets into their flames – many little, accursed, damned Guy Fawkes -, thus celebrating for the sixth year in a row the providential preservation of the King, Queen, Prince and Parliament, yea, of the whole of Britain as it was. Stratford too had organised a big gathering in the marketplace: the festivity would go on until the break of the following day.

The first of many bonfires had already been lit. An icy wind fanned the high flames, making them mount even higher and roar more ferociously. Two travellers, one tall and wide-shouldered, the other short and slim, both wrapped up in heavy cloaks with wide hoods which covered even their eyes, moved closer to the fire and reached out to warm their hands. They had spent the night in an inn at Atherstone and had just arrived in town. They drank a mug of hot spiced wine, that day offered by the Mayor, then walked down Chapel Street towards a fine big house.

Its landlord, Master Shakspere, gentleman, was already up, working in his office. No, they were not disturbing him, for, on that morning, no words would descend on paper, not even had he squeezed his brain with his hands; so much that he was contemplating the thought of putting down his quill and having a walk round his country property to check for holes in the hedges. No, he wouldn't go to toast the King and burn his Guy Fawkes; neither would he turn up at the special religious service, which, one must say, was not particularly popular in that area. And, yes, he was really happy to see Dick Burbage and Tim Rice. Still laughing, he welcomed them into the hall, then called his wife and his still unmarried daughter, who gave orders to serve them a delicious breakfast of hot sausages, eggs, porridge, warm bread, cakes of seeds and saffron. "Ale or mead, boys? Both home-made." Shakspere tried to look natural and even cheerful, but he knew well that his friends hadn't come all the way from London simply to pay him a jolly visit.

"And both we'll have, Will!" said Burbage. "My congratulations to Mistress Anne on all this divine food!" Anne smiled, blushing a little.

"Thou always hast the best of times at home, hast not?"

"Always, Dick. Especially in recent times." Will smiled listlessly. "Thou knowst how much I needed a long holiday." His gaze was lost in emptiness.

"Relax, Will, 'tis not that. I've brought thee thy part of the box office takings. A little worse than usual, with the neverending plague, and Armin who's left us, and the preachers who, egged on by the Bishop, have been putting us down. But, nevertheless, 'tis something: once again, the King hasn't grudged us his patronage. We'll shortly be called to Court, as thou well knowst, for the Twelve Days... We need thee, Will!"

"I know. I'm working from here, on something new for the winter season."

Dick laid his piece of cake on its dish and earnestly looked into his eyes: "There's something else, Will. For three days now, we've been without an Archbishop of Canterbury."

"What, is Bancroft dead?"

"Ay... and try to guess who's already been proposed for the Arch-chair."

"Not our dear George Abbott, Bishop of London?"

"Precisely! How clever thou art! This way he'll get even more powerful and make our life utterly unbearable. He's already drunk with power. So much that..." He stopped short.

"That...?"

Burbage lowered his voice. "Will, Abbott wants to suspend our licence for the new year: what do we do now?"

"Upon what ground?"

"Why, here in England!" They both laughed.

"No, seriously, Dick, for what reason?"

"Doubtful loyalty."

Shakspere looked down again, his hands on his forehead. "I'll come back, write a play the way they want it and show them we're loyal. I'm already writing it, actually. I don't want you all to pay for *my* problem."

"'Tis *our* problem, Will, for it concerns all of us. On the other hand, we surely can't starve to death. Something or other we'll have to do... Canst imagine me learning a trade, at my age, or going back to being a joiner and carpenter after more than thirty years? But we'll think of something, as we've always done. Something will turn up!" Burbage grinned wishfully. "What about the new historical cycle Cecil has commissioned? Hast started it? Were it well received, *that* could save us all. Knowst thou what I think? That the reason they're so patient with thee is that they sorely need thy four plays as a piece of propaganda. As if the lot of the monarchy as such were at stake..."

"As much as that! Indeed! Anyhow, I'm trying hard, Dick, God knows how hard. But everything that gets out of my pen seems to be desperately, irretrievably wrong. Wait, I'll show you both."

He went to fetch a sheaf of papers and showed them the first lines of a new prologue: "*I come no more to make you laugh. Things now that bear a weighty and a serious brow, sad, high, and working, full of state and woe...*"

"Dost see, Dick? As usual, my mind goes on by itself and creates things, almost visions. It shows me facts and scenes, makes me hear what my characters would say, so that, in the end, the result may be totally different from what I'd started with. Here, for instance, I am supposed to happily celebrate that pig, Harry the Eigth; what comes out of my brain, instead, is this tragic prologue, both serious and sad. 'Tis all wrong."

"However that may be, thou must come back, Will."

"Thou knowst, dost'nt thou, that the very moment I came back I would immediately have to take both Oaths: Cecil gave me six months, and now they've almost expired. I've asked Southampton for help, as I always do, but he's being elusive, this time. He's sworn, and so has Jonson. Young Montague still resists and has fallen from grace, fined and kicked out of Court, ... I'm scared, Dick."

Tim was sick at heart. He dared not move and was almost afraid to breathe, lest, on noticing him, the two men might realise this conversation not to be fit for his young ears.

"All in all, Will, I don't believe thou hast any more choice. Come back, take those damned Oaths and let's start again as before."

"Nothing will ever be the same as before, Dick. Even if, of course, I'll do all I can in order for your licence not to be held back for my fault. I'll write a letter to the great man himself, saying I'm slowly recovering from a serious disease, and I'll try to buy some more time by continuing to write from home. Although I know this can't go on very long..."

"What's the matter with thee? The pox? Or maybe consumption?"

"Who knows? I might've come down with the plague. I'll ask my son-in-law for a believable diagnosis. Above all, I'll tell Cecil that I've started the first of his histories, which is perfectly true: I'll only ask him for the time to stage my last fairy tale, next spring, and then I'll stop dithering forever. This I promise thee too, Dick."

"All right, Will. I'll give thee thy money and let's no longer talk about it." Burbage took a large leather purse from his bag and put it on the table.

The feast went on all day, in the fine Chapel Street dwelling, for Burbage's arrival from London. Its landlord improvised a little banquet to which he also invited his married daughter, with her husband and their three-year-old Bessie. Luckily for him, Shakspere didn't only live on plays. The plots of land he had slowly pieced together thanks to his London savings now granted him a good income. Therefore, there were crackling fires in all his chimneys, plenty of wood to burn, food and warmth for everybody.

After luncheon, Burbage went to rest awhile. Mistress Anne also offered a bed to Tim, who, however, was not tired.

"Will you go to sleep as well, Master Shakspere?"

The poet was quick to grasp the meaning of his begging expression. "I don't think so: I'd rather have a walk up to Snitterfield, where I've just bought a field. What sayst thou to coming along?" Tim's face lit up: "I'll be glad of it, Master Shakspere!" He was actually exhausted for the journey and the early rising, but he would still walk a whole day and night alone with his idol.

They donned their cloaks and took a path among the fields, soon leaving the little town behind, with its mixed sounds and smells of burning wood, roasting chestnuts and feasting people. They went uphill through a grassy lane, a high hedge running along one of its sides. The air was fresh and the sky was clear, while the green grass and dead leaves, still frozen where the sun hadn't reached them, crunched under their feet.

"And so, Tim, what sayst thou?"

The youth breathed deep. "I like the countryside, Master Shakspere."

"Hast always lived in London?"

"I have, Sir. London's fine too, but here 'tis diff'rent."

"It is. I'm fond of here, because I was born here. I remember the day I left, all in a rush, many years ago. I thought I could no longer come back; things, instead, have more or less come right again... let's say so. Sometimes, by now, I feel I belong in London; deep down, though, I know this is my home. 'Tis like a clash of loyalties, as if London were my duty and Stratford were my soul. I love them both, but I know they are becoming irreconcilable. I'm not sure thou understandst..."

Tim nodded. "How did you end up in London and start playing, Sir?"

"Ah, that was not a nice moment, lad: I had to drop everything, grab a bag and be off in a wink. As a youth, thou knowst, I liked looking for trouble. Here in Stratford things were quiet enough, as to that. One day, however, and all of a sudden, an uncle of mine (twice removed) was arrested. He was a rich man, Uncle Ned was, and quite important too. He'd crossed the Earl of Leicester, a most powerful and dangerous man, the old Queen's favourite. After being accused of high treason on a trumped-up charge, he was hanged, drawn and quartered; he, a spotless subject, totally innocent apart from his religion... He loved his country and wanted to serve it regardless: little did he think that his country would reward him that way. I was not yet twenty, then. I was part of his household, I helped him in everything and I knew all his papers and his business... Dear Uncle Ned..."

Shakspere shook his head. "So one day, thanks to friends I had in the right positions, I learn that the justice of the peace of this county, Thomas Lucy, a really staunch Puritan, means to question me over that alleged plot they say Uncle Ned has taken part in. What's more, one of my dearest friends, who had married Uncle Ned's daughter, was blamed for contriving it all: he was arrested and put to torture, but didn't even reach the scaffold, for he was said to have hanged himself in jail... I was blind with terror, Tim. I ran away at random, leaving everybody else behind: my sick father, my pregnant wife, my not yet two-year-old daughter... I sought shelter in London, where nobody knew me, in the house of a powerful man I'd met some years before. Since he had once seen me perform in a little play, as people often do in private houses, he came up with the idea of introducing me into his playing company, which his patronage sheltered from too close inspection. I liked it at once, of course: 'tis there I met Dick and some of the others. As a player, I started working with other poets to improve plays that didn't run smoothly enough... And the rest thou knowst already."

"Didn't that Lucy ever find you?"

"He didn't hear from me for three or four years. In the meantime, the Government had solved its greatest problem and killed off the Queen of Scots. 'Tis with her that my uncle's so-called treason was connected, so the matter gradually lost importance. And then, just imagine, there came the Spanish Armada and, in the general panic, everybody had worse trouble to think of. Lucy was old, moreover: he shortly withdrew into his estate and died... about ten years ago, I suppose. As for me, I was well established in London, by then: I had begun writing like that, not seriously, mainly to scrap up a bit more money, but now I was starting to be not a little successful."

Tim smiled. "And this is how, fearing a noose round your neck, you found yourself a famous and acclaimed poet, instead."

"Queer, isn't it? I've experienced firsthand what the uses of adversity may be. But tell me one thing: how's it going, down there, without me?"

"Sadly, Sir. Now Master Armin's had to go too, life's no longer the same. And you too, Sir..."

"We'll see, Tim."

"You're needed, Sir: 'tis just as Master Burbage told you"

"I'll come back: sooner or later, I will. I miss you all, too. It won't be easy, though, for I'll have to take a decision I've long put off. Thou seest, at times treason is even too easy, too subtle – almost natural, I would almost say! – and this grievous responsibility on my shoulders, of what you players say or don't say on stage, is becoming an unbearably heavy burden. I've always liked playing with fire, and then play dumb to get away with it, but the game's now got really dangerous."

"Don't be afraid for us, Sir. And, then, Master Armin wasn't sent away for your fault."

"But he was performing in one of my plays. And the Simpson brothers' company, up there at Gowthwaite Hall, Sir John Yorke's manor, got into trouble while playing my *Lear* and my *Pericles*. In these hard days, there's no safety: never lower your guard! Not that I don't trust you all, not that I don't trust thee, mind me: the matter is different. Dost know how they framed some of the toughest ones? By threatening to hurt their families." Tim's thought ran to Jack and his loved ones. "And so I'm afraid for myself and mine, here in Stratford, and for you too, who are my second family. Thou knowst me by now, Tim: thou'st become like a son to me. Thou knowst I have no son, dostn't thou?"

"I've seen, Master Shakspere, and I've guessed so."

"I used to have one. He looked a bit like thee: blond and lively. I wasn't at home when he died: I couldn't even get here in time for his burial. I didn't see him either being born, for I was already in London, or dying. I missed both his baptism and his funeral. He wasn't yet twelve: a bit like thee when I first met thee, if I'm not wrong." Tim nodded again. "I'd give all my goods, all my papers, my plays, my poems, everything, to call him back to life; for there's no worse thing than surviving your child. I'd give my life. And I also had a younger brother who followed me to London, the only one in my family, to be a player like me. He died too, three years ago, of the plague. He was only twenty-seven. Edmund, he was called, like... but let be, it doesn't matter now."

"I remember this." Tim had just joined the company, then. He remembered well that moment, and the great poet's tears, and his own wish to soothe him and not knowing how, and the splendid funeral Shakspere had paid for at St Saviour, near the Globe, for that brother who had almost been like another son to him, and the knells of the great bell which cost who knew how much.

"And how was your son called?"

"Hamnet."

Tim gasped: "Like the Prince of Denmark?"

"No, no, like his godfather, a dear scoundrel friend of mine, here in Stratford, with an unfortunate name. But, what wouldst thou do, the baby's name is down to its godparents... So, we named our twins after his wife and him. And they, in their turn, named their first born, my godson, after me."

They went round the new plots of land, checking the enclosure hedges. Master Shakspere stopped on the way to chat with several acquaintances, introducing Tim as his London apprentice, which made Tim very proud; then, towards dusk, they started to walk back.

"Thou seest, I believe our trade not to be a mere job, but almost a sort of mission." Tim nodded silently. "We are in close contact with people, with a wide audience, each day. What do we want to give them? What they want, like this, just to make them happy? Or else, what they need? Or else again, should we tell them something they don't know? All three things, I believe; otherwise the play's a failure, however successful it may appear."

"You're very good at it, Sir!"

"What I do is work in layers, like a builder or a miner, so that all those coming to see my plays find something they can get their teeth into."

"And they all have fun, too. Because they identify themselves with what they see, I believe."

"That's it. Players should stage real life, which is never either tragedy or comedy, but always a bit of both. That's why I always mingle them, on stage, despite our sour critics, who would have me fall in with all their rules. They believe I don't know any rules because I didn't go to university: the thing is, 'tis they as understand neither art nor life."

"You write your plays all by yourself, don't you, Master Shakspere? I mean: don't you accept other people's advice?"

"Well, we talk about them, as thou knowst and hast seen, but the final decision is mine alone. Little by little, the others have learnt to trust me. And that's another heavy responsibility… At times there are elements we absolutely have to include, of course – and thou knowst this too – by order of the Master of Revels, or even of the King himself, who has his will made clear to us through some important man; other times, instead, we argue with one another because some of us shareholders, to give thee an example, would like a different ending. Let's take the character of *Lear*'s Cordelia: why must she die? Because death is the test of love, I say. We don't need so many words, do we? Does she really love her father to that point? 'Tis different, but 'tis similar to *Romeo and Juliet*: love till death, which death can't stop. Who wouldn't want such a love? Even Burbage, who would have saved Cordelia at all costs, finally understood this. A Spanish mystic once said that love is the measure of our ability to bear crosses. Well, death is the utmost cross and, therefore, the utmost expression of love. Isn't it?"

"Is this why people love tragedies, Sir?"

"Well, it depends. Generally speaking, people love tragedies because they love bloodshed. But, without realising it, they also like reflecting on human nature and the mystery of existence... Although the ancients were not of this mind."

"What did the ancients say?"

"They brought up something called catharsis, a process enabling us to purify our evil instincts by contemplating other people's misfortune, such as violence against the innocent and the persecution of the good. What sayst thou to this?

"I wouldn't know, Sir: I've never looked upon the matter *that* way. I love tragedies for their solemnity and because I love great speeches."

"Thou'rt right as well."

"What about you, Sir?"

"To me, 'tis still different. As I see it, tragedy is a means to give voice to the endless woe we all have inside, to our anguish and helplessness before the mystery of death, or of undeserved evil in good people's lives. It gives voice to the dumb yell of despair that may surge inside us. Tragedy is a remedy to prevent our heart from breaking, it gives us the words we wouldn't have. I give people the words they look for, dost get me?" Tim nodded. "Because, at times, our apparently dull everyday life stumbles over such tragedies one could hardly dream of. Dostn't think so?"

Tim looked at him attentively, drinking in his words. Then he spoke: "'Tis right like that, Master Shakspere."

"But I never end my plays without a glimpse of hope, however tiny it may be. Almost never, I mean, unless I'm particularly distressed. Because I believe one can never say that everything's lost. Not even in death."

"Not even in our difficult time, Sir?"

"No. We are not the be-all and end-all, Tim, and neither do we know everything. Although 'tis hard to believe it, better times will come, if not for us at least for our children and grandchildren. I'm positive about that. What we must do is act for the best and then... keep our hope high. *There's a divinity that shapes our ends...*"

Tim smiled and completed the line: "... *Rough-hew them how we will!*"

"Tragedy springs from our inability to give a meaning to sorrow. From how easily we lose hope. In such times as this, it appears clearly to me that human history is like a long agony, a long crucifixion leading to death: that's why suffering is said to be a Calvary. But that's not forever, is it? Because 'tis followed by Resurrection."

"Let's hope so, Master Shakspere. At times it seems to me as if there were no way out... But two things my playing career has taught me. One, if a bloke in the audience is not tall enough, he can't see the same things as a taller man; I'm not sure I can explain this."

Shakspere smiled. "Dost mean we're all short? All dwarfs?"

"Ay. Dwarfs who believe they are giants who have already seen and known everything. But not so!"

The playwright laughed. "And the second one?"

"The second one is that things are seldom as they appear."

"That's it. Good boy!"

"And, at times, what appears so important to us is not important at all, but when we realise it 'tis too late. And what if one's already old, maybe on's death-bed? What if one realises he's been wrong all's life, I mean, he's followed something worthless or outright wrong, thus wasting all his days like the talents in the parable?"

"I don't know, Tim: I believe we shouldn't always blame ourselves. So little depends on us, after all. And, in any case, no one can refuse action for fear of doing wrong. I try to behave according to my conscience; the rest is not in my power, unfortunately; or, rather, fortunately! I like writing plays because 'tis as if, on a smaller scale, I imitated God, creating my characters and putting them onto the little world of the stage. Since they're my creatures, I love them all, even if I know that some of them will soon commit horrible deeds. I know that even the worst of villains has his human side, an aspect for which he is to be pitied: and so must it be for real people too."

"Master Shakspere, you have predestined your characters to be heroes or murderers, to live in happiness or die young. What about us? Do you believe what our Doctors in Divinity tell us, down in London?"

"About predestination, thou meanst?"

"Ay."

"After all, Tim, I am a puppeteer and my characters are my puppets. But on the stage of the world it is up to us to choose, and God is no puppeteer. Our tragedies haven't been written in advance. A single choice, right or wrong, may change the whole world's lot: this is the beauty, and the tragedy, of being human. And this is only in apparent contradiction with what I said before, mark me."

"All the world's a stage, Sir, as our motto says, down at the Globe: *Totus mundus agit histrionem.* Have I pronounced it correctly?"

"Thou hast. And 'tis exactly like that, Tim. So much that at times I'm not sure whether 'tis the theatre that imitates life or the other way round. Dost know what I was told by my patron and friend, the Earl of Southampton, when I finally could talk to him after he was released from the Tower? That the Earl of Essex had finally decided to take action, and to start his disgraceful plot, after he'd read my *Richard II.* That's why he asked us to perform it, on the eve of the rising: because he hoped Londoners would get down to the streets and acclaim him just as they had acclaimed my Henry Bolingbroke as he went to dethrone a tyrant. Dost understand? He hoped people to identify him with my Henry the Fourth, because *he* had first identified himself with him."

"Unbelievable!"

"Dost see what a responsibility I bear on my feeble shoulders, with thousands of people coming to watch my plays every week? On the contrary, if thou thinkst of it, in real life everybody has a part to play. Is there a moment when we can say we are exclusively and completely ourselves?"

"'Tis true, Master Shakspere."

"Our time, besides, is full of formidable actors: the King playing the part of the good sovereign; secret agents ferreting everywhere and pretending they are whoever is needed, playing a different part each day... The poor Queen of Scots, who ended up losing her head because they'd pinned a plotter's part on her, and even Campion, Southwell, Garnet and the others who were mangled and slaughtered as traitors: they unwittingly played the parts of villains, which they weren't, were they? Just like poor Uncle Ned... And isn't the scaffold similar to a stage? Life's funny, Tim!"

"Ay, Sir... 'tis funny, but it doesn't make us laugh. In this, 'tis not like the theatre."

They walked silently for a while. Tim had a question burning his insides which he didn't dare spit out. Then he braced himself: "Sir, do you know how the Powder Treason really went?"

"Ah, that was a great disaster. But more of this at a later time, Tim." Shakspere sighed.

They were in sight of the first buildings. The lit-up windows of the fine Chapel Street house looked at them invitingly and told them it was time to move inside. Here and there, in the chilly air, Guy Fawkes' bonfires burnt ever more brightly against the darkening sky, which was already twinkling with the first white stars.

Jack was standing in the library, his shoulders to the big table, waiting for Milly, whom he hadn't seen since escorting her to Hatfield the previous summer. Not that they had agreed to meet; but, as he had heard from palace servants that the little Countess was back, Jack was almost sure she would call to say hallo – if only to laugh at him -, and probably ask him to resume their lessons, a she had said back then. He had kept coming here quite regularly, meanwhile, partly in order not to arouse suspicion, partly to go on with his secret research. Actually, though, he had made no new discovery. More than the library, he would have needed a secluded place where he could think calmly and put his jigsaw pieces together. But too many of them were still missing and each time, halfway through his rebuilding of the Plot, his hypotheses got invariably stranded against a huge sandy bank of absurdity.

One thing was certain: there must have been at least one traitor among the plotters. One who had probably stayed on in London with Guy Fawkes and might therefore have written that anonymous letter to Mounteagle, not really to save him from the blast but because he knew Mounteagle would run to Cecil at once. He might even have meant to ruin Mounteagle as well, had he not run to Cecil. Provided that, as Tim and he had suggested to each other, Mounteagle had not written it himself, like that bastard Edmund in King Lear's tragedy… Maybe the two of them had worked together, maybe they hadn't: who could tell? Above all, who was this mysterious traitor? One of the names that were reported in the trial transcripts? Or rather someone else, who had escaped recording? If he had served the Government so well, Cecil could as well have his name disappear from the investigation, exactly as he had done with Mounteagle's name.

That traitor, therefore, whoever he was, had first written the letter, then waited for the Government to take action; finally, as soon as Fawkes had been arrested, he had caught up with Catesby, who had left London on that same night, to tell him the explosion *had* taken place. Did Catesby know the powder was decayed? Maybe he didn't. Fawkes, anyway, couldn't have ignored it. By now, though Jack had managed to read all the papers he had found in the library concerning the Plot, he had found nothing he didn't already know: it all felt like a vast dead end, or a sort of ensnaring marsh.

He walked once again up and down the room in impatience and dissatisfaction. Maybe Milly wouldn't come. He knew that Sir Robert had introduced her to high society and, over the Christmas season, even to Court. Lately, he wondered why, he had caught himself thinking about her more often than he would have liked to admit, and his tutoring task, which he had started almost as a sort of divine punishment, had gradually become more pleasant – so much that, by now, he would be happy to start their lessons again. But, had they done so, he and Milly were sure to resume their usual skirmishes and begin again, according to their old style of tit for tat, verging on abuse.

Maybe she had changed so much as to have clean forgotten about his presence in the library, and even about his lessons: over the winter, she might have met some young courtier of undoubtedly orthodox persuasion, one who might even have spent some time in Italy. She might have read Petrarch with him; the *Canzoniere* might have become "galeotto", as Arthurian romances had been for Dante's Paolo and Francesca, causing their love to blossom. They might soon get married and set off for Italy together. Well, what did he care? Surely, though, if Milly was no longer interested in his lessons, she'd better let him know. But good manners were known not to be typical either of Milly or of her class.

As he was thus lost in his thoughts, almost resolved to go, he heard a familiar voice behind him: "Hallo, Jack." He turned and saw her walk in smilingly. She was wearing a magnificent red dress bordered at the neckline with snow-white lace, which also lined her wide puff sleeves. The jewels in her hair and ears, and the golden miniature at her neck, were certainly priceless, while her hair had been put up on top of her head, her unruly curls, now iron-tamed, delicately cascading along her neck in orderly ringlets. She looked more adult, and her clothes were certainly those of a high-born woman. She even looked taller, though she actually wasn't. She had turned a little plumper and her eyes were deeper. He went to meet her but stopped short after a couple of steps, slightly in awe. "Hallo, Milly. How art thou?"

She could have offered him her hand to kiss again, but instead looked up to him: "Hey, don't tell me thou'rt still taller! No, maybe thou'rt not, but thou'rt certainly stouter. Thou lookst fine with a beard!" Jack, who was very proud of the short thick beard he had grown in his father's honour, smiled.

"Thou lookst well too." He wanted to add why, but couldn't find anything to say at such short notice. He surely couldn't start over-praising her eyes as if she had been Laura herself. "I've heard thou'st been leading a great Lady's life, lately. Dost like it?"

She snorted: "Let's say it's been both interesting and boring."

"Hast met the Prince?"

"I have."

"And what's he like?"

"Handsome. Kind. Cultivated. Clever. Dost need more?"

"I don't. Wilt thou introduce me to him, one day?"

"Ha ha ha! Ay, just guess! I'd have to take him here surreptitiously and in disguise: that would be the only way to let him get close to the son of one who meant to kill him."

"We can start joking, if thou wantst, but one day thou'lt see…"

"What shall I see?"

"Nothing. Shall we start our lesson? Let's see what thou'st been working on in these months."

"Nope! What shall I see? Meanst thou to kill me too?"

"Don't talk nonsense: thou'lt see and that's all."

"At times thou scarest me, Digby. Pity, for thou'rt not ugly at all." She laughed. "I actually noticed this at once, when I first met thee. Dost remember?"

"How could I ever forget? There, ay, I would have strangled thee. Thou canst not even imagine what I'd just been through."

"Well, 'tis not so hard to guess… But think of what the risk had been for the King, the Queen, the Prince and all the peers of the kingdom. And for my father as well, of course. Once thou'st uncovered treason, what wouldst thou do, spare the traitors?"

Jack exploded: "Enough, Milly, with this story. The powder was decayed!"

She stared at him, her clever brown eyes transfixing him: "What meanst thou?"

"I mean that no one ever risked anything! No one apart from my father and his friends, of course."

"This can't be true!"

"I've seen the receipt with my eyes, in the Tower Armoury. Thou canst go and seek it out for thyself: 'tis there, in everybody's reach. But why am I here, telling these things to thee of all people? Now thou'lt run to thy papa and tell him that I'm investigating the Plot and that I've found out several interesting things, that is, forbidden things. But I'm fed up with keeping silent and letting myself be covered with abuse. This has been going on since I was twelve, knowst thou? And now, at last, I'm discovering something to restore my father's memory."

Milly was silent for a while. Maybe she was shocked by his loud, trembling voice, by his latent wrath, by his eyes staring into hers: Jack, who had not realised he was almost shouting, had never looked at her so directly and for so long.

"All right. Now cool down, wilt thou? No, thou knowst I won't go to my father: I never have and never will. I'll always be a mischievous, sneaky, unreliable little creature in thine eyes, clearly. But if thou seekst the truth, thou'rt doing nothing wrong."

Ay, Milly had grown up. She had become less shrewish and self-centred, more reasonable. Less cruel too, perhaps. Definitely not mischievous or sneaky. Still upset, Jack sat down at the big table and curtly said: "Thanks. Let's no longer speak about it. Can we begin, if thou pleasest?"

Her Italian had considerably improved, her intelligence always quick and lively. Above all, she was deeply interested in the subject, which, besides, had for her the typical fascination of all that's forbidden. Petrarch remained her favourite author, and by now she could read him fast and well.

"*Passa la nave mia colma d'oblio…*"

"I still fail to understand how thou canst be so taken up by these stupid sonnets, which, by the way, are exactly the same as our English poets' versions."

"Not so! Our poets only wrote vulgar imitations. Petrarch speaks about pure love, while all the others have a more or less concealed down-to-earth interest. Wyatt himself only started to write to impress the Court ladies and try to bed Anne Boleyn. Just look at the two sonnets about the white hind: look at the difference between them! Petrarch wrote praising Laura even years after she'd died. 'Tis pure love: how canst thou not understand?"

"Well, I can't. He seems to me to be endlessly whining over himself. As soon as thou canst understand it, I'll have thee read some passages from Dante: then thou'lt see the true difference."

She smirked. "The one who claims he's been to Purgatory? But please! Purgatory is only a fairy tale!"

"Knowst thou, if thou couldst remove thy prejudices even for one minute, thy company would almost be agreeable."

"I no longer ask thee to remove thine, John Digby; yet, deep down, I like thy company as it is."

Her look was strange, enigmatic. He blushed and looked down at the open book. It wasn't clear whether or not she was teasing him, as she always did. He realised that, differently from before, he liked talking to her, and would have liked to know whether it was the same for her. Quite embarrassed, he mumbled: "Ay: thou only likest my company because thou likest laughing at me." Then he sharply changed subject: "If I ever managed to find it, anyway, one day I would like to bring thee one of my favourite pages from Dante. The finest ones are from the *Inferno*. There Dante speaks to Ulysses, who, like Guido da Montefeltro, has ended up in the circle of evil counsellors and liars."

"Poor Ulysses, what a bad end! What's his sin?"

"He deceived the Trojans, for example: thou wilt know that the horse trick was his idea."

"So what? The Trojans were his enemies. As to that, he also deceived Polyphemus, who was another enemy, nay, an oppressor."

"Art thou trying to justify deception and lying, when devised against thy foes and oppressors? Maybe against persecuting tyrants."

"Not at all: I was speaking about Ulysses."

"I'm speaking about our time, instead."

"Well, here 'tis you who are the deceivers by excellence; you and your equivocating Jesuits. Masters of lies, they are."

"But poor Ulysses was to be saved, while a man who's being tortured to death for his mere faith has no right to retain a secret he doesn't want to reveal, right?"

"My tutors have taught me that lying is wrong."

"Including to one's foes?"

"Including to one's foes."

"Then Ulysses is well there where he is. But Ulysses was not defending the truth and, in the horse's case, he was attacking, not defending. And 'tis different. You powerful people can draw no distinction and put all your enemies together, apart from some exceptions which are always established by you. We, on the other hand, only try to survive without selling ourselves, without disappearing from history."

Strangely enough, though clearly not convinced, Milly didn't reply. "All right, let's go back to the poem," she said, looking down and starting to read again.

When that sonnet was over, she asked him about his home: "Hast thou heard from thy family in the country?"

"More or less. We can't write our real thoughts to each other, of course, or mention what lies closest to our hearts, for Big John reads all my letters. All I know is whether they are in health or not. But 'tis already enough, with what my father is said to have done, thinkst thou not?"

"Art thou very close to thy mother and thy siblings?"

"I am. And to our estate, Gayhurst House, Buckinghamshire. I yet didn't know, but that was the only happy moment of my life. 'Tis strange, but happiness can only be recognised with hindsight... Especially now that I'm far away and can't go back, my home almost appears to me as a garden of Eden, I'm not sure thou understandst: 'tis like that mankind must've been before the fall."

"I do understand thee. I don't even remember my mother, so young I was when she died. And, even when she was alive, I didn't see her very often... Right, everybody has their troubles, dear Jack!"

"Thou canst well say it. Wouldst like to read the next one too?"

"Ay, let's, as there's still a little time."

"Try and concentrate more on pronunciation, though: thy translation is quite good, but thy reading would split an Italian's sides with laughter!"

"How knowst thou? Thou'st never been there, Mr Perfection!"

At the end of the lesson, Milly seemed not to wish to go. "I'll see thee next Wednesday, then," she had said; but she remained standing, next to the big table, between him and the way out. Jack was afraid someone might see them, as he could already hear steps down the passageway and some distant voices, some calls among servants. Milly eventually spoke: "Listen, Jack, I'm afraid I've never thanked thee for thy lessons, and for the time thou wastest for me, and for the risks thou takest... Thanks!" She went on tiptoe, put her arms round his neck, delicately kissed his cheek and disappeared, running as usual. It all took but a second and left Jack in shock, wondering whether it had really happened or he had dreamt it.

After a wait of several weeks, the King's Men had at last had their licence renewed, just in time for the Christmas festivities, in exchange for their taking the Oath of Allegiance. They had all sworn apart from Shakspere, who was said not to have yet come back to London, recovering as he was from a serious and dangerous illness. Others said that he was already back in town but was not keen on showing himself in public. For last winter's season, in any case, he hadn't written anything new. Big John, who had just come home from his mission overseas, had also admitted that, no, the famous poet had not yet taken the Oath, but that he was expected any time at the Palace: it would probably be only a matter of days. Like many others, Jack expected for the company to stage a new Shaksperean play at least by next spring: then, maybe, he would manage to talk to him.

Today Big John had finally decided to go and watch one of the famous company's performances. Jack ardently hoped he could have a word with Tim, at the end of the play, but he wasn't even sure he could make it to the tiring house. He just wanted to say hallo to him and, even through eye contact, to know whether he had anything new to tell him; as for himself, unfortunately, he had discovered nothing of significance.

It was yet another tragedy. Not at the Globe, this time, but at the Blackfriars, the new, respectable, elegant private theatre inside the City walls. Obtained many years ago from the chapter house of the ancient convent whose name it still bore, Blackfriars was the only private theatre to be run by an adult company. Only they wouldn't see anything Shaksperean, today, but rather Benjamin Jonson's *Catiline*, a brand-new play.

"There's another rascal-poet," Big John told him as they sat comfortably on cushioned benches in the pit waiting for the theatre to fill and the performance to begin, while two elegant-liveried servants were gracefully lighting an impressive quantity of tapered candles.

"Another? What meanst thou, Big John?"

"Eh, my dear, playwrights are all rascals, some more, some less... Apart from myself, of course, mind me! And nearly all of them, sooner or later, have been in serious trouble with justice. Weren't it so, we agents wouldn't have so much to do, ha, ha, ha! Well, this one, this Jonson, is impeccable as for style: he is, so to say, my inspirational model, my master, as I've always told thee: a great classicist! In real life, however, he's been a little less spotless, and not only in his youth, when both one's hot blood and inexperience may egg one on to inconsiderate deeds. He's ended up in jail several times, both owing to his seditious plays and for common crimes; once, just imagine, even for murder!" Big John opened wide his little hazel eyes, his fat cheeks wobbling. "Think that, while in jail, he let himself be perverted to superstition; so much that on his release he preferred to pay the fines, and suffer the penal laws, rather than conform. After which, he wrote a play, *Sejanus*, which took him to prison yet again..." Jack remembered this title: it was among Sherwin's documents, which wasn't surprising at all. Big John shook his head. "Eh, I was sorry, that time, 'cause the duty to report its seditious content fell right upon me. I would've liked to make an exception for him, had I been allowed to, but, of course, I just couldn't see and keep silent, could I? Well! In the end, to make a long story short, it took the Powder Treason to make him see reason – nice rhyme, that one! – and even to cooperate: since then, Sir Robert has welcomed him under his protective wing. But one can never tell, with such a one, he he he! 'Tis always better to have a little check, like this, to make sure..."

The small refined theatre was possibly still more beautiful and lavish than the Globe. Richer, cosier, better kept. And the entrance was much more expensive, of course, which made it a place for aristocrats, automatically excluding the noisy, smelly commoners. It was also far more comfortable than the roofless popular playhouses. At first, Jack found it queer to sit in almost complete darkness, but then he realised that this helped him concentrate on the stage, lit by that expensive thicket of candles. It was good for the night scenes, which became much more realistic, though it looked a bit artificial for day scenes: exactly the opposite effect of what he was used to. The audience was all made up of respectable, composed people, and thus more inclined to appreciate details, fine poetry, long descriptive speeches, dances, musical interludes, which, performed as they were by extremely refined musicians, were much more enjoyable.

But, against all odds, the first act did not please and, soon enough, people began commenting till a widespread buzz arose. An aristocrat sitting in front of them, beside a lady in a bulky dress wearing a black gold-rimmed mask, said that this Catiline had no serious political project and this Cicero was a deadly bore. "Cut it out, Cicero!" he shouted.

"'Tis interesting to notice," remarked a man's voice from behind them, "that this Julius Caesar is among the plotters and sides with Catiline. A criminal, therefore: so, of course, Brutus acted for the best when he killed him."

Big John turned round and snapped at him: "Brutus would have restored the republic! Would you like this for your country?" The man was struck dumb, surely biting his tongue for his own imprudence.

Towards the end of Act Four, a young man sitting beside them, who was probably a student at the Inns of Court, objected to the playwright's lack of style: "They call it a tragedy, but where are its basic features? I can't find any: no reversal of fortune, no fall from on high, no self-discovery through innocent suffering, to say nothing about catharsis… I expected something better, both from Jonson and from the King's Men."

A fellow who was sitting near the centre of the pit suddenly stood up and started whistling. "I want me money back!" he shouted. Others soon followed until the noise grew deafening. After Act Five, the players thought better than coming back onstage for the final dance. It was sad to admit, but the great Burbage and his men had flopped.

"How awful!" Big John exclaimed frowning, but with a slight patronising smile on his lips.

"I'm sorry for them," said Jack. "But, indeed, it's been a bit heavy. Maybe even thou couldst have done something better, couldst thou not?" he added, elbowing him.

"What meanst thou by 'maybe'? '*Even* me'? 'Course I could have! All one needs is dramatic energy! Thou knowst, my dear, I'm afraid the disciple has outstripped the master: Jonson is a setting star, by now!" They remained seated, waiting for most people to stream out. Then Big John craned his neck towards the tiring house: "Hast seen Shakspere among the players?"

"I don't think I have, but I'm far from sure. I don't remember his face well: I've only seen him once."

"'Twould be a shame if he weren't here: I've actually come to speak to him."

"Hast thou? Therefore, thou knowst he's here."

"Ay. Let's say 'twas my little secret! I've got mine and thou'st got thine, hast thou not?"

"Right, Big John, come on, stop it: you've been rubbing it on my face every day and by now 'tis an old story. Let's go and see if he's inside, or maybe in the changing room." Jack was thrilled at the thought of seeing Shakspere again and, maybe, even speaking to him. He wondered what Big John had to tell him: nothing unpleasant, he hoped.

"Wasn't there a little boy thou knewst, once, among these players?"

"There used to be... I don't know what's become of him, I've never seen him again. They'd called him for a substitution, I believe, and they probably didn't keep him."

Once in front of the tiring house, they stood on one side of the door, waiting. A man whose thick white hair looked like a lion's mane, and who was clearly one of the eldest members of the company, asked them what their business was. In all reply, Big John somewhat solemnly handed him a rolled-up, sealed parchment he had drawn from his satchel: "'Tis for Master Shakspere. If he's not here, let him please have it as soon as possible."

Bewildered, Heminges turned the roll over in his hands. He didn't have the time to reply as Shakspere himself walked out right at that moment. Jack recognised him immediately, for he was still almost the same, despite his thinning hair and greying moustache. The dramatist looked at Big John and smiled wearily, almost imperceptibly: "Ah, Fletcher!"

"The same, Master Shakspere. 'Tis with great pleasure that I deliver this to you"

Heminges gave him the paper; Shakspere broke the seal and unrolled it, his face darkening as he read, all his colleagues gathering round him. Then he lifted tired eyes and sighed. "I'd been waiting for you awhile: so, 'tis you"

"I've been overseas for work, Master Shakspere; but now here I am, ready to help and support you in your difficult mature years, when you are beginning to feel the weight of so much work."

"Well said, Fletcher, well said."

The King's men looked at them in silent expectation, both miserable for *Catiline*'s fiasco and worried about this over elegant, over self-assured, over smiling newcomer. Jack spotted Tim, behind everybody else, and motioned for him to make himself scarce lest Big John might recognise him.

Shakspere spoke out loud: "Boys, let me introduce you all to my new co-worker, Master John Fletcher, poet and dramatist, who graduated at Cambridge with distinction!" This was declared by the official document bearing the King's Privy Seal, which Shakspere showed everyone.

Jack felt all the tension of that moment, together with the ill-concealed irritation of the players, who had been waiting for this inevitable event in anguish and dark foreboding. He experienced the unpleasant feeling of not being wanted, as if he were Fletcher's lackey. Even Tim's face, behind Burbage's shoulders, was as blank as a wax statue: now more than ever, they belonged to two opposing fields.

The good side of it all was that, from now on, Jack could see the King's Men almost every day. He didn't feel welcome, of course, but for the time being he didn't much care. Shakspere, who maybe didn't want to let Fletcher into his private lodgings, had started to work in a small upper room at the Globe, alongside the lodge hosting the musicians during performances: there the two poets would write four-handedly the great historical cycle commissioned by Cecil.

Jack acted as a sort of page to Big John. Besides serving him, he had the task of befriending the players, which Big John didn't care to do, and report each and every suspicious statement he heard; which was perfectly clear to everybody, so that they all avoided him. More than once he tried to find himself alone with Tim; his player friend, however, and rather understandingly, behaved exactly like his colleagues. He probably didn't want them to learn about their friendship, just as Jack didn't want Big John to do.

Jack was waiting for Milly. He felt even more lonely, now that Tim too seemed to shun him, so that their Italian lesson often turned out to be the most interesting, heart-warming moment in the whole week. "There: I've reached an all time low," he said to himself.

While waiting, a new thought dawned on him: if Milly didn't come, he would be disappointed. Why? Ay, she was awfully spoilt and full of herself, but, on the other hand, she was also clever and, when she chose so, nice to be with. It wasn't her fault, after all, if she had always had everything she could wish for and if she had been filled with lies and conceit ever since she was a baby in arms. Could their relationship be considered as a sort of friendship? His heart said so, but his mind told him that Milly was always Sir Robert's daughter. Anyway, he had understood, by now, that their bantering would always stay between the two of them. All in all, she seemed honest: she had proven this several times, and it was probably true that the idea of informing agains him repulsed her. Or, maybe, she simply knew that if she reported him they would no longer be able to meet and she would get too bored; not to mention that she would have to justify their being well acquainted and meeting regularly, which Sir Robert utterly ignored. Keeping silent, by now, was convenient for both.

It was amusing, in a certain sense: the man who managed the most efficient secret services in the world hadn't noticed what was going on under his very own roof, right under his nose… That was, Jack hoped he hadn't. What if, instead, Sir Robert had always known about the clandestine lessons he had been giving his daughter and was only waiting for the right moment to jump on him and have him jailed? But no, what nonsense: would he be arrested for reading Petrarch? He then wondered what Sir Everard would think, if he could see his first born pleasantly chatting, and at times even joking – besides quarrelling – with the daughter of the man who had sent him to the scaffold. He looked up, at the vaulted ceiling, as if trying to see whether his father were looking at him from Heaven. "Please, lead me on, father!" he thought.

And what did that unexpected kiss mean? Was Milly flirting with him, now she was a regular guest at Court and had learnt their manners? Or might she really be grateful to him for his pains?

At last he heard the light rustle of a dress and Milly walked in almost noiselessly. "Hallo, Jack," she simply said this time too, but smiling sadly, her eyes lowered.

"Hallo," he said. It was as if that big, dark, mazy place had suddenly been flooded with light. But why didn't she smile more openly, more cheerfully, like last time? Why didn't she look him in the eye? Maybe she was beginning to find her studies too hard... Should he lighten her homework, so as to make those hours more agreeable? Or rather, might it be that she had grown tired of his lessons, now she was part of high society and was certainly revered by the most handsome, wealthy, interesting young men of the kingdom? Was she running out of time for that little stolen space? Did she think she had already learnt enough, so she didn't need him any longer and today had come to say "I regret so much to tell thee that..."?

He looked at her. Her hair was loose, this time, only held back by one tiny ribbon. She was wearing a splendid pink silken dress, the bodice all covered in precious embroidery interwoven with pearls, a soft white woollen shawl over her shoulders. Jack tried not to look, under the shawl, at her low neckline. They sat down one beside the other. Milly sighed and started to read. After half a stanza, while reading the line *con sospir mi rimembra*, she stopped and sighed again.

"What's up?"

"Nothing... Thou canst not understand. Let's go on with this *canzone*, which I really like. I'll start again: *Chiare, fresche, dolci acque...*"

"Thou'rt right: I still don't understand what thou findst so special in love poetry. But 'tis only natural, thou'rt a woman... What else shouldst think of?"

"Thou'st never asked thyself that, hast thou?"

"Not really."

"Because, apart from the fact that we've got more things on our minds than you men can dream of, you are not interested in love. We can only think of silly things, and love is one of them, isn't it? Because, to you, choosing a woman is like choosing a pair of pantofles. Because you can well marry one woman while loving another."

"Well, you are also well versed in this: just look at Sidney's beloved, worshipped 'Stella'!"

"That's not for me: I couldn't. I know it never happens, but the man I wish to marry will write love poems for me and will only think of me all through his life. And I would only think of him."

"Write poems to thee? Ridiculous!"

"No, 'tis not ridiculous at all: 'tis sad! Because I know all too well that my father's pondering who to marry me off to. And my opinion will only be a matter of formality. Because he's already told me that making marriage a matter of feeling is a most grievous mistake. That may be the reason why he's never wanted me to read love poems... So that I wouldn't think I lived in fairy tales. I don't know why I've told thee all this: now thou'lt laugh at me, I know."

"Why should I? 'Tis not *my* habit to laugh at other people's woes."

She chose not to rise to the challenge. "Because these may sound like women's trifles to thee. But I don't want to be an old courtier's bride in order to please my father. Just look at that poor girl who's married my revolting cousin Bacon. I thought she was satisfied with it, with the prestige, the money and so on, and I despised her in my heart. Then the other day, at a ball, we had the chance to talk awhile and I got to know her better. She's a poor frightened child, Jack, who knew not what she was doing. In love my foot! Bacon might well be her grandfather, dost understand? And now she's desperate. Disgusting! She didn't tell me so, of course, but I know that her only hope is for him do die soon and leave her a happy widow."

"'Tis not always like that, Milly: my parents got married for love. Even if, unfortunately, they weren't together for long."

"Well, rest assured: this is not the way it works at Court. And anyway, my father being who he is, I can never hope to choose a husband for myself! He's already done this with my brother William, who's been married three years already, even if he's never here, he's always away. But he's different from me: he simply asked papa to choose well among several candidates. His only request was for his wife to be pretty and not very shrewish: for the rest, he left him carte blanche."

"Really! I didn't know Sir Robert's heir was already married. Who is he married to?"

"Katherine Howard, Suffolk's daughter, who's only older than him by three years. It could've been far worse, couldn't it?"

Jack was startled but said nothing: so, Sir Robert had married his only son to his own mistress' daughter. But Milly was unlikely to know... Or did she? Hadn't she been so miserable, he could have tried to tease her about it, but now he could really say nothing.

Milly went on: "And then, just last night, papa told me cryptically that something will soon materialise for me too. He probably even expected me to be overjoyed... But I don't want an elderly husband! And neither do I want a youth whom I don't care a straw about."

"Hast thou not the least idea who he's chosen?"

"I haven't."

"Just mention to thy papa, then, that, whoever he is, thou wantst him not: tramp thy feet, whimper a little and thou'lt see that, as has always happened, he'll do as thou wishest."

"Ay, just imagine... Thou clearly knowst him not in the least: thou'st not yet had occasion to cross him. He simply does not contemplate disobedience. At most, he can let me choose among two or three of his candidates. But those I know are all disgusting to me! And, in any case, I didn't say no. I didn't say anything at all: I lowered my eyes, as I always do, and was silent. He took it as a yes, of course."

Milly covered her eyes with her hands and sat still, her elbows on the table, her little many-ringed fingers half concealed by the lace round her sleeves. Jack didn't know what to do. It was so unusual to see her in distress, and still more so to imagine her, always so sharp-tongued, being silent and submissive before her father.

He brought his face closer to hers. "Hey!" he whispered, delicately drawing a lock of dark curls away from her face and hands. "I thought thou wert stronger!" She didn't move and the curls fell back where they had been. To console her, then, without much realising what he was doing, Jack hugged her. Strangely enough, instead of boxing his ears and calling the guards, she hugged him back. They remained silent for some seconds, embracing, sitting one next to the other. Jack was surprised to find that she had melted into a flood of slow, silent tears.

"If I could... I'd take thee away from this world full of sham and hypocrisy," he then said, his own words sounding funny, as if uttered by someone else; but he realised that it was exactly what he meant. "I wish I could prevent this, Milly! But thou knowst well that thy father's got my life too in his hands. We're like checkers on a chessboard, and of different colours at that, which can but fight and devour each other. Thou knowst, he also told me that he's going to arrange an important marriage for me, since I'm totally broke, so that, if I behave, I can hope for a career at Court. But, exactly like thee, I don't want any of this."

The unhappiness surrounding them slowly ebbed like a tide all round the tiny rock which was that brief instant of happiness. They kept silent, still embracing, desperately clinging to that rock so as not to be overwhelmed by the waters, Jack's nostrils filled with the flowery scent from Milly's hair. She rubbed her face on his chest and said: "Thou'rt a filthy superstitious Papist, Jack, but 'tis thee I like!" It was a bolt out of the blue.

"Milly, 'tis impossible! Thou'rt mad!" He lifted her chin and looked into her eyes. "And then, look, I'll never write thee a sonnet!" She laughed in her tears. Jack went on: "At most, if Dantesque tercets are enough for thee…"

"In Italian?"

"Maybe. But only if thou promisest never to call me a filthy Papist again."

"And wouldst thou take me to Italy, if thou couldst?"

"Of course I would. Starting from Venice, so thou wouldst stop saying 'tis more or less like London!"

"Deal, then!" She smiled feebly, wiping her face with one hand. She kept looking at him.

Jack took her face into both his hands and shyly kissed her brow, then her cheek, then her lips.

Only then did he realise he was head over heels in love. With the only woman in the world he was absolutely certain he could never have.

The King's Men were taking advantage of this sunny feast day to tidy things up, no matter what the usual fanatics might say about Sunday rest. They had all rolled up their sleeves and were now going to and fro with buckets, brooms, little pots of paint to fix the spots where the colour was peeling off. Jack was hanging about the main stage, bored to death. Suddenly, he saw them cluster and whisper all together. That was quite a lively whisper, however. He thought he grasped some references to one of Speed's latest work, one of those Jack had helped revise: the ambitious *History of Great Britaine from Julius Caesar to King James.* He got closer in order to tell them that he had also had a part, however small, in that work: so that, maybe, they would start to accept him a little. But, as soon as he reached them, silence fell and, after some embarrassingly silent seconds, they changed their subject, some of them even turning their backs on him and stepping away. Jack felt frustrated and misunderstood and had yet another proof that, in there, he was not the son of a man who had given his life for a cause, but rather a spy's henchman. Determined to leave, whether or not Big John, from his office up there, might need him, he walked towards the gate. There he came across Tim, who was carrying a great heap of costumes down to the river to have them washed. But even Tim pretended not to see him and went his way.

"Rice!" he called. "What thinkst thou, that I've sold meself? What have I done to thee?"

"Nothin', Digby," Tim replied without stopping. "Thou'st only come along with a bragging, spying scribbler to encroach on a place where people are earning an honest living, to watch'em and threaten to report'em. But don't worry, there's no problem, go on with it!"

"Stop it, Tim! Thou knowst I've got no choice." Jack started to walk behind him.

"What I know is thy old tale, but it wasn't thee as invented it: 'tis typical of those like thee."

"I've never ever betrayed anyone, Tim."

"Well, then thou knowst not thy trade."

"I've done nothing wrong to thee. Thou'st no right to speak to me like this. And then, 'tis *not* my trade!"

"'Course it is! Thou'st not betrayed anyone, thou sayst: ay, we may be the first."

"What must I do to convince thee I'm not a traitor?"

"Ditch Fletcher."

"I can't."

"Then, sorry, 'tis all over between us. Thou canst not hang round with both. Now, then, after what has happened…"

"What?"

Tim threw the heap of dirty garments onto a stone bench on one side of the road and looked at him in fury. "A good spy, ain't thou, to miss the great news of the day. Even rocks and stones know what Speed's written in his history: the roof tiles are shouting it. Thou'st worked with him too, hast thou not? I'm beginning to realise who thou art, John Digby!"

Jack was stunned. "I have no idea what thou'rt talking about."

"He's written that Shakspere is the Papists' poet. Worse, the Jesuits' poet. Worse still, Persons' poet, who is now as dead as a doornail and can't deny it. 'Tis put down in black and white, understandst? We're deep in the muck, Digby, and don't tell me thou didn'tst know."

"I swear, Tim, I've only learnt about this now from thee. But 'tis all useless, for thou won't believe me."

Tim was calmer, now he had spilled the beans. He bent over the costumes, picked them up again and started walking downhill towards the river.

"Why on earth should I believe thee, Digby? And, then, even though thou hastn't wronged us so far, why shouldst thou not do so now, if thou wert asked? Why not perjure thyself, why not report seditious matters, why not ruin a troupe of jugglers, should the Gov'ment offer thee some great advantage, such as complete rehabilitation, a good deal of money, a plot of land, or permission to go home forever?"

"Because I'm a man of honour, Tim. And also because I thought thou wert my friend."

"Brutus was a man of honour too, and one who deeply loved Caesar. But, as he loved Rome more, he slew him."

"Thou'rt disgusting, Rice!"

"Look at thysel', thou stinker!"

Maddened with rage, Jack turned his back on him and walked off
without a word. That filthy commoner: he was just a filthy commoner
who had no idea what a gentleman was, what honour was. He could
have run him through with his rapier like a chicken, and no-one would
have objected in the least, because he was only a plebeian who had
wounded his honour. Never again would he go back to the Globe,
nor uselessly try to get information out of Shakspere, whom, in any
case, he had not yet managed to meet one-on-one. And neither did
he want to go on living with Big John. Wherever he went, he was
always a fish out of water. A Government agent to the players, a
Papist traitor's son to Big John, a piece on a chessboard to Cecil, an
obscure time-server to all of them. To hell with them all! He'd had
enough of it. He no longer cared about getting back a part of Sir
Everard's goods. He didn't want a career at Court, he didn't want a
good marriage, he didn't want anything from anyone, and no one
must ask him for anything.

He wanted to leave London for good: he didn't really believe Cecil
would bother to look for him, or to go to Gayhurst and hurt his
family, with all that he had on his mind. A man-hunt cost money and
had to be really worthwhile. One could never tell, though... it would
be a risk regardless. Above all, how could he leave Milly right now?
The idea of not seeing her anymore tore his heart, now he had so
many things to tell her, now he would have liked to see her every day.

Once again, his life looked to him like a dead-end street. It was like
being caught in a fishing net with no hope of flight. He would ask
Milly to flee to Gayhurst with him, then. "Fool!", he said to himself
at once. "You, a traitor's son, kidnapping Sir Robert's daughter and
taking her home with you? You'd get caught in a wink, and there'd be
enough to send your whole family to the scaffold".

What was to be done, then? Flee overseas, as Sherwin had done?
And the money? And what would they live on, once on the Continent,
even admitting Milly *were* willing to leave everything behind to follow
him? What could he offer her, besides a life of poverty, when she had
only known wealth and luxury all along? And what a queer paradox,
as one of Shakspeare's characters had said, for his only love to have
sprung from his only hate, the man who had ruined his family. He felt
guilty towards his loved ones, because the blood of the worst
persecutors of his people ran in Milly's veins: would he really manage

to love her? Anyway, the problem was non-existent, for a future with Milly would be utterly impossible and, nay, if he left Cecil he could never again go near her. He had been a worthless good-for-nothing in this too.

As for Tim, he didn't want to see him ever again. Never again would he go back to the Globe. It was true that fear could drive people mad; but he should never have turned on him like that. This meant that their friendship had always been on his part only, and Tim had never held him as a true friend. He bitterly shook his head and tried not to think about it. So, Tim wanted him to dump Fletcher in exchange for his friendship: very well, he would! But, after he had abused him so grievously, he would never speak to him again. He would throw himself into restoring his father's good name, instead. His only thought would be about the Plot, now, and about Prince Harry. He would write down what he knew and personally lay it at the Prince's feet, even should this be the very last thing he did.

In the end, then, he headed back to Little East Cheap, which was still the most reasonable thing to do. He sent Wat to the Globe to tell Master Fletcher he was unwell. Then, he slightly lifted one of the floor boards and pulled out a crumpled piece of paper: the plan of the work he meant to write. He sat down at the little writing desk, took out a sheet of good Flemish paper and, right in the middle, he wrote the title: *A True and Perfect Relation of the so-called Powder Treason*. He left some blank space to add a detailed subtitle and started to write an introduction, beginning from the implausibility of the Government version. Once that first urge had run out, in which he didn't blot one word, he stopped to tidy up his thoughts. He took another sheet where he listed the topics he would write about: Fawkes' absurd, persistent presence in the "cellar", the decayed powder, the fake news Catesby had brought to the Dunchurch gentlemen, the close relationship with the Essex conspiracy, Mounteagle's ambiguous role, the Jesuits' innocence and so on. This mere planning took up several hours and a lot of energy. He soon filled five sheets of very thickly written notes and dates. In order to go on, he would need to go back to the Salisbury House library: it had to be an absolutely rigorous research. He folded the papers and provisionally put them back under the floor board. He would continue his narration with fresh data in his hands and, if ever he managed that, after speaking to Shakspere, despite Tim's prohibition. Nay, he would try to approach the great playwright just to spite his former friend! He asked the servant for something to eat, then lay down on his bed, waiting for Big John to come back, as he usually did, for lunch.

He obviously had to find a perfect hiding place for the dangerous libel he had started. Where? The hollow space under the board wouldn't do: should Big John find it, he could never deny his authorship. Even less could he keep it under his garments, for, in case he were searched, it would be enough to send him directly to the block. That's where: in the place where no one would think of looking and, even if they found it, no one could ever prove it was his. It would be like a needle in a haystack, inside a book out of everybody's reach in Cecil's huge library. He would take the papers there tomorrow. Perhaps he'd better stay with Big John until he completed the first draft, but not one minute longer. Meanwhile, he would work out a plan to escape. As for Milly, there was no point in deluding himself: she was not for him, and they both knew it.

Big John didn't take long: Jack soon heard his heavy steps on the wooden staircase. It wasn't the smug smile that he greeted him with that showed he was exceedingly satisfied with himself: that was his usual style. It was rather the way he asked Jack how he was, and then the lively, gleeful manner in which he poured himself a drink and took off his boots.

"Well, how art thou feeling now?" he asked him again, peering into his satchel, then accurately buckling it and laying it carefully on the bed next to him, instead of throwing it into a corner as he always did.

"All right, Big John, I only had a headache. And then…"

"Then what, little one?"

"And then they had all got it with me because of what Speed's written about Shaskpere. Just imagine! And, 'Zounds, once and for all, wilt thou stop calling me 'little one'?"

Big John laughed out loud. "Ha ha ha! Right! But thou wert not really thinking of making thyself agreeable to them, wert thou? Because, were it so, thou findst thyself in the wrong boat, shouldst've known that! But what carest thou 'bout'em? What carest thou about all the losers of the earth? We're there for another reason, ain't we?

By the way, didst thou not get any interesting information? Any comments? Or exclamations?"

"Far from it: as soon as they see me coming, they seal their mouths. That's also why I've got back home. Only for this, to be more precise. I don't give a damn for them all!"

"Art sure, Little John? Not even for their poet?"

"Nay. I admire him because he's good, but I don't even know him. He's always up there, working with thee... He's never talked to me, not even once. What about thee? Now thou knowst him better, dostn't thou admire him, at least a little?"

Big John went serious. "Of course he's very good, even if he lacks discipline, as I've always told thee. I'm there to help him, and maybe even to save him."

"From what? Or from whom?"

"From himself, Little John. But he doesn't seem to realise this." He quickly, almost unwittingly cast a sidelong glance at his satchel. "We've put our hands to the historical play he's apparently unable to write: it's doing quite well, modestly speaking, thanks to me!"

"Anyway, I'm fed up with this life, Big John. Can I take the afternoon off? I just want to have a walk and think and unburden my mind: tomorrow, everything may appear to me under a different light."

"Ay, take it. Anyway, I'm not getting back to the Globe either, this afternoon." Big John winked at him and pointed up with his thumb. "Been summoned up above!"

"Remember to speak well about me."

"Dost doubt it, my friend? Thy loyalty's quite clear, by now... Apart when thou givest in to sentimentality."

"Well, they're human beings as we are, after all, thinkst thou not? Isn't it fair to feel some pity even for traitors, even for one who's hanging from the gallows?"

"Ay, little one (ehm, sorry, that was habit, ha ha!), but in the just measure. And then, of course, 'tis always a matter of hierarchy, that is, of priority: what comes first, in thy heart?"

Jack didn't answer but only smiled idiotically and mumbled an "Ay!"

Big John didn't have much time for him: after eating hastily the cold meat that Dave brought him, he pulled his boots back on, grabbed his satchel and hurried off, full of self importance. He would be out for the whole afternoon. Jack was happy of this. Shortly afterwards he was in the street too, breathing deep at that little whiff of freedom.

He didn't head towards the river, and neither towards the bridge. He walked in the opposite direction, instead, towards Cripplegate, hoping to meet someone who, exactly like him, had taken advantage of Big John's afternoon absence to have some time by himself. He went through various lanes, slightly uphill, to Lombard Street and to the little square where the pillory was, which today was fortunately empty. He remembered that once, as a child, he had seen a man there, whose ears had been nailed to the wood for speaking ill of the old Queen; the poor wretch could free himself, but only by pulling hard and reducing his ears to rags, while people kept throwing rubbish at his face: rotten eggs, mouldy fruits, steak bones and other leavings. He shuddered at the thought. He walked past the Haberdasher's Guildhall and found himself in Cheapside, the elegantly paved street all lined with poplars, in the middle of which, regularly distanced, were three marvellous gilt brass fountains. On his right, the ancient little church of St Mary le Bow struck two. He turned right in Wood Street, then left in Silver Street. He knocked on a fine, newly painted door. The housemaid who opened it looked as if she had been washed, ironed and starched. The house belonged to a Huguenot who made wigs and headgear, and a smell of fresh lavender came from inside.

"Is Master Shakspere at home?"

"Non, Monsieur. Oo's asking for 'im?"

"Tim Rice," said Jack unflinchingly.

"Vill you vait a minut, I'll go and see if 'e's back."

Jack was shortly invited to come in. He went up narrow stairs whose carven wood railing ran beside flowery tapestry. He saw an open door; he stepped across its threshold and found himself in a large, well-lit room, which had clearly been tastefully furnished by a landlady. Right now, however, it was in a total mess. Its lodger wasn't at the best of his looks either, for he was walking to and fro, barefooted and ruffled, his shirt unbuttoned, as one who found no peace. He suddenly started to fumble inside a trunk, not bothering to turn round on hearing Jack's approaching steps.

"I'd told thee to leave me alone, Tim. What's up, now?"

He turned and froze in horror to see it was not Tim. His face whitened. "What wantst thou?" he asked, almost calmly. "Is't thou'st taken it?"

"It isn't, Master Shakspere, whatever you're talking about. Please, forgive me for using Tim's name, but I must urgently speak to you. No one must know I'm here."

"Maybe some other time, Digby, if thou dostn't mind: I'm very busy right now and I don't feel well. Hast got a message from Fletcher?"

"I'll never work for Fletcher again, and neither for Cecil, Sir. I know you don't believe me, but I'm here on my own accord. You don't have to be afraid."

"I'm no longer afraid of anything, by now: I no longer have anything to fear. All is lost and I'm undone. I'm not sure whether it's been Fletcher or rather thee, but in the end it doesn't matter: I should have expected this, sooner or later. The damned fool I've been!"

"What are you talking about, Sir?"

"About a certain original script of a certain play: when I got back, not long ago, the room was like this and the manuscript was gone."

"A dangerous text?"

"Ay, of course. If I leave London now, thou'lt run to report me, wilt thou not?"

"I won't, Master Shakspere. I swear it on my mother. I beg you, trust me. Do so for my father, for his wounded name, for what can ever have bound you to him. Hasn't Tim told you about our friendship?"

"Tim's a babe in the woods. What did he tell thee about me?"

"Nothing, Master Shakspere. Not a word. And he perfectly knows what he's doing. He is far more attached to you than he is... than he was... to me. He loves you more than he loves himself. He's always stopped me from talking to you, because he was afraid for you. But now our friendship is forever broken, since he's accused me of something I've never done and never will. He says I've blabbered things to Speed, but I haven't! It hasn't always been easy for me to understand what to do: but then, I was but twelve when ... Be it as it may, Master Shakspere, you know that I never chose to work for Fletcher. Now I'm going to leave London for good, just like you, but

I must speak to you before I go. That is, I'd like you to tell me about my father and the mystery of the Powder Plot."

"Ay, that's surely all I need to end up straight on the gallows. Really, Digby, I couldn't, even if I didn't have Government agents on my back, even if I didn't fear being arrested every other minute. At most, thou canst help me tidy up just a bit in order not to raise suspicion. Then I'll pack my bags and go, if thou'rt so good as not to tell Fletcher."

"Believe me, Master Shakspere, I will never go back to him. Nor will I serve Cecil any longer. Now, please, tell me which text he has taken."

"*Macbeth.*"

"The lost play?!"

"Ay, that one."

"The one you said you had destroyed?"

"Ay, that one. I had it nicked from under my nose like a child. I thought I had hidden it well, but... Now all I would like to do is destroy it."

Only then did Jack realise what had been in Big John's satchel at lunch. The mysterious text, which so many people wanted to read for different reasons, had been in his own lodging, if only for half an hour, in his reach, and he hadn't dreamt of it.

"All you can do now is trust me, Master Shakspere. If it's really been taken by Fletcher, I'm the only one who can try and find where he's taken it. I'll do all I can to bring it back to you... In exchange for less than an hour of your time."

The dramatist looked at him awhile, as if trying to read his thoughts. Jack looked back earnestly, without lowering his eyes. In the end, Shakspere said: "Thou knowst, Digby, that secret agents may play double, triple and even quadruple, dost thou not? But of course thou'rt too young... I have no choice, Digby: done! But we must hurry. Let's go away from here, where they may come for me any minute."

They tidied up a bit, Shakspere packed a few things and they went out, heading for the *Mermaid*. The playwright knocked five times at special intervals on a little back door: Bill Thomson let them in without a word and led them to a little subterranean room which they found after descending a staircase, behind the cellar, among huge wine and beer barrels. Shakspere bolted the door, lit a lamp and sat down on a tiny stool at a little round table cut out from a barrel bottom. In the half darkness of the place, everything smelt of mould and wine must. He clearly trusted Jack, or he would never have taken him to that secret hiding place. Shakspere seemed to read his mind, because he said at once: "Don't be surprised, Digby: not that they don't know about this little room, after all their incursions. 'Tis only in order for us to buy some more time, for hence there's another way out and Bill will let me know as soon as he notices anything unusual. Now sit down and tell me."

"I don't know where to begin, Master Shakspere. Ever since I was a boy, I would've liked to speak to you, and ask you how come in your plays those who are accused of treason and banished are always good and unjustly blamed."

"Ay: how come?" A faint smile appeared on the dramatist's weary face. "Since thou'rt asking, it means thou already knowst."

"'Tis because you don't hold them to be evil who fight against a tyrannical authority, I guess. Now, I'm trying to understand what the Gunpowder Plot has really been, Master Shakspere. I want to write a libel telling the whole truth: all the world must know! If someone is guilty of betraying my father, and of accusing him of something he didn't do, I want them to pay."

"Thou wantst too much, boy. Thou'rt an idealist, just like thy father." He looked ever more hopeless, and wearier.

"Tell me about him."

"Oh, he was quite ingenuous, and he had a heart of gold. Even if he was often at Court, and saw many things there, he stuck to the belief that there's some good in everyone and that the Government persecutes Papist so grievously only because they don't know them thoroughly. So much that he had made many friends there, and even enjoyed the King's favour."

"Which displeased somebody, didn't it?"

"Of course. The game at Court is always the same: back-stabbing whoever might become a favourite and covering thy shoulders from other people's daggers. And, besides being a nice man, thy father was also good-looking: exactly what the King likes."

"What was his relationship with the other plotters?"

"He was close friends with Catesby, Tresham and the other Warwickshire gentlemen. I knew them well, for I'm from those parts myself. Just imagine: with Catesby and Tresham I'm even connected by blood. But they were all as if – afraid of Percy; maybe because they didn't know him so well, maybe because, differently from Catesby, who was always with his friends drinking, Percy was silent and mysterious, never wasted words, never laughed. Of course, he looked like one who knows what he's doing. Thou knowst that thy father was part of the Gentlemen Pensioners, just like him, and, even if he was superior to him by birth, he was his inferior by rank."

"I know. Percy worked for great Henry Percy, Earl of Northumberland, didn't he?"

"He did. As Captain of the Gentlemen Pensioners, the Earl had admitted both Percy and thy father. Thomas Percy said he was a poor relation of the Wizard Earl, but no one knows whether or not 'tis true. A very curious incident is that, just before the Plot was uncovered, Percy openly went to seek the Earl, and not once but twice, in two of his London houses, Syon and Essex House."

"I've seen it in the official documents: this was enough to frame Northumberland, the great Nortern magnate."

"Ay. They've apparently spared his life, so far, but he's not going to get out of the Tower alive, thou knowst this too. Exactly like his father, who was killed off in his cell. And knowst thou how much he was fined by? Thirty thousand pounds!"

"As if Percy had involved him on purpose... Why? To eliminate a powerful faction..."

"A powerful faction with wrong beliefs. There's no doubt that Percy meant to frame the Earl, with all the good he'd done to him. Because, for one thing, on the eve of the explosion he didn't warn him about the imminent danger and didn't tell him not to attend Parliament on the fifth of November."

"And what about my father? What did he know about the Plot?"

"Nothing. He thought he had to gather men and horse, weapons and ammunition to help his friends leave for Flanders, where they would form a brand-new mercenary force."

"There: I knew this! But why did they have to prepare all this in secret?"

"Because in theory our Government is neutral, but in practice they don't want English subjects to fight for the hated Spaniards against the Flemish Protestant rebels, whom England has been supporting for forty years. Before the 1604 peace, those fighting for Spain were guilty of high treason; now they no longer are, of course, but it is no secret that Cecil is still trying to prevent it."

"And Guy Fawkes?"

"He too believed he was guarding the powder for the Flemish expedition. That's why, when they arrested him, he didn't put up any fight and even slept soundly, on his first night in the Tower: he thought that, after a short questioning, he'd be released. After all, even if he had acted in secret and had used a pseudonym, he'd done nothing illegal. At most, had they discovered his real name, they could detain him shortly for fighting against the English before the peace treaty was signed... Instead, they almost tortured him to death and forced him to sign ignominious, utterly false declarations."

Lo and behold who notorious Guy Fawkes actually was: neither a hero, as Sherwin believed, nor a traitor or a fierce beast, as everybody else believed. He was simply a poor man who had happened to be in the wrong place at the wrong time. Jack gulped. Then he raised his eyes to meet the dramatist's. "Master Shakspere, did you know that the powder was decayed?"

The playwright looked at him in surprise. "No." He was silent. "Art sure?"

"I've seen the original receipt, in the Tower Armoury."

"Powder that could never go off?"

"Exactly. And Guy Fawkes can't have ignored this."

"He can't have."

"If Percy knew this too, that may be the reason why he never warned Northumberland: because he knew there would be no blast. Now, I beg you, help me reconstruct the whole matter. I've been talking about it to Tim Rice too, who, as you know, is... was... helping me understand. So: at Dunchurch, my father is preparing the weapons to embark new troops. While they are all together, there come Catesby and Percy, directly from London, shouting that the King's dead and the whole country's up in arms, and people want to slay all Papists, and they've got to flee in haste. Therefore, seized by panic, they take to horse and run... at random, foolishly, to save their skins. But taking arms without the King's warrant means levying war against him – in other words, high treason: this was the crime my father and his friends actually committed."

"Clever boy! If, on the other hand, as Catesby had said, the King is dead and so is the Prince, the country is most likely on the verge of civil war and everything becomes licit. But not only did thy father and the others ride through the country in arms: they also stole more horses for their flight and, were this not enough, even plundered Hewell Grange, adding common theft to that treason they knew nothing about."

"This is why, and I've heard this with my ears, my father publicly admitted he'd broken the law. But, now I think of it, he also said that his conscience had nothing to reproach him with. Everything's clear now!"

"Ay. But thou sayst they were fleeing at random, seeking support here and there: not so, Digby."

"That is?"

"They took the direction that their leaders had given them."

"Catesby and Percy?"

"Ay."

"But what exactly was their game? They can't have known 'twas all a fake. Who'd told them that the King had died? Was there a spy among them?"

"There was no one else, Digby. 'Tis the two of 'em as deceived all the others, leading them round the country like lambs to the slaughter."

"But... D'you mean that, at the Dunchurch inn, Catesby lied to them knowing he was lying? Did he betray all his friends just to go and get himself riddled with bullets like a quail? Why on earth? This makes no sense at all!"

"We are not all the same, Digby. And I assure thee, besides, that some means of persuasion never fail, even without resorting to torture. They could bring thee to betray thine own mother. That's why Tim Rice is afraid to trust thee."

"So, were Catesby and Percy agents provocateurs?"

"They had been "turned" into agents in the wake of the Essex conspiracy, when they'd had to buy back their freedom and their lives. Although, I believe, neither of them knew exactly what the other knew and which orders he followed. They worked together, but were no friends. Above all, they feared each other, as each was afraid that the other had orders to kill him. And, who knows, it might well've been so."

"But they died together, fighting back to back at Holbeach."

"Not back to back, really, and not even shoulder to shoulder: Catesby had been shielding himself, clutching Percy from behind, a dagger at his throat: most likely, he feared that Percy was the one to be spared. It was a fight to the death between them too. I know this for certain, since one of the sheriff's men besieging Holbeach is one of my cousin's in-laws, up there in Worcestershire."

"Therefore, 'twas one of them who set fire to the powder that had been spread before the fire: for *that* blast must have been intentional, Master Shakspere: damp powder that has been spread out will never go off."

"Maybe. Between the two, I'll bet it was Percy."

"But *what* was it, in the end? A suicide mission? Or did each of them really believe he could get away with it, once the other had been killed off?"

"It may have been in the deal. On their part, the Plot was the last resort they had to be spared from death. Knowst thou that, if one has done good service, he may be pardoned even with a noose round's neck? I remember several such cases, the latest one right at the beginning of His Majesty's reign."

"What they got, instead, was that they shut their mouths forever."

"Of course. Foolish of them, not to have realised this earlier."

"Because, to kill two with one bullet, one must aim very well, mustn't he? It can never be a coincidence..."

"All too well. In fact, they were *not* killed with one bullet, but with two bullets shot by the same musket."

"Weren't they! The one who shot had been ordered to bring them both down!"

"As to the gunfight, its only purpose was obviously to eliminate the two of them. Once the sheriff's men had surrounded Holbeach, it would've been enough to wait: there was no need for him to waste powder and ammunition, or to risk his men's lives, since they had put up no resistance from the inside, so few of them had been left."

Jack closed his eyes. The whole matter appeared to him now as it had been since the very beginning: a huge, great frame-up. A complex machination, a perfect mechanism to definitely destroy all the Papists of Britain. A trap carefully prepared which, on springing, had swept away in one blow all potential sedition, all concealed dissidence, both political and religious. Now, the Jesuits and all Papists were universally hated: now, thanks to the Gunpowder Treason, they had become, and would always be, a tiny, guilty, frightened minority.

Shakspere went on: "The bonfires that are lit every year mark the relentless hatred they are continually stirring up. And, thou'lt see, 'tis only the beginning. They keep blowing on those flames. But then, thou'rt too young to have seen…"

"Crazy." Jack had tears in his eyes. "I still can't believe it! But couldn' they have shouted from the scaffold that nothing of this was true?"

"Don't be naive, Digby. One: nobody would've believed them. If thou rememberst, thy father said something of the kind about the Jesuits, openly stating that they were not involved, but to no avail. Two, and this is fundamental: had they proclaimed to the world that they had been deceived, their families would have been literally swept away. Thou, thy mother, thy little brothers and sisters – including the little girl prattling about treason right here, above our heads: all of them. Like the Macduff family." Shakspere sighed, then went on: "I'll tell thee it all. I liked thy little sister's words in themselves, but I chose to include them in *Macbeth* as a tribute to poor Everard Digby. It was the least I could do, wasn't it?"

Jack had always known, deep down: Shakspere too was a dissident to the bone. He suddenly realised why, on the night of his flight, up there in Cambridge, Sherwin had entrusted those documents to him. It wasn't that those papers would incriminate Sherwin: it was the other way round. Finding them among his things could have put their authors into trouble. His precise words had been: "'Tis only important for them not to be found here." Sherwin too, therefore, had wanted to protect Shakspere and his clandestine work of handing down the memory of the downtrodden of history.

"I thank you, Master Shakspere, on behalf of all my family. I really thank you. But, in the end, who ever…?"

"Who could contrive in cold blood such a deadly and perfect trap, sending Catesby and Percy to destroy the others and then to die like broached chickens after sacrificing so many lives, thou meanst?"

"Ay. Who?"

"Thou already knowst who. The cleverest man in the kingdom. The one who gained more than everybody else from the whole matter. Throwing down Northumberland too, into the bargain, the last great nobleman who had the instruments to oppose him. And hoarding exorbitant amounts of money both into the King's coffers and into his own pockets."

"Cecil?"

"'Tis thou hast said it, not I! But of this I am absolutely sure: a truly reliable friend of mine, a baker, told me he'd seen Catesby walk into Salisbury House from a back door, one night, shortly before the Plot was foiled. Nothing new, anyway: thou'rt too young to've seen the secret services at work, in the time of the old Queen, under senior Cecil and his kite, Walsingham. 'Tis exactly the same mode of action."

"I should've realised this earlier. I used to believe that Sir Robert had merely seized a golden chance, a plot some simpleton had hatched. The point is, he looks such a mild man…"

"Thou shouldst see him when he presides torture sessions. He's a better actor than all of us put together. And he's an accomplished dramatist as well; a puppeteer, I daresay." Shakspere paused in reflection, then smiled bitterly. "Now everything holds together. The powder was decayed: this was the missing piece! They couldn't have been so careless as to put the safety of the royal family at stake for even one second… It was decayed, and they didn't even bother to conceal it: sayst thou 'tis in the registers?"

"I swear it on my father's memory. So, he did nothing wrong… Nothing! Because, if the throne is vacant as Catesby had told him, riding through the Kingdom in arms isn't treason and not even a crime. I must write about it and inform everybody!"

"What thinkst thou, Digby? That no one's ever tried this before? Dost presume thou'rt the first one to realise 'twas a fake? Or the first intelligent being to walk the earth? Ever since the beginning, when the plot was uncovered, clandestine libels and even some ballads started to circulate. They weren't logical argumentations, obviously: they'd been written with the instinctive rage of someone who's detected injustice. But they were all tracked down and destroyed, and their authors and printers, when found, executed."

Jack nodded: "I've learnt this from Tim."

"Thou hast no idea how many people paid, in those days, in every shire. Everywhere one could see a scaffold and human remains hanging in chains. I wrote *Macbeth* with all this still fresh in my mind and heart: that's why I was less cautious than usual. In theory, it was a play which had been commissioned by Cecil himself: he wanted to spread terror among people and even scare the King. As if it had been necessary! He'd given me some fixed points which I couldn't exclude, such as, of course, the reference to equivocating Jesuits. I put into it all he wanted, in a sense; but then, on stage, we sort of turned it upside down, and it came out marvellously! Ever since the beginning, moreover, I wrote two scripts: a shorter one, meant for the Government and for the London playhouses, and a longer one, meant for myself, for private houses and for future generations. To keep memory alive. That was the play I'd always wanted to write. We called it 'Secret Macbeth'. Because, thou knowst, at times I like to play with the idea that my works won't die with me and will reach our descendants."

"I believe they will, Master Shakspere."

The playwright became thoughtful. He sighed again. "Well, let's go on. The Master of Revels only approved the former, of course, and we staged it. One day, however, while performing at the Globe, our Armin smuggled into it some lines from the other play. Imprudent, foolish of him. As was to be expected, Cecil learnt about it at once. All the blame was laid on Armin, as it was thought to have been his own improvisation, so he was forced to withdraw from the scene forever. And Cecil ordered the script destroyed immediately. No more *Macbeth,* from that moment on. But I'd put my soul into it: that's why I publicly destroyed the more innocent text but not this one, which I hid in a safe place in my lodging. And now, right today, while Speed's accusations are on everybody's lips, the manuscript's disappeared: I am absolutely certain this is Fletcher's work, who, this morning, came to the Globe much later than usual." Jack remembered that Big John had sent him ahead, telling him he had something to do. "I don't know either how he found it or how he could have even imagined its existence: he must be much cleverer than I thought."

"Maybe someone told him. But who?"

"Not that I thought I could really get away with it... Of course, I *hoped* I could. While writing it, though, I trusted that, if I were ever found out, I would resist heroically, I would face death with an open face as so many of my friends had... Now, instead, I only wish I'd never written it, or that I had destroyed it: now, I'm scared." The great dramatist wearily rubbed his eyes with both hands. "There's no escape... Because one thing is hearing that a seditious play has been performed somewhere; another is reading its script, word by word, black on white, in my hand. *Verba volant, scripta manent*. Let me think about what to do: let them question me and try to justify myself, as I've always done? Right now that Cecil has it against me for everything else, for suspicious hints in my other works and because I still haven't taken the Oath? Right now that Speed has openly accused me of being the Jesuits' poet? Out of the question! Find a hiding place? That can be done, but not for long. Maybe, the best thing to do would be simply disappear for good, as so many have done already. Flee overseas and never see friends and family again... And how would I earn my living? Not to mention that 'tis so difficult to board a ship, especially now that all ports will be alerted, the streets watched... I need time to make up my mind, and I have none!"

"I still might do something for you, Master Shakspere, I've told you: All you must do now is trust me: I promise I'll do all I can. Meanwhile, now that the hatching of the Plot has come full circle in my mind, I'll have to proclaim the truth aloud. Mine won't be a simple libel merely accusing the Government: 'twill be a well-balanced, well-grounded, convincing query. As for spreading it, I'll find the way. If truth has failed once, it doesn't have to fail always."

"Thou knowst not what thou'rt risking, Digby; and then, by now, our people's opinion is formed. Even supposing thou shouldst manage it, who would believe thee? Listen to me: as to written records, the battle's lost. There's but one version, not only of the Plot but of our whole history: the official, Government version. For many years I'd hoped that what *has* been written down could be rectified through what has *not* been written down, what is carven in people's memories, what is declaimed in the ciphered language of the stage. For many years I urged people not to forget, to hand down our past and our present: that's why I wrote not only *Secret Macbeth*, but also all my other works. Now, however, 'tis become too dangerous. Not to mention that many people are forgetting, many have already forgotten. Cecil has won."

"But we *know* he's betrayed everybody else! Now we must find evidence against him, so that it will be impossible for people not to believe us! There *must* be a higher justice to address!"

"I've said this from the stage again and again: both Lady Macbeth and Goneril are sure they'll get away with their crimes exactly because they hold the power, and the law, in their hands. What do they care if ever people learn about their crimes, when no one can judge them or punish them?"

"Both Goneril and Lady Macbeth, however, end up quite badly, if I'm not wrong."

"That's fancy, Digby, just fiction: reality is different. I stopped believing in earthly justice long ago."

"There *must* be a way! If only I had some hard evidence... I could take it to the King... But the King will certainly already know everything and will have approved of the fake plot as well."

"Methinks not. His Majesty might not know anything about it. Even Mounteagle's letter was artfully written, in a language that wouldn't be too simple but neither too obscure, so that it wouldn't be too difficult even to one of average cleverness such as our James to grasp the hint at gunpowder. The King, and the Royal family with him, must believe it was a real plot: terror pushed him into Cecil's hands. 'Tis the same technique as had been used by Sir Robert's father, Lord Burghley, in the conspiracy that sent Mary, Queen of Scots, to the block: it was an utter fake, but our old Queen was so terrified as to sign that poor woman's death warrant. The Cecil mark is all too clear, by now. And 'tis not by chance that this plot, unlike that one, included gunpowder: the King is obsessed with it and fears it more than anything else, seeing how his own father died."

"How?"

"In a gunpowder attack, up there, in troublous, warlilke Scotland... But thou'rt too young to've heard about the famous Kirk o' Field murder. That was more than forty years ago, when I myself was but a child... That's why His Majesty is so terrified of gunpowder, for someone's said to have predicted that the same lot will one day fall on him too. Ha ha, he's not much of a lionheart, our

King, this is no secret: he had a difficult childhood, and doesn't seem to have yet got over it."

"One of Cecil's aims, therefore, was to scare him to death, in order to control him better... Well, if he still doesn't know the truth, I'll tell him myself. Because, in a sense, Cecil betrayed him as well, didn't he?"

"Sure he did. Knowst thou whence his family motto comes?"

"*Sero, sed serio?* I've already heard it somewhere, but I don't remember where."

'Twas conferred by our present King's grandfather to a Scottish mercenary captain who was fighting for the English and who, during a decisive battle, decided to support Scotland at the very last moment. He came late, but he seriously meant to side with his King."

"That's where: in the Scottish chronicles! His name was Kerr: an actual traitor, a turncoat, a two-faced hack."

"Exactly. With this motto, Cecil has turned vice into virtue. He too started quite late to support King James in his race to the English throne; now, however, the King can't do anything without him."

"As if he were admitting in anybody's face that he is a professional traitor. But when the King finds out this treason to've been his work, he'll throw him into the Tower!"

"Don't be so optimistic, Digby: the King owes him too much, even his throne. But, above all, he is afraid of him. He'll never move against Cecil, not even if he found out the truth. He would eat his heart out in silence, that he would, but he'd never say anything, just like the crawling coward he is."

"The Prince, then, as I had already planned: 'tis in him as our only hope lies. I must write for him and to him! Everything would change, if *he* knew. He can't brook indirect, sneaking ways."

"Who knows... However it is, there are too many unknowns, too many risks." Shakspere had stood up. "Now wilt thou excuse me, Digby, we'd better go. Do what thou canst without risking too much; I'll find myself a hiding place and wait."

"Good luck, Master Shakspere, and may God speed you!"

"Good luck to thee too, Digby."

They left separately, through the two different passages, and disappeared among the London crowd.

So, apparently, Jack was to spend some more time in London, after all. He went back to Little East Cheap, where Big John gave him a beaming welcome in rich, brand-new clothes. His satchel lay all floppy in its usual corner and told him that *Secret Macbeth* was gone.

"Hey, Big John! One would say life is smiling at thee."

"And maybe she is, my boy, ha ha ha ha! I'm glad thou'rt back: I've ordered a luxury dinner for the two of us alone, and it'd've been a real shame for thee to eat it cold. Where'st thou been?"

"I've toured all the printing shops, both round the cathedral and in Fleet Street, to look at the latest novelties. Nothing of great interest, apart from Speed's works and, of course, the general great expectation for King James's great Bible. How beautiful thou lookst!" Jack admired his velvet waistcoat, suede breeches and fine fur-lined cloak. "Has something turned up particularly well, old chap?"

"Thou canst well say so! All my painful years of trudge, obscurity, and humiliation are at last beginning to show their first fruits. Patience, one needs. Patience, and sooner or later, if thou'rt bright enough, thou'lt not've waited in vain!"

"Well, the very first fruit has been, after thy success as a dramatist in thyself, when thou becamest one of the two official playwrights of the King's Men, hasn't it?"

"Ay, ay... but that's the lesser part..."

"Then thou'st just rendered special service, I guess. Hast found something worthy of note, while working with Shakspere?"

"Well..." He grinned enigmatically. "I can't give thee the details, boy. Be it enough for thee to know that Sir Robert's put the right man beside thee! I wish thee the same fortune as I've met, Little John!"

Jack nonchalantly asked him whether he'd been to see Sir Robert.

"Sir Robert's out of town; otherwise, he'd 've been the one to run to me, ha, ha, ha!"

"Then, who didst report to?"

"To someone else, lad!"

"But hast taken something to him?"

"Ay, something, Little John. Something they'd been after for *some* time, up there above, something I was the only one to finally find."

"And whither didst take it?"

"Uh, how many questions! Hark: the door. I believe dinner's come. Be ready, as they'll bring it up in no time. I've spared no expense, this evening; and, thou'lt taste what a wine!"

The roasted goose and mutton pie were really something special; but Jack only took a sip of the precious Spanish sack, while taking care to always fill Big John's goblet to the brim. Even when tipsy, though, he didn't reveal anything of relevance about his afternoon mission. Jack then tried talking about directions, telling him that he thought he had seen him walking along the river.

"That can't 've been me, Little John, I tell thee! I was right on the other side."

"On the other side of the river?"

"No, on the other side of the City. But what's wrong with thee tonight? Thou'rt so slow… Thou hastn't drunk too much, hast thou?"

"I might have, Big John. That's why I suddenly feel so sleepy…" He yawned. "I thank thee for the dinner, 'twas really superb! I promise I'll pay thee back as soon as I manage to become as successful as thee."

"As me? That'll be utterly impossible, boy!"

"Ay, I'd forgotten how matchless thou art. But I'll offer thee a sumptuous feast regardless!"

Jack spent the night in a turmoil of thoughts. He wasn't sure he would manage to show the whole world that the Gunpowder Plot had never existed. What he knew for certain, though, was that everything in the world had changed for him and his family. Everything. Because, even admitting he couldn't divulge anything, the boulder that had fallen and crushed him that faraway fifth of November had suddenly been splintered into tiny pieces. Everything would be different, from now on. Sir Everard had done nothing, really nothing wrong, apart from trusting a treacherous friend. He had been overwhelmed and destroyed by a machination he could in no way have escaped, annihilated by superhuman cruelty and chicanery.

The sense of injustice that had slowly been smouldering inside him was now unleashing a rage he had never experienced before, lifting him forever from the mud of shame and humiliation. He wished he could go back to Cambridge, now, and brave all his erstwhile oppressors, not to a rhetorical dispute but to a true single fight, to begin with his pathetic roommates: he was sure he would defeat them all, one by one. Sir Everard and his friends were not burning in everlasting fire but, Jack was unflinchingly sure of this, had obtained mercy and were now in the peace of those who had given up their lives for their friends' sake. Even if the world should never acknowledge anything of this, the whole universe had changed for him.

As for Shakspere and *Secret Macbeth*, he had to spring into action at once: every minute he spent thinking about what to do, while continually changing his position in bed, felt like an eternity of wasted time. He wasn't deterred by the thought of fighting alone, he, a green, inexperienced youth, against a system of espionage that was as proficient as it was merciless, and that sacrificed human lives as if they were gnats and midges. The moment for action had come, and he was ready. The readiness was all.

The following morning, Fletcher worked alone, in the little office in the Globe attic, for Shakspere had sent word that he was still unwell and would stay home. Big John was not surprised at all: "Tell him not to worry: today, Henry the Eight will be all mine!"

Jack went up to him, studiously avoiding Tim, to ask for yet more time off. "I'd like to get back to Fleet Street and inspect the new books, to make sure none of them's been printed illegally, so I'll have both a walk and something to do: here everybody is so sulky, today! I wonder why, but not one of them's said a word to me. Thou knowst what, I'm afraid thy triumph is no secret and will mark the end of my career as a Government agent among these people."

"Dost say so, Little John? Shall I therefore have to fear for my life? Will they stab me in the shadows?"

"One never knows, Big John: 'tis no laughing matter. Nay, if thou letst me, I'll go home and tell Dave to bring thee something to eat and stay here watching thy door, so thou'lt be safer."

"Ay... This thou couldst do as well, though."

"I could, but I could never bring thee what's left of that splendid goose, nor serve it to thee as well as Dave. All right, then?"

"Uhm... Right, Little John. Tell him to bring some wine too."

"I will, Big John. Thanks!"

Jack walked quickly out, crossed the bridge and went home to tell the servant. Then he went down Watling Street, almost as far as the cathedral, then turned right and reached the area broadly corresponding to what he had understood about Fletcher's movements on the previous night. He found himself in Cheapside, with its leafy poplars and fine fountains. Who lived in this area? Not Northampton, not Munck, not Southampton, not Jonson. But the Archbishop of Canterbury had a palace near here: of course, it must be to him Fletcher had taken the precious manuscript.

This was already beyond him: what were his chances to pull *Secret Macbeth* out of Abbott's claws? That Puritan hater of drama might be reading it right now, marking down displeasing passages, as he always did, with red crosses on margins. That graveyard of crosses would end up on Sir Robert's desk in less than no time and Shakspere would find himself in the Tower before he, little, insignificant Jack Digby, could move a finger to prevent it. What should he do? Knock on the front door under any pretext, since the servants knew him as a censorship clerk? And, once, inside, where should he go?

The sky had become so overcast that it was almost dark, thunder rumbling in the distance. While meditating about what to do, and almost without noticing, Jack walked past another well-known house: John Speed's, who, with his newly printed history book, had raised such a fuss about Shakspere and the King's Men. Yet another Puritan and sworn enemy of drama... Jack wondered whether Shakspere might truly have been in close touch with the political "Arch-Jesuit", Robert Persons. Above all, it was over Speed that he and Tim had fallen out. Tim's snapping words, his gratuitous accusations, were still resounding in his ears, as sharp as blades, and like blades they kept wounding him.

Without thinking too much, and without exactly knowing why, he turned round and walked back to Speed's house, which was on a corner between the main street and a long, narrow lane. The old scholar was another of Cecil's men, after all: he might know where Abbott kept his most precious documents, and Jack was on more confidential terms with him than he was with the sour, haughty Archbishop. He resolutely knocked and had himself announced, hoping to find him home alone.

As usual, Speed was in his little office: his poor eyes didn't allow him much outdoors, by now. Jack had come to congratulate him on the publication of his *History of Great Britaine,* which had created a sensation. Speed was pleased. "Thanks to thee, Digby, for thy help. With thee checking my *Atlas,* I've been able to revise my *History* far more quickly! For, thou knowst, my sight is getting ever worse." His tiny eyes, set like fake jewellery between his bushy eyebrows and his swollen eye sockets, were covered by thick lenses as if they had been precious collection gems, but were veiled by an opaque film which certainly made reading and writing very hard to him. Speed offered him a chair opposite his, at the other side of his desk all encumbered with papers, quills, inkpots of different colours. "And how are things with thee, I wonder?"

"Quite well, thank you, Sir. You know, don't you, that Sir Robert has sent me to the playhouses with Fletcher?"

"I remember, boy, I do. Right between the devil's legs, ih, ih ih!"

"To tell you the truth, I haven't seen much of devils so far…"

"'Tis the activity in itself, as thou well knowst. Starting from the simple fact of men dressing up as women, as I may have already had the chance to tell thee: a devilish thing, and forbidden by the Bible. But above all, as the historian I am, I abhor their treatment of history and historical characters. Have I told thee already?"

"Ay, Sir, you have, and I've seen them rather worried about this: I mean, about what you've written about Shakspere and that Papist, Persons. Might it be about what you once told me about Sir John Oldcastle?"

"Thou canst well say this, boy: I've put everything down in black and white. And they're rightly worried, because 'tis all true: what I write is always true, after all. I can prove it, thou knowst. And I will!"

"Prove what, Sir?"

"That they were in touch. That it wasn't by chance if both of them, Persons and Shakspere, turned Oldcastle into a ruffian and a drunkard. That juggler-poet is in with the Jesuits: I've got enough to send him to the block!"

Jack shuddered. "Wow! Do you happen to have found a compromising letter signed by Shakspere?"

"I haven't yet, unfortunately: that's a prudent fellow, and I'm afraid he regularly destroys all his correspondence. But I know that one of

His Lordship's agents is looking among the Latin letters of that accursed Papist, Persons, down there in Rome. I'm certain he'll find something! Dost know what I'd like to do, one day? Collect all his plays and find the seditious elements connecting them all. 'Twill out, like a pattern in a carpet! I've mentioned this several times to His Lordship already: I'll surely find a lot of compromising material. I wonder how many references there may be to topical issues, how many burning-hot themes he handles wrongly. Because, thou seest, the thing is: he's always taken advantage of the impossibility to compare all his works together. What I'll do, instead, is trace back to all the mouldy copies of forgotten plays. Dost know that about fifteen plays he wrote have never been printed? 'Tis one of Fletcher's tasks, as thou wilt know: find all his manuscripts and rough papers." Jack nodded, as if he had always known. Speed went on: "Because I don't believe he's destroyed them all, as he says he's done." He was silent awhile, as if not knowing whether to go on. Then he spoke, lowering his voice: "And the worst of them is surely this one. Fletcher's admirable work, I must admit: this alone will be enough to nail him."

Speed pointed to a worn-out manuscript lying on the desk. Jack's heart jumped. There it was! *Secret Macbeth*! Of course: it was to him, not to Abbott, that Fletcher had taken it. How could he not have thought of it? He managed to conceal his shock and even to tell an outright lie. "I know, even if I wasn't sure I could speak about it, so secret it is: Fletcher's told me everything. Really a master stroke! Can I have a look at it?"

"'Course, thou canst. Read it, by all means. I've just begun it but will go on tomorrow, as by now, in this foul weather, there's too little light for my poor eyes. His hand is really horrible, besides, and I may take a quarter of an hour to read five lines!" Jack took the forbidden manuscript, his hand trembling, and started to read.

Yes, it did deal with a regicide which was eventually punished, as Jack remembered he had seen in the official version. It was about the restoration of justice and peace, and the dawn of a new age. But it was about many other things as well. Firstly, and differently from what had happened with King James and the Gunpowder Plot, no one managed to prevent the barbarous murder of the legitimate good king. He was not blown up, nor was he killed by a dissident, but, rather, by one of his loyal thanes. Good King Duncan, besides, didn't in the least look like King James, but his features rather reminded Jack about old King Hamlet, the ghost of an ancient world now lost forever. A very old man, an almost divine figure who took on a sacred, even Christ-like connotation. This was not the King of Scotland, but rather the ancient Church, disembowelled by a usurper who... had killed his first wife after confining her to a remote castle? Had married Lady Macbeth while his former wife was still alive? Wow, this was Henry the Eighth.

When, instead, Macbeth blamed the regicide on the two royal guards... here, maybe, Jack could see a reference to the Plot. He and his wife had drugged the two poor guards and smeared their daggers with blood. Macbeth had then killed them in cold blood before the other thanes could have them questioned or even tortured. "*O, yet I do repent me of my fury that I did kill them!*" the fiendish usurper said at this point. Differently from what took place in the official version, however, which Jack remembered well, here the two guards were killed on stage. Above all, they had names. They were two young Scottish gentlemen, one called Fox, the other Rook. Fox? What did it mean? Could this refer to Foxe, the Calvinist author of the *Book of Martyrs?* But why on earth? Where was the connection?

Jack looked up, trying to organise his thoughts. Daylight was waning, in the little chockablock office. In a corner above the window, a large spider was weaving its web undisturbed, as if confiding in Speed's poor eyesight. How patient spiders were: they built their little, frail, invisible masterpieces, then they knew all they needed to do was wait. And their patience, and their accuracy, and their secretiveness were invariably rewarded.

The chain of his thoughts was broken by Speed's voice: "Well? What sayst thou, boy?"

"Incredible!" Jack replied. "Could I go on a bit?"

"Help thyself, if thou'st the time and canst see. There, I'll light a lamp, but I'm not sure 'twill be of much help."

Jack went back to the play, and to those two names. So, a fox and a rook, accused of something they had not done... He got it: "Fox" was Fawkes! Guy Fawkes as an innocent victim accused of a crime he hadn't committed. Then, "Rook" could only be Rookwood, another of the plotters, a friend of Sir Everard's. Another country gentleman, another idealist who believed he would go and fight in Flanders, while waiting for tolerance as a gift from above, from his sovereign's bountiful hands.

He went on reading. Here was the chilling scene in which the porter, who had been temporarily turned into the porter of Hell gate – so that Macbeth's castle was Hell – refused to open it to the other Christ-like figure, Macduff. He imagined he welcomed someone who had been newly damned. Here, however, rather than a Jesuit equivocator – as Jack remembered happened in the official version and as Big John had explained to him to exhaustion – it was an accursed hunchback, an evil jester who had *"juggled with religion, with the king, queene, theyr children, with nobilitie, parlement, with friends, foes and generally with all."* Clearly, Robert Cecil. Jack turned page after page, drinking in everything he found. Even that one scene, anyway, was surely enough to send Shakspere straight to the block.

Now Macbeth's loyal friend, Banquo, fell under murderous blows because he knew too much. Here, however, his murderers had names too, or maybe nicknames: "Cat" and "Perch", and were later slain by Macbeth himself, again on stage, because they knew even more than Banquo did. "Cat" stood for Catesby, of course, and "Perch" for Percy: their aliases were even too clear and dangerous. Government agents, charged with a dirty job, killed off once their compromising deed was done.

Here was, instead, and almost exactly as he remembered it, the famous dialogue he had always wanted to read: the one inspired by the innocent words that had sprung from little Meg's sorrow and bewilderment, on that far away evening at the *Mermaid*. His eyes filled with tears, so he had to suspend his reading for a moment.

As for the witches, they had much longer parts, here. They chanted about Fate as Predestination and... During their sabbat they sacrificed a victim to their hellish demons and to the pagan goddess of Destiny, Ananke. It was a human victim, the personification of Justice. Before this, however, they forced her to undergo a fake trial. They chanted about quartering her and impaling her head on a stake; they sang a dismal, ghoulish song whose refrain obsessively repeated: *"The execution of Justice, the execution of Justice!"* But... It was impossible to be mistaken: this was the title of an infamous divulgative essay penned by William Cecil, Lord Burghley, Sir Robert's father. Ay, that was its title, *The Execution of Justice:* a famous treatise meant to publicly justify, before the whole of Europe, England's torturing and dismembering her dissident subjects. It was just like Shakspere to pun on the word "execution"… and the execution of justice had certainly taken place in England. Was it too late, now? Too late to retrieve any form of justice? Maybe it was. Justice had been unjustly executed, like so many English subjects.

Jack stared blankly before him, at the books and papers crowding the desk. In this version of *Macbeth,* Shakspere had finally come out into the open from the refuge he had built himself, from his hovel made of masked cross-references which only a part of his audience could grasp. As he had said, this was clearly not to be performed in ordinary playhouses, but maybe in some private manors; essentially, it was to be handed down to less dangerous times, like a ciphered message in a bottle destined to those who had the instruments to crack its code. Shakspere, who was usually so careful not to keep even one innocent everyday letter, had been so foolish as to keep this play, in the hope of passing it on to a future age as a historical record, a poetic exposure of the injustice of his time: as he had hinted to him in their short, intense interview, he thus hoped to make up for the gradual waning of popular oral memory. This was, therefore, Shakspere's most truly historical play: a poetic history of England from the time of the breach with Rome.

This was why the dramatist had deemed it worthwhile to put his own life at stake: as he had already written, almost prophetically, in Hamlet, it was in order to tell, *"th' yet unknowing world … of carnal, bloody, and unnatural acts, of accidental judgements, casual slaughters, of deaths put on by cunning and forced cause; and… purposes mistook fall'n on th'inventors' heads. All this can I truly deliver"*. After all, this was what Shakspere had always done: tell the world not what went on in Denmark or Scotland, not in a distant country or time, but in the modern kingdom of England, then Britain, in his own time. He wanted everybody to know how its Government had cold-bloodedly decided to clip all its subjects' wings, even at the cost of compromising the salvation of their souls, besides their earthly happiness. He wanted to tell how this persecution left no escape to those who didn't accept the new political and religious settlement. How injustice, poverty, torture and heartache were the everyday lot of those who refused to conform. How there was no way out left, other than abjure the kingdom. How the rest of Christianity had renounced the battle and given England up to its destiny. How no one was any longer willing to listen to them, let alone help them.

But, after all, it might not be yet too late. Jack's thought invariably went back there, to the young, pure Prince, who, although he would never lend his ears to dissidence or even tolerance, would certainly promote justice. Everybody knew, even if it was forbidden to speak about it, that the Prince had grown into a man totally unlike his father, and was attracting an increasing number of courtiers: those either who longed for a virtuous Court which had actually only existed in their dreams, or who had grown tired of corruption and bought-and-sold privileges; in short, those who were fed up with the Cecil supremacy. Once Harry Stuart became king, he was sure to give everything a new order. As bountiful and honest as he was, he could never be indifferent to the sad lot of those who, until a few years before, had been the majority of the population. If someone proved to him that all the accusations against Papists were groundless, he would surely be a very different ruler from his father. Anyway, one thing was certain: King Henry the Ninth would get rid of Cecil's nefarious influence. Cecil had realised this, of course; that's why he feared the Prince and probably hated him.

Jack was ever surer: what he must do was write a work telling directly the Prince the true story of the Gunpowder Plot. Since Harry was as clever as he was fair, this would have many concrete consequences. Of course, the best thing to do would have been to speak to him in person and convince him about the truth with well-balanced arguments, as Jack had been taught in Cambridge, but there was really little hope of achieving this.

An objective, reliable, book, faithful to what had really happened. A refined book too, well written and elegantly bound, maybe even illustrated. It would be the most important work of his life: like this, John Kenelm Digby would save his entire country.

His imagination had already begun to run wild. The new King covered him in honours, completely rehabilitated the family, appointed him Gentleman of the Chamber, and married him to a maid from an attainted family, the daughter of a traitor of his own country: Mildred Elizabeth Cecil, who was now universally despised and who looked up to him as her only saviour. Marry Milly... And finally take her home to Gayhurst, to his mother and siblings, and to Adam and Ellen, and they would all be so proud of him, so proud... As to Sir Robert, Jack would intercede for him before His Majesty, who would allow him to keep Hatfield, provided he didn't leave it as long as he lived. Because, of course, Milly loved her father in spite of his treason... Jack would do this for her, showing great generosity, despite all that Cecil had done to his father, to his family and to all of them...

But this was no time for idle dreams. The first thing for him to do was urgently take back the manuscript to Shakspere before Speed could complete its reading. How? It was as if the precious document were burning the tips of the fingers he had laid on it to make sure it was really there and wouldn't vanish before his eyes. Destroying it would almost be sacrilege; not doing, it, on the other hand, would certainly cost the writer his life. And, anyway, right now Jack could do nothing at all, with Speed sitting at the other end of the table.

"Hast finished it? What thinkst of it?" the old scholar asked him while fiddling with a quill and a penknife.

"Staggering! Hair-raising!" Jack replied. "It must reach Sir Robert at once so he can proceed to have that player-poet arrested without more ado. I can take it to him right now, Sir, if you will."

"Not so fast, Digby, not so fast: I still have to peruse it, then copy down all the lines I mean to quote in my future work. This done, I'll see to it personally... Too precious, boy, too precious, he he he! Sir Robert has been waiting to have such a thing in his hands for far too long." Despite Jack's dithering, Speed whisked the manuscript away and slipped it into a little drawer on his side of the desk.

"This document alone, though, makes your book about his other works superfluous."

"Ay: 'tis enough to frame him. But my comparative book, when I've managed to find all his plays, will storm the market even after his death. *Especially* after his death, I say, just as happened with that other Papist poet, Southwell. I remember his poems came out after his execution and were amazingly successful. Thou knowst, people love the thrill of a narrow escape from treason, and the mixture of art and blood. But my study will be especially useful to justify this player's execution before the commoners, who worship him like an idol and won't easily believe him to be guilty. It will go far, Digby, it will, should it be my very last work!" Speed seemed beside himself with glee. "Mine is not greed, Digby, mark my words: I am not subject to that temptation, although only hypocrites would say no to a little extra money. 'Tis not pride, either, although no one dislikes being known and praised. And not even personal resentment, hatred, or wrath, seeing that this poet and myself have never once spoken to each other. 'Tis sheer love of the true religion as sets me going. And of justice, of course, together with loyalty to my King. 'Tis unbelievable how our beloved sovereigns are always surrounded by traitors, and so closely! Traitors and hypocrites are hidden everywhere: but now, yet another viper's nest concealed among flowers has been unmasked, thanks to me, for God's greater glory! All I ask Him now is to preserve my eyesight till I've written the last word in the last line of that book; after which, He can take it from me forever."

His heart thumping like mad, Jack made an effort to think coolheadedly: how long would it take for the order of arrest to be given? Big John had told him Cecil was out of town: before sending soldiers to seek Shakspere – who, hopefully, in the meantime might have found a safe hiding place – the great man would prefer to read the play, or, at least, to leaf through it personally. There was still a little time left, therefore, but Jack had to act at once. A plan was needed right now. He got up, again congratulating Speed and recommending that he should require his service as soon as he needed him, then took his leave; he wrapped himself up in his cloak and went out, almost running, in the driving wind, thunder above.

He couldn't act alone. He went down to the river, called a wherry, reached Southwark. He headed straight for the Globe, where the performance of a play by Fletcher, *The Tamer Tamed*, had just finished. Its plot already heralded the new hard times: the same character who, in an old Shaksperean play, had tamed his shrewish wife was now tamed in his turn by his second wife, who was still more shrewish than the first. Was this a coded message? Was it Shakspere they wanted to tame?

He didn't take long to find Tim, intent on putting costumes away. "Hey, Rice!"

Tim turned round in surprise. Jack didn't leave him the time to speak.

"Follow me right now, for Shakspere's sake. I come not to apologise, and much less to make up a lost friendship. There's work to do: I know where the manuscript's kept." He turned his back on him and walked straight out into the street, making for the nearest alehouse. Tim followed. Jack sat down at a table and ordered two pints. Tim also sat, without looking him in the eyes. Jack told him everything he had learnt. "We must do it tonight, if we want to save Shakspere's life."

"I'm ready," Tim replied.

"How come? Dost happen to believe this story?"

"Jack…"

Jack looked at him.

"Jack, forgive me. I was scared. Canst thou ever understand?"

Jack thought back to when they had first met. It had been him, then, a totally helpless child, unprepared to what was to come, who had been confused, horror-stricken, devastated by sorrow. It had been his turn to see his worst nightmares materialising before his eyes. He thought back to the scaffold, the blood, people's cheers, and his own pure terror.

"Ay, I can," he told him earnestly and calmly, clasping the hand Tim was offering him across the table.

"We must do it now, as long as it's still there."

"All right."

"Let's meet soon after midnight at the northern gate of the bridge, hoping the moon's out."

"Right. But how wilt thou do with Fletcher?"

"If he doesn't wake up, there'll be no problem: I'll be back before he does. If he does, and can't find me … I know not, I'll do something. Anyway, I'm no longer afraid of him and in a very short time I'll ditch him forever. Now I'll pay a quick visit to Salisbury House to find out when Cecil will be back. I'll see thee at the bridge, then. Don't breathe a word to anybody."

"'Course."

"Ah, and once we've done it, if thou wantst, I'll tell thee exactly what the Gunpowder Plot has been. Shakspere has kindly given me the last pieces of the jigsaw, so that now, at last, everything fits."

"All right, Jack. I thank thee for everything and, again, forgive me."

"Let's no longer talk about it."

He got himself rowed back to the Strand. Cecil's palace guards recognised him at once and told him that His Lordship wouldn't be back before a couple of days. Once he'd got this precious piece of information, he left Salisbury House with a heavy heart, walking close to the walls to see if Milly happened to be at one of its wide windows, so that he could at least wave to her. But she wasn't. She was likely to be playing, singing or reading with her Madam Barrett, and she couldn't possibly imagine how everything had changed for him since they had last met. He sadly set off for home, readying himself to play his last cheery comedy role for Big John, that evening, at dinner.

Big John, who was still in high spirits, drank a lot and collapsed on his bed. Perfect, Jack thought: he would go there and back without him even noticing. They would do everything in less than an hour. He lay down in his clothes and waited, his mind in turmoil, his stomach churning. To calm himself, he tried to think of the comic side of it all: Speed's face, and Big John's, when they learnt that the precious document had vanished into thin air just when they had it in their hands. They would believe that Shakspere was a wizard, or had made a deal with the devil. Speed would start attacking all players and playwrights indiscriminately, hence coming to blows with Big John, who would defend the noble art of mimesis despite all the potential traitors taking refuge among players. He imagined Cecil's cold, controlled rage, the sense of defeat of the most powerful man in the kingdom, who thought he had finally framed a seditious poet only to end up empty-handed. For the time being, of course, he could say nothing to Milly about this, also in order to protect her; in the future, however, in the new reign, he would find a way to tell her.

He wondered what she would think, on having to face hard facts telling her that Jack had always been right about the Powder Treason. She would finally understand that English Papists were peaceful people, far too scared to go and look for trouble. Who knew? One day she might even forsake all the nonsense she had been taught as a little girl, and finally acknowledge that he was right in everything. And then, in a future that might not be too far away, if she still wanted him…

Meanwhile, the moon had risen in a providentially clear sky. At last, the belfry of St Margaret Pattens struck twelve. Jack stole out of bed and shoved a pillow under the blankets. He pulled on his boots, slowly opened the door and started to creep down the accursed creaky wooden stairs. Before opening the front door he paused briefly, listening. Big John hadn't stopped snoring and all was still from the servants' room as well. He slowly opened the door and closed it again. It seemed to him he had taken hours just to reach the street. He hastily headed for London Bridge. Tim was already there. They proceeded towards the City centre, keeping close to house walls so as not to be seen by the night watch.

"Where's Shakspere?"

"Vanished. Really, Jack, he didn't even tell *us* where. Doesn't want us to get into trouble, I guess."

Jack didn't believe him, but only said: "Ay. This way, not even from the rack can you tell them where he's hiding."

"Oh, but they'll find him, they will. Unless he's already embarked for Europe, of course."

"What do we do with the play once we have it? Where do we take it?"

"We burn it, Jack. No place is safe. Especially now Speed has started to read it, it must be destroyed. And, even so, after what that bastard has written about him, let's not take it for granted he'll be left alone."

"If we destroy *Secret Macbeth*, his will only be unproven allegations, from which Shakspere is used to defending himself. 'Twill be his word against theirs."

"Let's hope so… But now Fletcher too, besides Speed, can testify to leafing through it."

"Law is law, Tim. They can't arrest him without evidence. And, then, the people would rise."

Jack wondered if it was really like that. He tried to believe so with all his might.

They cautiously approached Speed's house, whose office overlooked a little rear courtyard. They climbed over the garden wall quite easily. Everything must be done quickly and silently, before the servants woke up. "That's the window, Tim. Mount onto my shoulders and try it."

Tim took off his cloak, carefully folded it and laid it on the ground. He then took a crowbar from his satchel and lightly climbed onto Jack's shoulders, thus getting exactly to the same level as the stone windowsill. He worked slowly, so as not to make noise, until the window frame gave in. "I'll go, Jack," he whispered. "Tell me exactly where the little desk is."

"'Tis dangerous, Tim. Let *me* go in and stay thou out on watch."

"I could never pull thee up, Jack. And, then, I want to do it mesel'. Thou'lt see, I'll be quick. Where must I go?"

"The little desk is straight on thy right, the drawer facing thee. If anybody comes from the yard I'll whistle, and thou must jump down immediately."

Tim disappeared into that black hole. Jack squatted below the window, his heart beating so hard he feared it might be heard. Waiting was so much worse than acting. What if someone had suddenly got in? What if Tim were caught? Would they manage to make him speak? Would they torture him? And what would he, Jack, do, then? Would he run off leaving his friend in there? What to do, otherwise, let himself be caught too in order not to leave him? Instead of watching the yard, Jack found himself staring at the small dark window, while every second felt like an hour. Meanwhile, a cold wind had risen, and the moon disappeared behind clouds. "Not right now, please!", Jack thought.

He couldn't believe his ears when he heard a sudden crashing noise, as of furniture smashing on the floor, followed by a scream and a loud call: "Alarm! Thief! Run to me, ruuuun!"

It was as if his heart meant to jump out of his mouth. Then everything happened so quickly he didn't have time to think. Tim rushed out of the window shouting: "Take me!" Jack grabbed him and they ran together towards the garden wall. Tim needed help and, while climbing, uttered muffled moaning sounds. While, inside the house, several lamps were being lit, he was still on top of the wall, staggering, as if afraid to jump down. Almost crazy with fear, Jack, who didn't understand, grabbed him by the wrist and pulled him down. But, once on the ground, he saw that his friend couldn't walk. He hoisted him on his shoulders and went to hide in a dark narrow lane, under an old, clumsy wooden staircase. The whole area had woken up, meanwhile, with a hue and cry, and the chase had started. Trying to run far away would be useless, nay, dangerous: they crouched down in the darkest corner of that lane, instead, covering themselves with Jack's brown cloak, hoping they wouldn't be noticed.

"We'll make it, Tim! Shut up, though." Jack spoke mechanically, as if they were running away from an orchard after stealing a few apples. But, he thought as soon as he had uttered those words, why didn't Tim shut up, he who was usually so cautious? Then he felt the hand he was holding under Tim's chest getting wet and warm... Blood. He'd been stabbed, in there. And, poor Tim, he was trying hard not to make a sound.

"Don't fret, Tim, and don't fear: we'll make it! Does it hurt much? Now I'll take 'ee home to thy ma', we'll dress it in bandages and thoul't be better at once, thou'lt see. Let's only stay here still a little bit longer, be patient till they've all gone." How he would take him home without making themselves noticed he had no idea, with all the blood Tim was losing and had already lost. It had started to rain, in the meantime: at least, their chasers could never follow that track.

"No, Jack, 'tis deep.... I haven't taken it... 'twas locked... then a servant came... I haven't taken it. Shakspere's undone!" Tim cried in utter despair.

"Don't worry, 'twill all go well. Don't think about the manuscript now: we'll do in some other way. Knowst thou what I'll do now? I'll go to fetch Burbage and th'others and get a horse, maybe a cart. I'll leave thee here in hiding, under my cloak, and I'll be as quick as a flash; if thou managest not to be heard, they won't find thee!" The soft pattering of the rain rebounding on the pavement turned into a roar.

"No, Jack, don't leave me, stay here... 'tis as deep as ... a well... as wide as a church door... I want thee near me still awhile... and then, leave me here and run... I'm scared, Jack! 'Tis over...."

"No, Tim, 'tis not! Thou'lt see! Does it hurt much?"

"Ay, much! Mum... mmmhhh!"

Under the cloak, on the cold ground, their words were whispers. Very slowly, Jack had him lie down, while the shouts and yells of their chasers faded into the distance. He lay down next to him and spread the cloak better to cover them both. But Tim's voice, by now, was rattling. "Art here, Jack?"

"I am, my friend. I won't leave thee."

"The manuscript!"

"I'll get it, I swear! Think not of it. Now, let's say a prayer." He poured into his ear all the prayers he could remember, while Tim was dying, there, next to him, on the pavement of an obscure, dirty city lane. He grabbed Tim's shirt more tightly with both hands, as if he wanted to pull him back, his mind shouting: "Don't go, don't go, don't go!", while whispering ever faster, without perfectly knowing what he was saying, chanting in English and Latin and in a jumble of both, until Tim seemed to get calmer. Until he calmed down completely and forever. It was then, only then, under that brown cloak in the dark corner under the stairs, that Jack burst into inconsolable tears, still holding the garments of that still warm body, shaking it every now and then. His friend, his only true friend, had gone. He had died for nothing, in the blink of an eye, at sixteen years of age, and all for his fault. Tim's blood, washed by the rain, flowed on the ground like a wasted treasure and was lost among the paving stones of the lane. Soon enough the bells of one church, and then of another, announced the beginning of daily activities and the opening of the City gates. Day had come; a bleak, cold, gloomy day.

Jack did not change position – rain trickling down his back through the rickety stairs – crying over his friend. Then, wet and numb with cold and hunger, he slowly crept out of the cloak and sat up beside the body, waking him for hours on end, while people went hurriedly to and fro under the driving rain. "'Tis all my fault, my fault, my fault!", he kept repeating to himself more and more obsessively. "I am the scum of the earth: I'm the only one who could've organised such a foolish enterprise. Lord, forgive me, if thou canst. Canst thou ever forgive me? Tim, forgive me! Forgive me, Mistress Rice, forgive me you all! If only my poor death could bring him back! I didn't know, didn't, didn't know! If only it were all but a dream, one of my usual nightmares!". He cried in silence, continually rubbing his eyes and nose into his sleeves. "What do I do now? What do I do?".

Time crept by without him taking any decision. No one seemed to notice them, in their dark corner. They probably looked like two harmless beggars on whose account it was even useless to call the guards. Then he began to think that he must take the body away. But how, and where? Who could help him? He was afraid of the King's men: as far as he knew, they might as well kill him as Fletcher's spy, maybe thinking that he had deliberately sent Tim to meet his death. But who else? And what else would Tim have chosen, if not to be buried by the friends and fellow players who he had shared everything with? They could kill him, if they chose to do so.

He reluctantly left Tim, then, pulling himself up on his cramped legs, and slowly staggered towards Bishopsgate, then northwards up to Shoreditch, towards Richard Burbage's house. He would tell him everything from first to last, and the great player would be free to believe him or not. He didn't care. He would only ask him for help to recover the body, and then... He didn't know. Probably, the moment to leave London for good had really come: Fletcher was certainly looking for him, since he had surely learnt about their failed nightly incursion into Speed's office and had certainly associated this with his strange absence. He could no longer go back to Fletcher, and neither to Salisbury House. And not even to Milly... He would desperately have wanted to explain something to her, so that she wouldn't think he was running away from her, as if he had changed his mind about her. Right then, he remembered another detail: the draft of his own manuscript was still under the board in the Little East Cheap lodging. Fletcher might even have already found it, and this was one more reason for him to disappear, now. But his mind wasn't clear enough to think straight: he could only think back on Tim, who he still had the impression he was holding in his arms.

Once he had got to the northern suburb of Shoreditch he started to run, until he found the house where Burbage lived with his wife and six children. Mistress Winifred took pity on his wretched appearance and let him in. Only then did Jack realise he was exhausted, starving, drenched to the skin. He flopped down on a bench in the entrance, trembling with cold, no longer able to move, whispering that he must urgently speak to Master Richard alone. The woman got scared to death on seeing that his hands, his clothes and even his face were smeared with blood, and ran to fetch her husband. Surprised to see him, and in this state, Burbage took a stool and sat opposite him. Jack told him everything, starting from his friendship with Tim down to all that had taken place the night before. Halfway through his narration he realised he had started crying and sobbing again. Burbage looked at him earnestly, without saying a word.

"'Twas all my fault! I'd told him that I wanted to be the one who got in, through that window, but he didn't listen to me. I'd told him!" Jack repeated, writhing among groans and tears. "Master Burbage, we must go to retrieve his body. Trust me, I beg you! I'm not Fletcher's spy! I don't want to look on his face again in my life. If only I could go back! I'd leave Tim out of this matter, I'd do everything by myself. I'd go back to Speed's, find the manuscript and save Shakspere's life, and Tim's…"

"And maybe ours too…"

"And yours too." Jack wiped his face yet again in his dripping sleeve. "Come on, let's go."

Burbage didn't budge. Only little by little, as he listened to Jack's words, did their meaning sink in, as he slowly realised that this wasn't sheep blood, or swine blood, like he was used to seeing on stage. This was Timothy Rice's blood.

"But is he dead, Digby? Are you really sure he is?"

"They've opened up his side, Master Burbage. Let's not leave him there. Let's go!"

But it was as if the great actor were nailed to his low stool. While something as scalding as burning-hot molten lead gushed up in his eyes and went rolling down his cheeks to wet his beard, one only sound echoed in his mind, as obsessive as a huge stage drum, and blew up his brains: *"O Horror! Horror! Horror!"*

That slim, clever youth and himself would no longer perform together, no longer talk about their shared passion for that art which had so violently entered their lives. No longer would they walk the boards side by side. Tim had stepped down the tragic stage of life once and for all; he hadn't had the time to become the great player he potentially was. Burbage shook his head.

"Poor, poor Tim! Who'll tell his poor old ma' now? As I've always said, he was too good at getting himself killed… He shouldn't have taken me literally." He smiled, among tears. "But he meant to save Shakspere at all costs. Now I realise why he was so cheerful, yesterday, despite all the bad news: he wanted to find a remedy to all our trouble! What presumption! When one is young, one's really crazy!" He shook his head again, took out a large kerchief from his pocket, dried his eyes and said: "And I daren't think about what they would've done to him, had they taken him alive. Had they taken you both, Digby!"

Jack had only briefly thought about this, there, below Speed's window. He shuddered again: whoever had been caught in such circumstances would have been tortured to death, just like Little John

Owen and Guy Fawkes. And, down there, in the Tower dungeons, what would have come out of their mouths? Jack preferred not to think of it. The fools they'd been.

"His last thoughts went to *Secret Macbeth*, Master Burbage. I have no idea where it's ended up. Seeing the risk, I'm afraid Speed may already have taken it to Salisbury House. What will you do, now, if they arrest you?"

"We'll see. We'll say we didn't know that text in the least. We've always put on stage the version approved by the Master of Revels. I don't believe the company to be in serious danger. The problem is Shakspere: his safety is really at stake, for Fletcher stole it from him, not from us, and 'tis in his hand."

"But where is Shakspere?"

"Vanished into thin air."

"You … you believe me, don't you, Master Burbage?"

"I do, Digby: you're not a player. I do, also because Fletcher came to the Globe, this morning, asking first for Shakspere and then for you. When we told him we didn't know where Shakspere was, he just grinned: but when he learnt you had disappeared as well, he looked really cross."

He remained seated on his stool some more time, his head between his hands; then he jumped to his feet. "There's no time to lose, now: I'll go yoke the horse. We must get through the gates and come out again before they're closed. Get changed, meanwhile: you can't come in this state."

"And do have something to eat, so you won't pass out on your way," added Mistress Winifred, who had come back, without Jack's noticing, carrying a bowl of hot broth and a bread roll, tears in her eyes.

They went out with Burbage's horse and cart. It had stopped raining, at last, and the wind was sweeping the town. Tim was still there, under the drenched cloak. In a flood of tears, his face like a tragic mask, stout Burbage lifted him as delicately as a mother would have done with her sleeping child; and in his arms, still wrapped up in the cloak, Tim did look like a child. He gently laid him on the straw of the cart, as if afraid to wake him up. Then, choosing secondary lanes, they slowly drove to Blackfriars, which was not far, and took him down to the dark cellar of their private theatre. They laid him out on the stone floor. Burbage closed his staring eyes and drew his soaked hair away from his face. Both in tears, they kissed Tim's forehead, then left him there, covered with a dry cloth, his hands crossed over his breast, as if he were sleeping. As they miserably went back to Shoreditch, Jack saw London Bridge looming on the river and against the pale sunset behind them; with a pang in his heart, he thought back to when Tim had last met him, right there – only a few hours before – in perfect health, smiling self-confidently, looking forward to springing into action, not dreaming that it would be his last action, the last act of his life.

Jack spent the night at Burbage's place, on a pallet in the attic, ready to flee through the dormer and the roof in case the house was searched. He cried himself to sleep, sinking into a dreamless interior night, like a stone thrown into a lake.

He left before dawn. He surely couldn't stay for his friend's clandestine funeral, which was to be held on that same evening after curfew, nor could he say farewell to Tim's mother, that poor woman who had trusted him and even admired him like a demi-god only because he belonged to the gentry.

As to *Secret Macbeth*, there was nothing to be done, by now. It would soon end up in Cecil's hands, if it hadn't already, and Shakspere would be hunted down as if he'd been the worst of criminals. Again, Jack felt he was a loser: he had promised the famous playwright that he would retrieve the manuscript, he had even held it in his hands, and not only had he let it slip between his fingers, but he had also brought about his one true friend's death. On top of all that, he was also a hunted man, now: he no longer had a place to go and risked his life by simply walking down the London streets.

But, perhaps, there might still be a moment of respite: if Cecil was not yet back, the palace guards might not yet have received the order to arrest him. Knowing Fletcher, Jack also knew that he would never anticipate any of his own discoveries: he would take advantage of the emergency to seek a personal interview with Cecil and show off before him. He certainly wouldn't let others take any merit for what he had achieved: not Northampton, nor Speed, and nor any other of Cecil's henchmen. Jack was sure he could read Big John like an open book. He would certainly seek an audience with the great man and, after putting on his best clothes, he would only reveal all the big news directly to him. First of all, he would tell him that he had tracked down the forbidden document all by himself; and then, that His Lordship's ward, Digby, the traitor's son – that boy on whom they had invested so much time, money and energy – was actually exactly like his father, a traitor to the bone, who had tried to steal that most important piece of evidence and had run off. Above all, Digby was writing a treatise on the Gunpowder Plot in which he tried to turn the plotters into innocent victims and the Government into the true guilty party. He might even tell Cecil that this treacherous youth had been sent to Speed's house, to try to steal the manuscript, by no other than Shakspere himself, who clearly was really in with all the worst Papists in history: obviously, Speed had always been right in this respect. Cecil would surely be very generous in rewarding Fletcher, both for his discoveries and for the forbidden play. Only then would he give orders to search everywhere both for Shakspere and for him.

So it was that Jack decided to attempt an extreme move. For the very last time in his life, after walking westward round the ancient City walls, he headed towards the Strand and Salisbury House. He would explain everything to Milly, before saying farewell forever: today was Wednesday and she should be in the library. After this, he would go… Where? He knew, deep inside, he had always known, that the only possible way was the same as all the English refugees: a ship bound to Douai. But what if Cecil took revenge against Lady Mary and the children? What could he do, now the damage was done? Only ask them to forgive him his ineptitude, far worse than Prince Hamlet's, and pray God, the defender of widows and orphans, to deliver them from all evil. Maybe it wouldn't be a bad idea to take the whole family with him in his exile overseas.

Once in view of Salisbury House, he didn't head directly for the front door, but, rather, he started wandering round it, waiting for some servant to walk in or out. After what felt like an eternity, a child-like scullery maid carrying a basket ran out, heading for Ludgate and the closest market. Jack talked to her, ready to read her expression and grasp even the least trace of wonder. "Good morrow, Jenny. I was just going to see Sir Robert. Knowst thou whether or not he's back?"

There was no surprise in the girl's eyes: so, after all, the law wasn't yet after him. "A good morrow to you, Master Digby. He isn't, unfort'nately: maybe he'll be home tonight. Master Fletcher's been seeking 'im too, didn't he tell you?"

"He didn't, Jenny, because I haven't yet met him."

"I hope he doth get back soon, 'cos there's old Hannah of the laundry who's in agony and wants to see 'im. I'm going for the pastor, afore I go to the stalls for groc'ries."

"I'm sorry to hear that. I won't detain thee. Good day, Jenny!"

"Life is short, Sir. A good day to you." Jenny dipped a curtsy and went her way.

Jack was, therefore, quite self assured when he walked to the front gate, though his heart seemed to be exploding in his throat. He no longer felt like Hamlet, now, but rather like Laertes, who had jumped into action without hesitation. The guards let him pass without even blinking. As usual, he went straight to the library, where he was almost certain to find Milly waiting for him.

He was not disappointed: she was right there. She beamed at him: "Jack, at last! I was afraid thou'd never come. Mayst have already repented about…"

Jack held her tight her and kissed her hair. "Don't talk nonsense, Milly. Only, this time, I've come to say farewell for good. By now, I risk my life in this house, but I couldn't go without seeing thee for the last time. Above all, when I'm gone, thou'lt be told horrible things about me: I've come to tell thee the truth."

"What happened?"

They sat at the big table and in a few moments Jack whispered everything in her ear: about the Plot, about the libel he had started and then hidden in Fletcher's room, about Shakspere's *Secret Macbeth*, Speed, and Tim: about their doomed expedition, his friend's death, the danger for all of them. Milly clapped both hands on her mouth. "My God, Jack! Did he die right in thy arms?"

"He did. And all for nothing, understandst? For my fault. Shouldst've heard his moans, and seen that open wound, and all that blood…" New tears slowly rolled down his cheeks. She took his hand into hers.

"I'm sorry, Jack, so terribly sorry! Right now that we'd reached some understanding… But, of course, thou must go at once. Solitude will be unbearable to me, now… And thou canst not even write to me. I wonder where thou'lt end up: Flanders, France, Spain, Italy…

Thou'lt marry a Mediterranean beauty, while my father'll marry me off to some old courtier for his own reasons." She smiled bitterly. "'Twould've been too good if…"

"We'd never've made it anyway, Milly: it could only've lasted a bit longer."

"Anyhow, it was surely silly of thee to write that stuff about the Plot and then hide it right in Fletcher's home."

"Milly, I'd have taken it here as soon as I could: here, no one would ever have found it. But events moved so fast…"

"So, in the end, according to what thou sayst hast discovered, thy father was no traitor at all: in a sense, instead, 'twould be my father who betrayed everyone including the King."

"'Tis quite indelicate on my part, but I'm afraid that's the way things really are."

"'Tis all nonsense to me; but I don't want to argue today."

"Thou seest, 'twas written in our stars for us to never get to know each other better, and not even agree for long."

"Know each other better? What meanst thou?"

"Well, that if my name hadn't been attainted, and if I still had all my father's estate, and if yours weren't so powerful, and if our families weren't bitter enemies, I could have asked for thy hand."

"Ah, that's what thou meanst…"

"And wouldst thou have said yes?"

"I would, Jack. I love thee. Even if thou'rt a filthy superstitious Papist. Ouch, sorry, I've said it again. Ours has been pure folly, but… but…" A sob choked her words. They embraced again. "Now go. 'Tis quite late and Bridgie will be looking for me. 'Tis really too dangerous for thee to stay."

"I'll go. When thou thinkst of me, if thou getst the chance, read Shakspere's famous play, *The Tragical History of Romeo and Juliet*: there, 'tis us. My friend Tim's also there; that is, a friend of Romeo's named Mercutio."

"I will. Farewell, Jack."

"One last thing: when thou art a middle-aged lady, married to the greatest nobleman of the kingdom, and thou hast the chance to speak to His Royal Majesty Harry the Ninth, tell him about me and, even leaving thy father out, tell him that mine was innocent: like this, maybe, I can come back. Like this, maybe, we can meet again. Ah, and ask him whether he remembers reading a little note of mine, which I gave him the only time I met him."

"I'll do this too." Her voice was trembling. "And I'll go on studying Italian by myself, and I'll even read that Dante, so I can tell thee what I think of him."

Jack kissed her for the last time.

"Remember me," he told her. Then he went out without looking back and was soon lost among the crowd that, by now, was coming and going along the aristocratic Strand.

After the show, the audience made their way gradually towards the exit, conversing in low tones about the play. It was the usual well fed, well dressed, perfumed bunch. Not many, among them, had noticed the working-class woman sitting in the last row throughout the performance. She had never taken off her cloak or lifted her hood, nor did she seem to have understood a thing about the play, and had probably not even followed it at all. Who knew where she had found the money to get in – and why in the world had she come, seeing that she was clearly not interested? Besides, she hadn't yet made a move to leave. Perhaps she was a beggar seeking shelter from the rain. If so, how on earth had she managed to slink in? Ay, it must be like that. The King's Men should be keeping closer watch, otherwise the riffraff would soon dirty and ruin the fine padded benches, along with being as much of a danger to the pockets of respectable people as happened in popular theatres.

Once outside, however, amid the crowd waiting for coaches, the hesitant who didn't want to get wet and those in a hurry, the strange woman was clean forgotten by them all.

She didn't even move when the company stayed behind the scenes much longer than usual to tidy up, nor did any of them tell her to leave. Then, when all was silent, she slowly stepped towards the tiring house along with a gentleman in a plumed hat, who had also stayed behind, seated in the third row. The leading player, famous Richard Burbage, embraced her; then he took her arm and led her down a short ladder to the cellar. There, in the half darkness of a few tapers, the corpse of a slender youth had been dressed for burial and was surrounded by all the other players and their women. He was barely recognisable. His blond hair had never been so neatly parted, while his constellation of freckles had all but disappeared, sort of sunken into his wax-pale face. The woman could barely stand on her feet. Still wrapped in her cloak, her face still covered, she began sobbing loudly, mumbling inarticulately. They let her cry it out: no one would hear her from there. She seemed to be telling her boy off for going out at night, in secret, without even saying good-bye to her.

"Why, why, why?" she kept repeating between sobs, kissing his dead face over and over. She still couldn't take it in. The last of her children, the only one who had survived the angina, the pox and the plague, had gone so quickly, cut down by a murderous hand while she lay asleep.

The gentleman in the third row who had come down with her donned his sacred vestments and was soon ready to celebrate that secret funeral. The players pushed aside a wooden board covering the grave they had dug that afternoon, after taking out six of the big stone slates paving the cellar. At the end of that brief, simple service, Tim was lowered into the grave that was to host him to the crack of doom, right below one of the playhouses he had loved so much. In the end, everybody knelt down on the cold stone and threw a handful of earth into the open grave. Then Richard Burbage's low, deep bass voice started to chant the ancient antiphon: "*In paradisum deducant te angeli…*".

The others joined him, slowly, as if in one voice: "*In tuo adventu suscipiant te martyres et perducant te in civitatem sanctam Ierusalem. Chorus angelorum te suscipiat et cum Lazaro quondam paupere aeternam habeas requiem*". Among them, a clear, fine tenor voice was easily distinguishable. It belonged to a short middle-aged man with a thin grey beard who didn't at all look as if he could sing like that. Just before the chant began, he had waded through the little crowd and thrown something into the grave, together with his handful of earth: a red fool's cap, symbolising what had united him to poor Tim. It was Robert Armin, their former clown, who, when prevented forever from performing, had gone back to his brother's goldsmith's trade.

So it was then that Tim Rice's body was buried properly on consecrated ground, underneath the ancient convent. As soon as it was over, his poor old mother collapsed to the floor and didn't seem to want to get up again. From then on, she went to live with Dick Burbage's family.

Jack never dreamed that leaving Salisbury House and the Strand forever would upset him so much. The thought of never seeing Milly again was burning him up. Every step he took led him farther away from her; but he walked on with the desperation of a hunted man. Tim's death, the separation from Milly, the fear of being taken, the worry for his family now he was an outlaw, all this produced such an inner turmoil as to neutralise his thought. Again and again did he try to clear his mind, but everything was darkness, and weariness, and sorrow, and hunger.

He didn't know where to go. His heart flew to Gayhurst, but he knew it was there they would first look for him. However, he certainly couldn't let his mother, brothers and sisters be tortured by his disappearance, nor could he leave them at the mercy of Government agents. If, on the other hand, a man-hunt started and he was found there, they would all, including the servants, pay for it with him. Yet, there must he go: he had to tell everything to Lady Mary and show her he was still alive. Then they would decide how she should deal with the authorities and Cecil, once he had gone forever. Friends and neighbours might help him embark and even give him a little money and some introductory letters for other friends, those living in perpetual exile, and Jack would soon start a new life, as so many before him had. He would leave everything behind, all the nearest and dearest, to leap into a void. It would be like dying a little, it already was, but there was no choice. He had already lived through this many times in his soul: he had learnt it in his childhood from the tales of his elders. Sooner or later, there were only two routes for those who wouldn't bend: the scaffold or exile.

In the end, therefore, he decided to head for Gayhurst, gambling on the little time he had over his pursuers: before they started looking for him there, even before they moved on to Buckinghamshire, they would need an order from Sir Robert. Going to the public stables for a horse was out of the question: he had almost no money and, besides, it wasn't unlike Big John to have already placed some men in the strategic points of the City. Walking all day and all night, he would reach home the following morning. He would only spend a few hours there, just the time to devise a strategy with Lady Mary; then he would go, never to return.

But what if Fletcher had already left for Gayhurst? No. Knowing him, he wouldn't leave the City before meeting up with Cecil: not before tomorrow, then. Still, he could certainly send one of his men to wait for Jack there. He had to be very careful.

He crossed the Fleet river, walked round the ancient walls, then took the Old Bailey and walked towards Smithfield. From there he took Aldersgate Street, losing himself among merchants and peasants coming and going with their mules and horses, carts and barrows, cattle and sheep.

The countryside was lush and green, lime trees were starting to blossom and in a few weeks they would fill the air with their sweet nectar scent. Jack thought back to the last time he had ridden in that direction, less than a year ago – even though it felt more like a century -, when, he and Big John had escorted Milly and her train to Hatfield. How many things had changed, since then. How many stupid and grave mistakes he had made. The faces of the two dearest people he had just lost, Milly and Tim, kept appearing before him. He rubbed his eyes till they hurt.

As he walked northwards, the country road remained unusually peopled. Jack remembered it was market day in St Albans. This was a stroke of luck: even if the man-hunt had started, he would be difficult to find among so many people. He liked St Albans' market: he remembered the first time his father had taken him there, on a bright sunny day. He was about six, back then, and fascinated by the colours, smells, voices, by the people, and all the good things to eat that were in array on stalls, inside both the public market hall and the main square, along the streets and even on some doorsteps. And, when he got tired, Sir Everard had asked for Locksley, his great dapple-grey steed, and had set him in saddle, he, a little chap on that huge beast, and all the people stared at them. How proud he had felt to be Sir Everard Digby's son! He remembered some musicians in the streets and even a group of jugglers: how well, from up there, he could see them! But now Sir Everard would no longer lead him, nor hold his bridle. Slowly, painfully, he now had to find his way by himself. He wondered what had become of Locksley, that his father had owned even before birth. It had surely ended up in the stables of some Court favourite.

In the afternoon he caught the first glimpse of St Albans' pointed belfry, far away in the distance. He reached the town towards sunset, when the stalls had already been dismantled and the merchants' carts loaded. Right in the centre of the main square, opposite the market hall, a scaffold had been left standing, the slender body of an old woman hanging from its gallows; the last sun of the day had just left the square but still hit the corpse.

"Who's that?" Jack asked two housewives driving home an ass laden with fruits and vegetables.

"That's old Gwynneth, that is, who was once our midwife, and cunnin' woman as well."

"Witchcraft?"

"Ay, Sir," answered the younger, a plump, red-cheeked woman. "'Cos she'd got poor, and short-sighted, and had no kilder, you know, and her hussbind long dead and gone. And so she lived on what she could grow and what we gave her, when we had summ'at. But we're told that poor folk must be provided fer by the law, 'tis not fer us to do it, 'cos if I give away a piece o' bread I won't go to Hevvin for that. What I still can't believe is that Gwynneth had made a pact with the Evil One, yet 'tis right so, as the Justice of the peace told us."

"The vicar said so too," added the other, a little thin woman whose hair was covered by a kerchief.

"What's she done?" asked Jack.

"She's done that one day the blacksmith's wife – Bertha, that is – is sittin' afore her door, a handful of chestnuts in her lap. 'Gimme some', quoth Gwynneth. 'Aroint thee', quoth she, 'cos today I got nothing fer thee. And the old woman insisteth, and Bertha saith, 'nay, begone!'. But afore she goes, Gwynneth tells her: 'Hevvin forbid rainy days to come fer thee too, now that thou'rt well and fine and wantst nothing, thou who as yet but take pride in thy good hussbind and thy li'l laddie: I once had a kild mesel', and now I have no more'. And Bertha's scared and saith she's cursed her with the evil eye or summ'at as bad. And so it is, 'cos a little month hadn't gone by when her kild, who had been all a-bloomin', falls sick and dies. Like this, in three days. And so they go and take her – Gwynneth, I mean – and she saith 'tisn't true nothing, that she hasn't done nothing, that she said what she said like that, 'cos she was cross, but meanwhile the kild is dead. A goodly kild, you know, Sir, rosy-cheeked, and chubby, as cute as could be. And, the day afore, her kine's milk had curdled up and butter hadn't set up good. And so, to be short, they put her on trial and it all comes out. On the one hand I'm sorry, 'cos afore this she ain't never hurted nobody, nay, she helped those in need. But they also said that her remedies, and the spells to be chanted afore taking 'em, come directly from the devil. And so, at last, it served her well: she'd been deceivin' the 'ole town for ages. Let's go, Kate, 'cos 'tis almost dark already. Pardon me, Sir, a good night to you!"

Jack looked up at the scrawny, puppet-like corpse, limply hanging at the end of the rope, still invested by the last sun rays, slightly swinging in the newly risen breeze. He wondered if she had really been a witch or she had simply made the wrong wish at the wrong time. However it might be, today people had had their entertainment to gossip about and their criminal to see hanged. He wondered whether a time had ever been when the scaffold was reserved for true criminals, robbers and murderers.

He dined in an alehouse on the main square, even if it cost him all his money, because he felt faint and still had a long way to go. He ate quickly, sitting in a dark corner, without talking to anyone. Then he resumed his journey northwards. He had at least twelve hours' walk before him.

Once out of town, he could hardly see his own feet in the dark. He walked slowly, warily, for the country road was deserted and the risk of having a bad encounter was high.

He walked about ten miles, quickly squatting behind a tree or in a ditch whenever he heard a noise, his ears easily deceived by the branches rustling in the wind. After about four hours, in the middle of the night under a drizzle, he reached Dunstable. He shunned the main road, which cut through the town centre, where someone might see him from their window. It was pitch dark, now. While crossing a field, he kept tripping against large stones which seemed to be everywhere round him. Exhausted, his feet aching, he crouched against a low ruined wall, wrapping himself up as best he could in the cloak borrowed from Burbage, sheltered by what was left of an old dilapidated roof. He meant to have just a few minutes rest; but, exhausted as he was, his lids dropped shut and he fell fast asleep.

It was still night, when he awoke, but the drizzle had stopped, the wind had cleared the sky and the moon shed her silver light enough for him so see his way. He noticed that this spot was really scattered with big square stones. He should have guessed this: the low wall that had sheltered him was part of an ancient ruined monastery, one of the many in the whole kingdom, one of the many stories of pillage and desolation. This one must have been quite large. As he got closer to the main body, he saw that a part of the nave had been recovered, perfunctorily fixed and turned into a shabby parish church: they had simply built a wall between the nave and the crumbling apse, its fallen stones – witnesses of a glorious past – now covered in moss. This merging of past and present, life and death, offered a living picture of dreariness and desolation.

Jack walked into the apse. It was like the empty shell of a huge walnut, the floor now covered in grass, the moon and stars looking down where the ceiling should be. Part of the wall was still standing, its fine pointed mullion windows desolately empty, like the eye sockets in a skull. He pitied those naked stones, still wet with the rain and lashed by the wind. He could still see, here and there, a few carved shapes, mainly monsters, ghastly in the moonlight, decorating the bases of what had been columns and were now going back to their natural state, sinking among nettles and thorns: the stonecutters of yore had only rescued them for a short time from the common lot of stones. Traces of frescoes might also be left, but, at that time of night, all the walls were just black. An inescapable fate had plagued a whole world, a fate of slow extinction, despair and death. There was no way out: all this only belonged to the past. Not to the present, not to the future.

Jack left Dunstable behind and resumed his journey, somewhat amused in his sorrow: had anybody seen this hooded, lonely figure wandering at night among the ruins, they were sure to believe they'd seen a monk's ghost coming to reclaim what was his.

Immersed in these thoughts, he kept to the side of the road, always on the alert for suspicious sounds, ready to jump into hiding at the slightest noise. As soon as it was light enough, he cut across fields and pastures, walking along border-hedges, among sleepy sheep, across moors brown with heather and yellow with gorse.

It was full day now. He was starving, but daren't ask for food at one of the small farms he spotted in the distance, as his family house was getting closer and he was afraid someone might recognise him, he was so much like his father: they might remember feeding him and report it to the authorities. And there was obviously no point, at this time of year, in seeking fruits in trees or berries in bushes. He kept walking, worn out, his body aching all over, the cold wind whistling in his ears, his cloak flapping. He lowered the hood over his eyes and bent as he walked, so that no one from afar might figure out his age or his height.

The sun was high, the day clear, when, after yet another flock of sheep, he finally saw the tips of the oaks and, a little later, the walls of the park emerge from the horizon. He quickened his pace, the wind still lashing his face. His was certainly a sad homecoming; nevertheless, his heart suddenly flooded with calm and surprising joy. He jumped across the brook where he used to play as a child. He didn't head for the open front gate, but rather walked round the park wall: no one must see him. He would climb over the wall from behind, then approach the window of Lady Mary's chamber and wait for her to be alone.

But yonder, at the end of the oak-lined alley, right next to the front door, stood a luxury coach, its coachman and several servants waiting, no emblem visible. His heart jumped. But no, this couldn't be one of Fletcher's men coming to arrest him in his own home: any London pursuivant would travel by horse, not by coach. As for aristocratic visits, they had become utterly unlikely by now. Who was it, then, and what did they want? It looked like a private visit. The mysterious guest must be in the great hall, the one with the carved stone fireplace. Very cautiously, Jack approached one of its windows. Lady Mary was sitting at the sewing table, where that unexpected visit had clearly caught her unprepared. Sitting opposite her, his shoulders to the window, was an elegantly dressed man, clearly past his youth. The man must be explaining something; Lady Mary had bent her head, her elbows on the table, her face in her hands.

Alarmed, Jack walked round the house again until he got to a climbing plant he remembered well; he clasped its boughs and nimbly, almost noiselessly, hoisted himself up to the roof. Once there, he pushed the frame of a dormer and got into the attic. As silent as a cat, he lowered himself onto the first floor, which looked deserted. From there he crept into a room above the great hall and, lying with his ear on the floor, he managed to hear the man's voice: "Lady Mary, you don't have to give me an answer right now: take all the time you need to think it over."

"I will not," she said. "I've told you already: my mind is clear on this. I really thank you for your generous offer: I'm flattered by it, Lord Henry, but I can't accept. You will not be offended, I hope." Her voice was trembling, as if she were moved or upset.

"I do not hope you can ever love me, Lady Mary. Think, however, about all you could give your children. A great estate each, with a title, liveried servants, horses and carriages, and, of course, wonderful marriages."

"Therefore, essentially, are we talking business?"

"For you, maybe: certainly not for me."

"You have already told me, Lord Henry. And I thank you again, but I cannot accept. I have decided that I will remain faithful to my husband's memory to my death."

"You have not made any vows, I hope?"

"I think I will, as soon as I can. And you know what a vow is, Lord Henry."

"I do, Milady. I want you to know that I admire you and I would sincerely like to help you"

"I thank you, Milord, but don't pity me: at this point, 'tis a choice."

"And have you the right, I wonder, to choose for your children as well?"

"'Tis not a right, Milord: 'tis a duty."

"Of course, Lady Mary. But, I pray you, do not exclude this thought forever."

The man, whose voice Jack had heard before but couldn't remember where, stood up and took his leave in a very formal way. A minute later the mysterious coach was running fast down the oak-lined alley and disappearing into the moors.

Jack forgot both weariness and hunger. He walked into his mother's chamber, waiting for her. He went to her small writing desk, took a piece of paper, dipped her quill and wrote: "Mother, 'tis Jack," so she wouldn't be frightened. He lit a candle to draw her attention, then hid behind the thick coarse curtains.

She wasn't long; surprised by the lit-up candle in full daylight, she ran to the desk, saw the note, turned round, whispered his name. Then Jack went to embrace his mother, who was still shaking like a leaf.

She wanted to hear about him.

"'Tis a long story, Mother. Tell me first about you. Who was that?"

"Henry Howard, Earl of Northampton. He wanted to marry me."

"I've heard."

"I refused him, Jack."

"I've heard that too. Why on earth did he want to marry you?"

"He says he's in love with me. I don't know…"

"'Tis disgusting, mother: he'll be more than seventy."

"As for me, the thought never even crossed my mind. But for you all… Perhaps I was wrong to say no. It would have meant an utter change of life, understandst? He's as rich as Croesus, never got married and not even does he have illegitimate children. This he had come to offer: his huge wealth in exchange for my person." Jack looked at her silently. "I lived through a terrible moment, Jack. What ever is my person before your future? And complete rehabilitation of your father's name? There were a few seconds, very few seconds, when I thought I had to accept him. He's an elderly man, he's come to offer us his enormous fortune for a few years of patience. Isn't it selfish, on my part, to say no to all this? I've thought of it, Jack."

"But he is Cecil's man, mother!"

"Ay. It was but a moment, as I've told thee, then I thought of who this mild, kind man actually is. He's one who has decided to throw all his life at Cecils' feet. He's betrayed his own family, he's sent his own brother to the block… He's ruined Ralegh and Cobham, he's taken part in the negotiations for peace with Spain; together with Cecil, and against his own conscience, he crossed out religious tolerance from its conditions. And then, of course, he's taken part in the trials of the powder plotters… How dare he come all the way here to propose to me! One might almost think that it looks like a form of atonement… Perhaps he's thinking of his own approaching death, when he'll have to stand before an incorruptible court before which nothing can go unnoticed. But it would be as if I married my husband's murderer, as that poor unfortunate queen of Scots did."

"She'd be our Queen now, mother, had they spared her... As to Northampton, if you married him, he'd put an end to our freedom. He would lead you all to Court and, in the few years that are left to him, would have me and all my siblings engaged to people of his choice. Muriel too, Robin too. So that, once he's dead, there wouldn't be anything left for you to choose. He'd smother our freedom and kill our dissidence, mother."

"I'm not sure he's really left me free to choose. I'm afraid he may come back, Jack, and with extremely convincing means of persuasion."

"If he came on Cecil's order, he is sure to."

Jack thought this could be a plan, seeing he had betrayed, to subjugate the whole Digby family. He shuddered at the thought: might the reprisals have already started? So soon?

"If he came on his own initiative, on the other hand, he may not come again," his mother objected.

Jack didn't hear her. He covered his face with his hands: this might not be because of him, but it worsened the situation still further.

"So, there couldn't be a worse moment... What will you all do without me? Because things have changed, Mother: I'm a hunted man, now. The time of ambiguity is over, I could no longer live like that. You're all in great danger, now, and I don't know what to do to save you. Apart from him, has no one else yet come?"

"No, Jack."

"They will, mother, and won't believe you when you say that you didn't see me, and they will search Gayhurst again, and ransack it, and take everything from you again... They'll take the children, this time... They must be protected, Mother: we must get'em away from here! And, among all this, out pops old Northampton, who'll exploit the situation to his own great advantage and, at that point, will force you to marry him. I'm a failure, Mother: I try to act for the best but everything I do is always, completely, desperately wrong!"

Once again, a scene from *Macbeth* flashed before his eyes: the one he had seen at the Globe so many years ago, the one in which he had first recognised Tim on stage as he repeated Meg's words. The little boy's father, Macduff, had disobeyed the tyrant and run away. What had the tyrant done, then? He had slaughtered his whole family: his wife, who was a lady just like Mother, and the children, all of them, one by one, like a hawk swooping on a henhouse. Might Cecil send murderers to Gayhurst because of him? Would they run their swords through all his loved ones and set fire to the house? Would what Sir Everard had so courageously managed to avoid, letting himself be dismembered for what he was not guilty of, eventually take place for his fault? He felt so dizzy he had to lean against a chair not to fall. "Mother, we must all flee, this very night!"

Lady Mary had gone very pale. She looked at him without fretting. "Calm down! Sit. There must be a glimpse of hope. Now I'll go down to fetch thee some food. Wilt thou collect thy thoughts, meanwhile, and start from the beginning?"

Jack sat at the little writing desk, his aching head propped up by his hands, trying to imagine what else could come to pass: the future was gloomier with every second and all hope was lost. Might Northampton, in his frustration for his mother's rejection, dare ask for Milly's hand? And who said that Sir Robert wouldn't grant it to him? After all, he had made Lord Henry one of the richest, most powerful men of the kingdom; without mentioning his ancient lineage and the Howards' renowned name, which the Cecils lacked. The two families had been bitter enemies, once. Now, instead, Sir Robert might choose such an unnatural marriage for his daughter to assert the upstart Cecils' victory over the ancient ducal family. Once again, *Sero, sed serio*. Where would Milly find the courage to refuse, since she didn't even dare look her father in the eyes?

Lady Mary came back with a jug of ale and a cake which was almost whole.

"We'll be left alone for a while: I've told Ellen to feed the children without me, for, after Northampton's absurd proposal, I'm unwell and I need rest."

Jack ate, then began telling his mother all that had happened, at the same time trying to put order into his troubled mind. Lady Mary tried to soothe him about Tim's death. "Thou'st acted for the best, Jack: at that point, there was nothing thou couldst do. Surely, the decision to go, the two of you, alone to that man's house, was a rash one, but who can always reason calmly and rationally? I'm so sorry for thy poor friend; but the decision was taken by both of you, not only by thee. You did all you could for a good end. Unfortunately, 'tis only in fairy tales that good intentions are always crowned by success." Jack thought about poor Cordelia's words, just before she was murdered: *We're not the first who with best meaning have incurred the worst.*

Lady Mary was upset, not desperate. She needed to think, she said. "Go and rest now and do not worry, son. I am proud of thee. Dost realise what thou hast discovered? Thanks to thee, it is finally, definitely clear what lay behind the Plot. Now, at last, everything holds together." She smiled. "The news thou'st given me of thy father's and his friends' total innocence is the best in my life, 'tis a load that has been lifted from my heart. About the rest, don't fret, don't fear: we'll find a way."

She silently thought of the other mother, a widow like her, whose only son had not come back from that rash expedition, nor would he ever again.

The sun was setting when Jack crawled back up to the attic, threw himself down on the straw covering the floor and fell asleep. For the time being, for everybody's safety, no one must know that he was back.

As soon as Jack had left, Milly ran to take refuge in the remotest corner of the huge library. All he had told her, about what he believed the Plot had actually been, and Sir Everard's innocence, and Jack's poor friend dying in his arms, and about the precious seditious manuscript, and the celebrated poet risking arrest and execution, and the role her father, Sir Robert, had had in all this... It was all too chaotic, too confusing for her poor brain. It was all so hideous, so complicated, so uncomfortable... the human soul could be so wicked... As for the Plot, though, knowing Jack's simplicity, it was very likely all bunkum – or almost: it made no sense whatever to her.

Right now, though, she had no wish to think, reson or reflect: all she wished was to stop time at the instant he had last kissed her. All she wished was to stop the hands of all clocks, the sand in all hourglasses, stop the stream of her thoughts, her very breath, even her blood circulation, and lose herself in that single instant. She knew she would only manage this for a few minutes, after which the tangled web of thoughts would overpower her, forcing her to face it. But right now she didn't want to look at it, let alone touch it: let it stay there, buried deep inside her, in all its mess. She wanted only to think about Jack's beautiful eyes, and the brown lock forever dangling between them, and the smell of his face, and his short, thick, soft beard rubbing against her cheeks and her eyes, and his calm, deep voice, his strong arms holding her, and the taste of that last kiss. It was as if life had to be one long painful walking away from happiness, from now on. A permanent exile.

She crouched on the floor, in tears, rumpling the fine turquoise dress she had chosen for him, that morning, full of joy at the thought of seeing him again. She closed her eyes. The smell of dust, leather, ink and old papers had become closely associated with his presence: now, she could no longer walk into any library without thinking of him, of their clandestine lessons, and of the still more clandestine love that had slipped between the shelves, emerged from the pages of some hidden book, mesmerising them, like Cupid, point blank with its arrow. What did she care for all the rest, now? For fine clothes, jewels, balls, carriages, the splendour of Court, the flattery of courtiers? Or for the compliments of some repulsive upstart old nobleman, newly elevated by the King, to whom her father might already have chosen to give her as a wife… She'd rather die! Because that wouldn't be life. Jack was life. She liked talking, joking, even quarrelling with him. If Time's winged chariot must run far from Jack, and turn him into a hunted man and her into a sated, disappointed old lady, she wanted either to get off that chariot or stop it forever. She looked down at the palm of her hand, where a thin paperknife cut was just beginning to heal. She opened it up with her fingers until it started to bleed afresh. She wanted it to be there forever to remind her of the last time she had seen the man she loved.

She had no idea how long she had sat in that state. It was with amazement, then, as if waking up from a dream that she heard Madam Barrett's voice calling her from far, far away, her words muffled, as if from another world. "Lady Mildred, are you here? Do come out, I pray you: there is need of you!" She decided to respond, in the end: whatever it was, it would distract her from the dangerous machinations in her mind that were now pushing to get out. She shook her head, dried her tears with her fingertips and stood up. "I'm yonder here, Bridget. What's the matter?"

"I wouldn't have come to disturb you, Milady, knowing how much you love studying in solitude, in the morning. But there's old Hannah, of the laundry, who is drawing her last breath and keeps asking for His Excellency your father." She had come close, while Milly had grabbed a book and lowered her head, her curls covering her eyes.

"But I do not believe she will live until tomorrow," Madam Barrett went on, "so the other servants beg you, if you find it not too annoying, to go yourself and listen to her, as this may give her a bit of relief in her last moments."

"All right, I'll go." She closed the book and walked to the door.

She had never liked dealing with servants, for they were rough, ignorant people who apparently ate nothing but garlic and, for the most part, were still anchored in the old superstitious ways. But now she was in want of something to distract her; and then, she had never seen anyone on the point of death. Her mother had passed away when she was not yet three: she only remembered servants taking her to receive her last kiss, and her young, fair mama lying very still in bed, but nothing else. As for her grandfather, great William Cecil, Lord Burghley, he had died the following year, but she didn't remember anything at all about him. She wondered whether the old Queen had really assisted him personally on his deathbed, as she was said to have done, and fed him with her own hands. If she had, then it might not be completely out of place for her, now, to go to the deathbed of someone below her rank. She also wondered what on earth this old servant might want of papa. She might have a prophecy to reveal to him: dying people's prophecies were said to be always true.

She had never even been to the servants' wing, so that this unprecedented circumstance made her excited and curious at once. She sighed. There: in an eye's wink, she had passed from total boredom to an excess of turmoil and restlessness; now her thoughts went to the bedside of an old woman whose face she wasn't sure she could remember, while Jack's kiss was still burning on her lips and in her heart. How would she carry on without him? She would think of this later. Now, she followed her former governess up a narrow staircase at the end of a corridor she wasn't sure she had never ever set foot in.

Even though it was daytime, there was not much light in the large women's dormitory. It was a bare, plain room, dark big rafters running across a low, sloping ceiling. Many women servants were clustered round a big iron bed, which would normally host at least two of them but where only one woman was now lying, her face whiter than the snow-white sheets. She was so skinny that, if Milly had ever seen her, she was now unrecognisable; her voice was a rattle, her toothless mouth partially open, her grey uncombed hair glued on her head and lank cheeks, her eyes half closed. She looked as if she were ninety but might well be younger: lower-class people always looked older than they were. The women round the bed were whispering a Latin chant in a uniform, hissing buzz, which they cut short as soon as they caught a glimpse of the two gentlewomen. Room was instantly made for them at the bedside. "The Lady Mildred is here!" one of them whispered in the dying woman's ear. Hannah's eyelids rose and dropped again. She spoke feebly, panting heavily: "I want to tell her… alone… Leave us alone…" All the women, Barrett included, walked out and closed the door. Milly sat down beside her on a stool. What was usually done in such situations? She saw her skinny hand, her thick, purplish veins sticking out, resting on the blanket; repellent as it appeared, she took it between hers and waited silently.

"His Lordship's not here..." the old woman panted.

"He isn't, Hannah. Thou canst tell me: whatever it is, I'll report it to him." In fact, Milly was quite sure about this, papa would never listen to the last ravings of a dying old servant, he who swayed the destiny of an empire. The woman went on without looking at her: "Tell him... That I... Repent..." Milly sighed. There would certainly be no point in trying to explain to this wreck from the past that deathbed confessions were utterly useless, even if she *had* been the Romish priest it was impossible to have; not even if she could administer, instead of a drug, one of their superstitious sacraments. God didn't need men's contrition, nor their works: good works, bad works, often both good and bad, more often bad than good. No human work, and not even repentance, could determine the eternal destination of souls; so much the less could be done by the obsessive babbling of those uncouth women in their dead language. God knew very well what he was doing, and it was only His omnipotence to predestine souls to joy or torment. Good people never worried about this, since they already knew, deep inside, that they had been saved despite their sins: saved by God's fathomless mercy.

Hannah spoke on: "I... ask forgiveness... I had an evil plan... I sinned in my thoughts, in my words and ... but then I didn't do it! I'll have to pay for this, but not forever, shall I?"

"Of course not!" Milly tried to soothe her, although she had no idea what she meant.

"'Tis at the bottom of my trunk... Go and take it... I have not betrayed... I've... not... betrayed... I've been... loyal. I'll be punished... for this too..." She panted ever more heavily.

"Thou wilt not, Hannah, don't worry. No one will be punished for being loyal."

"I will... Two masters... but I didn't do it... 'twould be pointless by now... Should've done it afore, yea... Pray for me... Someone may make an ill use of it... Take it! Pray for me..." Milly was horrified: what superstition, what ignorance, to think that men's prayers could change the Almighty's inscrutable will! But she equally said she would, for what it cost her. The old woman, who had slightly lifted her head, now dropped it again on the pillow; she closed her eyes in exhaustion and started rattling again. Milly stayed where she was for some more minutes; then, seeing that Hannah appeared to have told her all she had to, she delicately let go of her hand and stepped out on tiptoe. She told Barrett to let the other women in and to have Hannah's trunk taken to her own chamber: she would open it as soon as she had the time.

On that day, however, her mind was soon busy again, for her father came back with several precious gifts for her. She later learnt that old Hannah had died soon after talking to her, without saying another word.

John Fletcher, the famous poet and dramatist, was finally in sight of Gayhurst house. He was tired and hungry, but what he fancied most was a glass of cool, good wine.

"There we are," he said turning to the three men following him, and spurred his horse. The orders he had received entitled him to enlist a local militia and search the ancient manor-house from top to bottom. Confiding in his own intuitive and rhetorical skills, however, Fletcher first wanted to personally speak to Lady Mary and, as long as that was possible, behave as the gentleman he was. Should the woman's words be unconvincing, he would ride back to town and order the sheriff to put together a patrol. But how on earth were they going to feed and pay their men for all the days that would be needed for a thorough search, seeing that all this manor had was two cows and four chickens? He had no intention of putting his own money into it: everybody knew how slow the Government was in refunding. No: he would try to do everything by himself, as he trusted his wits enough for such a comparatively simple mission. He only had to be quick enough and play on surprise.

From the front yard, a little girl feeding the chickens spotted them at once and ran inside. When, a couple of minutes later, Fletcher and his men dismounted, they were met by the old manservant that Fletcher remembered well as a good-natured man. This time, though, he had something rude about him and glared at them balefully: he might have been made rougher by his long permanence in the country, of course; or he might not. They asked for the lady of the house; he let them in without hardly a word and without offering them anything to relieve the weariness of their journey.

Despite their haste and stealth, Lady Mary Digby seemed to be waiting for them. She was sitting at the large table of what had previously been the banqueting hall, which now displayed diverse works in progress: bunches of raw, partly wrought wool, a winder, a spindle, several pieces of cut cloth and other sewing material. From the poverty surrounding them, Fletcher understood that they were very unlikely to find any good wine here: well, he would be contented with a tankard of home-made beer.

She didn't stand up to welcome them. She was wearing a plain, faded black dress, her fair, almost unnaturally pale face covered by a thin, precious black veil lined with black lace, through which one could see a white ruff reaching to her shoulders. A veil of ancient times, whose use was forbidden: an old veil women used to wear in church in the time of superstition. 'Tis unbelievable, thought Fletcher: with all the searches these people have been through, they still manage to pull out – from God knows what secret cabinet – things about whose existence one would no longer suspect. They were cleverer than the devil himself.

Lady Mary, still elegant and dignified even in her now unhappy poverty, did not invite them to take a seat, neither did she offer them a glass of water, nor even wasted time on ceremonies, but coldly said to him, her clear, low, firm voice echoing in the huge empty room: "You are not welcome, Master Fletcher. Why do you come alone? Where is my son?"

In spite of himself, Fletcher broke into an almost embarrassed grin. "This is precisely what I've come to ask you, Milady."

"Your question surprises me: he was certainly not entrusted to *me*. What's become of him?"

"He's run away, Milady. 'Tis not my fault, if not in that I trusted him. He was clearly not worthy of my trust… But are you sure he hasn't come back home?"

"He would never have, had he really run away, since he knew perfectly well that you would come for him. But he couldn't come back regardless, because he's dead!"

Fletcher frowned. "How can you know, Milady?"

"He was stabbed, down in London, while he was in *your* custody. In the streets, at night. How can I know what he was doing out of doors at that time? Had he been here with me, this certainly would never have happened. A quarrel? A drunken row? I do not know: it wasn't me as took him to tour all the taverns of the City. A coarse dagger opened his belly and he went to die like a dog, he, a gentleman, in the ditch of a suburban lane. A beggar saw him die and received his last words. Jack made him promise he would run and tell me; as a proof, he brought me this!" She took from her lap a white lace handkerchief, all crumpled with clotted blood, and threw it on the table. "'Tis me embroidered this: I know it well! As a reward, that beggar will have taken all he had in his pockets and even his garments, leaving the poor body as naked as a beast's." Lady Mary lifted her veil and fixed on him inquisitive eyes, as black as her dress, as chilly as her voice: "Tell me: is't all true?"

Fletcher sighed. "Your version is in unfortunate concordance with what I know, Milady."

He had sunk into a small old armchair, without waiting for her to invite him to do so, while his three henchmen had remained standing behind him. "But I must tell you that your son was *not* hanging round to have fun, or to have a merry drink with his friends. He escaped from my lodging to surreptitiously enter an honest subject's house and steal a precious document from him, through which, I am afraid, he meant to blackmail someone."

While talking, he scanned his eyes first on the bare stone slabs of the floor, then on the mighty grey mastiff that had come to lie down at his mistress' feet and was now growling at them. "Unluckily for him, however, the room was being watched by a zealous servant, who certainly didn't realise he'd stabbed a gentleman; also on account of his high birth, however, Master John should never, for no reason whatever, have found himself in that place at that moment. I regret to tell you, Milady, but your son died while committing a crime," he concluded, raising his look.

She screwed her eyes. "A would-be criminal, therefore, wasn't he, like his father?"

Fletcher nodded slightly. She pressed him on: "Not, rather, a would-be secret agent like you? Do not think I don't know! Might it perhaps be while playing spies and sheriff that he lost his life? Or else, more realistically, on some absurd mission *you* gave him? I want the truth, Fletcher!"

"This is the truth, Lady Digby, however painful it may be. And I'll tell you more: he had an accomplice. There were two of them, on that night, climbing over the garden wall and breaking into that man's property. We still do not know who the other was, but we are investigating the whole matter."

She didn't seem to be listening. "I wonder where he died: I can never even bury him, as I couldn't bury my husband. He must have been left on the side of a street, then thrown into the river, or buried in a common pit, he who has a family tomb and crest… As it went with his father, I will never have a place where to mourn for him. Nothing is left for me now: my husband, my eldest son, my property ... Not even my family's good name." Her voice got gradually louder, and louder, until she was shouting: "YOU took Jack away from me, saying you meant to give him more: THIS is the result. I don't give a straw how your investigations will proceed: they can never give MY son back to me! YOU are not welcome, Master Fletcher! GO, now, and never dare come back again!"

Lady Mary stood up, while the dog started barking. Despite her minute stature, Fletcher was awed. He bowed, mumbled some confused farewell and walked out with his men. They mounted and were soon gone, galloping into the horizon.

So, Speed's servant had been right in saying the blow he had stricken against that petty thief was no scratch. So, he had done away with young Digby. But what if the woman had been lying and had concealed her wounded son in the house? No: he couldn't have survived. No: he couldn't have reached home alone, on foot, his side slit open by a dagger. At any rate, it wasn't worth organising a manhunt with the sheriff and the shire pursuivants. So much the better: he would save both time and money.

He made for the closest alehouse. The thought could certainly not have crossed his mind that, before rushing to Buckinghamshire, he had better ask Jenny, the humble scullery maid of Salisbury House, or the men who had been guarding it a couple of days before, in the early morning, who would perhaps give him a slightly different version of recent events. Fletcher couldn't have dreamt of this, and neither did he get to know. Also because, on getting back to London, he found Salisbury House in complete chaos, and for far more weighty reasons. So much that no one ever tried to look into John Kenelm Digby's squalid death. After all, he was but a common thief and a traitor's son.

Once the dance was over, the King's Men made their ritual bow. This had been a successful show and had pleased the high-ranking, elegant audience who, though generous in their applause, never let themselves be involved too much. The leading player, Richard Burbage, was not sure what they had liked most: their performance, the magnificent stage props, or the music and dances? This sedate tragicomedy was more similar to a masque, the kind of entertainment which, by now, was storming the Court: a beautiful, extremely expensive facade, full of good taste, but void, like a beautifully painted egg that someone had drunk up. All in all, this was also the least dangerous genre, both to applaud and to stage, and, to them, the most economically rewarding of all. Grinning widely, he bowed again. But what nostalgia he felt for the dirty, dusty history plays that had been so much cheered, and even participated by the *mobile vulgus,* by the blue-attired sour 'prentices whose stench of sweat and garlic came up to him from the pit. How he longed for those half-blood plots, full to the brim with coarse jokes and coded messages, slaughter-blood trickling down the stage. Now rich and famous, he pined for the time he had been poor, obscure, and free. Those low, smiling bows were becoming increasingly hard for him.

They broke ranks and, chatting, stepped down the wooden stairs leading to the tiring house. Burbage went further: as leading player, and main shareholder of the company, he was entitled to a room all for himself, which had been created at the end of a sort of small cellar in that ancient building. While crossing the wide main cellar, he walked past Tim Rice's grave, now perfectly concealed under the six large slabs which looked as if they had never been touched. He sadly crossed himself and, instead of stepping into his little room, walked by and took a narrow passage leading to the lower, deeper, huge Blackfriars dungeons. No one had ever explored them completely, for they were damp and chilly. Above all, they were said to be still haunted by the ghosts of the black friars who had dwelt in the large Dominican convent before King Henry VIII had it closed down and splintered into a thousand small properties to be either sold or rented away.

The prestigious private theatre, which had later been bought by Burbage's father, had been obtained from the chapter house of that big convent; right there, many years ago, the first church trial had been held against Katherine, Henry's Spanish queen. So that, this being universally known, no one could help but see Katherine tried again each time their company had staged *The Winter's Tale*, with poor Hermione's unfair trial. So much that the King's Men were now allowed to perform it at the Globe, and at Court too, but not any longer at Blackfriars.

The mysterious former inhabitants were said to be haunting the subterranean tunnels of their ancient convent, complaining about their sad lot: while most of them had given in, and had let their House be "dissolved" by the King, others had resisted. They had ended up in chains in those very dungeons, never to emerge again; so that, still today, people happened to hear queer noises and a strange clanking, as if of chains, coming from those tunnels, especially on All Hallows Even and on Christmas night.

Richard Burbage would have liked to be as brave as the great lion-hearted king whose name he bore, or even as he often appeared on stage, in the role of Henry the Fifth or Coriolanus, but he knew well he was not. Despite this, he lit a lamp, shrugged and went down yet another ladder. He was met by a gust of dampness and a musty stench. The ancient convent had been built at the meeting point of two rivers, great Thames and little Fleet, so that one descending would often meet puddles and water trickling. Burbage went further down as one who knows well his way, although he shuddered at the flight of bats which met him as he turned a corner with his swinging lamp. He went down a short staircase cut into live stone until he got to an opening, a sort of small cave. There he stopped, as if waiting, after sitting down on a rough bench that had also been cut into live stone. Opposite him, a niche hosted something like a sarcophagus, on which the friars had set two sitting skeletons. Over the niche were some roughly carved words: *Estis quod fuimus, quod sumus eritis*. It was one of the friars' *Memento mori*. No one, even had they gone so deep down, would ever dare remove it, and risk calling the wraiths' wrath down on their heads. Burbage stared at those grinning skulls which, comfortably sitting, and partially hit by the light of his lamp, seemed to be laughing at him and at all the woes of the living. And how could one forget about death? What need was there to be reminded? But, maybe, those had been different times.

He shortly caught sight of another swinging lamp coming from the opposite end of the tunnel, in the hand of a cloaked and hooded man who stopped before him and uncovered his face. It was Shakspere.

"Hey, Dick!"

"Hey, Will!"

"How did it go?"

"Not bad. And for St George we'll be at the Globe in the morning and here again in the afternoon, rehearsals in between. We miss thee, Will."

"I miss you too."

"Come on: thou'rt treated like a lord."

"Of course, I can't complain: they're dear folks. And their organisation is unbelievable. Thou canst not imagine how many people were saved thanks to them. Including 'Long John' Gerard, as thou knowst: 'tis here he was hiding while, in the Tower, they were torturing Garnet. Seest thou, once one manages to get here, he's safe."

"Don't speak too soon, Will, just in case. Just wait, before speaking."

Shakspere sat down beside him. "Only, I'm sorry for them: they've run out of money and their patrons too have been impoverished by the fines. While I'm here, an absurd thought is dawning on me: buy the place."

"Art out of thy mind?"

"Relax, Dick, that was but a thought. I wonder how much it may cost… I'll talk about it at home, to my women, in case I manage to get back there. Thou seest, I really owe a lot to these people. And then, I wouldn't mind the idea of becoming a small landlord here, inside the City. So far, I've only bought property at home, in my little village… Let's say it would be a spiritual purchase, for the good of my soul, which badly needs it. We'll see. What news?"

"Nothing, Will. Only…"

"I don't understand: how come nothing is moving? I expected a sudden order of arrest. I don't like this stillness."

"Listen to me. Knowst thou what happened a few days ago? Here comes Fletcher with his usual bragging, hiding some secret rage behind his customary idiotic smile, telling us that we've obviously been very lucky, but that winning a battle, and totally undeservedly, doesn't mean winning the war. What on earth did he mean?"

"Who knows? If thou dost not, who seest him every day..."

"Then he grins again and says he's almost finished the first of the four new history plays."

Shakspere's mouth had an unchecked twitch of pain. "*My* tragedy about Katherine. My last tragedy about my Katherine. She that, like a jewel, hung twenty years about that pig's neck, yet never lost her lustre..."

"Ay... I'm sorry, Will. He will have turned it into a complacent big drama with a happy ending. And we'll even have to stage it! He wants to entitle it *'Tis all true,* or something of the sort: ridiculous! Anyway, apart from *Henry VIII,* 'tis not clear what he's referring to. Something went wrong with him, but what? I don't know what you're talking about, I says, but he laughs in my face, 'cause, he says, we players are good dissemblers, nay, equivocators, and when one has anything to do with us nothing is ever certain. I just can't work it out."

"Maybe he's just bluffing, to get me out of my hole."

"I say! But why did no one look for thee, not even in Stratford?"

"I don't know, Dick... Art sure about this?"

"As sure as death."

"This unexpected calm frightens me. What has become of young Digby? Has he come back?"

"He hasn't. Let's hope he's not playing double."

"I don't think so. He'd found interesting details about the Plot: he was trying to rehabilitate Sir Everard's memory."

"I also believed he was really fond of poor Tim: he was devastated by his death."

"Tim... 'Tis as if I'd lost yet another son, yet another brother. He died for me, Dick, dost understand? He died to save me." Shakspere covered his face with his hands and cried. "Last night I went up to his grave and sat down beside him, as I couldn't sleep at his thought. I talked to him all night, as I used to do with my poor Hamnet, and then with Edmund. I felt like a barren flower, if thou getst what I mean. A flower blossoming by mistake on a dead stump." Dick nodded. "And I thought: How can I ever repay him?"

"By staying alive for as long as thou canst, Will. Just stay here in London some more weeks, out of safety. Then, when we learn some detail about what exactly has happened, go home for a while and stay put. Only when we're sure that the dust has settled wilt thou come back among us."

"'Tis over in any case, Dick. Apart from the fact that I simply *can't* work with Fletcher, if I ever come back to the company I'll have to take the Oath or be arrested. And I won't take it, Dick, for Tim's sake too. He died to preserve my integrity. Even if I didn't have any other reason, I could never let him down like this, for he's looking at us from above. Because, besides his being a good boy, there's no greater love than giving up thy life for thy friends. And now, just as Tim gave his life for my sake, Digby may well be risking his own for Tim's memory. And shall I falter before such heroism? I'm not made of martyr's stuff, Dick, and thou knowst this: none of us jugglers are. We chose to be living chronicles as long as we could. Now 'tis no longer possible, but this is not a good reason for me to bend down. I'm no *bending author* any more, Dick."

"I've taken both Oaths, Will, as thou knowst."

"No problem, Dick: it's become too difficult not to. What's more, thy life is here in London, with thy family, thy brother and all thy relations. Mine's no longer here, instead. At home, far from everybody's eyes, I'll manage to resist and won't take any oath."

"They've all sworn, by now: Southampton, Ben Jonson, Jack Donne and our old Rob Armin… Jack Donne's even pondering whether to take holy orders and make a career in His Majesty's Church now established. Right him, with the renowned forefathers he has; with all the blood they spilled for him too… His old mother is distraught, but he's decided to back the fastest horse."

"Well, that one's known never to've been a saint and not even a hero!"

"I would say so…"

"But saying he means to be a clergyman is sure to be just gossip: I know him too well."

"I know him too, my friend, and I think he will, instead. And what sayst thou about all the others?"

"That these are cruel times, Dick."

"I'll tell thee one more thing: if thou goest back home, retiring to thy little village, they'll say thou hast conformed, and people will believe it."

"What can I do about that?"

"Nothing. Now, I tell thee, just try and stay alive. For thyself, for thy loved ones, for Tim and for us all."

"Didn't Fletcher ask questions about him?"

"He didn't even realise he's no longer with us."

"Not that I doubted it... That's saying a lot about his skill as a Gov'ment agent!"

"'Tis also saying a lot 'bout the consideration you poets have of us poor players! Anyway, should he ask, we'll tell him that Tim left us a while ago and we know not where he is."

Shakspere stood up. "Better for thee to go, now, in case they look for thee. Let's meet again here on St George's day following your afternoon play."

"I hope I'll bring thee clearer and more comforting news, by then. Take care, Will."

They shook hands and walked off in opposite directions, each man going his dark way, each with his lamp swinging against the dismal walls of the ghastly dungeon.

Lady Mary Digby always rose before dawn, soon after Ellen and Adam. At night, when her heart was so troubled for everything that had happened and kept her awake for hours on end, action – whatever kind of action – was the only thing that could relieve her. While working, she felt that things were taking a good turn; when she was in bed, instead, she was overwhelmed by the fear that something terrible was about to strike her and all her children.

The wind and rain of the previous night had cleared the sky, which was now being slowly flooded with the purest morning light. She walked out, into the back yard, to fetch some water from the well, and filled her lungs with the cool air. She shivered, wrapped her shawl tighter and looked towards the horizon, wondering what this new day might bring. Then she stiffened in alarm. She looked southwards, where she was sure she had seen something move. Ay, something was moving in the park, and it was not an animal. Thanks be to God, it was surely not a troop of armed horsemen either. It was a solitary human figure coming out of the woods and slowly advancing, nay, staggering towards her. It didn't seem to be hiding. Her instinct told her that this was not a criminal. It certainly couldn't be the Earl of Northampton coming back to renew his proposal, maybe with some blackmail or other in his pockets; it might be one of his men, though. But Lady Mary was also used to helping and sheltering mysterious lonely travellers: more realistically, then, it was some runaway. Although she hadn't heard of any man-hunt in the area, she resolutely, fearlessly walked towards the figure.

It was a young boy. Small, frail, cold and drenched to the skin. Her mother's heart was moved to pity. "Who are you and what brings you here?" she asked from a distance, without speaking too loudly, as soon as she was sure he could hear her.

"Is this Gayhurst House? I'm looking for the lady of the house; please, take me to her!" he answered in a voice that was at once hoarse and shrill.

Lady Mary got closer. The young traveller's garments, however ruined and muddy, were of fine quality. "Are you alone?"

"I am. I'm on the run, please help me! Is your mistress still in bed?"

"I am her. Come." Lady Mary led him into the large kitchen, by the crackling fire, and invited him to spread his drenched cloak near it.

"I heartily thank you, Milady!" the boy said in a suddenly different voice, unclasping his cloak and uncovering his head.

Lady Mary was shocked at the damp, dark curls cascading from the hood – for it was a girl.

"My name is Mildred, Milady. Mildred Elizabeth Cecil."

Old Ellen, who walked in at that very moment, dropped the tin jug and ladle she was carrying to fetch some milk. The noise might have woken up the whole world, but Lady Mary appeared not to have heard anything, she was so stunned.

"I'm looking for Jack. I know that he's alive and he's here. No, my father knows nothing about this. Trust me! I've brought this for you, Milady, for you only. Do not be afraid." She gave her the leather bundle she had been clutching.

It contained a leather-bound book. It hadn't got wet, but its front cover was partly ruined, faded and discoloured in some spots. Lady Mary had a better look, lifting the book to the window which let in the first slanting sunbeams of the day. The lighter spots formed the features of a human face: a face she had known and loved, a face she would never see again in this life. Holding it with both hands, she fell to her knees, dumb with amazement, her eyes glued to it. She didn't understand. In a flash, she thought that trying to flee would be perfectly useless: if it was a trick, there was nothing in the world to do. Everything was lost.

"I'm looking for Jack, Milady, forgive me," the girl repeated gently. But Lady Mary was too stunned to react. Summoned by the noise of the jug and ladle, Jack peeked out from the back stairs.

He didn't dare believe his eyes. His distant, secret, forbidden love was right here, in his own home, materialised out of nothing, chatting in the kitchen with Ellen and his mother as if it were perfectly normal. Exactly as in his wildest, most beautiful, most foolish dreams; miles away from London, Hatfield and every other surveilled place. Milly, whom he had been absolutely certain he would never meet again, was now right here in front of him. Better still: she had left behind all the luxury, all the handsome youths with brilliant prospects she had met at Court, and had come to look for him in his poor disgraced family.

He wanted to run to her and hold her tight, also to know whether or not it was all true, but he didn't dare. He advanced slowly, shuffling his feet, slightly screwing his eyes, all three women staring at him. He stopped in front of Milly and stood there without a word, his arms along his sides, confusion on his face.

She did not speak either, looking at him with her usual teasing half-smile. She had mud on her face and even in her hair. The situation must surely be tragic: why on earth had she left her father's dwelling? If she was smiling, on the other hand, nothing was beyond remedy. His thought went to the King's Men and Shakspere. If Milly was smiling, they might not have arrested him, after all. If Milly was smiling, everything was all right. He tried to smile too, also because he didn't want his mother to worry. But when he looked at Milly's eyes, he was suddenly afraid she would laugh at him for the idiotic expression he felt was painted on his face. So, he decided to attack first.

"Hey! Dost know thou'rt ridiculous, dressed up as a man?"

She kept looking at him in silence.

"How silly thou art!" she said in the end, and threw her arms round his neck. Jack embraced her mechanically, as if still not believing either his eyes or his arms. It was not before some seconds had gone by that he realised she was crying – again, as she had done on that memorable day at Salisbury House. Only now did he understand that, if Milly had really run away from her golden cage, she could never go back. He was all that was left for her, now. Milly had forever given up her princely life to seek him out in his misery. He felt proud. He held her more tightly. Her hair smelt of moss and fresh earth.

"Fool, fool, thou'rt but a fool!" Milly went on softly, starting to sob. "You can't imagine the sorrow, the fear, all alone in the open country... The cold, in search of this house which I could never find, running away from everybody. By day and night... You don't know the weariness... How full of anguish I was!"

"I... I..." Jack mumbled. It was as if the whirlwind in his heart had jammed his words together. Fearing he might say something stupid, he said nothing. He looked round. His mother was shaking her head in disapproval. In the end, he spoke. "Milly, I was joking! I'm so happy thou'rt here, so happy!"

Lady Mary was quick to overcome her shock. She had realised there was nothing to fear. Not yet, anyhow. Now she was sure this girl wasn't concealing any deception. She gently put her arm round Milly's waist, told her to calm down, for everything was all right, and that she needn't explain everything right now. She and Ellen led her to her own room, prepared a hot bath and some food, then laid her to sleep in her bed. Jack, who knew not whither to go or what else to do, remained sitting in the kitchen to look at the fire, Milly's cloak spread out beside him, an unprecedented confusion in his mind. Clouds had gathered again, meanwhile, and it had started to rain. On the kitchen table, the precious relic-book with Garnet's face seemed to be looking at him and telling him over and over again that he hadn't been dreaming.

"Methinks thou owest me some little explanation, son," said Lady Mary as soon as she got down again, not knowing whether she felt more anxious or flabbergasted, resentful or, even, amused.

"Ay, mother," he replied without taking his eyes off the fire. "She's... the part I haven't told you. Because I thought it wasn't important..."

Royal forest of Royston, Hertfordshire, 15 April 1611

The sun peeped out from an opening in the thick layer of clouds and projected a glorious rainbow against the horizon. As day advanced, the air was getting warmer. Amongst dripping beeches and oaks, the dead leaves on the path, brown, red, yellow, were glistening with still water.

On his majestic steed, Henry Frederick Stuart, Prince of Wales, Duke of Rothesay and Cornwall, Earl of Carrick, Baron of Renfrew, Lord of the Isles and Great Regent of Scotland was cantering a little ahead of his group. He wanted to enjoy the peace and quiet of the woods by himself, without the racket of dogs, beaters, servants carrying dead prey and their typical smell of blood. He, however, the most important youth of the kingdom, knew that he wasn't free. An heir to the throne could never be alone, not even for a moment. There: even now, his young Gentlemen of the Chamber were hurrying after him, galloping on the drenched grass of the clearing. He gave a light spur and sent his horse to full gallop, letting them understand he didn't wish for company. They got the message and slowed down.

The Prince disliked hunting. He couldn't see what satisfaction one could get in defying feeble, doomed creatures. Weapons, and fights, were meant to brave and defeat attackers, foes, villains, oppressors. The good must fight against the bad, not against helpless beasts. This might be the very reason the King his father loved hunting so much: because it made him feel bold, great and strong. Because it enabled him to exert a supreme, ruthless power over inferior beings which were completely at his mercy. But, then, his father was but a despicable coward: the Prince would have liked to see him, who said he loved danger, hunting a bear, or even a boar, without his train of courtiers and only armed with a dagger, as the kings of old used to do during rites of initiation. He could hardly imagine that. The King his father only liked vast, crowded hunting parties where he had a chance to show off before the whole Court, chasing and killing the best stag, which others had found for him.

King James knew well how deeply his favourite sport was despised by his first born, who, even as a child, only wanted to fight against goblins and dragons, and save threatened princesses. That was why, years ago, he had had that famous portrait of him painted. That had been the first time the little Prince had dared squarely set his will against his father's and defy his judgment: almost as a form of punishment, then, His Majesty had had him portrayed with a newly killed stag while, little more than a child, he sheathed his sword. That universally admired painting was but a demonstration of the absolute power his father exerted over him, and through which he thought he could control, along with the members of family, all his subjects as well. God's delegate, the Lord's anointed. But now little Harry had grown up and it wouldn't be that easy for the King to force him to do what he didn't want to do. Just let him try, now! He would answer him back in front of the entire Court.

His first childhood memory flashed before his mind. It went back to long before that picture was painted. He wasn't yet three, then, and a churlish, repulsive manservant had just wrenched him from his royal mother's arms to take him far away, to be fostered in the Earl of Mar's castle. He was screaming as if under torture, while the Queen had gone down on her knees in a flood of tears, begging her husband to leave her child with her for a little, little longer: but to no avail whatever. He had only cried his eyes out, back then; he had only despaired, without wondering who the villain of the situation might be, apart from that repellent servant. Only later had it been explained to him that the King didn't wish his wife to exert a bad religious influence on him and had consequently taken the decision to entrust him to a guardian of the right persuasion. What nonsense: if the King really feared he might grow up a Papist – which, seeing his love for honesty, could never be -, it would have been enough to give his son the right tutors, as he had later done. What need was there to tear him from his mother at such a tender age? As to Queen Anne, Prince Henry didn't know whether she had ever forgiven her husband for what he had done to her. What he remembered well was that later on, as soon as the King had rushed southwards to take possession of his new English kingdom, his apparently submissive Queen had quickly put together a troop of armed men and had, in person, marched to Stirling to fetch her son by force, were it needed. Her plan had failed, though, the only result being that of losing the baby she was carrying in her womb. At this point the King, who had maybe taken pity on her, had graciously given Harry back to her as the King's special gift, so that all three of them might meet in London. But he was already nine, by then, his mother a total stranger to him, while his father was someone he couldn't even remember. And how could such a father, now, ask his son to love and revere him, he who not only had never done anything to be loved and revered, but whom it was utterly impossible to love and revere in any way?

By now, this was impossible for everyone not to see: subjects, courtiers, noblemen. A true sovereign must be a royal figure and set the example in everything. He must shine with human and Christian virtues, especially if he also wanted to be (and must be!) Head of the Church. He must be like Marcus Aurelius, who used to watch over his empire by day and night, heroically fighting against weariness and even against sleep, besides fighting against every other passion and temptation of the flesh. A true king must deprive himself of food and sleep for his kingdom's sake, not spend his nights in carousal and debauchery and his days chasing game, after delegating his kingly power to a slithering, insidious, creepy being who was as clever as he was false. The Prince despised Robert Cecil, the hunchback, not only because he could never bear arms or mount a war horse: he despised him because the fox's cunning must never go without the lion's strength and royalty. Because cunning without strength and virtue was a danger to many, a disgrace to everybody.

The Prince grimaced in disgust at the thought that one of his father's favourite ways to show his royalty was to gather the lowest commoners of the kingdom in a line before him, pretending he could heal them from scrofula, "the King's evil", through his holy touch. Pity that not one, in those eight years he had been on the British throne, had ever averred they'd been healed by him!

He looked behind and, seeing he was alone, slowed down a little. He touched his cheeks as he remembered the disappointment when he had last looked at himself in a mirror, a few months before. What a shock it had been when he had recognised in his own face the same features he loathed so much! The same long face, the same spacious brow, the same round-tipped nose. From that day on, he had ordered mirrors to be removed from all his chambers. As a child, he had looked so much like Queen Anne and his dear little sister Lizzie: why was he now becoming a living image of his father? Might God, who had chosen him for this all-important task of ruling over an empire, be giving him a lesson of humility? Might He be punishing him for not honouring enough the man from whose loins he had come? Ay, he might.

He knew well that he was grievously sinning against the Fourth Commandment: but he also knew that it was not in his poor human power to manage his loathing and respect this man. Therefore, he asked God for the necessary patience to triumph over this horrible devilish temptation. He asked Him to let him live long enough to change. It was humanly impossible, for he felt he hated him a little more each day, and, now he was no longer small and helpless, he no longer bit his tongue when he had something to say. He was no longer silent, even if His Majesty couldn't brook insubordination, nor the mere prospect that his orders should be questioned.

But a true king must also be endowed with the necessary humility to listen both to the Privy Council and Parliament, must he not? King James, however, apparently trusted no one apart from Cecil... Nay, almost no one: for his surrounding himself with universally hated favourites was more evident each day, and more harmful for his already marred reputation. The Prince saw dark clouds gather above the throne each time the King had an argument with members of Parliament, especially with Puritans. Unless he, as Henry the Ninth, managed to give a new course to royal policy, he didn't see a bright future for the monarchy.

In his father's eyes, every objection was dissidence, all opposition was sedition. Since, therefore, he was clearly unfit to rule, maybe it was better for him to spend all his time far from the Court chasing boars and stags. Meanwhile the true Boar, endowed with a hunch and crooked tusks like a fierce beast of the forest, ruled in his stead. But, as soon as he succeeded to the throne, Prince Harry would change many things. He would *put down the mighty from their seats, and exalt them of low degree* – such people of low degree as poor Sir Walter Ralegh, who had been confined in the Tower, a death sentence hanging over his head, for treason he had not committed.

The Prince was wrenched from the course of his thoughts by the insistent call of Robert Carr, a youth of obscure origins who had recently become the King's number one favourite. Harry would have liked to strike him down with his sword, he hated him so much. That special, intimate friendship had further contributed to widening the yawning gap already alienating the King from his Queen, who suffered in silence. And who was this Carr? A short, fattish, flabby man, neither cultivated nor clever, who loved everything the King said he must love and did everything the King said he must do. A lackey by nature, a flatterer, a spineless fop, an opportunist; and a plebeian, on top of all that. Of all the world, the last person he would want to meet or listen to, right now. Except his father, of course.

Carr, who sat in his saddle like a bag of turf, was galloping like mad, clearly frightened at his own speed. "Your Grace, please, stop, I beg you! The King your father commands that you go to him right now!"

The Prince turned his steed and without a word, wrath mounting inside him, followed that frilly youth who curled his hair with tongs. As usual, His Majesty didn't ask: he commanded. And, by sending him this upstart coxcomb, he was telling him to stay in his place. He launched his horse forward, determined either to give Carr the slip or have him tossed by that nag he couldn't control.

But he reached the rest of the group too soon, unfortunately. His Majesty was having a midday snack with all his Court: gentlemen, servants, beaters, dogs, horses. Sitting on a specially made stool, with his short legs and protruding belly, he looked like a juggler dressed up as a king; a player who, now the show was over, was having a bite before taking off his stage costume. The Prince unwillingly dismounted and went to homage his father, bending his right knee.

He soon found out why he had sent for him: to berate him! Lifting a half-nibbled chicken leg into the air, the King told him, loudly and quite solemnly, while everyone was looking at them, that he had not liked the way in which the Prince had kept apart during the chase; that dislike for the noble sport of hunting betrayed a dislike for arms, for fighting, for daily measuring oneself with the forces of Nature, as well as a scanty wish to test oneself. For the good of the Kingdom, therefore, he wished his son, who would one day sway the rod of the empire, to take a more active and enthusiastic part.

The Prince couldn't believe his ears: was his father – he of all people, he who trembled at seeing a bare bodkin even from a distance – calling him a coward in front of everyone? Was he calling *him* a coward, who got up at dawn every day, took daily exercise, was a better swordsman and tournament knight than anyone else, who often fasted to strengthen both his body and his spirit, who was unrivalled as a runner or swimmer? And how he hated his horrid Scottish accent! He lost control. He stood up, grabbed a stick leaning against a nearby tree and rushed at his father, who, from his low stool, gaped at him in fear. Harry was repelled by the expression of pure terror on his flaccid face, by that shapeless body, by those garments that were meant to be lavish and instead couldn't but make him even more ridiculous. He lifted the stick.

In the fraction of a second, the King realised that his son had been too quick, that none of his guards would have the time to protect him and that maybe, even if they had, no one would dare restrain the Prince. He realised that Harry would hit him with a stick before the whole Court, that this would be a terrible blow to his royalty, that he would lose everyone's esteem, that his son might even take the throne from him, without waiting for his death and without anyone objecting. He lifted his crossed arms, his right hand still holding his chicken leg, to cover his face, like a mischievous urchin before his angry father.

But then the youth lowered the stick and threw it far away: thank God, he had managed to master his wrath. He then turned his back on the King and, without a word, mounted and sped off. No one tried to stop him. The young gentlemen forming his train, who had not yet dismounted, simply turned their horses and followed him, and so did several other courtiers, quickly taking to their horses.

While riding away, the Prince breathed deeply, trying his best to choke the hatred that gushed forth from his heart and that now, had broken its banks and was flooding his whole being. What would that gormless grub do now? Disinherit him, exclude him from the succession, throw him into the Tower? He doubted it: seeing how popular his son was, he certainly wouldn't dare. Only then did he realise that, besides disliking him, his father feared him. He turned round: his entourage was surely larger than the King's. He had seen this before, in a sense, but today's hunt reflected on a small scale the whole kingdom. Had he chosen to do so, Harry of Wales could organise a coup and dethrone this king he was ashamed to call his father; as Zeus had done with Chronos, to hell with the Fourth

Commandment. Not unlike what the Earl of Essex had tried to do, ten years ago, with the old Queen.

Essex had failed, though, because he wasn't of royal blood, and also because he didn't claim the throne for himself. As for Cecil, who had stopped Essex, Harry would neutralise him before he could harm him.

Ay, *if* he had chosen to do so. But why force the hand of Destiny, since the throne was already practically his? Well, maybe in order to contain the damage: Great Britain, this artificial kingdom pretentiously created by his father, was to him like a sick body in urgent need of care before the death throes began. He didn't want to inherit a wreck, impossible to fix and launch again into the open seas. After all, the great Edward the Third, the knight-king of yore, had also taken the throne from a worthless father, deposing him for his very worthlessness and for his all too many male favourites.

The sky had cleared now, and the sun, high above, made everything shine: tree trunks, leaves quick and dead, puddles, and even some stones, while Prince Harry, frowning, thoughtful, continued to gallop at full speed, followed by his large entourage.

Milly rested for the whole morning and part of the afternoon. When she woke up, she was offered clean garments, Lady Mary all the while apologising for their modesty. She came down to the kitchen – from where Jack had hardly moved – smiled at him and embraced him again. Jack still couldn't believe it all. She was so fair, thus simply dressed in coarse wool and brown cloth. And it was strange, so strange for him, Milly smelling of the herbs Ellen used to perfume his mother's trunk with. This paradoxical combination told him that Milly was now part of him, just as Gayhurst and all its dwellers. The children came to meet "Jack's friend"; Milly embraced and joyfully kissed each of them.

Their mother entrusted each with a longish errand and off they ran. Sitting at the kitchen table, a mug of hot milk before her, alone with Lady Mary and Jack, Milly began her narration.

"On that day thou fledst, I was called to the deathbed of an elderly laundry servant. I couldn't see why, since I don't believe I'd ever said a word to her in my life and neither could I remember her face. I went, mostly out of curiosity, for they told me she wished to talk to my father at all costs, but, as thou knowst, Jack, he was away. Why on earth should a dying laundress want to bother him? Well, the woman is at her last. She sends everybody out of the room apart from me and mutters about repentance, and divine punishment, and tells me to look in her trunk. I try to soothe her as best as I can, then have the trunk taken to my chamber and, with one thing and another – because in the meantime my father had come back – I forget about it, and open it on the following day, and meanwhile she has died. I can't find anything unusual, only old rags and everything that can belong to a servant: cuts of cloth, some savings, some... beads, you call them? And then a couple of old silver spoons, such things, so I still can't understand. Then, some days later, I take some time and patiently start to empty it out. There, right at the bottom, carefully hidden among the folds of a shawl, I find a piece of paper on which someone had glued the torn pieces of a note or letter. They were tiny shreds, I wondered how long they'd taken to paste them all in their right position like as many mosaic pieces. It looked like the rough copy of one of my father's papers, but it was hardly legible, full of blottings and writings between lines, and all faded as well, as if it had been washed. What was it? Of course the old woman must have been speaking about this paper, which she was most likely to have found somewhere. Why was it so important as to trouble her at the moment of death? In the end, I managed to read some words. I'll report them to you: *'God and man hath concurred to punish the wickedness of this time…'*"

Jack's eyes popped in amazement: he had always known this, in a certain sense, but now could hardly believe his ears. This was the evidence he was looking for, the evidence he wished to present to Prince Harry! It was Lady Mary who exclaimed: "Mounteagle's letter! 'Tis Cecil wrote it… That is, Lord Salisbury, your father. I knew this! That was the rough copy!"

"Ay," Milly went on. "But I took some time to put things together in my mind. For, Milady, I couldn't bring myself to believe my father to have done such a thing. And then, Jack, forgive me, but I couldn't believe thou wert right all along! My esteem for my father was at stake, but it was also a matter of personal pride… But when I went down to the library to compare the two versions, and I saw it perfectly corresponded with the text that had been published in the transcripts, and that it was like a smoking gun in my father's hand, I felt as if I were dying. Because in the end I didn't want to believe it, but it was really as thou hadst said to me, Jack." She smiled and looked away for a second. "I've also come to say I'm sorry."

"Thank God," Jack replied. "Thank God that, having to say thou wert sorry, thou'st come all the way up here!"

"'Twas terrible, Jack. In one second I had to acknowledge that the true traitor, the one who had betrayed everybody else, was my own father. He, the most faithful of His Majesty's servants!" Jack thought of *Secret Macbeth*, which said exactly the same thing. Milly went on: "I could hardly believe it, but there was no other explanation. What was that letter doing at the bottom of a servant's trunk? The old woman had probably found the pieces in some of papa's pockets, while washing his clothes, and had carefully put them together, maybe in order to blackmail him; then, however, for some reason she hadn't done so. Maybe she'd been afraid."

"But could she read?" asked Jack.

"I have no idea. But she certainly knew what it was."

"And now, on the point of death, she might not want that crushing piece of evidence to be found by another servant, who could try and use it and put their lives at risk," Lady Mary suggested. "And then, once one found it, who would one take it to? The King? I wonder whether the King knew everything, he who, still now, keeps boasting about his great cleverness in finding the true meaning of this letter."

"I don't think he knows, Mother, and would get furious if he learnt that Cecil has cheated him too. Shakspere is sure the King's in the dark and believes he really risked his life: this has fostered Cecil's power still more. The King's afraid of him and would never do anything against him. This is why I'd take it to Prince Harry: he's honest and really noble-hearted. Hast thou still got it, Milly?"

"I haven't, Jack. And, anyhow, I could never let the Prince have something that would destroy my father. He's betrayed the whole country, he's cheated thy father, his friends and maybe even the King, but he's always my father. And then, by now, what for? Ay, truth. So, it probably was a thing to be done. But thou must understand me. I may need some more time. Dost get me? I don't like this: he betrays everybody, I betray him... Even if... Wait, I'll start again where I was. So: distraught by my discovery, deep inside I was still looking for an explanation to lighten his guilt. He might have learnt about the plot when everything had already been done, so he might have written the letter to expose it and create a dramatic effect. Thou couldst not be right, Jack, with all thy superstition and narrow-mindedness!"

"I thank thee."

"I'm joking. Well, on that very evening I went to papa in his office. He would certainly give me a satisfactory explanation, which would melt down all my suspicions like snow in the sun. Of course, he would tell me the letter had been his clever device to make those fanatic Papists' dark, deadly plot come to light at the right moment. Had it really been like this, don't you think it would have really been a most clever move?

"Well, I found him intent on reading and underlining a libel. He didn't seem particularly happy to see me, even if he hadn't talked to me alone for ages, but he probably didn't want to be interrupted in his reading. Nevertheless, he offered me a seat, telling me that he didn't have much time for me. But he'd already realised that something was wrong, for my voice was trembling. 'Please, tell me,

Mildred,' he said curtly. He never calls me by my full name. I showed him the letter and asked him what it was. 'Ahhh!' quoth he, and slowly takes it from my hand. He smiles. Then, without a word, very calmly, hobbling as he always does, he walks round his desk, gets to the fireplace and throws it into the fire. 'I thank thee, Mildred: it was something I thought I'd lost and had long been looking for. Nothing important, anyway.' He burnt it before my eyes, do you understand? I was horrified, I didn't know what to say. How stupid I'd been! And now he asks me where I found it. I find myself at a crossroads: either bend my head and be a loyal daughter, tell him about the servant and her trunk without comments and without questions, go back to my chamber after receiving a benevolent smile and a pat on my head – and a beautiful present on the following day, for sure – or else insist on an explanation, even if all this is far bigger than I am? Do I have the right to resist him, I, a woman, to meddle in high politics and in the affairs of State?"

"*To be or not to be?* – Hamlet would say. Let it be as it is or else react, even at the cost of paying personally?" Jack added. Lady Mary hushed him.

"After all, what did I care about what my father did when he was working? Had I spoken, I would put at stake everything I had: my certainties, my way of life, my culture, my very future. Above all, Jack, I was terrified about drawing his rage upon me: I know how terrible he can be. It would be the first time ever. All this went on in my mind in the fraction of a second. But then I thought that I mustn't be a coward and that what I wanted was truth, whatever the price. And I also thought about thee, Jack, and about everything thou hadst told me: that those Papists, among whom there was thy father, might have been hunted down and destroyed for something they hadn't done… Or else, were they guilty and all my father had done had been unmask them? I just had to know, 'twas all too important. Then, in the end, it may also have been a matter of pride: not that, because I'm but a woman, one can invariably leave me without an explanation and take it for granted for me always to obey, as if I weren't clever enough.

"I spoke out, then. 'Papa, what was it?'"

"'I've asked *thee* where thou foundst it,' he says coldly.

"'In the trunk of the servant who died the other day', I answer. 'Papa, what was it?'

"'I guess thou already knowst, Mildred, since thou askst,' he says.

"'Papa, it's all been a lie then! Mounteagle is *not* our country's saviour.'"

"'He isn't, Milly,' he says quietly. 'Even if he gets a nice life grant for this deed he never accomplished.'

"'And Fawkes and his mates were not traitors!'

"And what does he do, at this point? He bursts into laughter like a child, silently, hysterically. I was really horrified, Lady Mary. And says: 'They all are, knowst thou not? Maybe not in action, but they're traitors in their thoughts. Traitors in their bones! But I've framed them all!' He looked like he'd gone mad. Then he chills down and his face gets grim, ruthless. 'They hated our King, me, thee and our entire way of life, and our already precarious system of government. It was never enough, through the penal laws, to cut down that foul weed at the root every year: it was to be rooted out once and for all, ruining some of the soil if necessary, since every year those damned roots sprouted anew. For the preservation of us all. Do not try to understand what thou canst not, little girl! Thou hast no idea what keeping this accursed country together means, which for at least fifty years has risked falling to pieces from one moment to another. Thou hast no idea of the labour, the energy, the money, the heartache that lies behind it. Thou canst go, I thank thee, our conversation is over.' And he fixes his eyes on me: his eye, that is, while his other eye wanders away. And that eye of his tells me: I've already explained to thee far more than thou deservest, do not dare to speak back to me again. But I do not budge. I'm scared, my voice keeps trembling, but I go on. 'Papa, you've always taught me that truth is with us and lies are with our foes; that equivocation is their typical way and that *our* way is honesty and sincerity, straightforwardness and clarity, ay, ay, nay, nay. The rest comes from the Evil One… This is all false!'

"I expected anything but yet another grin. A subtle, chilly grin. 'Life is not as simple as thou thinkst, my dear. Knowst thou what Seneca once said? That a wise man will do deeds he does not approve of, using them as steps to lead him to higher things.'

"'Papa, this is Machiavellian!'

"'What knowst thou? Don't be ridiculous, in thy silly ignorance.'

"''Tis enough for me to know that those men died an atrocious death for a crime they had not committed, and that you knew everything! Not only did you know, but the whole thing was a trap *you* had set up!'

"'The realm was to be saved, Mildred, and let this be enough for thee. History is ruthless. Progress and justice have always claimed their victims. Now be a good girl, wilt thou, and go back to thy room as I've told thee: certainly, of all the people in the world, I don't have to justify my ways to thee.'

"Jack, papa had never glared at me like that. Before then, I'd been more or less as his little puppy, to be cuddled and spoilt; now I had suddenly been turned into his enemy and I knew that, had he deemed it necessary, he would strike me down as he'd done with all the others: Essex, Ralegh, Northumberland, even my uncle Brooke... All of them, dost get me? No one had had the better over him: how on earth could I think I would? Then, I say to him: 'Papa, do you believe in the life to come, and in God's Judgment?' And what does he do? He grins again! A horrible, disquieting grin. 'Thou refusest to understand this very simple thing: we can't go to Heaven through our poor human works. God has no need of them to fulfil his plans; and, anyway, he has made up his mind already. But, please, God's judgment!'

"Papa told me all this without ever raising his voice but, rather, sort of hissing, while glaring at me full of hatred and scorn. In that moment I realised that he even despised the tutors he had put beside me, those good pastors who'd taught me to hate falsehood and love truth. That, when he attacked Jesuitical equivocation, and said he was shocked by it, that was yet another lie, because he preferred outright, shameless lies to equivocation. I could never brave his eyes, and neither could I speak back again. I stand up, then, ready to go, but then I explode: 'I don't want to be part of all this: I refuse it with all my heart!'

"He, who had also stood up and had got closer, boxes my ear in response, leaving a red mark on my cheek. 'Go!' he said, hissing again. That's the last word he ever said to me. Well, I took it at face value.

"I burst into tears: 'tis terrible to see hatred in the eyes of those thou lovest and who thou thoughtst loved thee. At the very same moment, though, I lost all reverence and started to hate him back. In tears, I ran to my chamber without turning back. I didn't want to live under the same roof as him, and not only owing to the way he'd treated me: I didn't want to dwell with the unjust oppressor of his people, and eat, and be entertained, and ride in my precious carriage with the money we got from the penal laws, with what was bleeding His Majesty's impoverished, deceived subjects.

"That night I couldn't sleep a wink, of course; so, know you what I did? I got up and went back into his office snooping round. Not that I meant to find compromising documents to report him: this is unnatural and I don't think I would have gone as far as that. What I wanted to do was disturb him in some way; for once, maybe, foil some of his plans. The little book he had been reading when I had come in was still on his desk. I leafed through it. It was a play script."

"*Secret Macbeth!*"

"Right it! I threw it onto the still hot embers. Then, just to muddy the waters a bit, I also threw into the fire all the other papers lying on his desk. That was the point whence there was no way back: in any case, I'd taken my decision by then. So, I chose to come here looking for thee. This is one more thing I had to tell thee: that I've carried out thy poor friend Tim's mission. Shakspere has nothing more to fear."

"Milly, 'tis incredible! Thou'st been extraordinary!"

"They say thou'rt dead, knowst thou."

"I do. Big John believes *I* was the one who got stabbed, on that night, instead of poor Tim."

"That was my doing," Lady Mary smiled.

Jack would be forever grateful to his poor friend who had unwittingly saved him and his loved ones: like this, at least, his absurd death had been useful, so to say. Like this, he had not really died for nothing.

"Please, go on, young Countess."

Milly smiled too: "Just call me Milly, Milady. I went back to my chamber. Bridgie, my governess, was sleeping and hadn't noticed anything. So I put on some rags, of those I'd found in old Hannah's trunk; I took all the jewels and money I could find, then went down to the library to take this," she laid her hand on Garnet's book. "Then I hid in a kitchen corner, my face smeared with soot as a scullery maid's. As soon as the servants unbolted one of the back doors, still before dawn, I stole out to the street without anybody noticing me, then off towards Ludgate, which was already crowded. What a queer feeling, Milady! For the very first time in my life I was utterly alone, in the open air, without protection…"

Lady Mary nodded: she knew exactly what Milly meant.

"In this servant's disguise, no one seemed to notice me: it was wonderful, from this point of view. But then I thought that, if I must walk out of London and travel in the country, it might be better to dress up as a man. So I went to a stall of second-hand clothes, pretending I wanted to buy something for a brother of mine. Something quite dignified, in order not to risk being arrested for vagrancy. Then I went to the common privies, those near the river Fleet, and got changed. Then I walked into the City, towards St Paul's, then went out through Aldersgate and kept always northwards, every now and then asking for direction. Buckinghamshire, thou always toldst me, Gayhurst village and manor-house, near Milton Keynes. I almost never stopped, for I was afraid of spending nights in inns: by now, my father will be looking for me everywhere, I thought. I bought some food as I walked, and slept in forests and fields, but not longer than I needed to recover my strength and not collapse with weariness, then walked on. I lost the count of days. Then I got utterly lost and started to despair, thinking I would never find thee. Moreover, I started to think that, even if I found your home, thou mightst have already sailed for Douai... What would I do, then? It was a nightmare... More than once I came across troops of galloping horsemen... I was sure they were looking for me, so I hid... And once I even saw a gang of highwaymen from afar... But they didn't see me... I was so frightened... Well, in the end I've made it, and I've even found thee. And I've still got all the jewels!"

"You've been so brave, Milly!" cried Lady Mary.

"Lady Digby, I am sure I've acted for the best. But at times I feel bewildered... He's always my father, you know... But he has deceived me... He's deceived everybody... And he struck me because I told the truth. I hate him. At this point, I no longer know what to believe, and who to believe, and what to believe in... Can everything I've been taught be a lie? Can I have always lived a lie? Why?"

"It will take some time, Countess Milly. Yours has been a very courageous choice; as courageous as it is final."

"I know. What must I do now?"

"Your father will be turning the whole kingdom upside down to find you"

She addressed her son. "No place is safe. Jack, thou must take her away hence."

"I'm ready, mother." And he held tighter the little hand resting in his.

This was exactly what Sir Robert did: he turned the whole of Britain upside down sparing no expense, but he never said why. But the reason soon became clear to everybody, for the Salisbury House servants only obeyed for a few days the absolute prohibition, on pain of death, to speak about it. Little by little, one tiny drop at a time, they let the unbelievable news of the young Countess's flight leak out. Bridget Barrett was given the sack and even risked being thrown into the Tower, as Sir Robert held her directly responsible for what had happened, even though she had never had an inkling of it: to her, this sudden, devastating event had come out of the blue. So much the worse for her: that meant she had done her job in the worst possible way.

Sudden searches, by soldiers and Government agents, raged everywhere for several weeks. All ports were closed, all bridges chained, all public places alerted, as usually happened when the authorities were looking for dangerous criminals: traitors, foreign spies, Jesuits. This time, however, no portrait was divulged; no description, no detail whatever about who or what they were looking for. Someone was being hunted down who no longer had a name.

It was at the height of the searching, and of roadblocks, that an old peasant turned up at the Blackfriars, during the King's Men's dress rehearsals for that feast day, insistently asking for Master Richard Burbage. Condell tried to send him away, but the man was as stubborn as a mule: 'twas too important, he said. The leading player then stopped the rehearsal, came off stage and approached him in curiosity and slight irritation. He saw an old man like many others, coming to town to sell his cheese and sausages. The newcomer didn't waste much of his time: he gave him his message in a few seconds. He simply whispered in his ear, in his northern accent: "Let Master Shakspere know that the manuscript has been destroyed."

Burbage was astonished. He had a better look at him, but he was sure he had never seen this man before. "Who are you?"

"I can say no more. I swear, on the salvation of my soul, that poor Tim has carried out his task and *Secret Macbeth* has been devoured by fire."

Dick Burbage got the message: Digby alone could have mentioned Tim's name and called the manuscript like that.

"May God rest you merry, Sir!"

Old Adam turned round, went back on his not-too-steady steps and was lost among the crowd.

As he looked at him, Dick remembered Fletcher's indignant words, on that day he had arrived at the Globe badly concealing his fury: "A terrific lucky strike, Burbage, which won't be repeated, mark my words! Unless, of course, one of you, who's so skilled at making things and people disappear, is supported by some little supernatural help."

"Witchcraft, you mean?"

"One never knows: at times, methinks 'ts the only plausible explanation!"

"I do not know what you are talking about, Master Fletcher," Burbage had told him, a confused expression on his face which, for once, had nothing to do with his player's skills.

Now he understood why they hadn't dared send an order of arrest. Shakspere could come back, at last.

It was the dead of night and the great, half-empty manor was silent. Up there in the attic, however, someone was moving with very light steps on the wooden boards, behind the tiny dormer overlooking the roof, and behind the heavy black drape that obscured it completely. There, at the weak light of one small tallow candle, unbeknownst to the servants and even to the children, who were fast asleep in their beds, a clandestine rite was taking place in almost total silence. It hadn't been easy to find a priest, who, on learning about the extreme need of these people, had rushed here and arrived today from far away Lancashire, pretending he was a pedlar of lace and haberdashery. He was now wearing his vestments and had put up a regular altar on a little table against the wall. Then, in Latin, he started. So it was that, in such an unceremonious, hidden, hasty way, right on the fifth anniversary of Father Garnet's birth to Heaven, in the only presence of Lady Mary, and of Adam and Ellen, John Kenelm Digby married Mildred Elizabeth Cecil and swore to her love and faithfulness till death should part them, for better or worse. In their moments of joy, that hunted man told them in his short sermon, it would be as easy as drinking a glass of water, so that they might think they could manage everything thanks to their mere human strength. They should pray God, then, not to let them yield to the sin of pride. When the days of trial came, instead, they should pray God to increase their faith and help them bear their cross. Because, sooner or later, those days *would* come; because such a moment always came to everyone. Jack thought that, for the two of them, it might come very soon, maybe even tomorrow or on the following day. But he was ready. Because the readiness was all.

They rode away alone, heading for a little private harbour at the mouth of the Severn, in the estate of a friendly family, whence a clandestine boat was due to sail. For the first time in his life, while galloping in the dark, running against time, and fearing to meet Cecil's agents behind every tree or bush and squatting in every ditch, Jack felt really free. As he held his left arm round Milly's waist, who sat in the saddle in front of him, he had concrete proof that Cecil, the lord of their world, hadn't had the last word on their future. Sir Robert had torn him from his family when he was little more than a child and had treated him like a puppet for years on end; but Jack had turned out to be smarter than he was: he had managed to steal from under his very nose a more precious jewel than all those he had crammed into his precious Hatfield. More precious than rock crystal, ruby necklaces or golden chains. At the height of danger, therefore, he felt his heart being flooded by purest, spotless, undefiled joy, by an elation that was as paradoxical as it was unexpected. He was leaving all that was known and reassuring to him; he was leaping into the void; he was a wanted man, an outlaw who, if taken, would be doomed. But with her, and for her, he could brave any adversity.

"What's thy name?" he whispered in her ear.

"Me? Milly," she replied, quite puzzled.

"And then?"

She got it, and laughed: "Mildred Elizabeth Digby!"

"I'm happy, Jack," she told him as, on the little private wharf, they were waiting to embark. Behind the hills, at their back, an invisible sun already painted a small cloud with pink, while the stars were still as bright as ever above their heads. A strong, warm wind was blowing from the sea, the waves crashing frothily and noisily on the underlying rocks.

Jack embraced her and suddenly felt frightened by her happiness. But so it must be. He only asked her: "What about... when sorrow comes?"

"We'll face it together, Jack. After all, 'tis only fair for sorrow to be shared among mankind, isn't it? By now, I'm almost ashamed at my happiness. Especially if I think of the sea of woe that one can find in the world... In our country... If I think of the agony of all the innocent and helpless unjustly suffering, I think that we are so lucky, Jack, even though we've got nothing in the world. Not that we haven't suffered, thou in particular, but because we're still free, because we love each other, because we've got a totally new life to build for ourselves. We, that is, have the duty, ay, the duty to be happy for them too: for all the poor suffering souls."

"'Tis funny: as if happiness were a duty..."

"And it is!"

Milly was silent and looked round, filling her lungs with the sea wind which was ruffling her hair. She pointed at two crab trees near them, which the wind was mercilessly tossing to and fro. "Look, Jack: those trees are dancing for us!"

"They seem to me, rather, to be writhing in pain, torn by unspeakable tortures. As if they wanted to shout their pain."

"Don't be tragic: I'm sure everything'll be all right, as long as we're together. And thou must believe this too! By the way, knowst thou, I've read the tragedy thou toldst me about, the one about Romeo and Juliet. I had it brought to me at once, on the day thou fledst."

"And what thinkst thou about it?"

"'Tis unbelievable: we've got a lot of points in common with them. Only, we won't die in such a stupid way, I hope! Therefore, shouldst thou find me dead, one day, at least try stinging me with a pin before poisoning thyself! And don't be so hasty to reach me: wait some days, at least!"

"I promise."

"And, anyhow, apart from *Secret Macbeth*, this Shakspere is a really naughty boy and I don't know how he's managed to shun jail so far: had I not fallen from grace myself, I'd run to report him."

"And why, poor thing, after thou'st saved him?"

"Because that 'Romeo' is just like thee, a vassal of Rome, as his name says. And, when he is below his beloved's window, he says he wants to 'kill' the hateful, envious Moon, who, everybody knows, stands for the old Queen."

"Yet another seditious Papist, then, yet another terrorist ready to turn into a regicide, a bare bodkin in his hand?"

"Of course!"

They laughed. "When will you Protestants put an end to your witch hunt?"

"Well, I have already: I can even say I've entered a sabbat!"

"And why didst thou enter it?"

"Silly boy: for thee, of course."

"I'm joking, Milly, but not completely: what I mean is, if thou'st only chosen the side of the downtrodden for my sake, I fear thou mayst not resist. That is, if we still look like a bunch of superstitious, ignorant idol worshippers."

"Give me time, Jack: I believe I've got a lot of things to learn and, above all, to digest. But, more than what I don't understand or share, I've chosen to trust people. And knowst thou who's the one who's convinced me most?"

"Not me, I guess?"

"Apart from thee, who usually makest me angry."

"Who, then?"

"Thy mother, Lady Digby. Her bravery in disgrace, her constance, her calm determination. I know I can trust her: I feel I can share with her everything that is still not clear to me. What a pity, now, having to go…"

"Ay, what a pity. 'Twould have been such a joy to live at Gayhurst all together. Art scared?"

"I'm not, Jack. What about thee?"

"I'm worried for thee, Milly. But not for myself."

She looked into his eyes, as if to read his mind; he looked away, at the rough sea and the white foam, so that she couldn't read too deeply.

"Ay, thou'rt scared," she said.

"And what of?"

"Of having married thy foe's daughter."

Jack held her more tightly. "'Tis not that, Milly: The love I bear thee has covered thy father's wrongs just as this sea has covered its bottom. As my name has erased his. What I fear is not to make thee happy."

"What, art joking? I've told thee I'm happy already. Should I perhaps have stayed at Court, be Hatfield's landlady, proud of all its dead treasures, and maybe, I know not, marry old Northampton, whom thy mother refused? No no, I thank God every day for meeting thee, filthy Papist, and also for the idea I had of learning Italian."

"Knowst thou what I've thought? That if thy father hadn't had mine killed, I would never have met thee. 'Tis like this, in history, that some good may rise from evil. 'Tis as if he too, like Tim, hadn't died in vain. Because, when it brings such fruits, sooner or later one even manages to accept the unjust death of one's loved ones. 'Tis as if thou wert a present from my father at the height of unhappiness. And Shakspere too would have been undone, had I not met thee. Dost understand what I mean?"

"I do. And, had I not met thee, I would never have dared defy my father."

They embraced again. Euphoria and fear kept chasing each other, overlapping and blending in their hearts just like those foaming billows, like the gusts of that ruthless gale.

They set sail on a light, swift, vessel, full of young men bound for Flanders who had come in small groups from several counties. Like all the others, they started their new life of exile full of hope, thinking of the future, more than of the past, as the high coasts of Wales disappeared in the distance.

Royal palace of Whitehall, Westminster, 27 July 1611

Sir Robert had been extremely irritable for months. Today, moreover, he'd been sick. While working in his palace office, as he did almost every day buried among documents and surrounded by messengers and clerks, he had suddenly felt he was choking and had started gasping for breath. The crisis was almost over now, but His Majesty had equally wanted to send for the best of royal doctors, Théodore Mayerne, a Huguenot. This renowned scientist had recently arrived in London from the French Court, where his religious views were disliked, and had offered his service to His Majesty. Tall and lank, always dressed in black as the true Calvinist he was, Mayerne had a sour appearance and looked like one who knew what he was about. He now walked in, determined, totally indifferent to Court magnificence, and asked to be left alone with the patient.

Sir Robert had a swollen throat and, even now that he could breathe quite easily, he still couldn't stand up from the armchair where he had collapsed. The doctor asked him to undress and then dress again, after noticing red spots on the skin of his legs.

"Maintenant ouvrez la bouche, mon Excellence. There, good, like this." He lifted his patient's lips as if he were deciding about the purchase of a horse. Ay, these new followers of Paracelsus could be quite weird, but this man was said to be a real expert. The problem, Sir Robert thought, was whether or not he was reliable as a man, not merely as a doctor: he knew all too well that even the best physician in the world might yield to the power of money and, maybe, poison the patient he should have cured. This one, besides, was from France, Britain's traditional enemy... And it was certainly not pure fancy, on Sir Robert's part, to acknowledge that he had many an enemy: envious people, mainly, or those that had been defeated by his superior intelligence. All right, he would let himself be examined by this man: had he prescribed him some remedy, though, Sir Robert would speak to his personal doctors before taking them.

"Dites-moi, mon Excellence, have your gums been bleeding for long?"

"I'm not sure, roughly a year. Do you think some blood-letting could do me any good?"

"Absolutely not, Excellency. 'Tis time we put an end to this old tale of humours: c'est assez! Whatever your problem may be, 'tis not due to an excess of blood, and neither to any of the other liquids. Our diseases are a force attacking us from the outside, and they can be cured through the energy which the stars exert over natural elements. 'Tis not enough to take a remedy made of certain components: those components must be gathered at the right moment, under the appropriate astral influence. And so – c'est effrayant, n'est-ce pas? – the same substance might have either a good or a harmful effect. So much that the most powerful could well be either panacea or poison."

"So that one might end up poisoned by trying to be cured?"

"Not if he trusts the right specialist, mon Excellence."

"Your theory quite frightens me, doctor, together with the power your caste has. Noblemen, bishops, kings, emperors… all of them, sooner or later, give themselves up to your profession. You hold the whole world in your hands, even more so than priests do. Because 'tis untrue that you only deal with our bodies: as long as they hope to be cured, people also entrust you with the secrets of their minds, unveiling to you even the deepest corners of their souls." Mayerne didn't change expression or interrupt him. "And are you really sure that Galen's studies and those of his followers, which are the fruits of a thousand-year-old tradition, are all to be thrown to the pigs?"

"Absolument sûr et certain, mon Excellence, that's obsolete stuff. Modern science is based on the scientific study of substances and on the power of natural elements. The only thing to be saved of the old system is the correspondence between microcosm and macrocosm, that is, the human body, the world and the whole universe."

"Tell me, then, doctor: am I suffering from syphilis?"

"Non, mon Excellence: je dirais que non. Do you feel any pain?"

"Ay, doctor, in my bones: but I've always thought that was due to age."

"That may be and it may not, Your Lordship. Did you happen to hurt yourself, recently?"

"Ay, with a sharp quill, here on my finger-tip, do you see?"

"When was this?"

"About a month ago."

"And the cut took far longer than usual to heal, didn't it?"

"It did: far longer. But I didn't think... Tell me, is there any connection with today's crisis?"

"Je pense que oui, mon Excellence. You've told me that you feel tired, exhausted, don't you?"

"I'm always tired, doctor, as a man who never spares himself should be."

"Vous avez raison, Excellence. In order to make a diagnosis, I need to see you again: by now, I only have some suspicions. I'll give you a talisman to be worn round your neck and a therapy to follow, made of hellebore and spices, for which I'll leave the ingredients to the royal apothecary. Should the pain in your bones increase, I'll prepare some laudanum for you, the miraculous pain killer invented by our master Paracelsus. Be patient, but I prefer to distil it myself, for its ingredients are a secret of our guild. I may need some more spices, and also some pearls to crush into it. The more precious they are, of course, the more effective my remedy will be. I'll start examining, in my laboratory, the urine samples I have taken today. Be sure to drink the hellebore drug each morning, in the meantime. I'll meet you in a month to see how 'tis going. Do not undervalue these symptoms and try to rest, mon Excellence."

Doctor Mayerne left him. That evening, in his study, after he had performed an accurate uroscopy by analysing the aspect and translucence of the samples he had taken, and after spotting some slight nebulae in them, he carefully wrote everything down in his medical journal, for Sir Robert's case was surely an interesting one. While waiting for further checks, this was his conclusion: "*Nihil umquam siphillicum.*"

Sir Robert couldn't brook getting sick: he couldn't brook any unexpected, sudden event which took him away from all the urgent matters he had to deal with. He loved being the master of his own time and hated the idea of a triviality hindering him. He hoped that this sickness thing could be solved very soon and without more ado. Nay, it was probably all over by now: next time, he would tell this Mayerne that he was perfectly well and did't need him any longer.

Breathing slowly and heavily, he staggered back to sit at his desk; he took paper and pen and ordered that the next messenger be sent to him. And let all his clerks come in too, for Heaven's sake! Didn't they see that the doctor was already long gone?

Sir Robert also saw his personal physicians, Poe and Atkins, who clean refused to give him potentially harmful hellebore. As to laudanum, it would be sheer folly to accept a ready-made remedy, not specially prepared by the royal apothecary: Sir Robert had too many enemies for that. The problem was non-existent, on the other hand, as His Lordship was now much better.

Preparations were in full swing, at last, for a new Shaksperean play. The great dramatist was said to have finally come back, nay, and ready to walk the boards again: that's why the audience was so impatient, and many people had been waiting by the bolted gate since morning. When the servants finally opened, a crowd streamed into the pit like water at the lifting of a dam.

Below the stage, in the big changing room, Shakspere himself was putting on his costume, a splendid robe of the colours of the sky, night-blue all spangled with golden stars, his shoulders covered by a wide, glistening, grey mantle. He set his large pointed hat at the right angle and smiled weakly; but the sadness he had within filtered from under his smile and even through his costume, like a gory wound below a makeup layer. Richard Burbage, who wouldn't take part in today's play, was helping him get ready.

"Thou'rt sure of what thou'rt doing, Will, ain't thou?"

"Have I ever let thee down, Dick?"

"Almost never, old boy, I reckon; but I'll have to think about it."

"Don't worry now: the play'll be successful, you'll take it to Court for All Hallows' and everything will be all right. Prospero's part will be yours, of course, as agreed: I hope thou'st already learnt it."

"How can I, with thee giving it to me piecemeal?" Burbage was trying to look cheerful.

"Just learn what I've given thee so far; tonight, I'll give thee two more speeches and the Epilogue, which is in very easy rhyming couplets. I want those three passages to be a surprise to everybody, including you, under my sole responsibility: shouldn't they please, just tear them up."

The other two elders of the company, Heminges and Condell, had got close as well.

"Thou'rt beautiful, Will!"

"Thanks, Hem!"

Heminges, the oldest of the group, looked down, shaking his white, dishevelled hair.

"That it should end this way…"

"It must, Hem: time's up. Today's the expiry date. But you won't be involved. Next week you go to Court and do a wonderful job without me."

"With Fletcher, thou meanst?"

"Of course, Hem. You're the King's Men, aren't you? The show must go on. And, anyway, thou knowst: even if I took the Oath, and started to go to church each Sunday, and became an exemplary subject, I could never work with him."

Heminges shook his head and looked down again: "Nay, Will. Thou couldst not."

"There's no choice, therefore. They said I could choose: not so! One must know when the moment's come to hang up one's boots. Today, I will withdraw preserving my dignity."

"That's what thou thinkst, Will!" cried Condell, the youngest of the four, who, with his black ponytail and golden earrings, looked like a pirate. "Thou knowst, dost thou not, how Fletcher has revisited thy tragedy 'bout Katherine. He allowed me to read, and right this morning, a sickening speech he's put in Act Five, which Cranmer, the great Archbishop of Canterbury, will give in thy name. Boys, just listen to this: he apparently wants to play that part himself, walking on stage for the very first time in 's life: just imagine what a disaster 'twill be!" Condell laughed bitterly, showing teeth that were as white and sturdy as they were irregular. "Fletcher-Cranmer will say that 'tis Heaven bids him speak, not his love of flattery. And off he goes with a sugary little sermon extolling the horrid hag and our wonderful King. And there's a pun on thy name, too, when he says that this Queen shall be loved and feared, and her foes shall 'shake' like a field of beaten corn. That's thee, Will: people will think thou'st given in, in the end."

"But if I'm leaving! 'Tis clear I haven't. I would hardly say beaten corn is happy to cooperate: were it so, they wouldn't need to beat it up. Fletcher's more likely message is that I've been defeated, which, of course, is true. I know the play will bear my name. But, as long as you live, you'll tell everybody 'tis not so."

"What about after we've died?"

"Well, then 'twill no longer matter; even if I dare anyone to mistake even one of Fletcher's lines with my own. Have you seen how he rewrote *Macbeth*, together with Middleton? 'Gelded Macbeth,' would I call it!" They laughed. "And then remember, whatever we may think, that drama is *not* literature. A sonnet can make you eternal, a play can't."

"Not so, Will: it won't go this way. For thy plays will never die."

"Don't talk nonsense, Harry."

"I'm serious. Hem and meself've been thinking that we'd like to collect thy plays, right as Speed had started to do before he went blind, and publish them all together. Ben Jonson too is willing to lend a hand. And, I swear, we'll leave this big historical pastiche of Fletcher's out!"

"Don't thou swear, Harry," said Heminges. "We can't say for sure that we won't be forced to include it."

Shakspere went pale. "Have you lost your mind? Never, as long as I live! Nay, had I here a big book with all my works, I would drown it in the sea, just like Prospero is to do with his spell-book. For the theatre is art, after all, 'tis magic – although someone, out there, may not agree. But my magic will die with me."

"Right," Condell went on calmly, almost ignoring him. "This means we'll do so after thy death. Art thou in, Dick?"

"I am."

"Or, if we die before thee, we'll leave it as a mission to the boys. 'Twill be the King's Men's mission, those who will survive thee, I mean. We'll use the rough copies thou didst not burn, together with our memories. Thou'lt see from above, provided thou'lt ever get there, that thy *opera omnia* will storm the press, more than all epic poems and all sonnet collections put together. We're planning a great Folio!"

"A simple playwright's works in luxury edition? No one's ever heard of anything like that: you'll see, no one will be interested. But then, I won't care anymore, when 'tis done. Keep the rough copies. But do *not* store them all together and, above all, swear never to show them to anybody as long as I live. This is a solemn moment: what I need now is a cross-shaped sword, like King Hamlet's..."

"I'll find it, Will!"

"No, leave it: my magician's staff will do all the same. There, it may even be better. Do you see? This is the magic staff I've always amused myself shaking, so as to create a different world: 'tis the symbol of my production. Through it, I've shaken our little Globe world. I'm

called both Shak-spere as Shak-staffe, ain't I? Thou, Hem, put thy
hand here; Dick, thou here. As for thee, Harry, here. Now I'll play the
Ghost: 'Swear!'"

Amused at the idea, partly joking and partly in earnest, the three
elders of the company swore. At that, Shakspere slowly dropped his
staff, which went clattering to the wooden floor.

"Who will guess who I am now?"

"Uhm…" said Condell. "A fallen staff: a Fall-staffe!" They laughed
out loud. "No, that's impossible!"

"Thou'rt right: I'll never stoop so low." Shakspere picked it up and
got ready to enter the scene.

Out there, in the pit, the groundlings were even more restless than
usual; some had already started to fight for the best positions. From
below the stage, as they looked through a peephole at the galleries
being filled with important people, the King's Men saw John Fletcher
taking his comfortable seat, a nervous little smile on his face. He was
holding a big, gilt-rimmed book under his arm. Shakspere recognised
it: the new Bible, the one that had been promoted by the King himself
and was to replace all previous editions. Why on earth had Fletcher
brought it here? Of course: to administer the Oath to him. Fletcher
was sure to come and seek him out right after the play. Six pikemen
had come in with him; they placed themselves in twos by the gate, by
the tiring house door and near the stage. The groundlings stopped
fighting, but got even more restless and noisy.

He, however, the magician, didn't make much of it and, nay, felt
flattered. He gave the last directions to the musicians, up there, and
to the boy, Johnny Rice, who would play Miranda. Johnny was Tim's
cousin. Shakspere silently looked him in the eyes, then smiled at him.
"Art ready, boy?"

"I am, Master Shakspere!"

"While thou playst, think of Tim, Johnny, think of his sacrifice for
the theatre to be free."

"Tim didn't die for the theatre, Sir: he died for you"

"He died for both, Johnny. But thou'rt right: he was trying to find
a remedy to a serious mistake of mine, and I'll never forgive myself
for this. Try to become a great player: make his name famous. On my
part, I'll try to live the few years that are left me being worthy of his
memory."

"I will, Master Shakspere."

Dramatic fiction began. An unusual silence fell on the whole audience, including the groundlings standing round the stage. They had all recognised Will Shakspere, who had popped up from nowhere in Prospero's garments; they knew, for they felt it, that this was the old magician's last spell, the old poet's last creation. They knew they were living through the end of an age. Even the soldiers at the gate stood motionless throughout the show.

This was a strange play, dealing with dreams and reality, fact and fiction, art and life. It was about the power of magic of creating illusion, and about the wrongs suffered of yore, about love, revenge, repentance, crimes, atonement, reconciliation. And about extraordinary gifts, and about dead people brought back to life through the power of art. About spirits of air and fire, earth and water; about young people who were better than their elders. Until, when the moment came for the characters to say farewell to the magic island, the audience was all ears and held their breath.

Prospero came forward all alone and in a weird, ancestral chant, said farewell to the audience and asked for applause. What did he mean? Would he leave for good like this, as quietly as this, without explaining anything, without taking a position, not even a hint? The only certainty was, everybody felt it, that this was a last, final farewell.

He began announcing that he had overthrown all his charms. Some of the groundlings looked at the soldiers and murmured. He said that he had become a weak, simple man. "*Now, 'tis true, I must be here confined by you…*" He also looked at the soldiers. "*Or sent to… Naples. Let me not, since I have my dukedom got and pardoned the deceiver,*" he looked up, directly into Fletcher's eyes, who looked frightened. "*Let me not dwell on this bare island,*" he pointed down at the stage, "*by your spell!*"

What did he mean?

"*But release me from my bands with the help of your good hands.*" This was normal: an invitation to applause. They applauded. He hushed them with a wave of his hand.

"*Gentle breath of yours my sails must fill, or else my project fails.*" He stopped short. He brandished his magical staff. How often had he amused himself joking with his name: shake thy staff, Shak-staffe! But now, after shaking it vigorously, he snapped it. The crowd murmured again.

"... *Which was to please.*" He threw the two pieces to the pit and showed his naked hands.

"*Now I want spirits to enforce, art to enchant.*" He opened his arms wide.

"*And my ending is Despair!*" He stood like that for a moment and stared up high. He seemed crucified. People held their breath even longer. But then Shakspere lifted his arms above his head and joined his hands on his breast.

"*Unless... I be relieved by prayer.*" Hands could be clapped, of course, but one could also join them like that, "*Which pierces so that it assaults Mercy itself, and frees all faults.*"

He slowly opened his arms again, as if he meant to embrace the whole of his audience. "*As you from crimes would pardoned be...*" He paused again. He reached forward, his palms up. He breathed deep, then raised his voice. "*Let your indulgence... set me... FREE!*"

Burbage wouldn't have been surprised if, at that point, Shakepsere had grown wings and had begun hovering above them, flying away, high up, out of the wooden "O" of the Globe, forever disappearing from their sight. No such thing happened, of course. "Prospero" bowed deep, applause pouring like rebounding hail and apparently never wishing to stop. Then, with calm, theatrical gestures, Shakspere unfastened his magician's mantle, which slipped lightly on the boards of the stage in a silken, airy spiral. He took off his pointed hat, which he threw behind, and his star-spangled robe, which he lowered to his ankles, ceremoniously leaping out of it as if from a magic circle, while applause turned into anxious exclamations, yells, whistles. Under his stage costume, he had kept his best clothes. He bowed again.

Behind the wings, the leading player was crying quietly. It was all over. With this, Shakspere had already left them, truly and finally, and Dick knew that his heart had already flown home, in Warwickshire, forever.

Of course, he would manage to learn this part in a few days: that wasn't a difficult thing to do. And it would certainly be successful, at Court. The King would appreciate that polite, restrained farewell which, as all speeches, might be pronounced in different ways and had several levels of interpretation. His Majesty would even feel flattered, had he interpreted this imploration as addressed to him. Ay, just imagine… the pompous ass!

Those thermal waters had done no good whatever to Sir Robert, who lay, all twitching and full of sores, behind the white muslin curtains of his litter. Despite the warm weather, he was all wrapped up in a precious fur blanket, shivering with fever. To think that he had so much longed to go to Bath to take the waters. Now, instead, he wished he had never moved from his soft London feather bed. Nay, he should only have moved thence in order to be taken to his magnificent Hatfield, whose last touches he was looking forward to admiring. He hoped it was exactly as he wanted it, at last. As long as he had some more time left: it would certainly be paradoxical if he had provided it with so much splendour, so much beauty, never to enjoy it. Now he knew this for certain: it was to Hatfield he should have gone, rather than to that vulgar thermal resort, almost as if he'd been a superstitious pilgrim of yore, asking for a miracle which, of course, hadn't come. He clumsily, painfully tried to change position, but to no avail. His movements only resulted in the sores on his right side starting again to secrete their foamy humour mixed with blood and ruining the snow-white linen sheet the servants had only just changed. The mixture they had applied on them, made of mercury, lard, bee wax and medicinal herbs, hadn't been of great use either.

His two doctors, Poe and Atkins, had followed him in his long, painful journey. They were the best in the whole kingdom – together with Mayerne, of course. As often happens, however, they were jealous of this French newcomer and didn't in the least agree with his Paracelsian theories. Tradition, they said, is the only safe, trodden way: those who leave the old ways for new ones do so at their risk. And shall we use such a man as Sir Robert of Salisbury as a guinea pig? Never! That was why they had disapproved both of hellebore and laudanum, and also of the astrological talisman with angelic names that Sir Robert stuck to wearing at his neck. They had bled him several times, on their way to and from Bath, trying to bring his humours to a balance, even if they knew very well that this was unlikely to do him any good. The renowned French doctor could say what he chose, but to them it was clear, and their hypothesis was confirmed by the colour of his urine, that Sir Robert was dying of syphilis. Now, as they examined him once again, they exchanged quick meaningful glances, then smiled blankly to him: Sir Robert must not worry, for they had already sent a young servant up to London, on the fastest horse they had, to find some "holy wood" – guaiacum, that was – which was said to be truly miraculous. Meanwhile, since his state got worse with every hour and even travelling in a litter had become extremely painful for him, they would stop at the village of Marlborough, in the hope of finding a decent enough house to receive both him and his large train. The rumbling thunder was getting closer and the leaden sky looked as if it were going to crash onto the wind-swept heath, making it even more urgent to find shelter for both the healthy and the sick. The litter bearers tried to hurry without shaking him.

The charming little village turned out to be nothing but a cluster of huts and hovels: no respectable manor-house, no reasonably well-to-do gentlemen, no dwelling fit to host them. Sir Robert, therefore, who kept groaning and couldn't proceed one step further, was put up in the rectory, which had been obtained from an ancient priory. The parson, who still couldn't believe his eyes and ears, was more than honoured to yield his own and his wife's bed to the King's right-hand man, while servants and soldiers were distributed among poor folk's cottages.

Once in bed, however, instead of finding some ease, Sir Robert started to pant, and moan, and tear at those rough cotton sheets, no position apparently giving him any comfort. Encumbered by Mayerne's large talisman, he finally ripped it from his neck and threw it to the floor. It had gotten very dark, meanwhile, and the most violent storm a man could remember had broken out. A roaring, impetuous wind was followed by flashes of lightning, booming thunder and torrents of rain which made the window panes tremble as if they were going to burst; beyond them, it was as if the whole world had been liquefied.

Covered in purulent, festering sores, Sir Robert of Salisbury was but the shadow of his former self: his throat was all swollen with tumours and even his gums were bleeding, releasing his teeth like useless ballast. His speech was a hardly comprehensible splutter. He seemed to have shrunk, irretrievably bent double as he was, so that he was all humpback by now. His yellowish skin so taut on his protruding cheekbones, his too-long, all-white hair thin and sticky.

His face, ever more skull-like, was all eyes, his left one already wandering in search of the life to come. Those bulging amber eyes, now as large as ever, looked on everything and everybody, always watchful, more eloquent than his lips. He realised that this was the end: it was as though his bodily decay had made his mind even nimbler and quicker.

Words that were as ancient as the earth were incessantly echoing inside him: *I said in the cutting off of my days, I shall go to the gates of the grave...* The world, now, and life, and death also appeared to him under a new light, even colder and more realistic: it was all but an absurd, frantic dance towards the grave. A dance just like the one he had seen as a child, one day. That had been a fresco on a graveyard wall near Theobalds. How strange recalling about this now, after so many years. It featured many people: noblemen and commoners, rich and poor, kings, bishops, popes, craftsmen, knights, men, women, all of them holding hands with as many skeletons (or was it each with their own skeleton?) leading them towards graves looking like chasms to a bottomless abyss, like jaws ready to swallow the whole world. This was human history: men preying on one another like monsters of the deep, till the earth gobbled them all.

I am deprived of the residue of my years... My wounds are putrefied and corrupt...

He pretended to believe that the famous, costly decoction from that exotic plant could do him some good: what did he care, by now? The world was ending for him: it had already ended. Apocalypse? Doomsday? Nay: more simply, everything came to an end, everything faded until it was extinguished, like this, slowly, softly. Why hadn't God sent the end of the world while he was still alive? So that, at least, he would never die. By now, instead, there was nothing to be done. *You have cut off my life like a weaver.* A leap into the dark. If it must end, better to end it right now and shorten the pain: what was the use of suffering? *Mine eyes are tired of looking up on high.*

The wind howled, the rain stormed agains the panes: he wondered if he would ever see the sun again. So what? Even the sun had wearied him. Let it explode... What did he care, now, if a massive charge of gunpowder destroyed the whole planet? Like that, at least, he would take everybody else with him, while jumping into the abyss: a grand funeral train, worthy of the man he was, *id est,* of the man he had been.

So the evening and the morning were a new day: always the same old song dragging on incessantly, wearily, pointlessly, since the beginning of creation. Since then, each and every day had been exactly like the previous one, never bringing anything new: life, death, joy, sorrow, unequally distributed in handfuls according to who knew what scheme. *There is no new thing under the sun.*

So the evening and the morning were a new day. A new day? Nay, just another one, a repetition of all days past. Had it been of any use to him being endowed with more cleverness than all other humans put together? Of course, it had been a useful commodity to build himself a life full of privilege. And how he had enjoyed crushing the handsome, the fortunate, especially that big spoilt child, Robert of Essex! Yea, it had been amusing. *But the same death expected both the cunning and the foolish.*

Sir Robert had once considered his superior mind as a clear mark of divine predilection – and, as such, of predestination to salvation – at least as much as the deformity of his body seemed to predestine him to damnation. Because the body is made of flesh, and is connected to concupiscence and evil, whereas nothing gushing forth from the mind, which in its turn springs directly from God, can ever be evil.

Already several years ago, however, he had started to fear that Heaven too, just like Purgatory, might be but a superstitious invention. A place of joy? What joy? Let's say of boredom, rather. What did one do, up there, all day, all night? *So the evening and the morning were a new day*, and the cunning and the foolish jumped together into the abyss holding hands. Not out of love, for sure: out of fear.

History had always been like this: men were born, and went running, panting, rejoicing, suffering, dying, and it was only a matter of time: why did they live? Empires rose, spread, crumbled, and map borders were continually moved, shifted, erased and drawn anew, but they were always provisional, as if they'd been drawn on wax tablets, to be covered by a quick spatula stroke in a wink. Royal houses also rose, from dust and blood, unexpectedly brought up high by Fortune, who turned her wheel grinning. They enjoyed their power, their glory, their wealth, until in another wink they sank down again into the same dust whence they had once risen. And they sent men to the wars, to shed their blood over that dust, blood to be mixed with mortar to build the next empire. This way, history ground the centuries away exactly as a watermill built on a river continually ground its corn. *So the evening and the morning were a new day.*

The same could be said about all the wealth of this world: riches coming from the Indies, being hoarded in Flemish and Italian banks, and in the State coffers, and in the King's treasury; gold found in mines, then molten in coins. What was the use of riches? They had been useful to him to have a life of ease and luxury. He had always had everything he wanted, including the finest women, he, whom people compared to a toad. But now he saw that life had been but a grand game of cards in which one always lost: all the counters, in the end, must always go back into their casket. *Vanitas vanitatum.* With all his wealth, due to this ironic trick of Fate, he would now die in someone else's bed, naked like he had been at birth, unable to avoid suffering, powerless to add even one minute to his life. There must be, in some part or other of the kingdom, some eighty-year-old loon who was still sound and healthy, since Death, fumbling in all dark corners with his small lantern, had not yet found him. Death, who unleashed his dogs along men's roads every day – starvation, the plague, and war. Old commoners still in health, while he had to pack up and go... Where? And he was not yet fifty. 'Twas all true, there was no justice on the earth; but neither in Heaven. *The time of our life is threescore years and ten, and if they be of strength, fourscore years...* Who said so? Even Scripture itself, in the end, was full of lies.

So the evening and the morning were a new day, and others would come to enjoy his riches and the beauty of the world. Why leave room for others? He had never realised how quickly time passed: it had simply gone. His amber eyes rolled once again, not with fear but with rage. He turned his head and spat out a mouthful of blood.

He was suddenly aware of several human shapes standing round his bed. But were they human? Or, rather, were they demons coming to claim his soul? He'd seen them before, in a series of prints that had been found while searching the Dowager Countess of Southampton's house. He had had them thrown into the flames, of course. These must be those very monstrous devils who had now come to take revenge and, as patiently as kites, were now waiting for his last breath… To take his soul… How long had they been there? Who had let them in?

But no: rather than devils, they were those who should cure him and, instead, filled his ears with lies and his stomach with revolting remedies. He heard them whisper and then speak to him; he decided to ignore them. What nonsense, to think of devils: he must be really weak in body.

The revulsion they felt in approaching him could almost be touched. *My lovers and my friends stand aside from my plague, and my kinsmen stand afar off.* No one, however, dared contradict his orders, and even less dared they be disrespectful; for his son, his only heir, was on his way. *As the arrows in the hand of the strong man: so are the children of youth. Blessed is the man, that hath his quiver full of them.* Sir Robert had always known that one's offspring, the children of one's loins, were the only strength of a dying man. He didn't exactly have his quiver full of them, but at least he had a son; and that one son would make the difference. Unlike when the old hag died, whom everyone pretended to worship like a goddess but who was actually universally hated and, in her last days, even despised.

Sir Robert, or what was left of him, remembered well the Queen's last moments: ten years had not yet gone by, and he had been very much present, very anxiously present. Nothing in the world could have prevented him from being there at that pivotal moment, when the fate of the kingdom, and of much else, would be decided. It felt like yesterday.

Like a wounded beast, the old woman had realised that, had she taken refuge in the den of her royal bed, she would never get up again; she had therefore refused to lie down for several days, while the looks of all her ladies-in-waiting expressed either silent endurance or outright scorn. She stood in a corner, even refusing to sit down, a ghost from the past, one finger in her mouth as if she'd been an infant. "That's for her toothache," Lady Scrope, Gentlewoman of the Royal Chamber, had whispered in his ear. "She's never wanted to be cured, so now her teeth're all rotten." She had stood like that for fifteen hours, moaning, without speaking or even feeding. Which had been rather uncomfortable for everybody present, for no one could sit down if she did not.

Then she had collapsed on the floor, where her ladies had laid some cushions, and there she had remained four days and four nights.

"You must go to bed, Your Majesty," he had then told her. And she, as the harridan she'd always been, had tried to box his ears, endeavouring to sit up and rolling her small, bloodshot eyes in his direction.

"'Must' is not a word to be used to princes, little man..." She panted, in her effort. "Thy late father... were he here... would *never* have dared to speak such a word to me... Ah, but ye all know I must die... of course... and it makes you all presumptuous... God's death, you all disgust me!"

And she had dropped back on her cushions, as limp as a rag. Cecil had said nothing, only grinning triumphantly. It served her well, the old witch! Nor had her sickness purged her of this foul vice of teasing him.

Too weak to protest, but continually, stubbornly groaning and shaking her head, she couldn't stop her ladies from putting her to bed. In her regression, she was afraid of the dark and wanted two lit tapers beside her, thus untimely turning the royal chamber into a mortuary chapel.

When the end was near, while the Virgin Queen could hardly breathe from her rotten lungs, everybody was sort of distracted, already taken up by something else. Sir Robert had then invited them to leave the room; he had a little armchair brought in and sat at Her Majesty's bedside, waiting for her to lift her lids or give any other sign of consciousness.

"Name your heir!" he kept whispering in her ear. "Your Majesty, you're dying. You're dead already! *Dead!* You're no longer with us! What will become of the kingdom?" But she said nothing: the next succession had always been a forbidden topic. The dying woman had at last opened her eyes: "I don't give a damn..." she had said, in a barely audible whisper. Back then, Sir Robert had been enraged; now that it was his turn, instead, he could understand her very well: let the kingdom be consumed in everlasting fire! What did he care?

Those had been the Queen's last words. Sir Robert's patience was at an end: all his diplomatic efforts risked ending in nothing if that obstinate old spinster didn't appoint the candidate he had been in secret negotiations with for several years now. So, he had grabbed her night-gown, just below her neckline, and had shaken her with both hands. What if anybody had seen him? Well, no one in the world would have cared a straw.

"Old hag, thou *must* tell me thou'lt give thy throne to James of Scotland! Say it! Say it!" She kept groaning but said nothing, headstrong, stubborn to her last. He would have liked to slap her face. Right in that moment, Lady Scrope had crept in and had approached him. "Has Her Majesty told you anything, Sir Robert?" Right in front of the dying Queen, then, unflinchingly, shamelessly, he had unflinchingly replied: "She has: in a weak but well audible voice, she's named the King of Scotland." Lady Scrope, who belonged to his party, then got closer to the Queen, who was shaking all over as if she wanted to object. Without waiting for her last breath, she took the precious blue sapphire ring from the dying Queen's finger and dropped it from the window. "My brother Rob's down there, already on horse, waiting: he'll be the first to break the news to our new King. A man, at last. A man capable to sire an heir!" Sir Robert and Lady Scrope had exchanged fraternal looks, completely ignoring the being whom, up to a few days before, they had pretended they worshipped religiously and who now heard everything but could no longer speak.

A few moments later, pure terror in her eyes, Gloriana had breathed her last. Her servants had then quickly snuffed out those pointless tapers and, after throwing a coarse cloth upon her face, had forsaken the poor body in the huge, majestic royal chamber. Still more than during her agony, everybody had far more important things to do. Richmond palace was soon in such a frenzy that it looked like an anthill stricken by a stick.

Sir Robert's memories were interrupted by Dr Poe, who obsequiously brought a cup of the precious decoction to his lips.

"My shon?" Sir Robert spluttered to him. He then sipped it and started to cough and spit. "Dishgushting!"

"Your Lordship, you must be patient, if you want to be healed. As for your son, young Master William, I believe he won't be long now. And, Your Lordship, even though you are unlikely to ever need him, would you like me to send for the parson?"

"Let be, doctor, ... I need none of his advishe..." He coughed again. He expectorated. "Be healed? Bah! ... and then... God already knowsh what to do with me, doeshn't He?"

"Ay, Your Lordship, whatever you wish. As to… your daughter, the young Countess? Do you have anything to tell her, in case she were found?"

"I have no daughtersh, Dr Poe. I've only got a boy, whom I named William after my father." He panted. "Ash for that … trollop … who pretended to be my daughter for sho long… I confirm her banishment from this kingdom… on pain of death!" He panted again. "She hash deshtroyed… Shtate documentsh… betrayed my trusht… shtolen my money and prisheless gems… Banished, dishinherited and curshed! And what 'bout thish?" He painfully took from his finger a big diamond ring which could still sparkle in that scanty light. "Do you have an… idea of itsh worth?"

"It must be priceless, Your Lordship."

"More than… a thousand poundsh… Well, … give it… let it be taken to… the Countessh of Shuffolk."

He slumped back on his pillow, utterly exhausted. His mind went back to his secret – not too secret, actually – encounters with his favourite mistress. Because, in the darkness of night, beauty and ugliness disappeared altogether. Not even of those did anything remain. *Vanitas vanitatum*. And, now he came to think of it, he wouldn't have liked to see her again, nor would he have wanted her to see him in this state. He had nothing to say to her.

Then his thoughts turned once again to that creature he had always considered beautiful and empty as a precious china doll, to use as he pleased in his schemes and alliances at Court. He thought of the documents Milly had burnt, then of the marvellous jewels she had taken: how he would have wished to see her dead, those jewels in her coffin! A viper in his bosom, she had been. He wondered how long she had planned her treason. *They also that seek after my life lay snares, and they that go about to do me evil talk wicked things and imagine deceit continually.* She was not unlikely to have planned to blackmail him, through the shreds of Mounteagle's letter. Stupid hussy! And, just to spite him, she had even unwittingly saved that hateful, seditious, unbelievably lucky juggler. After that, unfortunately, with her flight, his sickness, Speed's blindness and a thousand other things, Sir Robert hadn't been able to concentrate on that poet: otherwise, he would certainly have managed to frame him regardless. To crush him like a slimy slug, let the uncouth commoners say what they would: they were always complaining anyway.

Above all, who had that bloody witch run off with? With a man, of course: a girl alone, who, moreover, knew nothing of the world, could never get far. Of all the various courtiers and noblemen's sons, however, none was missing. Had she, then, eloped with a commoner, even a servant? The mere thought drove him mad. What a paradox: the only person in the world who had managed to cheat him was the fruit of his own loins. And so it must be, on the other hand, as no outsider could ever compete with his intelligence. Obviously, although he kept denying this to everybody, he knew very well that Milly was actually his daughter, not the fruit of his good wife's betrayal or a changeling in the cradle. "The pox on her, now! Who, who has she run off with? And whither?" This he would have to tell his William, as soon as he came: never underestimate the cleverness of women; nor their perversion and malice.

He tried to turn on one side; he curled up like a baby. He was so small that the parson's bed, of modest size, looked huge. He tried to stretch his legs but bent them again in a twinge of pain.

"William! Call... William!" His voice was barely audible in the raging storm.

"He's coming, Your Lordship, resist!"

But His Lordship didn't resist. He stretched his legs again and there, in an anonymous bed in a little country village, consumed by hatred and resentment, the little great man stepped beyond the threshold of the undiscovered country from whose bourn no traveller returns.

He was buried at Hatfield, as he had desired. Nay, it was his official decorator, Rowland Bucket, who prepared the funeral banquet, so that everything was really flawless – apart, perhaps, from the need to summon a troop of soldiers to keep down the village people, who had risen to claim back the common land round which Sir Robert had planted a high, thick hedge. In the end, after this rising had been crushed too, the magnificent dwelling sank back into quietness, a huge, beautiful, cold mausoleum.

* * *

John Kenelm Digby led his young wife to the Brussels Court of the Archdukes, keeping their true identity secret: they were just yet another couple of English refugees risking starvation. Archduchess Isabella was really surprised, therefore, by the wonderful pendant they gave her as a present, which, they said, belonged to their family. This proved they were high-born, for they certainly didn't look like thieves.

His mastery of Latin and Italian came in very useful to Jack, who made a career as a Court diplomat and soon also started to work with several commercial enterprises with contacts in Italy and other Mediterranean countries. Milly became one of the Archduchess' ladies-in-waiting, for Isabella liked her wit, her liveliness, her noble manners and her surprising embroidery skills.

Jack couldn't finish his *True and Perfect Relation of the so-called Powder Treason,* as his rough-copy papers, with the dates and the chronicle he had begun to write, had remained under the board of the Little East Cheap lodging and had probably fallen into Fletcher's hands; nor could he use the official documents he had read, to refute them one by one as he had meant to do. Instead of the thick book he had in mind, he had to make do with a short libel in which he listed his discoveries, from the decayed powder to Mounteagle's letter; which detail, out of respect for his wife, he only added after learning about Sir Robert's death.

In the summer of 1612, Jack and his English exile friends started to look for a way to let the Prince have the libel that, in a not too distant future, could change the fate of all British recusants.

People, though, might consider this booklet of his as one of the many biased libels circulating throughout Europe: so much that no Flemish printer agreed to publish it. Who cared, by now, about an old English plot that had been foiled seven years before? Well, Jack and his friends wrote many manuscript copies, which started to circulate and be copied. He didn't sign them with his own name, but rather with a pseudonym; partly out of safety, partly to be more credible, as he was believed to be dead. So it was that the thinning Continental recusant community learnt about the details of the Plot and, at least, stopped hating its contrivers and blaming them for their ruin. As for public opinion in Britain, the damage was done. But something could be handed down, through the people, through memories entrusted from father to son, from mother to daughter.

One copy Jack signed with his real name: it was meant for the Prince and was accompanied by a dedicatory letter with a brief summary of his life. He hoped the future King, the most fortunate and powerful youth in the world, remembered the boy who, on that far-away spring day, at Cambridge university, had handed him a little note begging him to accept his humble services despite his father's treason. Well, now the Prince must learn that his father had been no traitor, and that the boy of the note, who had now grown into a man, renewed his promise to serve him loyally to the death, if only he would let him return. Jack felt that complete rehabilitation, both for Sir Everard and for all of them, wasn't far away.

The libel, and its long introductory epistle, secretly sailed on a merchant ship heading for Dover in the month of August. The carrier of the precious, dangerous bundle was a brave seminarian going back to England as a secret missionary. His name was Sherwin, Ralph Sherwin, and he had apparently made it up with God. His nimble, clever mind would think of a way to get it through to the Prince, maybe during an official ceremony.

Those were months of anxiety and trepidation.

* * *

When Milly told him that she was expecting their first child, Jack shuddered. For a split second, his eyes saw a perfect reproduction of Cecil, a little insidious, treacherous creature that he could never love. His natural worry for his wife's health was therefore made more painful by secret, choking anguish. He tried to persuade himself that their story was a different one, that this baby would be their child, more than Cecil's grandchild. And then, deep down, what did it matter? In the name of his love for Milly, he would never be ashamed of a little hunchbacked cripple; nay, he would sport him proudly. Thanks to his sharp mind, he would soon become Secretary of State in Flanders, and the Archduchess would call him "my elf". He quite unsuccessfully tried to hide his fears from Milly's penetrating eyes, as days and months crawled by.

It was not a little hunchback: it was a beautiful, grey-eyed little girl they named Mary. She was followed in a few years by little Everard and little Timothy, both healthy and strong. They all grew up with the dream of going back to England, sooner or later, to tell everyone the truth about what the Gunpowder Plot had really been.

EPILOGUE

Jack never went back to Gayhurst. Neither did he learn whether his precious documents were ever delivered. No one ever did, because Sherwin was arrested shortly after landing and disappeared into the jaws of the Tower, most likely to leave his mark of blood there.

Anyhow, it was no longer of any importance. Because the scion of Britain, the pride of the kingdom, the hope of the Stuarts for the future, the spotless, fearless prince, noble Harry Frederick Stuart died that autumn. In such a silly way, especially for a prince. In such a reckless, careless way. One day like many others, while joking with some of his gentlemen, maybe to show them how fit he was, and how strong, and how he scorned danger, he dived into the Thames. He should never have done so, as he knew perfectly well that his life was not his own only: it was the life of the whole kingdom. The great, proud river didn't forgive him for braving it and gave him typhoid fever. Even stones knew that those were treacherous, infectious waters.

The Prince's strong body desperately resisted, like an oak before an axe, for several weeks, between bloody vomit and diarrhoeic discharges, while, at the end of their wits, Théodore Mayerne and the other royal doctors helplessly wrung their hands. Not even a brew of *Teucrium Scordium* had worked. Young Princess Elizabeth locked herself up in her rooms, refusing to eat and never stopping crying. To think that, as soon as spring came, they were both to have been married. Now, instead of a double wedding, full of joy and laughter, there would only be mourning and despair and, instead of a bridal bed, her brother would have a royal grave. Queen Anne restlessly haunted St James' palace in her night gown, her hair all dishevelled, followed by her ladies who could do nothing to soothe her. Her cry, a continuous, monotonous moan, broke one's heart, while all the town's bells tolled for her son.

Harry tried to hold on to his last without complaint. He must die a hero's death and, above all, set an example – to those who would never become his subjects now – of a virtuous death in God's grace. He would have so much liked to be Head of the Church, besides being King of Britain: he would have done his best to direct his people in the ways of virtue and goodness. But this was not to be. Worn out like an old rag, his lungs filled with holes, His Grace the Prince of Wales passed away in the first hours of the sixth of November, in the dead of night, while, out there, Guy Fawkes' bonfires were slowly dying out with him. Someone was still around, down in the streets, as drunk as a lord, singing at the top of his voice, as if accompanying him in his journey to the life to come. The Prince had coarse songs instead of litanies.

At the break of day, everything was extinguished, hope included. Just then came, falling from a whitish sky, the first winter snow, too early not to be interpreted as a bad omen, the first sign of the chill that was to invade the hearts of all subjects.

When news of his tragic death became known, some didn't accept the idea that noble Harry had been defeated by such a mundane sickness. Rumours of poisoning began to spread. Nothing was proven, of course; also because his main enemy at Court, Sir Robert of Salisbury, had gone before him. Who else would profit from this?

His exemplary death, a godly death, was a clear sign that the youth had been predestined to Heaven ever since birth: he had been too perfect to live long. Few heirs to the throne of England were so widely, so deeply mourned. His embalmed body lay in state for his subjects' last farewell in St James' palace for as long as four weeks, the diadem of Wales with its three feathers on his head, a sceptre in his hand, his St George round his neck. Then he was delicately laid on an open hearse pulled by six magnificent black Holstein horses, preceded by a red velvet canopy below which his many heraldic emblems were carried. Behind the noblemen and courtiers, as many as two thousand people formed a mile-long cortege winding through the streets which, accompanied by fifes and drums, followed him to Westminster Abbey in an ocean of tears. During the burial service he was laid near the altar, under a beautiful wooden pyramid-shaped frame all overwrought with sculpture and held up by six tapering ionic pillars. There the Archbishop of Canterbury, Dr Abbott, held a two-hour sermon celebrating the virtues of the Treasure of Britain. It was a State funeral like no-one had ever seen; a funeral in which His Majesty, King James, did not take part.

Henry Frederick Stuart left his titles, and his succession rights, to his frail, inexperienced brother, twelve-year-old Prince Charles, who, in all possible senses, had never been able to move as skilfully as him. What should one expect, on the other hand, from one who had only learnt to walk at four? One who, despite his elder brother's continually teasing him for his rickety legs and his stutter, had never stopped worshipping him. One who, as the Sun of Britain was setting, and his mother and sister seemed to be dying with him, had defied contagion and had turned up full of hope at his brother's deathbed only to give him a small metal horse which would no doubt console him, if not even heal him... Poor Charlie had always been a little slow-witted: what should one expect from such a one? But beggars can't be choosers, and little Charlie was the only surviving male heir.

In time, King James patiently took to teaching the new Prince of Wales the art of good governance. He must take his father as a model in everything, so that he would always find himself happy. Let him never stoop to compromise with the Puritans, of the kind which Parliament was swarming with: nay, he should keep them at a distance, instead, for in the depth of their hearts they were nasty Republicans and never loved any sovereign. Prince Charles, who was much meeker and more amenable than his headstrong brother, tried his best to follow his father's orders. Days came when he bitterly regretted this.

* * *

Lady Mary remained at Gayhurst, which, under her second son, Christopher, slowly started to bloom again. The precious relic-book with Garnet's face, bound in his own skin, was handed down from generation to generation as the most precious family treasure.

The Earl of Northampton never turned up again: if he had ever thought he could exert some pressure on Sir Everard's fair widow, his plans were wrecked by the sore need not to founder, after the decline and death of his powerful patron. Because the Court was always full of envious, devious people. His health too, on the other hand, was fast declining: he soon lost his self-sufficiency and had more pressing matters to think about; such as, for instance, which faith to choose at the extreme moment. He died a bachelor, at seventy-four, two years after his master, finally denying the State Church and embracing again what had always been the faith of the Howards, of the Dukes of Norfolk, and of his country.

*

Shakspere went back to Stratford, and never took the Oath. Neither did he ever complete his four-play history cycle, which never proceeded beyond the first one. As they had been promised, the King's Men, who by now had totally conformed, were left alone by the authorities and proceeded from one success to another, together with their new, ambitious young dramatist.

The great history play about Henry VIII, which was entitled *All is true,* bore the joint authorship of Shakspere and Fletcher, but remained in a cupboard for more than a year, because, with one pretext or another, Burbage, Heminges and Condell kept putting its staging off. It was dramatically weak, they said, lacked coherent development and had too many characters; it looked like a sort of big mixed stew, and badly needed thorough revision. His Majesty had to personally intervene to make them perform it at the Globe, in June 1613, as a popular play. Were it to be as successful as the Master of Revels expected, it would then be brought to Court.

On that very day, on the feast of SS Peter and Paul, the private citizen William Shakspere, gentleman, was in London on business: with the money he had got from his theatrical share, he had just bought a dwelling that was as large as it was ancient, Blackfriars Gatehouse, and had to define a few last details with its tenant, a brother-in-law of Burbage's, to whom he gave it for a pepper-corn rent: strangely enough, he had no intention of living in it.

It had been the biggest purchase of his life: one hundred and forty pounds it had cost him, but he didn't regret a single groat. No one knew the reason for that mysterious purchase, nor did the poet choose to give any explanations to those who didn't already know. He just smiled sadly and mysteriously: a spiritual bargain, he would say. Some small atonement for all the mistakes he had made in his life, and for one in particular. It was time to rest on his oars and think of his soul.

On that day, he said nothing to his former fellow players and joined the crowd at the Globe entrance: after the play, he would go and greet them in the tiring house. What a surprise this would be to them! When his turn came to pay at the box office, Mistress

Winifred's jaw dropped, her eyes widened; before she could say a word, however, he winked at her and put a finger to his lips. Then he lowered his hat over his eyes and stepped in. He calmly went up the wooden staircase enjoying every step, contemplating his beautiful theatre, and went to take a seat in the gallery. It was so strange, so painful to take part in the life of the Globe as a member of the audience: as if he were a spectator of his own life.

A great flourish started the performance: Kit Beeston, dressed up as Prologue, bowed and started the first speech. "*I come no more to make you laugh. Things now that bear a weighty and a serious brow, sad, high, and working, full of state and woe... Such noble scenes as draw the eye to flow we now present...*"

Stupid Fletcher: if he had to glorify the old tyrant, he had better alter or even cross out those tragic lines. But then he told himself that today he was a mere spectator and, as such, he tried to exclusively concentrate upon the performance, not on the script. He mostly couldn't. He was apparently smiling and unmoved, cool and collected, but actually quite annoyed at this jumble of comic and tragic scenes no longer arranged in the typical organic order of yore, but rather perfunctorily thrown here and there in a casual sequence. He admired his friend Dick, who remained the greatest player ever walking the boards. All in all, he was not totally dissatisfied because, despite Fletcher's clumsy tamperings, the character of King Harry emerged exactly as he would have wanted it: a cruel, megalomaniac hypocritical jerk. After the Duke of Buckingham's judicial murder, there emerged "the King's great matter" – that was to say his divorce – and Dick Robinson, as Lord Chamberlain, confidentially said: "*It seems the marriage with his brother's wife has crept too near his conscience.*" Shakspere laughed with all the others at Rob Gough's words who, as Duke of Suffolk, winked at the audience: "*No, his conscience had crept too near another lady!*"

Again: stupid Fletcher. He should have crossed out that quip too. Or, maybe, he *had* crossed it out, and the players had put it in again to make people laugh.

The best part remained his Katherine (played by Johnny Rice), the virtuous Spanish queen who the King set aside because she was barren and no longer young: she went to die a royal, dignified, saintly death at the end of Act Four. After this, Shakspere knew nothing of how the play developed and really wanted to see how Fletcher had continued it. Above all, he wanted to listen to the sycophantic final speech which, as Harry Condell had told him, his beloved fellow playwright had put into Archbishop Cranmer's mouth to extol both the Tudors and Stuarts. He couldn't wait to see if Fletcher would really play that part. He wondered whether that speech really included a pun on his name, with the Queen's foes who "shall *shake* like a field of beaten corn." He too had always liked punning on his own name.

However that was, Fletcher – unlike him – had never been a player: his, therefore, was sure to be an awful first performance. How could this audience, who had once been his own, imagine him choosing to write such rubbish?

But Fletcher's final speech never came. Because, at the beginning of Act Five, just as Dick-Henry was entering in great pomp, a piece of ordnance was shot off from the upper stage and probably sent a spark onto the thatched roof. Fire ran round like a train and the great Globe was soon turned into a huge ring of fire, its roaring flames as high as towers, fanned by the wind blowing from the sea. And then it was all one scream, one mad rush to get away, a stampede in which many risked being injured or killed. While trying to step down the narrow stairs, Shakspere saw Fletcher dressed up as Archbishop fleeing in terror, brutally pushing and treading over anything or anyone obstructing his way to the gate.

* * *

There were no casualties, thanks be to God. But in an hour's time all that was left of the great playhouse overflowing with passion and memories was a heap of smoking ashes, a black skeleton which seemed to lif up its arms to the sky, as if complaining of its sad, undeserved lot.

William Shakspere had managed to reach his friends almost at once, wading upstream through the maddened crowd, and all together they had tried to save what they could. Now, sitting on the ground, covered in soot, acrid, pungent smoke stinging his nostrils and throat, the old poet was coughing like a hag while contemplating, yet again, the tragedy of life, his tears leaving cleaner trails round his eyes and down his cheeks. Beside him, his head in his hands, sat Dick Burbage, the greatest player of all times, his King's costume all blackened and torn, his hair and beard scorched. More and more people were crowding all round them, as if, on seeing the black smoke, not only Southwark but the whole City of London had poured onto the right bank of the great river.

Dick raised his head only a little bit and cried amid sobs: "Thou seest, this was its doom: once thou wentst, he died too! 'Tis over, Will, over!" He was holding between his knees a sheaf of scorched papers: the rough copies of the plays.

Shakspere smiled, his face all smeared with soot and tears like some sort of grotesque makeup, his eyes all reddened. "My friend," he said to him, "*Thou dost look, in a moved sort, as if thou wert dismayed. Be cheerful, Sir. Our revels now are ended…*" Burbage looked at him in surprise. Then, once he had identified the passage, he sadly smiled back. Shakspere-Prospero went on: "*Like the baseless fabric of this vision, the cloud-capped towers, the gorgeous palaces, the solemn temples, the great Globe itself, yea, even our own great Globe, and all which it inherit, shall dissolve. And, like this insubstantial pageant faded, leave not a rack behind.*" He shook his head miserably. "*We are such stuff as dreams are made on, and our little life is rounded with a sleep…* Dick, I am vexed. Bear with my weakness. My old brain is troubled, but be not disturbed with my infirmity. Let not thy heart be troubled!"

Dick looked at him in silence, his sorrow partly soothed by the poetic power of those words that stated men's great, tragic impotence before all that was painful, overwhelming, inescapable, and made it sublime. He rubbed his eyes and nose into one of his sleeves, which had originally been gilt but now, instead of cleaning his face, made it even dirtier. They looked like two devils who had run away from Hell.

"All the world's a stage, Dick," the dramatist went on, "And all men mere players. They mount the stage, they strut and fret for the time they've been granted, whatever its length, then step down and are seen no more. Everyone has their part to play, everyone, from the king to the peasant. But all of us only have one, and we must play it to the end. And, on stepping down, we are welcomed by applause or whistles. And so runs the world away, so history goes on, a long play through the centuries."

"The City of London is a big stage too, Will. Because, as the Puritans maintain, one must necessarily be false in order to be a good player, mustn't he? Well, what I mean to find out now is whether this fire's really been an accident, as it seems, or one of those 'godly ones' has put his hand to it. Nay, I'm beginning to suspect that that damned cannon had been overcharged on purpose. Ay, it must be so! If I find out who did it, I'll… I'll…"

Shakspere was no longer listening. He picked up a handful of grey, warm ashes, then he opened his hand and looked at them being scattered in the wind. *Memento, homo, quia pulvis es, et in pulverem reverteris*, echoed in his mind. Maybe the time had really come for him to step down the stage of life, as well as down the players' stage. He was afraid to present himself like this, with those few, worthless works of his, before the Great Enterpriser. For all his labours now suddenly appeared to him as this little heap of volatile ashes, absolutely meaningless. What had become of the golden talents he had received free from charge? They were his most precious goods, and he had loved and hated them at once. Because, ever since he had discovered he had them, he had only felt at ease when working. It had all been like a sweet slavery, at times even perceived as a curse. What had become of those talents, now, at the moment of the final reckoning? Had he traded well with them? Or, rather, had he hidden them in the earth out of fear, or, worse, out of cowardice and sloth? Had he been a good and faithful servant? Because deep down, but really deep down, the readiness is all.

The following day, while digging among the rubble, they found the wooden statue of Atlas (or maybe Hercules?), half charred, its top still covered in gold paint. Below the terrestrial Globe, now all blackened, the old sign still read: *Totus mundus agit histrionem.* All the world's a stage.

TABLE OF CONTENTS